DEAD MAN OHIO

ALSO BY T. M. SIMMONS

A Dead Man Mystery Series

Dead Man Talking

Dead Man Haunt

Dead Man Hand

Dead Man Ohio

Dead Man Series Collection 1: Dead Man Mysteries Books 1, 2 and 3

DEAD MAN OHIO

A DEAD MAN MYSTERY
BOOK FOUR

T. M. SIMMONS

ePublishingWorks!
love what you read.

Book and cover design by eBook Prep
www.ebookprep.com

August 2022
ISBN: 978-1-64457-346-4

ePublishing Works!
644 Shrewsbury Commons Ave
Ste 249
Shrewsbury PA 17361
United States of America
www.epublishingworks.com
Phone: 866-846-5123

To
Miss Molly and Trucker

CHAPTER 1

I almost didn't answer the phone after I glanced at the display screen and saw who was calling: My ex-husband, Jack Roucheau. Our last call had ended on a sour note, and I wasn't sure I was even speaking to him right now. But a movement across my office caught my attention. *Great-Grandmére* Alicia, a ghost relative who seemed to have appointed herself my conscience, stood beside the window, tapping her foot, an admonishing look on her face. Beside her, Howard, my head ghost, showed off his latest fish catch, lake water dripping on my hardwood floor.

"Howard, take that fish back to the lake," I ordered aloud, although he could have heard me if I'd used telepathy. Instead of replying, he pursed his lips in a grump, since Howard's a ghost of few words. Then he disappeared, fish and all.

Ghosts appearing in my home didn't surprise me. I see ghosts. I talk to ghosts. And at any one time, up to ten paranormal boarders share my lakeside log cabin in Six Gun, Texas. Not that they take up much space in their non-corporeal bodies.

The phone shrilled again, and *Grandmére* lifted a finger and pointed at it.

Normally, I was in charge of my supernatural residents, meting out discipline and punishment if they didn't abide by the Alice and Howard Ghost Agreement rules. Each one had signed a copy of the Agreement before I allowed them to *live* with me. But *Great-Grandmére*, my own ancestor, was different. She had only sniffed and declined to even read such poppycock. It's only polite to respect our elders, and she was quite a bit more elderly than me—in fact, well over two centuries—so I didn't insist.

Grudgingly, I reached for the receiver and pushed the green "on" button. Grumpily, I said, "Yes?" instead of, "Hello."

"*Chère*, don't hang up," Jack said immediately. "We need to talk about Twila."

"We agreed to always talk things out a few months ago," I broke in. "When we decided to try being more than friends. Yet you still pull those stubborn silences."

"We can talk about that later—"

"That's the point," I continued. "There never seems to be any later—"

At the sharp tone of my voice, Miss Molly, my Siamese, who was curled up beside my computer monitor, opened one blue eye and glared at me for interrupting her snooze. But I didn't apologize. Miss Molly slept away the biggest share of most every day.

Then it dawned on me what Jack had said. Something about my Aunt Twila, the dearest person on earth to me next to Jack. Well, next to how I used to feel about Jack.

"Quit inserting yourself when I'm trying to think," I murmured aloud in response to my mental Jack-thought before I remembered he could hear me.

"Who are you talking to?" Jack asked. "One of the ghosts you hang around with?"

"I don't *hang* with them, they hang...stay with me," I corrected. I looked over at the window. Satisfied at my obedience, *Grandmére* knelt beside my Rottweiler, Trucker. Trucker lay on his side, offering his tummy for her to scratch and glorying in the sensation. As with many ghosts who had been around a while, *Grandmére* had developed the ability to materialize well enough to touch things firmly. She was always petting the animals or scratching some spot they enjoyed. I could hear Trucker's rumbles of contentment from where I sat.

"What were you saying about Aunt Twila?" I asked Jack, bringing my deliberations back on track. "Is she all right?"

"I don't know." Jack paused and sighed. "You know how private she is, especially about all this hoo-doo stuff you and she—"

"Dealing with ghosts isn't hoo-doo!" I interrupted again, then loosened my hold on the phone before I crushed it. "You're confusing it with voodoo. Tell me what's going on!"

Fed up with my strident voice, Miss Molly stalked to the edge of the desk. She jumped to the floor and headed for *Grandmére* to get her share of attention.

"Well," Jack began cautiously, "Jess let somethin' slip when we were fishin' yesterday—"

"You and Jess were fishing? Where are you?"

Another deep sigh, and I could imagine him closing those deep chocolate eyes in frustration at my continued disruptions.

"Sorry," I said instinctively, "but what's going on?"

"I'm tryin' to tell you," he muttered first, then, "I'm actually in Ohio. When you couldn't get away from your work to spend some of my vacation time with me, I decided to come up here and visit Jess. You know he's my best friend."

Friends, I thought, this time silently. *Like Jack and I agreed to try to be, only as a foundation to perhaps building back into a permanent relationship. We haven't even gotten to the friends-with-benefits stage yet. And it's sure getting frustrating....*

I mentally slapped myself in the face and said, "Quit beating around the bush, Jack. What did Jess say about Twila?"

"I'm tryin' to tell you," he repeated, then went on before I could think of a defense to his runaround accusation that I was the one delaying his explanation. "Twila's been rather absent while I've been here the past couple days. I always enjoy visitin' her, too, y'know. And I

3

was hopin' she'd bake me one of her special meatloaves. She's a damn fine cook."

"Jack!" I nearly shouted. "What's wrong with Twila?"

"That's just it. I don't know. And Jess got this worried look on his face when I asked him if she was gonna fry the fish we caught. Not that we caught any, but Jess doesn't have an outdoor cooker up here, like I do down home. And Twila's not one to put up with me makin' a mess in her kitchen. She says Jess does enough of that."

"What the hell is wrong with Twila?" This time I did shout, and every one of my animals, including the other five cats scattered around my office, made a beeline for the doorway. I even noticed a couple of other ghosts, who had been lingering at half-materialization while they eavesdropped, disappear completely. I didn't get a good look, but I thought it was the two kids, Shannon and Rick. A moment later, I was alone in my office. Even *Grandmére* had gone back to her own dimension.

"Jess just said that she was busy helpin' out a friend," Jack finally explained. "I got the impression it was another one of those deals where she goes out and tries to take care of some ghost that's causin' problems. Jess told me once that when she gets involved in somethin' like that, she makes it her priority. Like you do with your writin'."

"My writing is my income," I reminded him for the ten-thousandth time. "And Twila has been helping people with ghosts for as long as she's been alive. Why, she had her first experience when she was five years old, Jack. What's so different about this one?"

"If I knew, I'd tell you, *Chère*. And I'm not sure there is anything wrong. Just a feelin' I get from the way Jess is actin'."

I frowned. "You're not just saying this to try to get me to come up there and be with you, are you?"

Jack lowered his voice to that soft growl I'd heard so many times, but I battled the thrill that threatened me. After all, we were fighting right now. The barriers weakened though, when he said, "If I thought it would do any good, I would lie to get you here. It would be a lot more enjoyable. But you were pretty clear about needing to finish whatever you were workin' on before you took some time off."

4

"It's my income," I repeated. "You know, for things like real estate taxes, utilities, cat and dog food."

He remained quiet for a few seconds, then almost whispered, "If we both lived in the same house, we could share expenses like that."

I wasn't about to get into that time-worn argument right now. We couldn't even agree on whether it was time for that or not, let alone if Jack would move in here or continue to try to talk me into sharing his place in Longview, should we decide on a yes. He kept reminding me over and over about the drive he'd have to make—at least an hour each way—and saying that I could work anywhere on my writing. But he didn't understand creative atmosphere.

Jack might be able to let our relationship problems sidetrack him, but he'd already said enough to get me worried about Aunt Twila.

"It will take me at least two days to drive up there," I said finally.

"Can't you fly?" he asked.

"With a cat and dog? I won't leave Trucker and Miss Molly, although the other cats are fine with a sitter. And—" I added in a childish jibe, "—the ghosts get along fine without me. But you know how Trucker and Miss Molly hate flying. They still haven't forgiven me for loading them in their crates to go to Albuquerque with me a few months ago."

"I think maybe you should get here as soon as you can, *Chère*. But I don't like the idea of you drivin' that far alone. Maybe you could ask Granny to come with you."

"I might just do that," I agreed, pondering the vague nuances in his tone. Prodding him, I asked, "What aren't you telling me, Jack?"

After a pause, he said, "You know I don't see those things you and Twila chase after often. But...well, when she left this morning in her little red car, there was somethin' in it with her. Somethin' I don't think she was aware of. As soon as it looked over at me and realized I'd seen it, it disappeared."

"What did it look like?"

"Nasty," Jack said. "Really nasty."

* * *

Granny and I stopped halfway between Texas and Ohio that next night. It had taken me the rest of the evening after Jack called to arrange a cat-sitter for the other five cats and get packed. As I'd told Jack, the ghosts could take care of themselves, although I'd reminded them that Howard was in charge. Also reminded Howard, and asked him to spit out a few of his scant words to assure me he had memorized my cell phone number.

It had only taken a few seconds, though, to get Granny's agreement to go with me.

My next-door neighbor, Granny Chisholm, is tiny, barely five-foot, but full of vigor. A widow in her eighties, she's as hale and hearty as me, more so at times. Deep wrinkles line her face, but some mornings after a late writing night, I noticed furrows plowed on my forehead nearly as substantial. I could only hope that the attractiveness I allowed myself to believe was mine followed me into the ages, as Granny's had. It wasn't only her bright blue eyes, which shone with knowledge and life. Her face still mirrored the beauty that had to have made her one of the most gorgeous Southern Belles in the South.

Hearing was Granny's only major physical problem. It didn't bother her as long as she remembered to wear her hearing aide, as well as keep the batteries changed. I couldn't blame her infrequent forgetfulness on age, since I suffered periodic bouts of that myself.

Granny loved to travel, and I could always count on her as a companion for trips with or without Twila. From a large family herself, she had borne several children and her extended family consisted of grandchildren, great-grandchildren, nieces and nephews. One of them could always be counted on to cat-sit and care for our houses while we were absent.

I called Twila's home as soon as we settled in the motel. I hadn't told her I was coming and had sworn Jack to secrecy. Jack was right about one thing—Twila was a private person. She would do anything for anyone she cared about, but hated to impose for herself, unless she was truly in need. If she hadn't called me for help, she either didn't know about the nasty entity shadowing her or felt she could handle things.

Jess answered. "Is Twila there?" I asked.

"Who is this?"

I kept forgetting that Jess didn't always look at the Caller ID display when he picked up the phone. "It's Alice, Jess. I really need to talk to her."

"Oh, O.K."

She practically sighed my name when she came on the phone. "Alice. I hope you and Granny are enjoying the drive. Don't get in such a hurry that you forget to stop and let Trucker and Miss Molly out."

Obviously, her psychic senses had already picked up on the fact I was on the way. One of these days, I'd quit trying to fool my aunt. Or maybe not.

"Don't worry," I assured her as I glanced over at Trucker lying beside my bed in the double-queen room. Miss Molly had already used the litter box Granny helped me set up and was sprawled on a pillow on Granny's bed. "You've travelled with my pets and me enough times to know that Miss Molly can set up a howl that will threaten your eardrums if she or Trucker need to take a potty break. I swear, the two of them have a psychic communication as strong as you and me."

"I wish I could read Jack as well as I do you," she muttered. "What the heck's got his bowels in an uproar so bad that he asked you to come rescue me?"

I hesitated. "First, tell me what you're involved in up there. I probably shouldn't say this— but maybe you already knew that Jess was worried."

"I didn't. Well, not really. I've noticed him being a bit grumpy lately, but he's a man. He gets like that. I really haven't had time to sit down and...." Her voice trailed off, and though I waited quite a few moments, she didn't go on.

"Twila!" I insisted. "Talk to me."

"Huh?" she said, as though she'd forgotten we were speaking. "Oh, Alice. Sorry. Fact, is, I was thinking of calling you anyway."

"What about?" I prodded when she fell silent again.

"Um...I'm not sure if I want to get into it over the phone. You know how *things* sometime listen in on our conversations."

That was true. We had to be careful when we chatted. Some of the ghosts we dealt with were advanced enough to use their own telepathic abilities, even to the point of eavesdropping on a phone conversation. Usually, we were able to tell when that was happening, both with our own senses and by hearing a telltale sound over the connection. I hadn't heard any suspicious noise this time, though.

"Can you at least give me a hint? So I won't worry so much?"

"Maybe. Think of the couple other times we've run into interesting situations. Jefferson and Cimarron? Remember?"

"Of course. But those turned complicated pretty quick."

"This one isn't *complicated*, if you know what I mean." I could sense the wink-wink in her tone. Given her warning of a possible listener, I didn't want to tell her about Jack's concern directly. Still....

"Is it something dangerous?" I asked cautiously.

"I don't think so," she said, then went on resolutely and frankly, "but to be honest, I don't know...yet."

"Look, my new car has one of those sync things, which connects my cell phone automatically whenever I get in the car. You can call me and I won't have to pull over to talk."

"You'll get just as distracted if you aren't holding that phone to your ear," she said. "Or almost."

"You call me if you need me," I ordered. "Do you hear me?"

I didn't even bother to chastise myself for being so bold as to actually tell my aunt, the senior ghost hunter of our partnership, what to do. After all, she was only four years older than me. Sometimes I was more right than she was. Well, once in a while. All right, infrequently, but it had happened.

"What can you do from a few hundred miles away?" she asked with a faint laugh.

"I don't know, but at least whatever you're dealing with will know you have backup," I insisted.

"That makes sense," she said, and I inwardly gave myself a point for this being one of my *I'm-right* times.

I sensed she was getting ready to hang up and I couldn't let her do that without at least a hint of warning. "And do me a favor," I went on. "Whatever it is, stay away from it until I get there."

For a moment, I thought my cell phone had dropped the call, but Twila finally said, "I'm not sure I can do that, Alice. But don't worry. I really am glad you're coming. Bye."

"Wait, wait!" I insisted, and I gratefully heard her sigh, indicating she was still on the line. "Do me another favor, then. Be sure and check your car over before you drive it."

"Hmmmm," she mused as I silently sent her one of the telepathic communications we used only in a dire emergency: *There might be something hitching a ride with you, something not nice.*

"I understand," she said. "My car needs a good going over anyway. It's been a while since she's had a tune-up. I might even burn some sage in her."

"A good idea, the sage," I said, relieved that she had indeed picked up my alert of a possible troublesome entity.

"Have a safe trip the rest of the way," she said. She disconnected this time, and I stared at the phone for a long while. Finally, Granny interrupted my contemplation of what could be going on in the quiet countryside in the state of Ohio.

"She's into something worrisome, huh?" Granny asked.

Unlike Twila and me, Granny only has a slightly above-normal sixth sense. Her blue eyes held more than a hint of anxiety when I looked over where she sat on the side of her bed, already in her long, flannel nightgown. Trucker had moved over to lay his huge head on her knee, and Miss Molly had crawled onto her lap. The animals always seemed to know when they needed to offer support and comfort.

"She won't tell me all of it," I said as I walked over and sat on my own bed, across from Granny. "But from the hints she dropped, I think she's looking into one of the situations like we had in Jefferson and Cimarron. You know, when we got called in to help with ghosts who wouldn't cross into The Light."

"And also got mixed up in a new murder right 'bout the same time," Granny reminded me.

"Twila assured me...or at least, I think it's what she meant...that's she's just seeing what she can find out about a troublesome ghost. But she's glad we're coming."

"Then why don't you look all calm, cool and collected about what she told you?"

"Oh, Granny, you know how brave she is. She never lets anything we run into in the paranormal realm get to her, no matter how nasty. But she claims she's not sure what she's dealing with this time."

"If'n she don't know, given how much experience she's got under that red hair of hers," Granny mused, "mebbe you should've brought your satchel of heavy-duty protection stuff."

"I did," I said with a nod. "And also my consecration supplies. Before I go to bed tonight, I'm going to re-consecrate and re-bless every darn thing in the bag. Right down to the last quince seed."

CHAPTER 2

I didn't bother to set my cell phone alarm. Granny always rose way before sunrise, and although she tried to be quiet when we were staying in the same room, I couldn't ignore the difference in the atmosphere. Perhaps my psychic senses picked up on the change; perhaps I was a lighter sleeper than some. It never woke me at home when the animals prowled the bedroom...well, unless Trucker stuck his wet nose under the covers or Miss Molly yowled in my ear because her water dish was empty.

To get myself going, I showered and choked down a cup of in-room coffee. We walked the animals and put them back in the room before heading for a breakfast buffet next door to the motel. As much of a hurry as I was in, I'd never make the drive successfully without more caffeine and something to eat.

Besides, Twila and I always justified our overeating on trips as there being no calories in food we consumed then. Lies, but I intended to stuff my tummy, since I'd eaten here before and knew the food was awesome.

They must have hired a new cook since our last trip.

"Ugh," Granny said as we left after reluctantly paying the bill. It wasn't only that the price for the buffet had doubled, but we'd had to ask for a stack of additional napkins to soak up the grease on dishes like bacon and fried potatoes before we could eat them.

"Bet I know where you could get a job cooking," I told her.

"I'll keep it in mind," she responded. "But right now...lookee there!"

She pointed at the new C-Max hybrid I'd bought just last month. Not one, but two of the tires were flat!

"What the hell?" I muttered as I stomped over to examine the damage. Not only were the tires flat, but someone had keyed the side of the car. A faint scratch marred the light gray-green paint listed as Seafoam on the sticker. It ran from the driver's side front fender to the rear taillight.

"Wonder if it was that fool you tee'd off when you forgot to check behind you and pulled out to pass that slow eighteen-wheeler?" Granny mused.

"Could have been that asshole," I fumed as I took out my cell phone and snapped a dozen pictures of the damage. I stowed the phone safely in the glove box before I marched into the motel office.

A teenage male stood behind the counter, his short blond dreadlocks sticking every-which-direction as he stared downward.

"Someone damaged my car," I told him.

He barely looked up from where he was furiously thumbing a message into the cell phone I now saw in his hands. He nodded a head-flick at a sign on the wall that read: *Not Responsible for Accidents to Your Vehicle or Belongings.*

Lucky for me, unlucky for him, he wasn't protected by a wall of Plexi-glas like at some of the lower-class motels I used to have to stay at. I reached over the counter and jerked the phone out of his hand.

"Hey!" he shouted, making a grab for it back.

I handed the phone to Granny and leaned in to face him, nose to nose, ignoring the garlicky smell of his breath. "I happen to be a lawyer," I lied. "And I know that sign up there doesn't mean diddly squat in court! Where's the security guard you had on duty when I stayed here last?"

The kid backed up a step, but not—I was sure—out of respect. "They had to cut the budget when the economy tanked," he blurted.

"Well, who keyed my car and flattened two of my tires?" I demanded. "You can see out the window behind me, and I'm parked right in your line of vision. That damage wasn't done when we went over to breakfast, and now it is. How long have you been on duty?"

"Two hours," he said before it evidently dawned on him that he probably should keep his mouth shut to a supposed lawyer. He hastily added, "But I...uh...went to the bathroom once."

"Yeah, and the rest of the time, you were texting!"

"Uh...no I wasn't," he lied in his turn.

"Is the manager here?" I demanded. "I want to file a claim."

He shook his head negatively. "She'll have my hide if I bother her right now. She's in the back with...uh...someone."

"Someone? Someone not her husband?"

His eyes widened. "Are you a PI instead of a lawyer?"

"Are you going to call her or am I going back there?" I asked, heading for the connecting door beside the desk.

He rushed over and turned the lock on the door. With a barely concealed smirk, he said, "If you'll wait about fifteen minutes, I'm sure she'll be back on duty."

I turned to share my disgust at his outsmarting me with Granny, but she wasn't standing behind me. Instead, she had walked over to what appeared to be a pull-down fire alarm handle on the wall. At first, I took it for just a decoration, but evidently Granny didn't.

Turned out, she was right.

"Noooo!" yelled the teen, but his shriek didn't cause Granny to so much as pause as she yanked down the gray lever set in the middle of that red metal box.

AHOOOOOO. AHOOOOOO. AHOOOOOOOOOOO! the alarm shrieked. And above us, the ceiling sprinklers let loose. Within seconds, our hair was soaked through. Not only that, but another shriek joined the continued blares of the alarm as a tiny blond woman in a filmy negligee she was still sliding into barreled out a doorway behind the office area.

"What the hell's going on out here, Bobby Lee?" she yelled as she slid to a halt. She was probably fifty, if a day, because she had the beginning of faint jowls beneath her chin. She hadn't resorted to one of those lifts advertised on television yet. She may have had liposuction, though, since she looked fairly firm in the belly and thigh area. At second glance, she might have had a boob job, too, but given her slight build, she should have opted for a C rather than double D.

The deluge of water turned that wrap, and the flimsy gown beneath it, totally transparent, and Bobby Lee—which I guess was the teenager's name—stood there with his mouth agape.

I tried not to, but I glanced down at the front of the kid's baggy jeans. His erection stood out so strong, it was a wonder it didn't pop those metal buttons.

"Bobby Lee!" she demanded, but she dropped her eyes and noticed his protrusion, pointed right at her. Her face reddened as her anger intensified, but she glanced over and saw Granny and me. At the same moment, it seemed to dawn on her what was going on, especially the working ceiling sprinklers. She didn't glare at them. She ducked her chin to stare down at herself ...all of herself totally exposed under the translucent material.

The door she had exited opened a few inches as someone back there apparently tried to see what all the commotion was about...at the same moment Blondie whirled and raced back the way she had come. Her arms were out to push at the door, which she did. It hit something with a *kerthunk*, but she didn't let that stop her. She leaped over whoever was on the floor and disappeared.

The water from the ceiling wasn't really that cold, so I continued to stand there. I could see through the open door, and little man lying there untangled his limbs and tried to stand. He finally reached up to grab the doorknob. Using it for support, he pulled himself to his feet...and stood there in his briefs. Very brief briefs, which barely covered more than a jockstrap would.

Maybe he thought it made him look sexy. Maybe it would have, on a man forty years younger. This guy had to be at least seventy. His spindly legs descended beneath a protruding tummy—one of those physiques that you see when an older man has to wear his trousers belted above where his waistline used to be. His chest was concave, and he hadn't taken time to put in his teeth before set out to check on his lost bed partner. He probably wasn't expecting to be seen.

Suddenly the alarm died a silent death, and Granny handed me an umbrella as she said, "Hank Peters! Does Callie Jo know you're foolin' 'round with that there young heifer?"

I'd looked behind Granny to see where she'd gotten the umbrellas. The stand with two left in it stood beneath that alarm lever, so I presumed she had been the one to turn it off. But when she spoke, I jerked my gaze back to the elderly man. He stood there as though in shock, which I'm pretty sure he was. His stare centered on Granny.

"Wha...what are *you* doing here?" he sputtered. "You...you're in Texas."

"And Callie Jo's in Tennessee," Granny said as she held her own umbrella with one hand and propped her other one on her hip. Her foot, clad in the white sneakers she loved to wear, tapped a cadence on the tiled floor. "She's livin' not too far from here, from what I recall. And last I heard, you was still married to her!"

I wasn't surprised Granny recognized the elderly man. She knew hundreds of people, and was related to a high percentage of them through her wide-flung family. Hank, though, remained frozen like a deer in headlights at her recognition of him and his philandering.

An arm snaked out from behind the door and dragged Hank out of sight. The door slammed, and a deep silence descended, broken only by the continuing patter of water drops.

"Uh..." Bobby Lee said. "You two mind if I turn off this water?"

"You can do that?" I asked. "Go!"

He walked over to the desk and pushed a button beneath it. The water ceased, except for a telltale drip now and then. Remembering why we were in this mess, I heaved a sigh as I shook the umbrella free of water and re-closed it.

"You ladies want some coffee?" Bobby Lee asked before I could demand he get Blondie's butt back out here. He motioned to where a pot sat on a shelf against the rear wall. From what I could see, the coffee had boiled dry long before and was caked on the bottom of the glass pot.

"No," Granny and I said together, and I went on, "Go back there and tell Blondie I want to file my claim!"

The second siren outside the building announced the arrival of a huge red fire truck, which squealed to a stop behind where I was parked. After it, a smaller truck, with *Ambulance* written backward across the front so drivers could read it in their rear view mirrors, pulled in. The rescuers on the tanker truck threw open doors and leaped off bumpers to grab hoses and immediately start unlocking two fire hydrants in front of the building. Their frantic actions indicated they weren't going to bother to ask what was on fire.

I grabbed Granny and lifted her over the desk, then followed her. Blondie hadn't locked the door she'd used to escape, and I half-carried Granny through it. After pushing her to safety, I couldn't help myself. I peeked around the door.

Bobby Lee was staring after us. Behind him, I noticed a tiny spurt of smoke from the coffeepot. It must not have been one of those safety pots, which turned itself off if left too long. Or perhaps the sprinkler water had shorted something out. I barely got my mouth open to shout a warning to Bobby Lee about standing way too close to the malfunction before flames erupted. Flames that licked dangerously close to his baggy pants.

"Move!" I shouted at Bobby Lee.

I didn't really expect his teenage brain to process the warning that quickly, but it did. Or maybe he smelled the smoke. He jumped away from the flames, and the next thing I knew, he was behind the door with me, watching as the firemen rushed in, the hose already spewing a deadly stream of water that destroyed everything in its path.

The water splintered the door Bobby Lee had locked earlier and hit the small table behind it, which held a printer, fax, and various other pieces of office equipment. Then the two firemen aimed the hose at the flames and smoke coming from the coffeepot.

It didn't take long for the fire to die out, and before I realized it, the firemen were glancing around to see if there were any other places that needed their attention. The problem was, the hose was wandering with their gazes. Bobby Lee, given his teenage body, was able to make one leap and get behind the protective door before the water hit us. I, with my older, slower, body, couldn't move as fast. The next thing I knew, I was sliding along the floor on my back, trying not to drown in the water rushing over me.

My head hit something with a thump that sent those stars I'd only read or written about winging through my consciousness. I knew I was going to drown, because I couldn't muster up enough strength to roll over. Then the water abruptly ceased.

Two paramedics hurried toward me as I regained my senses. I could tell by the looks on their faces they were ready, willing and able to do whatever it took to save my life.

Despite the pain it caused in my head, I rolled over and got to my knees. With the help of the wall, I rose to my feet.

"Ma'am!" one medic said. "Don't do that. You're hurt!"

I hate it when someone not that much younger than me calls me *ma'am*. I held out a forestalling hand and said, "I'm not hurt that bad. Both of you leave me alone."

"We can't do that, ma'am," the second medic said.

Granny toddled over to me and said, "You lissen to me, Alice Carpenter. You set yourself down on that chair over there and let these here nice doctors take a look at you."

"They're not doc—" I began, but Granny tapped my lips with her finger and gave me one of her don't-mess-with-me looks. I sat where she indicated. At least it was a metal chair without a sopping wet seat. Not that I was dry myself. I stared down to make sure I wasn't as exposed as Blondie had been, but I'd put on a jacket against the cool mountain air that morning and it was still zipped up.

The medic lifted my chin, and the darned flashlight he used to examine me burned into my eyes. I tried to close them, but he forced them open with his thumb and forefinger, first one, then the other. As far as I was concerned, he should have been able to see if my pupils were enlarged, indicating a possible concussion, a good ten seconds before he finally shut off the light.

"You'll need x-rays—" he began

"Look," I told him as I gratefully accepted an ice pack the other young man held out to me and gently laid it against my head. "I appreciate your care, but I'm not going to the hospital. I'm not dizzy or confused. And I've got far more important things to do than take time out from my trip to be x-rayed for a non-existent concussion."

"You can't know for sure," he insisted.

"I'll sign your waiver," I told him as two blue-clad policemen walked into the lobby past the open door and stood with their hands on their hips, examining the damage.

The policemen strolled back to where we were gathered, and one of them nodded at the paramedics. "Kyle, Andy. What happened here? Do I need to call the Fire Marshall?"

"Naw," the younger man replied. "Looks like that coffeepot shorted out."

"'Cause the sprinkler water hit it," Bobby Lee said. "Plus the water probably destroyed the computer and fax and...." His eyes widened and he glared at me. "What did you do with my cell phone?"

I instinctively felt my pockets before I recalled handing the phone to Granny. When I looked over at her, she dug in her own jacket, which was as dripping wet as mine, and pulled out the phone.

"Uh oh," she said. "I heard mebbe iffen you put a wet one of these in rice, it'll dry out."

"No!" Bobby Lee rushed over and grabbed the phone. He stepped back and pointed at Granny. "She's the one who started all this. You need to arrest her for a false fire alarm."

One of the firemen who came through the door in time to hear Bobby Lee said, "There was indeed a fire, so there's no false alarm. That coffeepot could have caused this entire building to go up. And how many guests do you have in residence?"

Bobby Lee defended himself by saying, "The fire started because of the water from the ceiling hitting the wiring."

"Not from what I saw," the fireman said. "There was burnt coffee in the bottom of that pot. That causes plenty of fires. How long were you texting instead of watching to make sure the coffee didn't burn?"

Bobby Lee hung his head, obviously out of accusations to sidetrack his own guilt.

It was my turn now. "I'm glad you're here, Sergeant," I said, recognizing the rank on one policeman's sleeve. "I need you to get the owner of this place out here from her adulterous rendezvous in the back so I can file a claim for damage to my vehicle. Did you see it out there?"

"The hybrid with the two flat tires?" he asked. "I had a cousin who owned one of those. Those tires on them cost a bundle."

I sighed at that unwelcome information, and added, "There's also a scratch someone keyed into the side of my car."

"Annette's not the owner," Bobby Lee muttered. I guessed he was referring to Blondie, and I made a note of the name for my claim. "The guy who owns the place is the one she's...with back there."

"Hank?" Granny asked. "My, him and Callie Jo has come up in the world."

"I think he won one of the smaller lotto jackpots," Bobby Lee explained. "And bought this place with it. Annette manages it for him."

"That's not all Annette does for him," Granny said snidely.

"What's Annette's last name?" I asked in a mild tone of voice.

"Jones," Bobby Lee provided. "She claims she's a distant cousin of George's, but nobody believes her."

"Look," one of the paramedics broke in. "This is all very interesting, but we need to get this lady to the hospital. We might get a call on something more serious."

"You go right ahead and find a more serious incident," I told him. "Just give me your waiver to sign, since I know you won't leave unless I do that. Then you can be on your way."

He shook his head in resignation as the two of them gathered up their bags of medical supplies and walked out.

"Now, I want to get restitution for the damage to my car, so I can get new tires and be on my way," I told the policeman. "Can we get Annette and Hank out here?"

My request wasn't necessary, because just then Annette came through the door. She'd obviously showered and repaired her make-up...and her cleavage. She now wore a bra, but her tight sweater clearly indicated she was totally proud of her endowments.

"I'm right here," she said to me. "And I happened to overhear what you wanted. We aren't responsible for damages to guests' vehicles. We're very clear on that. You'll have to file a claim with your own insurance."

Granny tapped Annette on the shoulder, and the younger woman turned a glare on her. But Granny, being Granny, only stuck her nose up to give Annette back scowl for scowl.

"You weren't here when I was a'talkin' to your lover boy, Hank," Granny said. "'Pears I know him 'cause he's a cousin twice removed from my dead-and-gone husband. May he rest in peace. My husband, I mean, since Hank's still prowling for pus—uh...prowling 'round outside the marriage bed. And I just happen to know Callie Jo, too. His *wife*. Won't take me long to call one of my younger sisters and find out how to get hold of Callie Jo."

"No, no, that won't be necessary," Hank said as he hurried through the door to join us. He, too, was dressed again, in a wrinkled white shirt and...yes...those trousers belted on his lower chest. He already had his wallet in his hand, and he thrust a handful of cash at me. "I've already called one of the local boys to bring you two brand new tires and put them on your car, Miss. And this should take care of any paint damage."

I looked down at the money. All I could see were hundreds, and there must have been at least four dozen of them. I started to protest that it might be too much, but Granny gave me a warning glance. So I stuffed the money in my jacket pocket, deciding I'd split it with her later. She could always use a supplement to her tiny social security check.

"Thank you," I said, just as one of the paramedics returned with a clipboard holding a paper and handed me a pen. I hurriedly scribbled my name on the waiver and started to give him back his ice pack along with the clipboard.

"You can keep that," he said. "And when we came through the lobby, Bobby Lee said to tell you there's a wrecker out there putting new tires on your car."

"What about all the damage to our office stuff?" Annette grumbled. "From what I saw when I rushed into the lobby, these two women were the cause of the sprinklers going off."

"Why, honey cakes," Hank said as he led her away, "we'll just have to close down for a few days until things get fixed. Maybe take off to do a little sightseeing while Callie Jo's off tending to her new great-grandbaby."

Too bad he could not hang around and teach that old man what honor meant. But he must stay with the Alice woman and make sure she and the grandmother made the trip without further delay. Even finding her vehicle disabled had not sent her into a woman's fit of crying, headed back the way she had come. Had he known she was so strong, he could have saved himself a trip.

In his time, women kept their places. Did women's jobs and what they were told. Still, it was not so bad now. He had been about ready to try to persuade the Twila woman to do what was necessary. He had seen her perform the wondrous procedure more than once. However, perhaps the Alice woman was part of it. Otherwise, he would not have been in the right place to overhear the conversation between her and the man called Jack. Not been able to use the abilities he had mastered to travel to where the Alice woman lived.

He supposed it was Jack's fault the Twila woman had blocked him. So it was only fair Jack aid in bringing another woman to help. Or two, as these two traveled together. And, truthfully, he was enjoying the journey. Too bad he had taken a walk in these wondrous new surroundings and missed catching the renegades who vandalized the Alice woman's car. But at least the dishonorable man had been made to pay, even if he was not the one who did the damage.

He had had several centuries to learn to function in this state of being. It was easy to stay invisible on the roof of the car the Alice woman drove. Their journey was taking them through more mountains now, and were it not for that wide, level road beneath them, he could almost imagine he was back in his time.

The houses the intruders had built and the land they had cleared were hidden by a forest the signs called a national park. He had never been one to just drift through life...or death, as it be. He labored when needed, as well as kept his mind active. He had, though, even learned to read the language over the years.

He had forgotten how beautiful the countryside used to be. And he had to admit, riding on one of these vehicles beat the olden way of horseback travel, both in smoothness and speed. Yet the pleasure of it made him inattentive at times. He grabbed hold of the side of the roof just before he slid off.

The Alice woman sometimes started gabbing like a woman and didn't watch out for those pothole things in the road! No wonder he had heard men in these times complain about women drivers. More than once, he had thought about riding inside the vehicle. However, even invisible, Alice might sense him.

CHAPTER 3

Given our late start to the day, it was after dark by the time we pulled in at the beautiful old farmhouse where Twila and Jess lived. A porch with a spindle railing wrapped completely around a two-story, white wooden house with dark green shutters beside each window. Beds of flowers were laid out along the front.

Huge old oak trees shaded the house, and two more grew on each side of the front yard. Security lights shone from both of the outlying trees. The same type of lights glowed on the detached garage to the right of the house, which held not only a vehicle, but Jess's man-toys, like four-wheelers and a boat. The vehicle, Twila's little red Cavalier, was parked in the nearest stall; Jess knew better than to take up the space she had claimed for it. However, three other pickups, including Jack's truck, had to be left out in the weather.

We'd been in touch by cell phone as Granny and I travelled, so there were lights burning to welcome us and three people waited on the porch. I recognized Jack immediately, of course, even though he stood in the shadows behind Twila and Jess. I'd seen Twila just a few months earlier, and her red hair was carefully styled, as always. She wore our favorite clothing, jeans and a casual shirt.

Jess wasn't as tall as Jack, and his years in the cabs of eighteen-wheelers had left him with just a bit of a pot gut, which Twila's cooking kept in place. He never wore anything except jeans, either, and tonight he had on one of his black t-shirts. His hair had grayed over the years, but he still wore it long and in a ponytail down his back. He kept his beard trimmed neatly, and it curved down past his neck.

They stood in front of a wooden swing attached to the porch ceiling with chains. Twila and I had spent many a night sitting there talking until the wee morning hours. The entire place brought back lovely, warm memories.

Until I recalled Jack's concern about what might be going on here. I carefully scanned the surroundings, trying to see or sense a fourth being waiting in the shadows, real or non-corporeal. I didn't find anything, but some ghosts or nasties were notorious for being able to hide their presence.

Granny scrambled out as though she hadn't spent the last fourteen hours sitting beside me in the car, except for our potty breaks—human and animal—and stops for food—human and animal. I groaned as my own muscles told their age when I slid out. I started to open the door for Trucker, but Jess called from the porch, "Hey, Alice. We better introduce our animals before we turn them loose on each other."

"O.K.," I replied as I turned around...and bumped straight into a broad chest I'd nestled against a zillion times in my life, awake and asleep.

"Hey, *Chère*," Jack said in a low, welcoming voice. Before I could stop him—not that I tried very hard—he tipped my chin up with his fore-finger and kissed me briefly.

All right, I kissed him back, too, deciding immediately that our little argument back in Texas wasn't worth bringing with me to Ohio. Since everyone knew Jack and I were thinking seriously of having another go at a forever-relationship, no one would be surprised if we lingered alone a while at the car. In fact, I heard the screen door close and assumed they had gone back inside.

"Jack," I said as soon as I got my breath back, since his kisses do that to me, even short ones. "Have you seen that thing with Twila again?"

"Nope," he told me. "But I've noticed she has one of those protection packets you two carry with you sometimes tied to her rear view mirror."

"Good," I said, just as something nudged my leg and I looked down at a pink nose with two holes in it on a long snout protruding from a bristly head.

"Oink, oink."

Thankfully, my lunge at Jack didn't take him by surprise. He steadied both himself and me as the pot-bellied pig sat back on its haunches and welcomed me to its territory with loud grunts. But Trucker wasn't as accepting of this strange animal. His roars of displeasure erupted inside the car, and the door actually shook as he threw himself against it to try to protect his mommy from whatever was too near her.

"Oops," Jess said loudly so we could hear him through the noise. He hadn't accompanied Twila and Granny inside, and he reached down to slip a leash on the harness I now saw on the pig. "I was hoping Harley and your Trucker would get along. Looks like that might not happen."

I knocked my fist on the window. "Trucker! Sit and shut up!"

To my relief, my dog obeyed, although the yard lights shining into my car showed me his pouting, hurt face when he plopped down on the rear seat and laid his muzzle on his front legs. He took up the entire seat, and I stared around, searching for Miss Molly. She was curled up on one of the suitcases in the hatchback, not a bit worried about anything with Trucker on guard, not even whatever was upsetting him.

"I'll put Harley in our bedroom, and we can introduce them tomorrow, when we're all rested better," Jess said.

"Uh...your bedroom? The pig sleeps in your bedroom?" I asked.

"He's litter box trained, just like your Miss Molly," Jess assured me as he walked away, leading the pig. "You should come on in. Twila made meatloaf and noodles."

"Yum," I said. Granny and I had only been snacking since lunch. We figured Twila would have a spread ready for us, and neither of us wanted to ruin that.

After Jess disappeared into the house, I opened the door and let Trucker out. Given the strange surroundings, and the fact Twila and Jess had numerous other animals around, I reached back in and grabbed his leash from the floor.

"I'll start carrying in y'all's luggage, *Chère*," Jack said as I led Trucker off.

I had to pull my dog away from sniffing the ground where Harley had been sitting, but Trucker was usually a pretty obedient animal. Given his probable size, I'd made sure he realized who was boss from the time he was a puppy. I walked over to a patch of grass and let him smell around to find the appropriate place to do his business.

April in Ohio is a beautiful month. I'd actually lived in the state for the first part of my life. Our trees down south had leafed out well over a month ago, but the ones up here were still budding. Yet there were daffodils and crocuses blooming along the front of Twila's house, and the air carried the scent of lilacs, one of my very favorite flowers. I couldn't see her lilac bushes from here, but I'd visited a few times before and knew they were planted in the back, where she could open her bedroom windows and enjoy their delicate perfume.

I'd left the car door open, and Miss Molly wandered over to join Trucker. The two of them were hardly ever far apart. I even had pictures of Miss Molly curled either on Trucker's back or inside his huge paws as they slept. I wouldn't have wanted to be the one who tried to tease or hurt Miss Molly with him around. Whoever dared would find a hundred and fifty pounds of snarling defense snapping at their throat. And Miss Molly had some extremely sharp claws, since I'd never had her declawed. She had been known to show her displeasure herself when necessary.

The screen door opened and closed again. Trucker still hadn't decided where he wanted to relieve himself, so I watched Jack head back to the car for more suitcases. Knowing him, he was probably grumbling under his breath about what all a couple women needed to bring with them when they travelled. I'd seen him head out on a week-long trip with not much more than what he could stuff into a bag the size of the one I used for overnight necessities. This time, he carried only a suitcase and my laptop with him. He glanced over at me as he headed back to the house, and I felt his pleasure at my being here even at that distance.

Or maybe it was my psychic senses. Whatever. His smile and nod filled me with that warm feeling I'd never lost whenever I was with him.

Our divorce seemed such a stupid move now. We should have worked it out. Twila and Granny agreed, but didn't judge us. They'd made their own share of mistakes in life.

But if it's so right, I mused as Jack closed the screen door behind him again, *why are we having so much trouble deciding whether or not to move in together again? Let alone sleep with each other.*

Sleep together? Mentally I counted Twila's bedrooms, although I already knew there were only two guest rooms. Granny would want one, and I was certain Jack had already been given the other. There was one other upstairs room, a small one, but Twila used it for her own projects. She had a slew of pen pals, and she refused to learn to use a computer, so she kept her local post office in business with stamp purchases. The room contained a desk and file cabinets for her correspondence. She loved to collect different things at different times, so her shelves were usually full of knickknacks, as well as boxes of stationary.

I was focusing on things like that, though, to keep from wondering if she expected Jack and me to stay in the same room. She knew exactly where we were in our strained attempt at a new relationship; I had to have someone to talk to. I wouldn't put it past her to give us a nudge.

Trucker didn't even have time to warn me. At first I thought Jess had forgotten to pen up another one of his animals when something hit me and the ground came up at me too fast to even get a hand out so I wouldn't hit hard. I landed on my back, and the next thing I knew, Trucker stood over me, Miss Molly perched beneath his legs on my chest.

Funny thing. Neither one of the animals made a sound.

"What the...?"

I tried to sit up, but Trucker refused to move. My nose would have landed right beneath his short tail if I forced the issue, so I laid back down. Then Trucker did start to growl, a low, wicked noise that would have frightened me to death if it had been turned on me. Next, Miss

Molly emitted one of those nasty cat-growls that make a person's hair stand on end.

Or maybe it was something else making my hair react as though there were some sort of paranormal energy in the area.

I wasn't really hurt, since I'd landed on the soft grass and the ground hadn't hardened in summer heat yet. Trusting in Trucker and Miss Molly's warning to me, I stared around as far as I could see in my position, but I didn't spy one other living thing except the plants, trees and flowers. That didn't bode good.

"Trucker, move," I ordered. Their actions indicated whatever was prowling and attacking was *not* something that had died carrying a nice personality. I sure as hell didn't want to meet a nasty entity flat on my back. But the dog only stiffened his legs and held firm when I tried to push him off with hands on his broad rear haunches. This was one of the infrequent times he'd decided to disobey, if even for my own good.

Then I heard footsteps approaching. For just a second, I stiffened, because yes, ghosts do make noise sometimes when they walk. But Trucker and Miss Molly didn't sound an alarm, and I quickly recognized the cadence my Cajun used when he walked, albeit this time Jack was hurrying.

"Alice," he said as he knelt beside us. Trucker agreeably ambled off me, but Miss Molly only turned around and licked my cheek with her sandpaper tongue. Jack gently lifted her to the ground, then helped me into a sitting position.

"What happened?" he asked. "Did you slip and fall?"

I debated whether or not to tell him the truth. Jack definitely didn't enjoy the paranormal the way Twila and I did. But then, neither of us relished some of the crap we ran into.

"I think it was something supernatural," I admitted to Jack, and actually drew back when the cloud of thunder darkened his chocolate eyes to the color of coal. "But—"

"I'm gonna talk Jess and Twila into comin' down to Texas for a while," he said in a too-quiet voice. He stood and reached down to pull me up, but he didn't let loose. Holding me in his arms, he stared around

28

as he said, "Whatever this thing is, it's not somethin' I want you foolin' with, *Chère*. Y'all know enough folks to call someone else in to take care of it."

I pushed back, slapping at his hands when he tried to hold me. "*You* don't want me fooling with it? Since when have I started asking your permission to do something, Jack Roucheau? That's one of our problems, your need to try to control me."

He shook his head, then bit his lip as though holding back what he wished he could say. "Let's don't go there," he said instead. "It'll swing into one of the areas we still have to work on. Anyway, I didn't mean it like that. I worry about you."

I wasn't quite ready to back down. Still, like Jack, I didn't want our conversation to deviate into one of those conflicts that appeared to have no solution. Especially since I'd truly been glad to see him when I arrived.

"I apologize for my tone of voice, Jack. And I'll give you this. Whatever is around here isn't something I'm real anxious to deal with, either. But that has to be Twila's decision. I'll give her my honest input, but whatever she decides, I'll be there to back her up."

"I know you will, *Chère*," he said with a sigh. "Just make sure you stay safe. And don't be too stubborn...uh...sorry, wrong word. Don't be too proud to ask me or Jess for help, if there's anything we can do. Or some of your other friends who deal with this stuff."

I held out my hand in a teasing manner, indicating we should shake on it. But he took my hand and laid it back on my chest, in a gesture we'd used more times than I could count.

"O.K.," I said, moving my hand in a cross as I said, "Cross my heart and hope to die, I'll ask you for help if Twila or I think we need it."

"And Jess," he added.

I traced the cross again and said, "And Jess. And anyone else we think we might need to consult."

"Now let's get inside before the meatloaf gets cold," Jack said.

Realizing I'd dropped Trucker's leash, I glanced around to see where he had wandered off to. Actually, he was right there by our feet, Miss

Molly beside him. When he saw that he had our attention, he walked over to a nearby bush and hiked his leg.

Trucker didn't want to wander off to pee until we were aware he wasn't on guard, I thought worriedly, not wanting Jack to know what I'd concluded. But it didn't work.

"Whatever this damn thing is, it's even got the animals on high alert," Jack said.

"We have protections for the animals, as well as ourselves," I assured him. "Twila and I will anoint them as soon as I get in the house."

"Good," he said as he picked up Trucker's leash. He waited until I had Miss Molly settled in one arm, then took my hand.

I bravely opened my senses as we walked toward the house, but there wasn't even a hint of anything close enough for me to pick up on— malicious or otherwise. Now would have been a good time to see *Grand-mère* Alicia here with me, but so far, she hadn't made her presence known outside my log cabin. I had had a ghost or two, or more, travel with me, but she seemed more of a homebody.

* * *

After the Alice woman and Jack disappeared in the house, he glared around the yard. Now what was happening? He had only been gone a short while, and whoever flew through here and knocked Alice down was not familiar. Or if he was, he had moved too fast to detect his identity.

This presence was a new problem to deal with, an unwelcome annoyance. He had encountered other beings similar to himself over the eons as he tried to solve his own matter. All he had ever had to do was threaten them to make them move somewhere else, away from this land he once called his own. This new one, however, did not stay long enough to decide if he was indeed like himself or made of unknown workings. He frowned as he reflected that the rush had seemed as much a confused dash as anything else.

He tolerated the two living people here now, the Twila woman and her man, Jess. They were good. Treated the land well and took very good care of the animals. Even when Jess hunted, he did not kill just to see the animals die.

They ate the animals when Jess's shots rang sure and true. Which they did, since Jess did not want to make the game suffer. Once he had even watched Jess spend hours tracking a wounded deer, both not to waste the meat and also so the animal would not continue in pain.

Even Alice's animals did not appear to tolerate this new being. Or perhaps they were angered because the woman they cared for was attacked. There was no way right now to know if the attack had indeed been deliberate, or perhaps unintentional. It could have been a result of confusion. He would have to find the other one before more damage occurred. Then try to make him see why it would be best to leave this area. If he would not see reason...well, it would not be the first war path travelled.

Twila, Jess and Granny chatted away in the kitchen as though they hadn't seen each other in months, which they hadn't. Twila had joined Granny and me in Cimarron the previous December, but it had been over a year since I'd visited with Jess. Jack set Miss Molly down, and she paraded over beside the back wall, where Twila had already placed food and water dishes for both animals. I unleashed Trucker, and he followed his buddy. Neither one paid much attention to the overflowing food bowls. I knew they were expecting table scraps as soon as we all sat down. Which they would get, of course. We were softies when it came to animals. They did, however, each lap up some water.

It was such a friendly atmosphere, I didn't want to mention what had happened outside right away. But Twila took one look at me and frowned.

She didn't give me a choice. Taking my hand, she led me onto the back porch off the kitchen. "Go ahead and start eating," she called to the others over her shoulder. "Alice and I will be back before the food gets cold."

On the porch, she shut the door securely behind us, then turned to face me. There were security lights burning in her back yard, but none on the enclosed porch, and she didn't bother to flip the nearby switch. We could still see each other clearly, and the glare in her eyes wasn't something I wanted directed at me. Luckily, I sensed it wasn't.

"Was that effing thing out there?" she asked. Twila hardly ever swears, and if she'd said the actual word, I would have been even more concerned.

"I think so," I said. "It scared the crap out of Trucker and Miss Molly and knocked me down."

She nodded. "Did you get any idea what it could be?"

"Not even a hint," I admitted. "But I'm going up and get some oil to anoint the animals before I even sit down and eat."

"Good idea. I'll do Harley, too."

From inside the house, I heard a low growl from Trucker. For some reason, I stared out into the back yard over Twila's shoulder instead of checking on my dog. In the distance, I caught a movement. When I gasped, Twila jerked around.

"Did you see that thing?" she asked.

"There was something there," I told her. "Something pretty darned big. Do you have an Ohio Grassman hanging around here?"

She laughed. "You know I don't believe in that Grassman."

"Well, maybe it was something dressed up to look like him. Or Bigfoot. I only saw if for a second, though."

The door opened behind us, and Jack stuck his head out. "The food's getting cold."

"Jack," Twila said. "Will you walk outside with us for a second? Your pistol is hanging there under your jacket on that coat tree in the corner. Bring it, too."

Jack tensed but didn't argue. He strode over and grabbed his jacket off the prong to get to his pistol and shoulder holster. Draping the gun belt over his head and chest, he positioned it so he could reach the pistol before he walked over to the back door.

"Where did you see something that has you worried?" he asked.

I answered, "Over there by the fence. Just this side of the tree line. Whatever it was came out real quick, then ducked back out of sight.

But..." I didn't really want to say this in front of Twila, as worried as I sensed she already was, but....

"I think maybe it left something there on the ground. It sort of knelt down for a second, and when it got up and went back into the woods, it didn't seem quite as big."

"You two stay here," he ordered.

"Fat chance," Twila said. "This is my property and I'm not one to hide from a trespasser."

Jack sighed, then went on out the door, Twila and I on his heels. It was at least a hundred yards to the woods behind the house, and none of us spoke during the trek. We were all staring ahead, concentrating on the tree line. Jack had his hand on his pistol butt.

I didn't want to believe what I finally saw. The closer we got, the more it looked like a long, dark shadow lying on the ground. A human-shaped shadow. We were still a ways off when Jack grabbed our arms and halted us.

"Y'all both wait right here and don't even think about goin' against my orders." His tone of voice made it clear he was now in cop mode.

By then, I could see what looked like a dark pool of something glistening in the moonlight beside what did appear to be a man's body. I don't do blood well at all, and even concern for another human being's welfare can't usually make me overcome the nausea it produces. Twila's nursing career brought her into contact with bodily fluids, but I noticed she didn't take another step, either. On her part, I imagined it was as much shock at seeing a possible corpse on her property as anything else.

Jack knelt and felt the man's neck. He immediately stood and came back over to us. With a firm hold, he turned us to face the house.

"Go inside and call 9-1-1," he commanded.

"Is he...?" Twila couldn't finish, but Jack anticipated her query.

"Yeah, he's dead, and the knife the perp used is lyin' beside the body. Tell them to send a medical examiner along with the medics, cops, and a crime scene team."

Even I didn't have a disobedient thought in my mind. In the moonlight, whoever was lying there looked to be still oozing blood. Lots of blood.

"Be sure and tell them I'm out here with a gun," Jack said. "And that I'm a lawman. Tell them I'm only securin' the scene. I don't want to get shot myself."

CHAPTER 4

"What's going on?" Jess asked the moment we walked into the kitchen and Twila headed for the phone hanging on the wall.

Twila nodded at me to explain. I sat down at the table with him and Granny. The smells wafting from what I knew to be delicious food nearly distracted me, and my mouth watered. I realized it was only because I didn't want to think about what we'd found outside, but I reached for one of the yeast rolls sitting in a basket next to a tub of real butter. Before I could touch it, Jess shoved the basket away.

"What's going on, Alice?" he asked again.

I sighed and sat back in the chair. "Sorry. I didn't realize I was so hungry. But I probably shouldn't be, given what's out there on the corner of your property."

"What?" Jess said, rising to his feet. "Never mind, I'll go see for myself."

I grabbed his arm. "Please don't. It's...Jack's out there. We think there's someone...all right, we don't think. Jack checked, and the guy lying there is dead. Jack doesn't want anyone contaminating the area."

"Dead?" Instead of rushing out the door, Jess sank back into his chair.

"What happened?" Granny asked.

I could hear Twila talking to the 9-1-1- dispatcher in the background, giving them her address, along with directions on how to find the house.

"I don't know, Granny. I...." I glanced at Jess, who, unlike Jack, did have a belief in the supernatural. But I wasn't sure about his views on what I thought I'd seen. So I waffled. "There was something in the woods, too. We need to let Jack and the authorities handle it."

"Yeah," Granny put in with a snort of disbelief. "Like you always do."

I bristled at her. "I mean it this time. We may have something else to deal with around here, and I need to focus on that."

Oops. I'd forgotten Jess wasn't aware of whatever was dogging Twila. Or, given the expression on his face, maybe he was.

He stared at me directly. "I hope you keep that in mind, Alice. I don't know what the fuck it is that's showed up here, but I ain't happy with the situation. Maybe it's also got something to do with what you found outside."

"It's possible, Jess," I admitted just as Twila came over and laid an arm around Jess's shoulders.

"Please don't worry," she said, giving him a hug. "If it turns out to be something we can't handle, we'll leave for a while and let someone else take care of it."

"Yeah," he growled. "And leave all our animals to face it. No way."

Twila sighed, and I rose to go out on the porch again and check on Jack. I stared out the screened in window towards the woods and saw him waiting a good distance from the shadow on the ground. I yearned to go stay with him, but two things stopped me. One was his cop attitude, which I'd learned not to toy with over the years. But that didn't halt me as much as the thought of being near that pool of blood.

Jack had said the man was dead, but he couldn't have been in that condition too long, or the blood wouldn't still be seeping out enough to show that much on the ground. Still, Jack hadn't attempted CPR, and he had enough medical training to determine if that would give someone a chance or not.

Maybe there was another wound I couldn't see from where I stood. Oh, God.

I clenched my fists in reaction and turned when Granny nudged me.

"Here," she said, handing me a paper towel around a roll stuffed with meatloaf. "I heard your belly growlin' clear on the other side of the table."

"Thanks," I said, but when I lifted the roll to my mouth, my stomach rebelled at the thought of putting anything in it right now. I laid the roll on the windowsill.

"I can't," I told Granny. "Sorry."

"Well, here then," she said as she gave me a glass filled with light amber liquid. "Found Twila's bar, I did, and this here's Crown and Seven."

Gratefully, I grabbed the glass. This time, I didn't give my stomach a chance to protest as I gulped down a huge swallow, then another. Immediately, the tension eased enough for me to handle things better.

"Who you think that poor soul is?" Granny asked softly.

I shook my head. "Jack didn't let us close enough to see his face."

Sirens sounded in the distance, and I instinctively turned toward the noise. All I could see, of course, was the inside of the kitchen, where Twila now sat beside Jess, their heads close together. Even in profile, her face radiated worry. She rose and patted Jess's arm before she walked out of the kitchen, on a path to the front door to meet the officials about to descend on her peaceful acreage.

* * *

All that lovely food had grown cold while we dealt with the questions and demands of the rescue squad paramedics and the sheriff and deputies. Law enforcement in this small county was just as efficient as any in a large city. Even though the sheriff appeared to know Jess and Twila both, he directed us to please not talk among ourselves until one of his deputies got our statements.

That had taken less time than anyone imagined, since none of us knew anything other than the body had appeared here.

Except for me, of course. The sheriff himself took me aside into the living room and invited me to sit on the couch while he settled on the other end. He looked to be about my same age, but I didn't recall him from when I lived in the area. He definitely hadn't gone to school with us, unless he had changed drastically. All of us back then had kept a close eye on the cute guys, and he still looked good in his uniform. Like Jack, his black hair had just a hint of silvering at the temples, but he had green eyes rather than Jack's dark brown.

"Twila raves about your books," he said. "Have to admit, I haven't read any of them. She says they're crime mysteries."

His face was friendly and open, but unfortunately, I'd been questioned enough times by lawmen to be on edge, waiting for him to morph from good cop to bad. Shoot, I'd even had Jack pull that on me a time or two. After the second incident, though, he'd known better than to go down that road, unless he wanted to sleep on the couch for a while.

Of course, he ended up sleeping a lot further away from me than that.

"I don't think I got your name," I said.

"Sheriff Hoof." He chuckled. "Yeah, like a horse's hoof. I don't know how, but my German granddaddy somehow let that bastardization of his family name happen over the years."

"Probably makes for some interesting campaign materials when you run for office," I mused, knowing he must have moved into the area after I left. I would have remembered that name.

He shrugged. "Haven't had to worry 'bout that the last few elections. Guess maybe it's too quiet around here to give folks much of a worry about who keeps the crime in check. We got the druggies, like everywhere, but most of them eventually head off to some other part of the state where there's more money to be made. This is the first murder we've had in five years."

"Do you know who it is yet?"

"Gotta notify the next of kin before I can let that out," he said. "You being a crime writer, you should know that."

His continued reference to my *crime* writing was setting off some sort of distant alarm bells, but I couldn't figure out exactly what it meant. Still, I said, "I write mysteries. There's crime in them, of course, but the story is about solving it. Bringing the bad guy, or guys, to justice."

"Or gals," he said as he eyed my face, giving me the impression he was watching my reaction.

"Or gals," I said, giving him back a shrug as nonchalant as the one he'd used. Then, getting tired of his procrastination, I added, "Do you want to record my statement? Or will I have to dictate it to one of your clerks to type up?"

He gave me a look with a smidgen of respect and pulled out a small recorder from his shirt pocket. He set it on the coffee table in front of the couch, but before he pushed the *on* button, he asked, "You want some coffee or something? I think there's a pot brewing in the kitchen."

"Not really," I said. The Crown and Seven was long gone, and I'd much rather have had another one of those. However, I didn't want to ask for a drink until after my statement. "I'm more of a latte person."

"I see." As he finally turned on the recorder, he explained, "This is one of our newer ones. Got some stimulus money a while back and updated a few things. It can pick up a whisper at twenty feet, so you don't have to talk real loud."

"Do you want me to start now?" I prodded.

With a sigh, he spoke again himself, identifying the date, where we were, and giving both our names.

"Now, Miss..." he began before halting and asking, "Do you mind if I call you Alice? Doesn't seem right to be all starchy with such a pretty lady."

Was he flirting with me? Didn't he realize there was a dead man outside, and this wasn't the proper time to try to hit on one of the witnesses? I started to make a smart aleck remark and ask him if I should call him Horse to go with Hoof, but I bit my tongue and nodded a compliance.

"O.K.," he said. "Alice, can you just go ahead and relate what you saw this evening that led you folks to discover a dead body on Mrs. Brown's property?"

I didn't understand why he gave Twila the measure of respect of addressing her as Mrs., but I didn't call him on it.

"Twila and I were on the back porch talking—"

"About what?" he interrupted.

I wasn't about to explain to this man that we were worried about some sort of nasty entity up to no good around Twila. Sometimes my mind doesn't work really fast, though. Someone once accused me of having an ice-water brain, and that was especially true when I was worried or upset. This was definitely a situation that had me both.

I must have let the silence linger too long, which always makes a law enforcement type start eyeing you with suspicion, because Sheriff Hoof cleared his throat.

Hurriedly, I said, "We hadn't seen each other for four months, although we talk on the phone at least weekly. We're both paranormal investigators, so—"

"You mean like those ghost hunters on TV?" he interrupted.

This guy was pushing his luck. Twila may have gotten the red hair, but there was enough auburn in my own locks to reflect the temper I tried to keep in check. I struggled to maintain a measure of calm, though, since I'd learned a time or two that defying men in certain positions of authority didn't always bode well.

"Not really like them," I said. "We don't use all that fancy equipment. We just help people who ask. And, like I was saying, we were just chatting and I heard Trucker growl."

"Trucker's that beautiful dog you have in there, right?"

"Yes. But when I looked away from Twila, I caught a motion off on the edge of the woods."

"I don't understand," Hoof interrupted once again. "Was your dog outside?"

"He was still in the kitchen," I explained. "Why?"

"I'm just trying to get everything set in my mind. Seems if he growled in the kitchen, you'd be looking back in there instead of out towards the woods."

"You're right," I said, and he couldn't hide the surprise in his eyes. "And I don't know why it happened like that, but it did. Unless maybe it was because I have what some people call a Sixth Sense."

His eyebrows rose in question. "Like seeing ghosts and stuff like that?"

"It's a lot more than that, Sheriff. And more than I can get into right now. Believe me when I say I don't know why I looked at the woods, but I did. Whatever came out of there was big. Huge. Large and bulky. I've thought about it, and maybe he was carrying the body when he came out."

"Why do you say that?"

"He knelt down and then stood up. And he was smaller then."

"Seems a funny thing for a killer to do," Hoof said. "Most of them hide their murders so they won't get caught."

You're discussing a lot of stuff that I wouldn't think you should be letting a civilian in on, I couldn't help thinking. Still, I wanted to get this over with and go check on the others. So I ignored his comment.

"Have you called in someone to try to track whoever it was?" I asked. "He did go back into the woods."

"Actually, we do have a dog on the way," he said. "My deputies will take care of all that. Can you give me a good description? Or was he too far off?"

I actually laughed, and he regarded me with a frown that told me exactly what he thought of my levity.

"What's so damn funny about a dead man?" he asked.

"I'm sorry," I said, holding up my palms in entreaty. "I didn't mean it that way. It's just...well, you're not going to believe me."

"Try me."

I sighed, then said, "It looked like an Ohio Grassman."

He dropped his head and chuckled. "All right, Alice. You got back at me for being snarky. Now tell me what he looked like."

"Actually, I am telling you the truth," I said as frankly as I could manage. "He was big, and it wasn't really a clear human-like outline. It was like he was wearing a bunch of weeds or grass or something all over his body. In fact, now that I think on it, there was a little bit of a breeze, and I could see what looked like maybe vines trailing down over him and swinging back and forth."

"How do you know what our supposed Grassman looks like?"

"Things like that are all over the internet and YouTube, places like that. There was even a TV show a while back that showed what the hunters thought was a Grassman captured on video."

"I don't watch stuff like that," he said.

Just then I noticed a tense-faced Jack appear in the living room doorway. He leaned against the doorjamb and crossed his arms, evidently not worried about the sheriff asking him to leave while he questioned a witness. Hopefully, only a witness. I'd been a suspect once before, also, but surely this time I had plenty of witnesses to vouch that I wasn't the huge, hairy thing that dumped that poor man on Twila's property.

"I understand you and Mrs. Brown went with Detective Roucheau when he went out to discover the body."

"Yes."

He appeared to expect me to elaborate, but I'd also been questioned enough times to know that an interrogator would let a silence linger, hoping the person being questioned would fill the gap in conversation.

"Sheriff," Jack said to announce himself as he walked over and stood beside us. "Sorry to interrupt, but the tracker is here. And there's something weird goin' on out there. One of your deputies asked me to come get you."

Hoof stood up, a worried frown on his face. "What could be wrong with putting the dog on the trail?"

"Well," Jack said, "your men assured me that you'd used this tracker and his hounds before. He's got two dogs with him, but neither one of them will enter the woods after the suspect."

"What?" Hoof growled. "Did they say why?"

"No. I was out there when they tried to put them on the trail. In fact, they found a patch of hair they think was left by the suspect. From the looks of it, he was probably wearing some sort of stupid suit for a disguise. Your lab will have to decide if the hair is human or from a costume, though. The dogs sniffed the footprints they found and sort of whined. Looked like maybe they would do what they were supposed to. But when one of the men waved that hair under their noses, they cringed to the ground and wouldn't move."

"I'll be damned," the sheriff said before he looked at me and added, "We'll have to finish this later, Alice. Come on by the office tomorrow. I'll have Kindra fire up the latte machine."

He started to walk out of the room, and I said, "Trucker might not be afraid of whatever dropped that poor man here."

Jack stared at me for a moment, then nodded agreement as Hoof paused in contemplation and gave Jack a questioning look.

"I think she's right," Jack said. "We could give it a try."

"He won't work without me," I put in.

"Now, Alice," Hoof said. "We can't have a civilian out there being in possible danger."

"Isn't the man handling the other tracker dogs a civilian?" I asked in what I hoped was a reasonable tone. I really wanted to get out there and see what was prowling around Twila's property. I hadn't lied, though. Trucker was primarily obedient to me, although he did like Jack. My dog considered several of my closest friends part of his circle of love, yet I was the alpha of his pack mentality.

"I'll go along and stay with her," Jack said. "Trucker might work for me, but it will be much faster with her."

Hoof reluctantly nodded, then scanned my body. "You might want to put on some better shoes. We had some rain yesterday, and those tennis shoes will get soaked through pretty quick. Plus even in April, our temperatures drop at night."

"I've got hiking boots in my luggage. Which room are my things in, Jack?"

"The double guest room," he told me.

The information relieved me. Maybe. I guessed. Oh, shoot, that was what I wanted, wasn't it? One of Twila's extra bedrooms had twin beds.

Evidently, Granny and I would share those, while Jack had his own, separate room.

"I'll be right back," I said with a sigh before I realized Jack was staring steadily at me, obviously interested in my reaction to the sleeping arrangements. I hurried out without giving him one. Or hoped I did.

When I came back down a few minutes later wearing my hiking boots, I also carried a jacket with a hood. Voices indicated people were gathered in the kitchen, but Jack and Jess sat in the living room, where I'd been with Hoof moments ago. Since Jack was going with me, I started over to tell him I was ready.

"No!" Jess said as he lurched to his feet. He stormed over to the fireplace on the far wall, Jack dogging his steps. Jess drew back a fist, and I gasped. Oh, no! It looked like he intended to crash his fist into the fireplace bricks!

Jack grabbed Jess's arm. They briefly struggled, but Jack finally spun Jess around to face him.

"I'm sorry, partner," Jack said. "But you had to know sooner or later."

"I've known Patches my entire life!" Jess said. "He wouldn't hurt a flea, even if it was biting his ass. Why would someone kill him? It doesn't make sense. He doesn't have an enemy in the entire county. The whole state!"

"I don't know," Jack said, then saw me standing over by the couch. He was busy with Jess, though, and I didn't want to interrupt. "I'll tell you what. I'm going to insinuate myself in this investigation and help them find out. I liked Patches myself when I met him a few days ago."

Jess pulled back, and Jack tensed as he let go.

"I'm O.K.," Jess said "Well, not O.K., but I need to be alone right now, Jack. I'm going out to my workshop in the garage. Tell Twila where I am, will you? But tell her I really don't want any company right now."

"I'll do that," Jack agreed.

Jess didn't even seem to notice me as he walked past. Instead of going through the kitchen, he went out the front door. It was a longer walk to the barn that way, but knowing Jess, he would rather go that way than have to explain himself to anyone.

As Jack approached me, I asked, "So they know who the dead man was?"

"Yeah, but it's not public information until they find his next of kin and get a formal ID," Jack said. "His name is Patches...or that's his nickname. He runs...ran the bait shop where Jess and I stopped before we went fishing. He was a really good guy."

"Just Patches?" I asked.

"I think the sheriff said his last name was Henry, but he wasn't sure of the real first name himself. Everyone around here called him Patches for years."

I stared at the front door where Jess had disappeared. "I'm so sorry for Jess. It sounds like they were close."

"Yeah." Jack sighed. "We better get in there with the sheriff. Are you sure you want to do this, *Chère*?"

I wasn't, but I needed to for Twila. Jack had this protective streak, though, and I couldn't voice my reluctance. Instead of answering with what would have been at least a white lie, I went into the kitchen. As Jack walked over to speak to Twila in a low voice, I looked around until I found my two pets. Granny sat at the table, a glass in front of her that probably contained her second drink of the evening, Miss Molly on her lap. Trucker laid on the floor beside them, head on his front paws, his gaze pinned on me.

I pulled the bottle of oil I'd retrieved from my satchel out of my jacket pocket and knelt in front of Granny. "Miss Molly's not real tolerant of this," I said. "Want me to put her on the table so she doesn't scratch you?"

"Not 'tall," Granny said as she tucked an arthritis-gnarled finger under Miss Molly's chin and lifted her head to stare into those blue eyes. "You'n me's gonna handle this just fine, ain't we, Miss Molly? You don't use them sharp claws on me and I won't forget where the Kitty Kisses are when you starts whining for a snack."

Miss Molly blinked and didn't even move when I took the cap from the oil bottle. It wasn't that pungent, but her sense of smell always picked it up immediately. I wet my forefinger with the consecrated oil and traced a cross on the top of her head, then tipped the bottle up again and added one on her back. My cat never twitched a muscle.

"Good girl," Granny said as I turned my attention to Trucker.

"What is that?" Jack asked.

I hadn't noticed him approach, and when the back door opened and closed, I saw Twila was gone. "I thought Jess didn't want her to come out there with him," I said.

"Men don't always know for sure when they do or don't want their women around," Jack replied.

I stared up at him for a second, caught in the sincerity of his expression, then nodded.

"This is oil that's been consecrated and blessed," I said as I tipped the bottle up to put more oil on my finger and traced the cross on Trucker's head. Unlike Miss Molly, he tolerated the procedure, although he did sneeze when I inadvertently got the open bottle too close to his nose. I added the cross to his back as I went on, "If there's something nasty out there, it won't be able to get through the protective barrier it places around my animals."

I didn't bother to see if Jack believed me as I stood. If he did, fine. If not, it wouldn't surprise me, given his skepticism regarding many of the paranormal incidents I dealt with every day. "And since Twila's busy with Jess, we should anoint her pig before we go. She must have forgotten."

Twila and Jess had remodeled the downstairs of the farmhouse to add a large bedroom for themselves. I led Jack down the hallway and cautiously opened the door to peek in. A bedside lamp shone, and Harley was sprawled on top of the spread on the king-sized bed. As soon as he saw us, his head jerked up and he scrambled off the bed, leaving a trail of disgruntled oink-oink's in the air.

Harley had to weigh at least fifty pounds, and luckily Twila's bedroom was carpeted. Otherwise, his low-hanging belly would have made a loud splat, and his sharp little hooves clattered on a hardwood floor.

I laughed. "I guess Twila doesn't allow him on the bed, so he sneaks up there when she's not around."

"How can that pig get up on that bed?" Jack asked before he noticed the nightstand drawers open beneath the lamp. "Oh."

As we watched, Harley walked over and nudged the drawer he'd used for a ladder closed, then sat back and stared at us. I swear he looked as innocent as a pig could pull off.

We both laughed aloud, and Jack shook his head. "That pig's exactly the type of pet I'd expect Jess to have."

"Well, I'm not used to dealing with a pig," I said. "So you hold him while I anoint him."

Jack squatted by Harley and grasped the harness the pig wore as he said, "You be good, Harley, and I'll tell Jess you behaved. Maybe he'll give you a PBJ sandwich."

The pig jumped to its feet and nuzzled Jack's shirt as though searching for his treat right then. While Jack was busy keeping it from climbing onto his lap, I traced the protective crosses. The pig's head and along its back were as bristly as they appeared, but I noticed it was a lot cleaner than I expected a pig to be.

As I recapped the bottle, I said to Jack, "PBJ?"

"Jess said this pig eats about the same things he and Twila do, and he's partial to peanut-butter-and-jelly sandwiches. They gotta go light on the peanut butter, though, 'cause his tongue sticks to the roof of his mouth and Harley sort of goes crazy until he works it free."

I reached down and scratched one of Harley's ears, and that darn pig closed his eyes and leaned against my leg as he emitted a noise that sounded close to Miss Molly's purrs.

"What a sweetie," I said, changing my mind about how good a pet a pig would make. "If Jess gets tired of you, you might come live with me. You can have the peanut butter, though. I'm allergic to nuts."

"No way, love," Jack said with a laugh. "I don't think a pot-bellied pig would fit in with your half-a-dozen cats and Trucker."

"Let alone my ghosts," I agreed.

Not surprising me, Jack didn't respond to my last comment. That was another one of the problems Jack and I had to work out. When we were married and lived in New Orleans, we didn't share the apartment with ten ghosts. Jack hadn't mentioned anything to me about maybe getting the ghosts who boarded with me to move on, but one day he did ask me where ghosts went eventually. After informing him that the best thing was for them to go into The Light, I didn't bother to tell him that several of my ghosts had indeed crossed over during the time I'd lived in Six Gun. However, others usually turned up to fill that empty spaces in my paranormal boarding house.

"We better get out there with the sheriff," Jack said. "You go first. I'll make sure Harley doesn't sneak out. Jess said the pig's good at that."

CHAPTER 5

Granny informed us that Hoof had gone back to the crime scene. Leaving Miss Molly in her care, Jack, Trucker and I walked across the back yard, towards the woods. I noticed the light still on in Jess's workshop inside the huge old barn. Evidently, he and Twila were still there.

Whoever, or *what*ever, had been carrying Patches' body had emerged from the tree line where Hoof waited for us. Even though the body had evidently already been removed by the medical examiner, I bypassed where it had lain, keeping my gaze averted from the dark stains the moon illuminated. Beyond Hoof, a trail led beneath tall hardwood trees. Rather than appearing spooky and desolate, especially given what had happened here, I thought of a poem by one of my favorite poets, Robert Frost: *The woods are lovely, dark and deep.*

I had roamed woods like this in my tomboy youth, never once being afraid. Yet like Frost, I had a promise to keep. Hopefully, I wouldn't have miles to go before I slept, because after the drive Granny and I made that day, I was looking forward to even that lonely twin bed.

Jack had halted a ways back, and I gripped Trucker's leash tightly. My dog already showed an alertness that usually indicated he was ready for bear...or ghost, whatever. He wasn't paying as much attention to the clear, wide trail beneath the limbs, though, as he was sniffing the air and growling low.

Kneeling at the juncture of woods and trail, Hoof shot me a look that indicated he had his doubts about whether an animal without the word "hound" in its name could perform in the tracking business. I tugged Trucker over and shone my flashlight on the deep footprint Hoof wanted the dog to zone in on.

"Trucker, look," I said, crouching for a closer look myself.

"Isn't the command *find?*" Hoof asked as Trucker quickly sniffed the print, then lifted his nose in the air again.

I didn't bother to answer such a dumb question. My dog wasn't professionally trained. He would, however, give his heart to anything I wanted him to do and understood my commands. Sometimes I even thought he had the same psychic ability as Twila and I did, since he followed directives as though reading my mind.

As I waited for Trucker to decide which way he was going to drag me, I studied that footprint. It sure did look like a Bigfoot print, at least, the ones everybody always posted on line to supposedly prove they had encountered one of the legendary creatures. It looked just like a human footprint, albeit a huge person. It had to be at least twenty-four inches long, a foot across, and the toes protruded several inches. I didn't know that much about gauging a thing's weight by its track, but this footprint had sunk into the dirt at least an inch and a half.

The one Hoof squatted beside was headed into the field where we were, but the flashlight illuminated another a few feet away, pointed into the woods.

I'd always been interested in monsters and wished someone would find positive proof of their existence. After all, there were such things as ghosts and demons, so why not monsters? I hadn't decided yet how I wanted my evidence of a monster delivered. Definitely not by someone actually murdering one of those awesome beasts. And given my shaky confidence in standing up to a mean, nasty ghost now and then, even with Twila at my back, I sure didn't want to actually see a living one. Not without an extra pair of underwear in my pocket.

There were various names for Bigfoot: Sasquatch, Yeti, Skunk Ape, even just Wild Man of the Woods. What I'd read on the Ohio Grassman indicated it appeared similar to Bigfoot. Stories gave its height at seven feet or more, its weight a lot more than I ever wanted to weigh.

"Well?" Hoof prodded. "Is your dog going to track or not?"

I gave him an irritated look and glanced at Trucker. He still had his nose pointed in the air, and I noticed a flutter an inch or so above where he could have reached.

"How well did your men search the area?" I asked Hoof as I stood.

"As good as we could without being able to smell like a dog can," he replied sarcastically.

I aimed my flashlight beam at what had caught Trucker's attention. "That piece of fur is visible enough that you shouldn't have to smell it to find it," I spat back just as caustically.

Hoof's eyes widened. He started to reach for the fur caught on the end of a prickly briar. Before he touched it, he jerked his hand back and dug in his pocket for a nylon glove. I continued to have respect for these local officials' investigative skills, although their bedside manners—at least Hoof's—left a lot to be desired.

The gob of hair was dark green and three or four inches wide, a couple inches across. The Grassman supposedly had vines and grass growing in its fur. Vines and grass were green in the spring, and it was springtime right now.

"Probably just a wandering bear or wild hog," Hoof mused as he examined the hair in his own flashlight beam. "Worth checking out."

"A green bear or hog?" I asked with a raised eyebrow. "I've never seen a green bear. And you must have a new breed of hog here. Green hogs with fur on them."

As Trucker stood there unmoving, his muscles tensed as though held in check, Hoof removed a plastic evidence bag from his pocket. He wore a jacket with numerous places to store stuff and seemed to have everything at his fingertips.

"Like I said." He put the hair in the bag and sealed it. "I'll have it checked out. But right now, we need to get on down the trail. You still want your dog to try tracking, or should I see if I can get our other tracker and his dogs back?"

I heaved a sigh and laid a hand on Trucker's head. Pointing at the ground again, I shoved gently on him, and he obediently bent his muzzle to sniff. Then, without my even asking, he started down the trail.

Hoof followed me, and when I glanced back, I noticed another shadow behind him. I assumed it was Jack, since his protective instincts wouldn't allow me to wander off somewhere in the dark without him there to oversee me. I'd never bothered to tell Jack how many times Twila and I prowled deep darkness both outside and inside shabby, rundown buildings without a big strong man to guard us.

Every few feet, there would be another footprint. Few feet might be an understatement. Whatever this huge beast was, it had an enormous stride. I counted two or three of my own steps in between each of its imprints. Trucker continued to lead us down the trail until it ended...at a wooden fence bordering a county road. There, he sat and looked back and forth from me to the asphalt, as though to say, "Now what?"

"Crap," I said. "It either crossed the road or got in someone's car."

Hoof shone his light on the ground just beyond the fence. "I'd vote for the car. Those are pickup tracks in the dirt on the other side of the fence, and they're fresh."

"We should cross the road and check," I ventured.

"Probably, but I doubt we'll have much luck." He proceeded to climb over the fence.

Trucker ducked under the bottom board, and I slid between the top and middle one. When I stood up, I turned around to wait for Jack.

But there was no one on the other side of the fence.

I gasped.

"What's wrong?" Hoof asked.

"Where's Jack?"

"Back at the crime scene."

"But...but...he was behind you," I insisted.

"Never was," Hoof denied. "He stayed back where we found Patches."

I bit my lip to keep from spouting off a denial and maybe making a fool of myself. After all, Hoof had been behind me. Surely he would know if someone had been following him.

However, I'd glanced back at least three times, and even though I didn't shine my light, each time I saw a black shadow of someone behind Hoof.

"What makes you think someone was with us?" Hoof asked.

There went my intent not to show myself a fool. I didn't know what Hoof's beliefs were, but if he was like Jack used to be, until proof was thrust under his nose, he would surely scoff at what I was about to say. Jack hadn't believed until he actually started seeing ghosts himself.

"There was someone following you," I said hesitantly.

"There wasn't," Hoof denied. "I would have heard him."

"Not if...." I still wasn't sure I wanted to discuss this with him.

"If it was a ghost?" Hoof asked. He shone his flashlight back the way we had come. "Huh. You think maybe Patches is trying to help us find who murdered him?"

"Please, no," I said, not realizing I'd said it aloud until Hoof spoke up again.

"Why not? It sure would help us cut down on the investigation time if the victim's ghost would just tell us who'd murdered him. Or at the least, where to look for clues."

I sighed. "It doesn't work that way, Sheriff."

"I wish you'd call me Harv," he broke in.

Oh, My. God. This time I was able to keep my mouth shut, but it took an effort to keep from spurting out the laughter the name Harv Hoof fostered.

"It's...uh...an official investigation," I managed to say without a gush of hilarity.

"Well, I'll let you get by with that for now." He actually winked, which I saw clearly because his light was near his face. "But afterwards, we'll have to see."

I debated for an instant whether or not to reveal that Jack and I were a couple again. Despite his hilarious name, though, the sheriff was a somewhat handsome man. It might do Jack good to be a little jealous. Maybe we'd get over this hump of compromises we needed to work on.

No, I couldn't play that game.

"Look—"

"We better get on over there and see if your dog can pick up the trail."

Hoof's words overrode my attempted explanation, and he took my arm to lead me onto the asphalt. The only thing that kept us both from suffering possible mortal injuries was Trucker jerking backward on his leash, which I still gripped tightly. The jolt sent me stumbling into Hoof....

...just as the rusty old pickup roared around the bend in the road and headed straight for us.

Hoof lost his balance and tumbled to the ground, leaving me without support to crash down after him.

The driver never even touched the brakes. The tires didn't even squeal. It barreled past as I fell, and I immediately tried to lever myself off Hoof and see if I could get its license plate number.

Unfortunately, I levered with my elbow. It dug into Hoof's stomach and air gushed out of him in a whoosh. He kept enough air to yell an expletive that I never said no matter how pissed off I got.

I didn't pay much attention to the sheriff's rudeness, though. I rolled on over and stumbled to my feet, gaping down the road. It ran straight ahead of us, and there wasn't a sign of the pickup anywhere. No way had it had time to travel far enough to get out of sight.

Trucker whined and sidled up to me. I laid a hand on his head and kept staring down the road as I waited for Hoof to get to his feet. When he only laid there moaning, I glanced behind me.

He was curled in an embryo position, and suddenly it dawned on me that I'd landed lower on him than I'd thought. That wasn't his stomach I'd used my elbow on.

"Good lord, I'm sorry," I said as I crouched beside him. "Is there anything I can do?"

"You've already done it," he said around his groans. Then he managed to straighten his legs and sit up. "I know you didn't mean it, Alice. But give me a few minutes of privacy, will you?"

I stood and walked back over to the asphalt. I doubted we'd be going on across the road now, since Hoof probably wasn't in any shape to keep on hunting the Grassman, or Bigfoot, or whoever or whatever we'd been trailing. I grimaced at the squishy sensation I now recalled. My elbow had dug in his privates pretty deep.

And frankly, finding a legendary monster was the furthest thing from my mind right then. That pickup crowded out all other thoughts—not because it had tried to run us down, either.

I mentally replayed what I'd see in my mind. The truck had been an old model, one of those from maybe the late 40's. It had a rounded hood and top of the cab, a short bed. It was painted orange and as rusty as all get out.

I'd had no problem telling that. A cloud of bright mist had surrounded it, lighting it as clearly as if it had been daylight. Lighting up everything except the windshield. It had been as black as coal, hiding the inside of the cab. Except....

...the passenger window had been down. I'd only had a glimpse as I fell, but the man hunched over the steering wheel looked a heck of a lot like the man I'd seen lying back there just outside the woods an hour or so ago. Looked a heck of a lot like the man dead man I'd seen earlier. The one they called Patches.

Or his ghost, anyway.

But where had he gotten the pickup? And how was he driving it? It didn't seem like he'd been dead long enough to have developed the ability it took for that. But then, who was I to judge how things worked in the paranormal world? How long it took a new ghost to learn to use its paranormal abilities? Plus it wasn't as if I hadn't seen a ghost driving a ghost pickup once before in my paranormal career.

Trucker nudged me again, and I absently petted his head. "What do you think, boy? Did we just see what I thought we saw?"

"Woof." I'd heard my dog bark a lot louder than that before. It sounded like he was as confused as I was.

Hoof spoke right beside my ear. "Can you identify the driver?"

I jumped as though a ghost had touched me and whirled on him. "Darn it, don't sneak up on a person like that!"

"You don't have to be scared now. Whoever it was is gone."

"A lot more gone than you think," I muttered.

"So?" he prodded. "Did you?"

I stared at him to watch his reaction. "It was Patches. The man whose body you just found back there."

He shook his head. "I'll have to talk to Jack. We didn't release his identity yet."

"I overheard him telling Jess, who has a right to know since they were good friends," I defended. "So Jack didn't deliberately let information slip. And did you hear who I said it was?"

Hoof actually reached out and patted my shoulder. "There, there, Alice. You don't have to tease me. I'm really not mad at what you did. Or even if I am, I'm getting over it. The pain's almost gone."

"I'm not teasing," I said flatly. "What sort of truck did Patches drive?"

Hoof frowned. "An old 40's Ford. He had it painted a...." His mouth dropped open. "It's painted sort of a dirty orange color. And the brief glimpse I had before you knocked me down was of an orange pickup. But his pickup's at his house. Has to be."

"Did you also see a cloud of bright white mist around it?"

"Come to think of it....Naw. Look, Alice, I was pulling your leg when I asked you if it could have been Patches' ghost back there. I really don't believe in spooks."

"It flew past as we were falling, so I was still upright enough to see in the passenger window." I pointed down the road. "Plus I was on top, and I saw it disappear about fifty feet down that straight highway there."

I swear I heard him whisper, "civilians," but I didn't confront him. This was going to take some contemplation on my part, too. I hated these situations. I'd come here to help Twila with one ghost—or maybe something worse than a ghost—and here was another newly dead person interfering. It had happened before, three times, and I'd hoped the third time—the charm—meant it was over with. After all, three was a significant number in the paranormal.

Three knocks on a house door where someone had recently passed.

Three times three in Wicca beliefs.

Three crosses in Christianity.

Three blind mice....

Oh, crud. Tiredness was making me silly.

One thing I was sure of. If Patches had revealed himself to me, he was intent on me getting involved with whatever quest he was on. Instead of going into The Light, which was where every darned soul should go when the body died, he'd remained behind for a reason.

"You got a radio on that belt?" I asked Hoof.

He nodded and removed what looked like a small walkie-talkie from his gun belt. "I know what you're going to say. I'll call a deputy out here to pick us up. I'm not in any shape to walk all that ways back, and we'll wait until the other canine unit gets here before I send anyone on into the woods across the road."

I wholeheartedly agreed. I'd had enough murder, mayhem and paranormal for one night.

* * *

The deputy pulled up in front of the farmhouse, and Trucker and I got out and went in without detouring to talk to Jack. I didn't feel any obligation, since Hoof could pass on whatever he felt anyone else had a need-to-know.

Trucker padded up the staircase with me, and I headed straight to my assigned room. Twila sat in there with Granny, and they both looked up expectantly as I entered. Before I said a word, I went over and collapsed on the twin bed Twila sat on. Trucker flopped down at Granny's feet. Miss Molly was already curled up on the bed pillow, and she opened her eyes and uttered a low meow of welcome for her buddy, then went back to sleep.

Twila and Granny were patient, waiting without urging me to

divulge what I'd been up to the past hour or so. I finally drew in a breath in an attempt to overcome the tiredness draining me and asked Twila, "How's Jess?"

"Upset," she confirmed. "They were close. They fished at least once a week, except in the winter. Then they found something else to do."

I gnawed my lip and averted my gaze. I couldn't decide whether or not to bring up the new ghost now prowling around in addition to whatever the other thing was that we hadn't had time to discuss. But she always seemed to know when I was trying to hide something. She cleared her throat to draw my attention and lifted an eyebrow in question.

I sighed. "Patches didn't cross over."

"Uh oh," she replied, and Granny sat straight up on her bed.

"You mean there's another new dead one we're gonna have to deal with?" Granny asked. "They're always a bunch of trouble."

"This one's no different," I confirmed. "He already tried to run me down with his old pickup."

"What?" Twila grabbed my arm. "What did the truck look like?"

I grouched, "Shouldn't you be asking whether or not I was hurt first?"

"You're obviously not hurt," she said. "What color was it?"

"Orange. An old 40's Ford. Hoof agreed with me."

She nodded. "That's what Patches drove. You mean the sheriff saw him, too?"

"He saw the truck. He didn't see the driver."

"Why not, iffen you did?" Granny asked.

"He...uh...we fell down as we got out of the way. He was in pain."

"There are grassy berms all along our county roads," Twila pointed out. "He shouldn't have gotten injured that badly. Not badly enough so he couldn't jump up and get a look."

"Just take my word for it," I said, then went on to keep them from demanding I go more in depth about what happened, "Seems to me it's awfully early after his death for a man's ghost to learn to drive again."

"Are you sure that's who it was?" Twila asked.

"I suppose I'm not positive," I admitted. "I only got a glimpse of him lying out there in your field. But it sure looked like the same person."

"Just a ghost version, huh?" Granny put in.

I shook my head. "He looked as real as that darned pickup that tried to run over us. That would have run over us, if Trucker hadn't jerked me back out of the way."

"That would have scared the crap out of me, too," Twila assured me.

"Speaking of scaring the crap out of someone...." I turned to face her directly. "I've already told Granny what Jack said to get me up here. And you evidently think there's something nasty going on yourself, since you put a protection packet in your car. What on earth are you involved in?"

"I've been carrying a protection packet in my pocket at times, too," she said. "But whatever it is, it hasn't revealed itself."

"You're saying *it* and *what*, " I pointed out. "We don't refer to a simple ghost that way."

She frowned. "I'm just being open-minded. No, I don't think it's a negative entity, a demon or devil. No matter how people glory in telling about things like that, you and I both know they're not prevalent. We've only run across a couple our entire lives."

"That doesn't mean this can't be one," I said.

"True. But if we went on that assumption, instead of keeping an open mind, we could miss some obvious clues as to what it truly is."

"O.K.," I agreed. "So what's our next step?"

"You means you ain't gonna try to help them there law officers find out who murdered Jess's buddy?" Granny asked.

I swiveled and gaped at her. "Bite your tongue! You know what happens whenever I get involved in a murder investigation. Shoot, I've come close to getting arrested myself once or twice!"

"Just so you remember that," Granny reminded me, and I realized I'd missed her sarcastic tone.

"We're here for Twila," I said. "And before we get sidetracked by a new murder and a possible negative entity...." I stared back at Twila. "The impression I got from Jack was that you were working on something. One of those help-me calls you and I get. And you were driving off to do that one day when, by chance, Jack happened to see something in your car. So are you tangled up in one of our attempts to help out some poor person who's being bothered by a troublesome ghost? Or something else?"

I noticed she suddenly wasn't paying any attention at all to me, and the hairs on the back of my neck stood up.

I whirled around to see what was watching us from the corner of the room.

CHAPTER 6

"What?" Jack said from the doorway. "I was just checkin' up on y'all."

I ignored him and scanned the room. The bristly feeling on my neck hadn't been from Jack standing there. Something else had been in the room with us. However, the feeling had already subsided, and though I opened my senses, I didn't pick up on anything paranormal at the moment. I glanced an inquiry at Twila. She only shrugged, indicating she wasn't feeling whatever it had been right now, either.

"Well?" Jack said as he came on in the room and sat down beside Granny. "Are you?"

"Are we what?" I asked inattentively.

"All right," he said.

Instead of answering, Twila asked, "Are the cops gone?"

He shook his head. "It'll be a while. It's a murder scene, and Hoof said their best evidence guy is half in the bag from drinkin' after a fight with his wife. Hoof called in a favor from the sheriff the next county over, and he's sending his CSI tech."

He centered his gaze on me. "I hear you think Patches is still hanging around."

"No thinking about it, Jack. I saw him."

"I'm not arguing with you, *Chère*. In fact, Hoof wants me to ask if you'll ride along to where Patches lived. See if the pickup parked there is the same one."

"He can identify it as well as I can," I told him. "I'm busy here."

Twila patted my arm. "You go on. I need to check on Jess anyway. I left him in our bedroom with Harley and Jim."

"Jim?" I frowned, then said, "Oh, Jim Beam. Yeah, you better get in there. But I'm too tired to go anywhere else tonight. I haven't even had supper yet. Plus I just told you and Granny that I had no intention of getting involved in this investigation. We've got one of our own to take care of."

"I agree, *Chère*," Jack said, surprising me. He stood and headed for the door. "I'll take a picture of the truck and send it to your cell phone. You get some rest."

I swear that man understood exactly how to manipulate me! He knew I'd be inclined to do exactly the opposite of what he thought I should. But this time, he was wrong. Twila and the situation here were more important.

Not that a death wasn't vital. Still, there were priorities, and Hoof had a whole arsenal of help at his disposal. All we had were Twila, Granny and me.

"I think you should go," Twila urged.

"What?" I stared at her. "Why?"

She rose from the bed, an expression on her face that indicated she wasn't up for an argument. "I'll fix you a meatloaf sandwich to eat on the way."

She left the room before I could protest again. I hadn't even noticed Granny get up, but she was right behind Twila. Miss Molly only curled up in a tighter ball; cats were a lot less tolerant of anyone giving them orders than most people were. And now that the bed was vacant, Trucker lunged onto it and turned around once before he settled down beside the cat.

"Well, crap," I muttered. "If someone as elderly as Granny can keep going for a while tonight, I guess I can, too. At least I'll get something to eat."

In the kitchen, though, I cornered Twila as she was making my sandwich.

"What the hell was up there in the bedroom?" I demanded. "Tell me. Or instead of eating in the back of a cop car, I'm going to sit down over there at the table and enjoy my meal."

She wrapped the sandwich in a paper towel and handed it to me, then took a red thermos from the cupboard as she said, "It's still not letting me see it. It's just making sure I know something's there. And you, too, since you sensed it."

"I did," I agreed, peeling back a corner of the towel to take a huge bite of sandwich as she poured milk into the thermos. "An it din fet gob."

"Don't talk with your mouth full, Alice. And I agree, it didn't feel good. I'm still not sure it's negative, though."

I swallowed and forced myself to put off another bite of sandwich, although the meatloaf was delicious. "It doesn't have to be a negative entity," I said, using the name we used for something that wasn't a ghost, an entity that had never *lived*, like humans had. We used that connotation for the nasty ones, although she and I also believed angels hadn't ever been human. They were energy beings of their own origin, the good that helped battle the evil on the other end.

"No, it doesn't have to be something negative," she agreed. "It can be a really vicious dead person."

"Or someone who had a horrible life and is out for revenge before he, or she, leaves this dimension for good."

She held the thermos out, and I took another huge bite of sandwich before I accepted it.

"It hasn't caused much trouble yet," she said. "And it's been around here for a while. It can wait a bit longer before we deal with it. Getting the investigation into Patches' death going in the right direction is more important."

"How lang...." I swallowed and said, "How long has it been around here?"

"A while," she admitted. "I was sensing something, and it's obviously been around long enough to develop. It's able to keep behind whatever boundaries it has so I can't recognize it. It wasn't until Jack told me what he'd seen that I started paying more attention."

"He said it looked like something really nasty."

"These things can appear to be vile as easily as they can look as innocent as a newborn babe, Alice. I don't need to tell you that."

I sighed. "And you don't need to tell me that you're not going to discuss this right now with me, either, do you?"

She gave me a gentle shove. "Go on with Jack and Hoof. Let me know what you find out."

"Just tell me one more thing. Do you think it has something to do with whatever you're working on for someone? And why won't you tell me what that is?"

"That's two things," she said. "Go on. I promise you, we'll get off by ourselves and talk when you come back."

I headed out of the kitchen, but turned and asked, "Where's Granny?"

"She went down to talk to Jess. And I better get in there before the both of them finish off that Jim."

"Oh, lord," I said. "I think I've got the easier job here. If Granny's already had more than one drink with Jess, you're going to have your hands full."

* * *

There were more people invading this land than came down the river in those boats! The filth was infecting not just the soil. People were also spreading evil. He could not, and would not, stand for this. Not here.

He had almost decided to talk to the Twila woman and demand her help. He had watched her over the past few years. She did good work. But she was not easy to command. She did not even obey her man.

He was not one to take back-talk from a woman, though. When he decided to tell her what he needed, he would not let her deny him. For now, it would be

64

impossible for them to do his wishes. Not with the other one trying to get his needs met.

Crowded. It was getting far too crowded. Something had to be done, and quickly.

* * *

The little bait shop sat on an inlet in a beautiful, small lake. Surprising to me, who was used to Texas lakes where people coveted shoreline property, there were no other houses or docks anywhere in sight. It looked to be perhaps a quarter-mile across the lake, and a half-mile from one end to the other.

The little shack was constructed of weather-worn logs, light gray in the overhead moonlight. Overturned wooden rowboats lined the shore in front of the shop, another one tied to the only dock I could see projecting onto the water. The sign overhead merely said, *Patches*.

Hoof stopped the car in the gravel parking lot beside the bait shop, and I blew out a nearly silent, "Whew." Although Jack had joined me in the back seat, I didn't like being trapped behind the heavy mesh protecting the driver from backseat prisoners who might turn violent. Plus, the rear doors didn't have handles, and I knew for a fact that wasn't to make them childproof. Unfortunately, I'd ridden in a cop car or two, once for research, once for....

No sense going down that mind trail. Hoof got out and clicked something on his keys, which telegraphed a reassuring *clunk* beside me a second before he opened the door for me to slide out. Jack scooted across the seat and exited behind me.

"I don't see his truck," Hoof said to Jack, ignoring me.

"Where's he usually park?" Jack asked.

Hoof nodded at the rear of the shack. "Right behind the bait shop. He's got a little room in the back that he lives in."

"One room?" I asked in astonishment.

"Some folks don't need at lot of material possessions," Hoof said grumpily. "There's been times when I wished I had the guts to live like Patches."

"He's not living now," I said before I thought, then hurriedly said, "Sorry."

"But you're right, *Chère*," Jack said. "And that's why we're here. That truck missin' could mean he was killed somewhere else. Or transported out of here in his own vehicle afterwards."

"Well," Hoof said with a deep breath. "We need to get inside and see if we need to call the CSI techs over here."

I cringed. I hated blood, and if Patches had been killed here, I didn't want to look at the scene. I'd probably disgrace myself by upchucking and contaminating it. Yet I didn't particularly want to wait out here alone...in the dark. I wasn't afraid of ghosts and whatever else might happen to be prowling around. Well, not too afraid. But there was a murderer out here, too. Likely as not, someone living. Twila and I still didn't believe ghosts could actually kill a person.

But what about that thing I saw carrying Patches? Was it the Grassman? They could very possibly....

Jack slipped an arm around my waist, cutting off my thoughts. "If you want, you can wait in the car," he said.

I glanced at the cop car, then the shack, wishing I'd thought to bring one of my protection packets. However, there had been a few other things on my mind before we left. Yet Twila and I had our ways, which we practiced unfailingly.

Given the unyielding choice now, I decided not to let fear invade. Fear did a lot more than frighten the person experiencing it; it gave fodder to an entity's energy.

"I think I'll wait down on the dock," I said to Jack.

"Are you sure?" he asked. "I need to go with Hoof."

"I'm sure," I said, slipping out of his arm and giving him a gentle push. "I'll be fine, really."

Hoof was already walking slowly toward the bait shop, gun in hand. Jack bent and kissed me briefly, then pulled something from behind his back.

"Here," he said as he handed me his Berretta.

I accepted it, but smiled. "Bullets don't stop ghosts."

"Believe me, I have no qualms about you dealin' with any ghosts that show up," he said with a wry grin as he turned and followed Hoof.

I blew a kiss after him. Since I was trained in various weapons, including pistols, I was grateful for the Beretta. I tucked it in my jacket pocket and stood there for a while. By the time the two men were inside the shack, I had called down enough protection to feel secure in venturing down to the dock. As I walked onto it, lights came on inside the bait shop, then another security light illuminated the lake area.

There were two benches at the end of the wooden planks, where I assumed people rested while they fished. I wandered out and sat down on one. The moon's gold circle reflection shone on a quiet lake surface, flat and still, not even marred by a stray breeze ruffle. Bright stars filled the overhead sky. A few even sparkled like pinpoints on the black water.

Since I loved fishing, I found myself wishing I could sit there, maybe with Howard, and forget all the paranormal problems we were dealing with, along with the loss of the man who owned such a nice little slice of a peaceful paradise. Jess and Twila both would be grieving for quite a while, Jess even more so than Twila.

"The best thing I can do for them is try to find out what's going on and why it's happening," I mused in a barely audible voice.

I didn't even experience a scant feeling of approaching energy before I heard, *You might just be able to do that.*

"Huh?" I jumped to my feet and stared around. I had no doubt what —or who—had spoken: something paranormal. But no matter how hard I stared into the shadowy recesses beyond the dock, I didn't see a fully-formed being, or even anything ethereal.

I propped my hands on my hips and narrowed my eyes. Whatever it was, I wasn't going swimming in the lake to get away from it if it tried to block my path off the pier.

"Who the heck is here?" I demanded in a stern voice.

You don't need to know my name yet.

"The hell I don't," I contradicted. "If you want my attention, tell me who—or what—you are!"

I am not a what, the thing responded in an irritated tone. *No one has ever dared call me a* what!

"I just did," I replied. "And unless you agree to communicate properly, and politely, you can go on back to your own dimension and leave me alone."

I reached in my pocket and pulled out a small packet of salt I'd picked up at one of the fast-food outlets where Granny and I had stopped. I had those type of packet stashed in about every jacket and sweater I owned. In a pinch, a pinch of salt worked extremely well to chase off a troublesome entity.

Just as I tore the top off the tiny packet, the siren on the sheriff's car split the air. Then the lights on the vehicle started flashing on and off, on and off, on and off. Next the bubble lights on the top of the car threw blue and red stabs of light around, and the horn blared an accompaniment.

"What the...?" I stuck the salt back in my pocket and ran down the dock. At the end of it, I felt a gush of icy wind, indicating whatever had been standing there had hurriedly escaped my path.

Wait! I heard.

"You wait your turn!" I called back.

Jack and Hoof emerged from the front door of the bait shop as I ran up the small bank from the dock. They beat me to the car.

"Stay there!" Jack yelled at me. When I ignored him and kept on heading his way, he stalked away from Hoof and intercepted me.

"You are somethin' else," he said, shaking his head. "Anyone else would dive for cover if they heard this goin' on. Here you are, headed right into the fray."

"Because it's probably a paranormal fray," I told him. "Hoof can't manipulate all those things on the car with a remote control, can he?"

"Probably not," Jack admitted. "And—"

"Help!" Hoof screamed. He jumped out of the car and raced across the parking lot, batting at his head. As Jack and I both hurried toward him, he fell down and rolled around in the gravel.

Jack rushed in to grab Hoof and settle him down just as the sheriff's feet swept a circular path. Barely in time to avoid getting tripped, Jack jumped into the air as though someone had swung a jump rope beneath his feet. Hoof rolled a good five feet away, and Jack lunged toward him again.

I didn't even bother to try to stop Jack. Instead, I threw the little bit of salt I'd poured into my hand as I yelled, "Begone!"

Ouch! someone screamed as the noises from the car died. Even in the silence, I doubted very much if Jack or Hoof caught the word, or what else was said: *Darn you! You'll pay for that!*

"You just try, you piece of protoplasm," I snarled. "Get out of here!"

This is my place, the ghost said.

Now that Hoof wasn't writhing around, I opened my senses and recognized what I was dealing with. Up here in the parking lot, anyway. I still didn't know who, or what, had been on the dock. Besides, the ghost's words gave away his identity.

"Patches," I said while Jack helped Hoof up. "Patches, you're dead. Don't you know that? So you can't own anything."

Hoof held out his hands and backed away, a look of horror on his face. However, Jack actually moved closer to me.

"Patches?" I repeated, but I could tell the ghost was gone. Either the salt or the demand to begone had taken effect.

"Shoot," I said. "Well, when he shows up again, I'll try to be a little more tolerant and get some additional information out of him."

"Again?" Hoof had backed all the way up to the patrol car trunk. The look on his face, illuminated by the overhead moon, indicated he would have gone on through the car, had it not been so solid. "That was Patches attacking me?"

"I think so. Why does he dislike you so much?"

"He's just one of those country hicks who doesn't like lawmen. Probably doesn't want me prowling through his stuff in the shop."

"But he has to know you're investigating his murder."

"He won't care. I'm still the law. And you're saying he'll be back?"

Hoof rushed around to the driver's door and jumped in. Given his fear, I assumed he meant to start the engine and get out of there. However, he left the door open, so the dome light shone, and I watched him scrabble around in the seat as though searching for something.

He jumped back out and shouted, "Jack, where the hell did I put my keys?"

"I haven't seen them," Jack replied.

"Patches probably lifted them," I told Jack in an undertone so Hoof couldn't overhear. "Or whoever was on the dock."

Jack stared down at me. "There's more than one ghost here?"

I nodded. "I think they're both ghosts, anyway."

"What did the one on the dock want?"

But before I could answer, Hoof screamed at us, "Get the hell over here and help me find the keys so we can get out of here!"

I frowned as I stared toward Hoof and said, "Interesting."

"What?" Jack asked as he started to walk toward Hoof.

I followed as I explained, "Hoof wasn't that upset out there on the edge of the woods when that pickup came at us. Why's he acting so scared now?" Then it dawned on me. "Oh, out there on the road, he only got knocked down. He didn't really get attacked. Patches was walloping him this time for some reason."

We'd gotten to Hoof now and he was bent back inside the vehicle, digging his hands down in the back of the seat. Then he dug beneath the driver's seat, tossing out what he encountered: a flashlight, some fast-food wrappers—it seemed he was partial to Wendy's rather than Mickie Dee's—and....Uh oh. That looked like a condom wrapper.

Hoof noticed the last item about the same time I did. He grabbed it and stuffed it in his pants pocket. It took me a split second to decide whether or not to embarrass him, but I chose the side of politeness and hurriedly turned my head as though I were looking at the shack.

"You probably dropped the keys inside," I said to explain my interest in looking elsewhere.

Hoof stood and stared at the bait shop. "No way. I always...*always* put those keys in my pocket. And they're gone." He stuck his hands in his pants pockets again, but instead of taking a chance on pulling out that condom wrapper, he moved his fingers around inside the confines. Had there been a set of keys, they would have jingled. There wasn't even a clink of coins.

"Still, we'll have to go back in and look," Jack said.

"I'll radio the crime scene tech," Hoof said adamantly. "They can check things out."

"We didn't see any sign that Patches was killed here," Jack said. "The lock was even engaged, and we had to pick it to get inside."

"Yeah, but...." Hoof's words trailed off and he bit his lip.

I couldn't resist. I'd given him the condom wrapper without embarrassment, but....

"He's afraid the ghost that was attacking him might be waiting inside now," I finished for Hoof.

I could almost have sworn steam rose from the red flush on Hoof's face, and, if possible, the glare he turned on me would have burned a hole in my forehead.

"There ain't no such things as ghosts!" he flared.

"Then what were you battling?" I asked in as calm a voice as I could manage around the laughter I kept barricaded in my chest.

"Nothing...uh...just...maybe...."

Jack took pity on Hoof and said, "The patrol car started actin' up just when we found what looked like a spot to hide somethin' in," he said. "If it was Patches, maybe he didn't want us to discover what was inside it."

"We need to know what he hid," I said. "It might help me deal with him."

"I don't want to go back in there," Hoof whined.

"I'll go," Jack said. "You can wait here."

"I'm going, too," I said.

"You're both civilians in my territory," Hoof said, although not very resolutely. "I can't let you go in there alone."

"We won't tell if you don't," I said.

"Well...." Hoof glanced at Jack.

"I'll go alone," he said. "At least I've got law enforcement training."

"And I've got paranormal training," I reminded him.

"Just wait here, *Chère*." Jack turned away.

"Either I go or I'll rescind my promise not to tell," I said. "And not just about you investigating outside your jurisdiction. It's always a comic tale about a ghost picking on someone."

Jack halted and Hoof gasped.

"Take her with you, Jack," Hoof ordered.

I lifted an eyebrow, and Jack stifled a grin. Darn him, he'd only been teasing about not taking me.

"Or else," I said as I tagged along after him toward the back door of the bait shop, "instead of teasing me, you figured you might need me if Patches decided to attack you when you snooped in his hidey-hole."

"Maybe a little of both," Jack said with a chuckle.

The back door stood open, and Jack stopped in front of it.

"Do you still have my pistol?" he asked.

"I'd forgotten all about it." I took the Berretta from my jacket pocket and handed it to him.

"That shows the difference in someone being trained or not," he said as held the pistol in his hand. "A cop never forgets his gun is handy."

"Get him, spooks!" I whispered loudly to tease him. I got a lot of satisfaction when he briefly jerked to a halt before he shook his head and walked on inside.

Lights still burned, and the small room was a lot tidier than I'd expected from a man living alone. But then, stuff would have had to be kept in its place in such a small area. Otherwise, there wouldn't be room to move around.

On the left was a tiny apartment-sized gas stove. A table that held salt and pepper shakers and a roll of paper towels was in one corner, a nice side-by-side refrigerator in the other. On our right, the small twin bed was made up neatly, not even a wrinkle in the covers and the pillows plumped and in place. It waited for the occupant to slip in for a night's sleep, but the sleep Patches would experience now was a never-ending one. The dresser at the foot of the bed held an alarm clock and a few framed photographs, the people in them not identifiable from where I stood.

"Surely he has a bathroom," I mused.

"In front of the store," Jack explained. He only paused in Patches' little apartment long enough to scan the room with cop's eyes to make sure no one was waiting to ambush us—alive or not. Then he walked toward the doorway in the rear. Beyond it, I glimpsed some shelves beneath windows across the wall closest to the lake. When I entered the shop, I paused. This would be a gorgeous view any time of year, summer, fall, winter or spring.

No wonder Patches is still hanging around, I thought.

My log cabin sat near a lake, also, but a road ran between it and the shoreline. My view was best in the winter, after the trees along the bank lost their leaves.

Shelves also lined each side wall, shorter ones on the left. A glass-fronted cooler took up the rest of that wall. Beside us was a small table with a cash register on it, a chair pulled up behind it. Small logs were stacked next to the chair, ready for the well-used potbelly stove.

Jack was right. A small addition had been added on the other side of the cash register and stove. That had to be the bathroom. It only had one sign on it: *MEN/WOMEN.* At first, I wrinkled my nose at the thought of having to share a bathroom with a bunch of men who were probably beer-drinking, farting and burping fishermen. Then I studied the tidiness that carried over out there. Patches evidently was...had been...a neat fellow, so he probably kept the bathroom clean, too.

Jack walked over to the chair. Above it hung a picture of the lake outside the bait shop, with one lone rowboat near the shoreline. A few feet of the dock protruded, just enough to give an idea of the location of where the photo had been taken. At first, I assumed the hidden crevice, or safe, was behind the picture. But I kept studying that wall.

Jack glanced back at me. "Do you see it, *Chère*?"

"Ha," I said. "You think since you're *trained* and I'm not, I can't tell there's one more board beneath that picture than there is on top of it. That must be where the hidey-hole is."

Jack grinned. "Actually, I thought you'd see it. You might not be trained in the same manner as me, but I've read your books. You know a lot about crime scenes."

"My readers would kill me in the reviews if I screwed up and did something totally out of whack with what's on TV," I said with a laugh. "They don't know reality is a little different. So I have to tread a balancing act."

"Well, balance yourself on over here and have the honor of opening the hidey-hole," Jack offered.

I nodded jauntily at him and took a step forward. Then screamed and jumped away before I could stop myself.

CHAPTER 7

The entity standing before us even sent Jack staggering back a couple steps. To give him credit, Jack thought of protecting me first. He grabbed my arm with one hand and pulled me against his chest, while he raised the pistol and took aim.

"Don't bother, Jack," I snarled as I dug in my jacket pocket, hoping to find another salt packet. "He's not real."

The thing in front of us drew himself up and glared at me. I could tell it was male—or at least projected a male appearance. Bare skin gleamed in the overhead light as though he'd smeared himself with bear grease, and there were no breasts other than the small brown nipples on his muscular chest. The rest of his body rivaled pictures I'd seen of men with toned but not over-blown bodies. He exuded maleness, even beneath his outlandish façade. Still, no amount of projected masculinity could overcome my senses. Mr. Muscles had been dead for a long while.

"How dare you?" he said loud enough for me to glance at Jack and see if he had also heard. I couldn't tell, but his pistol never waivered. The ghost continued, "I am real enough!"

Rather than giving the ghost the satisfaction of arguing, I just cocked my head and studied him. What had startled me—all right, the damn thing had actually scared me until I engaged my senses and figured out it was not a demon—was its bizarre appearance.

He stood about six foot, and his head was shaved bald. The only adornment on it was a band of what appeared to be chicken feathers sticking up about four inches above the back of his skull. What really made me blink was the red paint covering his head and smeared down his entire face and across his shoulders. A mask of black paint surrounded his eyes and extended past his ears.

He wore a wide leather band around his neck, a silver medallion at least three inches across and with some sort of etching in the center of it. The two-inch silver band circling his upper left arm matched the medallion.

Three various sized pouches hung from leather straps threaded across his chest. Another skinny leather band encircled his waist, and below his flat stomach draped a brief loincloth, which didn't cover much more than a Speedo bathing suit. His upper legs were bare, but he wore thigh-high boots, perhaps made from tanned deerskin, and decorated with beautiful beading. Some woman had taken months to make that intricate design.

The flintlock rifle in his left hand could instill a pound or two of fear in a person, even me. Held upright, butt to the ground, he and it were the same height. The rifle would be worth a fortune on Antiques Roadshow, not that it would ever find its way out of his dimension into this one. However, I wasn't completely confident this Native American hadn't found a way to shoot a bullet across time.

I didn't know that much about Ohio Indians, but I retained a faint memory of history. This guy looked like he belonged to one of the fierce Wyandotte tribes that once roamed the wilderness here. That meant he'd been around a few centuries, and it sometimes amazed Twila and me what ghosts with this much experience at being dead could do.

"Are you done examining me?" he said with a sneer. "Do you think I am going to haul you over my shoulder and carry you off to scalp you?"

I pulled my hand out of my pocket and held the salt packet out on my palm. "Want to try it?"

"I'd advise you not to even think about it," Jack said.

"So you can see and hear him?" I asked. I never could tell about Jack. Sometimes he could see the ghosts I encountered when he was around. Sometimes he couldn't...or at least, wouldn't admit to it.

"Yeah, I can see the creep," he said, his pistol still aimed at the ghost.

Before I could stop him, the ghost flicked a finger and Jack's pistol flew out of his hand. That did it. I ripped the salt packet open, but rather than throw it all on red-head-and-shoulders, I just picked up a few grains and tossed them.

"Ai-yi-yi!" he yelled. Instead of lunging at me, as I halfway expected, he backed up a step. A measure of respect showed in his black-outlined brown eyes. "I may have underestimated you. You seem to have some of the same strengths as the woman who is trying to assist my brother."

I immediately gleaned who he meant. There weren't too many people around who would agree to work with ghosts.

"You know Twila?" I asked as Jack walked over and picked up his pistol. This time he held it by his side, rather than pointed at the ghost.

"Not yet," the ghost said enigmatically.

"Look, I don't have time to chat with you right now. Jack needs to see what Patches has inside that wall. So move out of the way."

He frowned and looked over his shoulder at the picture. "Perhaps it's all connected."

His comment caught my attention, but he took that moment to obey me. Instead of just moving, though, he disappeared before I could blink.

"Where the hell did he go?" Jack asked.

"I'm not exactly sure," I told him. "Twila and I think it's another dimension. But it's not the same dimension as the one on the other side of The Light. Or there could be more than one dimension over there. We don't know, of course, won't until we cross over. And where he's at is not our dimension. We're separate in this one while we're alive. But—"

"*Chère, Chère, Chère.*" Jack gently put his left index finger on my lips. "I'd be glad to listen to you explain more about your ghosts at some point. Now, though, you were right. I need to see what Patches hid in that wall."

"Oh," I said and stepped back to wave at the picture. "Well, have at it. I can't wait to get back and talk to Twila, anyway. I want to get her take on that gorgeous Native American guy."

"Gorgeous?" Was that a tinge of jealousy in Jack's voice? "With that goop smeared all over him? That shiny stuff was probably grease. He probably smelled to high heaven, too, if we'd been able to smell him."

"Yeah," I said in a feigned dreamy tone. "But did you see that body?"

"Ugh," Jack said as he reached toward the wall. "Didn't do a thing for me."

"I'm glad he didn't turn you on," I whispered in his ear, and Jack jumped back at least a foot.

Then he narrowed his eyes. "So you want to play, huh?"

Laughing, I backed away. "We have serious business to take care of here."

"What I have in mind is totally serious." Jack took a slow step toward me, then another. Before I could escape, he reached out and captured my arm, then pulled me close. "I'll show you how serious—"

Varoooom!

We jerked apart. The noise sounded so close, it seemed to be right outside the shack door.

"What the hell?" Jack headed through Patches' living quarters toward the rear door. "Is Hoof too scared to wait for us?"

Jack wasn't fast enough to see what was going on. Outside, the engine noise revved again, then tires squealed, sounding as though the vehicle was moving away. Only for an instant, though. There was no mistaking the next sound. The noise headed straight toward us.

Jack turned and reached for me, but I was already diving for the floor. He came down beside me with a thud that had to have hurt. The engine noise surrounded us, but whatever had come in hadn't even made a tiny splinter in the wall it passed through.

"Gosh darn it!" I scrambled to my knees amidst the noise, but Jack jerked me back and held me tightly.

"Let go of me!" I twisted around and pounded on his chest. "I'm going after that damn orange pickup. Let go!"

Jack held on, a look of worry in his brown eyes. "I didn't see a truck."

"But that's what it was!" I could tell the truck was now stopped in the next room, the bait shop part of the shack. The engine noise ran in an idle, but only for a few seconds. Then tires squalled again, fading off into the distance.

Jack loosened his hold and I started to get to my feet. However, the table in the small room rushed at us, legs digging deep scratches in the linoleum. Jack grabbed me again and rolled us aside as it crashed into the cabinets behind where we had been lying.

Even before I got to my feet, I heard the telltale splintering of a wall in the bait shop. Then silence.

"Crap," I muttered as I lunged to my feet. Jack right behind me, I raced into the other room. We slid to a stop and stared at the splintered wall where whatever Patches had hidden had been concealed. Now there was only a gaping empty hole above the picture that lay on the floor, frame splintered.

Under his breath, Jack muttered a word I hardly ever heard him use, but I only shrugged. "I don't think we've seen the last of Patches. One way or another, I'll find out what he's trying to hide." I turned and faced Jack, shaking my finger at him. "And although I appreciate the heck out of your trying to *protect* me, next time leave me alone. I could have caught him."

"And done what?" Jack demanded.

"Who knows?" I admitted. "Twila and I never know what we'll do until we confront something."

"Or what the damn ghost will do, either," Jack reminded me.

"Touché," I said. "But sometimes it's not a ghost. Sometimes—"

"How'd you know it was that pickup?" he interrupted before I could go into another long, involved supernatural explanation.

I frowned as I thought. "I didn't see it," I told him. "It was just a sense. And even though I'm not a car buff, it sounded like the same engine as on the one out on the highway."

"Logic has me agreeing with you," Jack said. "It came in here where

Patches lived. And took somethin' that perhaps he didn't want us to find."

I chuckled. "And since women aren't bothered by logic, but men are, what we come up with together makes sense."

"Yep," he said with a smile. "Right now, we better get out there and see what happened to Hoof." He pulled out his pistol again.

I hesitated a split-second, a thought rushing through my head so quickly, I barely caught the tail end of it. I could have sworn there were two different entities in the bait shop this time. First, Patches and the pickup, next the one that shoved the table at us. There had been a definite gap in time from when the pickup left and the wall shattered. But then, the Wyandotte ghost had been there, too.

Before I could make my tired body and mind puzzle out this mystery, Jack heaved a sigh at my dawdling and took my arm. Pistol leading, he pulled me with him out the door. I didn't protest the weapon at all. It wouldn't bother either of the ghosts, but a murderer roamed around somewhere, and it didn't hurt to be on guard.

We emerged from the back door, but didn't see Hoof anywhere.

"There," I said, pointing at the car. "I can see his shoes. He's underneath. I hope he's not hurt."

We rushed forward again, and I breathed a relieved sigh when I heard noise coming from beneath the patrol car. Granted, it sounded like whimpers of fear, but at least he was alive.

Jack knelt and called to Hoof, "You all right?"

"Is it gone?" Hoof asked.

"Yeah, it took off. Both of them," Jack said. "It's safe to come out."

"Are you sure?" he whined.

"I'm sure," Jack told him. "Come on out."

"Ask Alice if it's gone," he said.

"Oh, for—" I dropped down beside Jack and stuck my head beneath the car. "There's nothing left to bother you. I ran them off. So scoot your butt out here."

Technically, I hadn't ran either of them off. The Native American had disappeared on his own, and Patches had fooled us and gotten away all

80

by himself. But if it would calm the sheriff down enough to wiggle out from under that car, I was willing to take the credit.

It took Hoof a few more seconds, but finally he crawled out. Jack helped him to his feet and brushed at some dirt on Hoof's uniform shirt as Hoof asked in a shaky voice, "Both gone? Two of them?"

"Let's secure this place and call for your crime tech," Jack said. "Then we can talk."

I burst out laughing, and both men stared at me as though I'd just kicked a kitten—not that I'd ever do such a dastardly thing. My laughter escalated at their expressions, and I pointed at them, then the shack as I tried to control myself. Still, I couldn't speak.

Jack shot me a disgusted look and asked Hoof, "You got crime tape and stuff like that?"

"In the trunk," he said as he glared at me for a second, then led Jack toward the rear of the car.

I managed to call after them, "You want me to consecrate the tape, just ask."

Hoof swiveled and said, "What's that supposed to mean?"

"Your yellow tape isn't going to keep out those ghosts unless it's consecrated," I explained, my giggles finally abating.

Hoof snorted in disbelief, but Jack nodded.

"She's right," he told Hoof. "But I don't think it's going to be necessary. Patches...or whoever that was...already took what we were after."

The two men discussed possibilities as they worked—without asking me to do a consecration. I mostly focused on Jack, and not because he was the man I still loved.

Well, partly it was because of that, and the complications that kept us from having a solid relationship. Had it been a few years back, even while we were married, Jack would have had fifteen different explanations for the paranormal entities we'd just encountered. It was only after our divorce, when we were thrown together on another murder investigation, that he actually *saw* his first apparition. Admitted he had, anyway, although with Granny and me as a witness, he hadn't had much chance to deny it.

Since then, he'd not only confessed to other actual experiences, but also become more accepting of what Twila and I did, something that was such a huge part of our lives. Anyone who denigrated us and didn't believe we could actually communicate with other-dimensional entities wasn't a person who fit in our circle of close friends...or lovers.

At first, it hadn't even dawned on me that Jack was a non-believer. I was so starry-eyed and wrapped up in our growing love affair that I didn't have time to mess around in the paranormal. I did keep my writing on track, but it just happened there were no calls for paranormal assistance during the time Jack and I dated.

And to the detriment of our marriage, neither of us had become embroiled in a career situation that called for us to give our undivided attention to something else while we dated. I'd taken a break from deadlines for a few months while I researched my next book, and New Orleans, where Jack worked as a homicide detective at the time, hadn't experienced any murders over and above the sadly normal statistics. The ones that did come in were deaths the lesser ranking detectives investigated.

The problems started after our marriage, when one of us wanted the other's company or attention and it wasn't available. I dived into semi-seclusion while I wrote, and suddenly there were several slasher-type homicides Jack had to investigate. It grew worse when one of the investigations Jack got called in on was a serial child murderer.

Then on one of Twila's trips to see us, it finally seemed to dawn on Jack what we did, and I overheard him chatting with Jess one day about how outlandish our imaginations were. To his credit, Jess tried to explain that what we did was real, but Jack never seemed to grasp it. That, along with all the other rough spots we'd found in our relationship after we married, escalated until things deteriorated into divorce court.

Now, despite the gravity of the situation and the murder, I found myself enjoying the fact Jack was a part of this with me.

Another cop car pulled in, and I realized I'd been standing there for some time while Jack and Hoof unrolled their yellow tape. They had also evidently gone inside to examine the bait shop again, since I didn't see them. They must have heard the new vehicle, though, because they emerged from the shop together.

Hoof went over to the new cop, and Jack guided me a distance off, where we could talk without being overheard. Still, he kept his voice low as he said, "*Chère*, Hoof asked me if we'd keep quiet about the supposed paranormal things around here."

"Supposed?" I asked with a squint of annoyance.

"Supposed to him," Jack assured me. "I agree with you. There was more here. But I think it makes sense to keep that part to ourselves for now. We might be able to get some clues and evidence in a different way."

"Well, I don't need to stay around as a...consultant, if you will. You can handle that end of it. Maybe not as well as Twila or I, but good enough." Jack grimaced before he could hide it, and I immediately knew he wasn't real happy about his fairly new abilities. I went on, "I'd like to get back to Twila."

"I already asked Hoof to have a deputy give you a ride," he said. "And that car there is bringin' Hoof another set of keys. I promised Jess I'd do what I could to help find Patches' murderer, so I'll hang around here and come back with the sheriff."

I nodded. "That's fine with me. These cops aren't keystone by any means, but you've probably got a heck of a lot more experience than most of them."

"Hard hitting experience," Jack mused, and I ran a comforting hand across his cheek.

To cheer him up a bit, I teased, "And you've got a heck of a lot more experience in another way, too."

"Witch," he said as he squeezed my hand.

"No, I'm a paranormal investigator," I said and pursed my lips. "Witches are—"

Jack dropped a quick kiss on my lips to stifle another one of my long, involved explanations. "More seriously, he said, "You and Twila be careful, hear? I think that Native American guy's what I saw in Twila's backseat that day. Hell of a lookin' thing, ain't he?"

83

"You're better looking," I teased again.

He couldn't suppress his smile. He turned me away from him and gently slapped my butt. "Git. I'm busy."

* * *

The cop let me ride in the front seat, and to give my fertile brain a break from contemplating murder and ghosts, I did something I enjoyed; I asked him about his more interesting arrests. He regaled me all the way to the farmhouse. Then, as I thanked him and started to slide out of the car, he said, "Oh, man. I almost forgot. Can you wait a sec, please?"

He dug under his seat and pulled out a copy of one of my books. "When my wife heard you were coming, she asked me to get you to autograph this."

I took the book as I said, "I've only been here a few hours. How did your wife know I was going to visit?"

"Oh, she's friends with Aunt Bess, and Aunt Bess knows Mikala," he said as though I should recognize each person. "You know, Miss Twila's working to help Mikala, so she won't get hauled off to the funny farm or old folks home."

My tiredness had increased on the drive back to Twila's, and I'd had to concentrate on my questions and his answers in order to stay awake. So I didn't feel like sitting through a longer explanation of who was who right then.

"Do you have a pen?" I asked.

He eagerly pulled a pen out of his shirt pocket and handed it to me. After getting his wife's name, I inscribed the book and gave it back to him. He didn't bother to see what I'd written, and I bit my tongue to keep from telling him what I thought when he shoved the book beneath the seat.

"Thanks," he said with a grin. "Now maybe I'll get off the couch, where I've been sleeping since last Saturday."

All right, I had to know. "Why did you get banished to the couch?"

"Must have been her hormones," he said as he revved the engine, which I took as a hint to get on out of the car.

I totally disliked it when men blamed women's emotional ups and downs for lack of tolerance of their own transgressions. I narrowed my eyes. "And?"

"Aw, I was just a few minutes late getting home from work. The guys and I stopped off to have a beer."

"How many beers?"

He shrugged. "A few. She can't go out with me right now. She's due in another couple months."

"She could drink soda or water," I said.

He looked at me as though I'd grown a third eye. "In a bar? Besides, she's big as a—" Evidently, he realized he was talking to another female and shut up, fast. "Uh...I guess maybe I should take her somewhere now and then."

"I guess you should," I spat as I got out of the car. Then I bent back in and snarled at him, "And get my damn book out from under your seat and treat it with respect!"

"Yes, ma'am," he said quickly, and did as I ordered. At first, he started to toss the book on the passenger seat, but after a glance at my face, he laid it down gently. "Good night, ma'am."

I slammed the door and stomped away. After I climbed the front steps, a voice called my name from the shadows. I recognized it, so it wasn't a ghost.

"Where are Granny and Jess?" I asked Twila as I sat beside her on the swing.

"Both asleep," she told me. "Are you hungry? Do we need to go in the kitchen and talk?"

I looked out into the yard, then at the beautiful sky littered with diamond pinprick stars. The moon had descended a good distance by now, but it still hovered well above the treetops outlining the western skyline. It was hard to imagine what had happened in the last few hours here in this quiet, peaceful place. But now and then, we had both had strange experiences in places where you would least expect it.

"I'm fine," I said. "What should we talk about first?"

She sighed. "They—whoever that darned *they* is—they say start at the beginning. But that's too far back."

When she bit her lip and didn't go on, I asked, "Well, who are Aunt Bess and Mikala?"

She glanced at me in surprise. "How did you hear about that?"

"I didn't hear what it was all about," I admitted. "The cop who brought me back from the bait shop mentioned their names. He said something about you helping a woman named Mikala."

"True," she said, then settled back in the swing.

CHAPTER 8

"Mikala's husband was in the nursing home where I worked for a while," Twila said. "I met her when she came to visit him. You know how it is sometimes when you meet someone and just click."

"Yes," I agreed.

"Mikala's husband passed on," Twila continued, "but she and I continued our friendship over lunches and visits. She's in her eighties, probably close to Granny's age. However, I wish I was as sprightly. She keeps that old house she lives in clean as a whistle, and I'd rather eat lunch at her house than any restaurant we've ever been in."

When Twila fell silent again, I prodded, "There's some problem?"

"Yeah," Twila admitted. "She and her husband are Native American."

"Omigod," I said, then clapped my hand over my mouth, ticked at myself for interrupting her story. She had to know what I'd experienced the last couple hours or so, but I'd been waiting since I arrived to hear her side of things.

She frowned, and I knew we'd have to have one of those tit-for-tat discussions and try to fit all the pieces together.

"What's *omigod* supposed to mean?" she asked.

"Oh, man," I said. "I haven't told you what happened out at the bait shop."

"Is it connected with what I've got to tell you?" she asked, which brought to mind Red-Face's words: *Perhaps it's all connected.*

"Probably," I said. "Tell me this. Is there a Native American ghost at Mikala's house?"

"How'd you know...never mind," she said. "You and I neither one believe in coincidences. So Patches' death has something to do with Mikala?"

"No, no, it's not that," I said. "At least, I don't think so. It's just that I think I met Mikala's ghost's brother."

"His brother. Hmmmmm," Twila said. "Wyandotte?"

"Yep." Her question didn't surprise me, and it didn't have anything to do with our shared psychic senses. It had to do with non-coincidence, and her sharp analytical powers. Powers she and I both had to keep honed to deal with some of our encounters, as well as to assist people who called on us.

She nodded. "O.k. Let me tell you what's going on at Mikala's, then you can add in the stuff from the bait shop."

At last, I thought, and listened closely as she went on.

"Mikala's kids are all three *professionals.* You know, white collar types. She and Major—her husband's name was Major—worked their tails off putting those kids through college. But the one blunder they made, which Mikala admits now was a mistake, was not teaching them about their heritage. So when the paranormal stuff started getting out of hand around her home, the kids decided their mother was becoming senile, or maybe had beginning Alzheimer's. They've been trying to put her in a nursing home ever since."

"Started?" I asked, referring to her comment about the paranormal.

"Let me correct that," she said. "Things were always going on where Mikala lives. The kids, though, didn't seem to see or feel the periodic incidents, so she and Major never bothered to talk to them about it. The kids did, of course, know they were from a Native American background, but you know how it is sometimes. People's racism isn't necessarily restricted to African Americans."

"Or Hispanics," I added.

"Yeah. After the kids were all through college and set up in their careers, Mikala decided to pursue something she'd been interested in all her life. She took a class in genealogical research and traced hers and Major's heritage. She said hers was rather innocuous, but Major had some pretty important people in his background. Two of them were warriors who were in the Battle of Fallen Timbers, up near Toledo in 1794. When that British general, Anthony Wayne, defeated them in the last big battle, the Wyandottes still tried to hold onto their Ohio territory."

Some of my history lessons were coming back to me. I loved research, and I couldn't count the number of times I had to pull myself away from this fascination and write the darned book. Twila and I also loved travelling to historical sites and absorbing the past events, as well as chatting with the long-deceased former residents of the areas.

"Like most of the Native Americans who were displaced by white settlers," Twila said, "they were really upset over losing their land and the lives they had built. The Wyandottes did manage to hold onto a few strongholds in Ohio for another fifty years: around Columbus, Lancaster and Zanesville. But a few years after the two brothers died, the remaining tribal members were pretty much banished to a small location at Upper Sandusky. Until 1843, when they were even forced out of there."

I mused. "Native Americans truly honor their ancestors, and it had to have really saddened them to leave the graves behind."

"Exactly," Twila said.

"Did you learn all this from Mikala's research?" I asked.

"Not all," she said. "Some came from Walking Bear, one of the brothers. He's also Major's many-times-great grandfather and the ghost at her house who won't cross into The Light. She thinks maybe Walking Bear's brother, Major's great-uncle Free Eagle, is probably part of the problem, too."

"I am not a *problem*!" the red-painted ghost from the bait shop said from where he stood at the bottom of the steps, his hands spread on his bare hips and a glower on his face. "Walking Bear is the one who is the *problem*."

"Ah, you finally decided to show yourself," Twila said in a castigating tone. "I'll thank you to wait your turn and speak when I say you can!"

Free Eagle, since I assumed that's who it was, shot her an irritated glare. When he opened his mouth, Twila pulled a protection packet from her jeans pocket and threaded her index finger in the ribbon loop to dangle it. Free Eagle vanished immediately, but not without an angry growl of annoyance.

"Now, where was I?" Twila asked. "Oh, Walking Bear won't explain why he won't cross over. For some reason, he's not communicating very well. Usually...well," she corrected herself, "a lot of times, ghosts develop abilities as they linger on this side of The Light. Oh, I don't have to tell you that. But there's something strange about Walking Bear. He seems to want to talk, but he gets frustrated when I don't understand him. And he does have enough ability to cause things to happen around there."

"Like what?"

"Things that Mikala can't hide. She decided to quit telling her kids about anything, pretend things were fine and she was just suffering a grieving spell over losing Major. They'd been married sixty years. But Walking Bear shredded the wallpaper in one room. Before she could get it replaced, one of her daughters dropped in. Another time, he hid Mikala's garage door remote control. She had to call one of her sons to bring his over, and he found her remote in the mailbox when he checked to see why the flag was up. Her kids have been 'dropping in' unannounced now for several weeks."

"Wow," I mused. "He's making it look bad for Mikala."

"Yeah. Another time, he scattered the contents of Mikala's pantry on the floor. Catsup, flour, peanut butter, you name it. It was all in a gooey pile. She called me and we got that cleaned up before her kids saw it."

"Why can't you just cleanse the house and banish the ghost?" I asked when she fell silent.

"I tried," she admitted. "And there are a dozen protection packets at Mikala's house, plus several St. Benedict and St. Michael medals. I have no idea why he's still able to hang around."

That was scary. Between us, we'd always managed to figure out how to protect people who asked for our help, even when they were experiencing something we hadn't run across before. Sometimes it took us weeks, like the time we had to research how to close a portal some idiot had opened with a Ouija board, but we were always successful.

"How long have you been trying to banish this ghost?" I asked.

"A couple months."

"It's never taken either of us that long to figure out the answer to a troublesome haunting."

"I've even called Cat Dancer in New Orleans."

Tired and groggy, I nodded. The first Cat Dancer we had known about was a woman dear old Uncle Clarence had loved his entire life. She had died a few months before Uncle Clarence did, but her daughter was also named Cat. Twila and I had made it a point to visit Cat Dancer the daughter after our uncle passed on, and we'd found a woman well-versed in things we needed to learn. We'd both taken lessons under her guidance, and become close friends as a result.

"We might need to call her again," I said when Twila fell quiet.

"She's rather busy right now," Twila explained. "Her daughter is having a troublesome pregnancy. Cat's been wanting to go stay with the daughter, but she's adamant she wants to be on her own as long as possible. Independent, you know how some of our kids get."

I didn't, since I didn't have any children, but I had plenty of friends I'd listened to over the years.

"So is Cat checking with her friends to see if they have any ideas on how you need to proceed?" I asked.

"Yeah," Twila said. "She'll call if she finds out anything, but she frankly said she hadn't run across a ghost like Walking Bear, either. Now, that brings you pretty much up on what I've been doing. What happened out at Patches' place?"

I pushed against the porch floorboard with my foot to set the swing swaying while I gathered my thoughts. I didn't want to go off on one of my long, involved explanations, which everyone, including Twila and Jack, knew I was prone to do. I decided to start at the beginning, which in this case was when I'd left with Jack and Hoof.

At one point, I sensed Twila stifle laughter as I described poor Hoof's fear and resultant attempts to escape the paranormal antics of the two ghosts who had showed up at the lake. But we both knew how serious this was, especially if we had another ghost we couldn't control. Walking Bear was bad enough, but with Patches also causing turmoil, we could end up with a mess on our hands before long.

Before I quit talking to let Twila contemplate for a while, I even managed to get in a little rant about the deputy's irreverence for my book. Then I sat in silence for a few minutes. It was too late in the evening to hear the spring peeper frogs in the pond on their property, and the peaceful quiet was soothing after what had happened since I arrived.

Frankly, I thought to myself, *I haven't felt this relaxed since the phone rang two days ago in Six Gun.*

I watched one of Twila's outside cats return from a night roam and head toward the barn. I'd lost count of how many animals she had, and there hadn't been time to update me. I did know there were several cats that mostly hung around the barn, but she didn't kick them out if they happened to drop in at the house. I also recalled a wild mustang named JJ that she and Jess had adopted. She didn't care for feathered things, so there were no chickens, ducks or guineas wandering around her yard.

They usually had a dog or two, also, but they had lost those pets recently. Perhaps Harley the pig was taking the place of a new dog for a while, but I'd be willing to bet she would head for a shelter to adopt again soon.

Eventually, Twila said, "It's weird. You saw what just happened with Free Eagle. I was able to control him when he tried to butt into our conversation before we were ready to talk to him. So why can't I dominate Walking Bear?"

"We'll have to resort to talking to Free Eagle at some point." I covered my mouth to hide a yawn. When I wrote, the hours flew by without notice. At times, the sunrise would startle me as I looked out my office window. However, other times, I needed my eight hours, and it was well past bedtime for me. Ohio was an hour ahead of Texas, so I'd lost another hour as we travelled.

Twila rose. "You need your rest and senses about you to help out. Go get some sleep. Things will wait until morning."

* * *

They didn't. I managed to get a shower and change into my pajamas before the antique dinner bell in Twila's backyard started clanging to beat the band. I'd just pulled back the blanket on my bed, laid down, and snuggled into the pillow. My eyes flew open as the noisy bongs split the air,

Trucker lunged to his feat and lumbered over to howl at the window.

"Gosh dang it, dog, shut up," Granny ordered as she sat up in her bed. "Ain't you never heard a bell toll a'fore?"

Trucker plopped down on his rump and shut up, although he didn't move from the window. I sighed and sat up on the side of my bed. "The middle of the night's not a time for a bell to ring," I reminded Granny.

"Sure ain't. Prob'ly one of them there dad-blasted ghosts. We best git down there and put it in its place!"

Granny had to dislodge Miss Molly in order to get out of bed, and my cat growled an irritated sound as she leapt to the floor and stalked over to Trucker.

"Maybe we should let Trucker and Miss Molly handle the ghost," I said as Granny and I grabbed our robes and headed out of our room.

"And mebbe we should leave them here," she replied as she firmly closed the door on the bedroom before Trucker could get out. "We don't know what we gonna be facin' down there."

Trucker whined once with displeasure, then subsided, and I breathed a sigh of relief when he didn't start digging at the door. I could imagine

Twila's face if I had to ask her to find someone to repair the damage his dog-claws had done to that beautiful old hardwood.

The bell continued to clamor as Granny and I descended the stairwell. Rather than surge ahead, I stayed beside her, just in case she had any trouble navigating the steps. I'd seen her walking stick beside the front door when Twila and I came in a while ago, so I assumed she was having one of her "good" times, as she referred to them when her arthritis wasn't bothering her too badly. She didn't throw me an irritated glower, so I took that to mean she didn't mind me hovering. This time, anyway.

Jess and Twila were already in the kitchen when we got there. Jess had a double-barreled shotgun in his hand, and they were both ready to go out the back door.

Twila glanced at us and said, "The bell's ringing on its own. Or something invisible's doing it."

"Has that ever happened before?" I asked.

"No," she answered. "As far as I can remember, I've only used it for one thing since I rescued it from that old homestead being torn down. I'd call Patches and Jess in from their fishing trips down at the river. They'd miss supper if the fish were biting."

I read the conclusion on her face. It was probably Patches out there.

Jess strode onto the porch. I knew him well enough not to try to stop him. This was his property and he was the man of the land. No darned ghost was going to intrude on his peace, even if it was an old friend. Twila was right behind him.

I grabbed a box of salt from the stove, and Granny and I followed. Outside, I could see the bell Jess had positioned about fifty feet from the back porch. The post was an upside-down L, the huge black bell hanging from the branch on top. Made from steel, the resonating noise from the clapper could be heard a long ways off. Right then, it swung back and forth wildly, as though a hurricane was ripping past it...except it was the only thing moving in the entire yard.

Boom!

I flinched as Jess shot in the air. I'd seen him raise the shotgun, so it didn't completely shock me. Still, the noise was loud enough that it, too, echoed.

The bell continued to clang.

"Damn it, Twila," Jess said. "You got any idea who it is?"

Twila and I both stared toward the bell. Closer now, I could make out a very faint outline beneath the L. Whoever it was held the pull rope, and the rope twitched back and forth rapidly.

Twila reached for my hand. "You and Granny wait here, please," she told Jess.

I handed Granny the box of salt, since this was a situation where we wanted our senses completely unclouded to identify the perpetrator. We weren't totally foolish, however. Twila and I spent a precious few seconds grounding ourselves and calling down some protective White Light before we took our first step toward the noisy bell. We both practiced protective measures daily, so it didn't take much for us to do what was necessary. If we needed them, we also always had spirit guides close by.

Now, we felt secure enough to stroll toward the bell without hesitation. Steadfast resolution on our part would show whoever was messing around that we were not going to put up with his or her tomfoolery.

We were almost at the bell when the image beneath it disappeared. The rings ceased, and the rope dangled motionless. Yet that didn't keep us from our pending confrontation.

"Stay!" Twila demanded, reaching out a hand in a grasping motion. "I don't think your abilities are strong enough yet to escape us!"

A small ball of orange light a few feet from us whirled and writhed. *Let me go!* I heard telepathically, and I assumed Twila had heard it also.

She said, "Patches, what do you think you're doing? Talk to me!"

No! Lemme go!

"You're the one who woke us up, Patches. So tell us what you want." Twila dropped my hand and walked toward the orange ball of light.

I waited where I was, since her releasing my hand indicated she wanted me to stay behind for the moment. Also, I'd never seen Twila use this new ability she had acquired, only heard about it when she called a few weeks ago. One of her pen pals had actually shared the knowledge the ability existed—and taught Twila this particular skill. I was very interested in seeing how it worked, and hoping she would teach me before I had to head back to Six Gun.

A second later, Granny joined me, and whispered, "Jess went back inside soon as he heard Twila say it was Patches. Then he shoved this out the door to me and closed it again."

I glanced down to see her holding out a bottle of Jim Beam. I took it and lifted it high enough for the security light to show there was still a good half bottle left. When I looked over at Twila, I saw her in a tug of war with that ball of light. It would writhe a few feet away from her, then she would manage to pull it back.

I walked slowly toward Twila, in order to give her plenty of time to sense my approach. Behind me, I heard Granny's less firm steps following more slowly. The sound of her footsteps ceased at least ten feet before I reached Twila and held the bottle out toward the orange ball.

"Hey, Patches," I said. "Jess sent you out a drink."

The ball quieted. Twila dropped her arm, but I knew she could call on her ability to restrain the ghost in a split second. It was something she would have repeatedly practiced until it became second nature, as did a lot of things we used in our paranormal ventures.

I wanna talk to Jess alone. You gals need to stay out of my business.

Twila shook her head and whispered to me, "Patches was a huge chauvinist." Raising her voice, she went on, "You know as well as I do that Jess isn't going to talk to a ghost, Patches."

I caught the whiny tone in the next communication from Patches. *Does he know it's me?*

Rather than answering that question, Twila asked, "Then you do know you're de— passed on? That someone murdered you?" When Patches remained mute, she added, "Do you know who did this to you?"

Wish I did, he replied.

Before I could stop myself, I asked, "What was it that you hid in the wall at the bait shop?"

"Now, Alice," Twila said as she turned to me, then said, "Crap."

96

I had kept my gaze on the orange ball...which wasn't there any longer.

"You made me lose my concentration when you butted in," Twila said in a chastising tone. "You know better than that. Now he's gone. And he knows I can bind him, so he won't show himself anywhere I'm near again if he can help it."

"Sorry," I replied. "I won't do it again." I held the bottle of whiskey out to her. "Should I leave it as a peace offering?"

She chuckled. "We usually don't attempt to make peace with a ghost, but this time, maybe it's worth a try. He can't drink it, but maybe just having it will remind him of some good times."

I set the bottle down and said, "Again, I'm sorry about the interruption. It's just that whatever he took from the shop probably holds the key to all of this. Maybe even his murder."

"You didn't know Patches," she explained as we turned and walked toward where Granny waited. "He's not about to discuss something he considers men's business with women. He had no qualms about coming here and eating whatever meals I fixed for him and Jess. But one time I mentioned maybe going down to the river and enjoying the sun while I watched him and Jess fish. I thought Patches was going to have a brain rupture trying to think of some excuse not to let me tag along."

"What did he come up with?" I asked as Granny walked with us back toward the house.

"He said he'd seen a big snake down by where they fished. That I'd better wait until he got rid of it. I could come then."

"Never found the snake, huh?"

"Nope," she said with a laugh. "And I never tried to horn in on their man-time again. Jess would have had no problem with me coming, but I didn't think it was worth it to insist. Patches would have been on edge, afraid he might let some man-secret out. He wouldn't enjoy the day."

We walked across the back porch and into the kitchen. Jess had made a pot of coffee and the smell lingered in the air, drawing us to the pot like flies to honey. The level in the pot was down, so someone, probably Jess, had already drank a cup or two, but I didn't see a sign of him.

"We're going to have to figure out some way to get Jess to sit still so we can talk to him," I said as I took three cups from the cupboard. It didn't appear that we would get any sleep for a while, and I direly needed the caffeine.

Granny and Twila fixed their own coffee and joined me at the table. Twila set her cup down, then returned to the refrigerator and pulled out a package of rolls. My eyes widened.

"Nichols maple rolls," I breathed with a sigh of happiness. "Oh, wow."

"Harrumph," Granny said with a sniff. "Packaged stuff ain't never as good as homemade."

"You've never tried these," I said. I quickly opened the package, took out one of the long, rectangular rolls and bit into it. "Omigod, heaven."

Shaped like a long-john, the roll was iced with yummy maple frosting and contained a creamy, pudding type filling to die for. The rolls were fresh, too. It must have been delivery day when I arrived, since the bakery only produced the maple rolls twice a week. I remembered one visit when Twila and I would meet the bakery truck at the local grocery store and buy up every package of maple rolls available to that store for the day. Other days while I was there, I'd have to settle for white- or chocolate-iced rolls, since I froze some of the maple ones to take home.

The roll disappeared before I'd even drank half my coffee, and I reached for another one. Finally, Granny decided they were worth her time and took a roll. I noticed Twila had already finished one herself, since she loved them as much as I did.

The rolls took my mind off the ghost and murder problems for a few minutes. It all intruded when Jess wandered back into the kitchen for another cup of coffee. He poured his cup full, then sat at the table beside Twila.

"Well?" he asked.

"Patches wants to talk to you," Twila said.

"No," Jess said flatly. "I can't do it. No way."

She patted his arm. "I know, sweetie. We'll figure something else out."

CHAPTER 9

By the Great Spirit, he would not divulge to either of those two women why their bag of tricks wouldn't work against his brother. Despite his disadvantages, Walking Bear had been a great warrior, just like himself. As long as he stayed close to Free Eagle, anyway. And he had vowed to never abandon his brother, no matter what.

Still, he had to admit he was tired and ready to be with his ancestors. How could he explain to Walking Bear they would find everyone he was searching for if they would only walk up that golden path to where their family waited with the Great Spirit? Walking Bear just couldn't seem to understand, and now he was avoiding his brother.

Walking Bear had killed when he went along on hunting parties to feed the tribal members. Once he had even saved Free Eagle's own hide when a band of Iroquois ambushed them at a waterfall. His brother's lacks did not preclude him learning how to shoot an arrow with a skill even greater than Free Eagle's own. His brother just did not comprehend death. He had to find him and once again try to make him understand.

For a minute, he thought he might have spotted his brother over by his many times great grand-niece's house. Then he realized....

"What are you doing here?" he roared. "You have no business at this place!"

The one they called Patches, the old man from the bait shop, whom he had watched fish with the Twila woman's husband, limped out of the woods into the yard. Although this one did not know of him, Free Eagle knew about Patches. At times he grew bored trying to find and reason with Walking Bear and roamed around. He had always enjoyed the fishing season when he lived, and this one and the Twila woman's man Jess fished often. They were never boring to watch or listen to.

Free Eagle still had keen vision, and he saw Patches had already managed to clean himself up. When he'd first caught sight of him, the new ghost in the territory had been covered with blood and walking unsteadily. Now he must have realized he could bathe in the water or, if he wanted, use his mind to change his appearance. Even his beard was combed.

Patches wasn't that big, but Free Eagle had to admit he had a large amount of courage. When Free Eagle rushed at him, the smaller ghost stared right down the muzzle of the rifle. He probably knew, also, the gun could not harm either of them in their condition.

Or...could it possibly? Free Eagle had never tried to kill another of his type. Not kill, he guessed, since they were already dead. But perhaps destroy. Contemplating, he pulled back the hammer on the rifle, then remembered he had not had any ball and shot for many seasons.

Patches had only existed in this manner for a few hours, so maybe he did not know either whether the gun could hurt someone.

"I still get confused some," Patches said. He stared down at his right leg and flexed it. "Also still can't get used to having my leg here back, instead of that prosthesis thing. Guess I'll quit limping soon."

Free Eagle nodded. He had seen Patches remove his fake leg on the riverbank at times. Now the man was whole again.

"And put that damn rifle down," Patches ordered. "I'll bet you ain't fired it in two hundred years. And even if you did try now, the powder probably ain't no good."

"Three hundred years," Free Eagle admitted, but he lowered his rifle.

This one might be able to lessen the boredom of this existence. He hadn't run across any other ghosts in a long while. Those he had encountered went on to the higher level as soon as they realized they could do so even if they had ignored the path the first time.

"I nonetheless want to know what you are doing here. Confusion is not an excuse, and this is my land."

Patches glanced at the house. "Looks like Mikala's house," he said.

"I am her ancestor," Free Eagle said, "so it is still my land, also. And I will defend her, should she be in danger."

"I just had someone tell me we can't own nothing the way we are now. And I won't bother Mikala. From what I heard, she's getting nutty, so I feel sorry for her. She's a fine lady. I just took a wrong turn in the trail while I was escaping from that darn Twila. Jess never told me that much about what she did when she was messing around with ghosts, 'cause he was scared to death of them himself. But I heard stuff from others in the county. 'Pears Jess's old lady has lots of stuff she uses to block us when we end up like this. But I still gotta get past her and talk to Jess."

"Mikala is not going...as you say...nutty. It is my brother who is causing the problems."

Patches contemplated him for a few seconds. "You got a brother who's wandering around like you and me? Same age as you?"

"My brother and I were alive together, yes."

"Where's he now?"

"He is here somewhere." He frowned. "You ask many questions."

"Until I can talk to Jess, there ain't much else to do. I got an idea who did this to me, but I ain't got no proof."

Free Eagle laughed. "You are still thinking as you did when you were living. This is not like those shows on that television. Now we do not need such things as proof in order to challenge someone we feel has wronged us."

Patches grinned. "You interested in a little fun and games? Or you too busy looking for your brother?"

* * *

"That's what they call their fishing camp down there on the river," Patches told Free Eagle. "It's about the stinkingest place I ever smelled. I don't care if they are my relatives, I never allowed none of them to come into my bait shop."

Free Eagle stared at the scene. The river made a bend there, so he could only see a short distance each way. A sandbar stuck out a ways, and several men sat or lay on it. On the shore, far enough back to escape high water during spring rains, stood a rickety shack. It evidently was empty, since not even lantern light glowed in the windows and no smoke feathered from the protruding metal chimney stack. More possibly, they did not have that new stuff in it, that electricity.

A campfire still burned, giving off enough light to see empty tin cans, plastic bags, and beer bottles, along with other trash, despoiling the land. Several men sat around the fire, drinking from a bottle they passed from hand to hand. A couple other men in a small boat were checking a trotline strung from one bank of the river to the far one. One of them must have already drank his share from a bottle, since he stood in the boat and wobbled as he jerked on the line.

The other man grabbed for him, but missed. The first man splatted into the water, then surfaced with a wild yell of pain. Sound carried across the water, and they both had a higher hearing ability in their states, so it was easy to understand the conversation out there.

"You all right, Eddie?" the man in the boat called. He reached out for Eddie's arm and tried to pull him back into the boat.

"Stop it, Hardy!" Eddie yelled. "Damn it, don't! I'm caught on one of the hooks!"

"Ah, shit," Hardy said. "Them's two ought gauge hooks. They'll hold five hundred pounds."

"You don't have to tell me! I helped you lay out this damn line. Get a knife and cut me loose!"

Hardy leaned back and scratched his head. "We mess around like that, we might lose any fish we got on the rest of the line."

"Damn it, you're not gonna leave me here treading water while you run the rest of the line! Get me the hell off this trotline!"

Hardy laughed and took a knife out of a tackle box at his feet. "I was just funning, Eddie. Hang onto the side and let me get at you."

A second later, he helped Eddie out of the water. The hook protruded from the rear of Eddie's jeans, and when he tumbled into the boat, he landed on his butt.

"Ouch! Shit! Damn it!" Eddie scrambled around and held onto one of the seats, his rear end stuck out in front of Hardy. He looked over his shoulder and said, "You're gonna have to cut that hook out."

"The hell with you," Hardy said. "I ain't cutting on another man's ass."

"Then how am I gonna get it out? I can't reach it!"

"Guess we'll have to take you to the hospital."

"No way! My old lady works there. I ain't gonna have her laughing her ass off at me getting hung up on a fishhook. Just hand me that bottle we brought with us and let me drink some. Then pour some on your knife and the hook and cut it out."

Hardy picked up the oars. "Tell you what. You hang on over that seat so you don't try to sit down and drive that there hook in further. I'll row us back to shore and get Doc to take the hook out."

"Doc?" Eddie shouted. "He's drunk as a skunk. He's stayed drunk since he got his medical license pulled...because he was drunk at the hospital! He might miss the hook and carve off the wrong thing."

Hardy shrugged and continued rowing. "Chance you'll have to take. I ain't cutting on your ass."

Free Eagle joined Patches' laughter as they watched the boat land and the man called Hardy get out and walk over to the fire. There, they could hear him try to explain to the man who lay on a sleeping bag on the ground what had happened.

"Come on, Doc. You need to sober up and help Eddie."

"Eddie shoulda got hooked before I got my buzz on," Doc said. "Tell you what. I'll supervise, but someone else's gotta do the cutting."

"Shit," Hardy said, but he helped Doc to his feet and picked up a lantern. Both Free Eagle and Patches decided to watch the rest of the show. They couldn't be seen, so they moved on down the hill, sat, and propped their elbows on their knees. They were both still chuckling.

Patches said. "Come close to something like that happening a time or two when me'n Jess had a couple more beers than we should've had while we was handling sharp hooks. But glad it never actually happened to me."

"That Eddie man probably wishes the same thing," Free Eagle replied.

At the boat, Hardy set the lantern on the rear seat and explained to Eddie what they were going to do. Then he reached under the back seat and brought out a bottle of booze. Eddie took several slugs before Hardy pulled it away from him.

"We ain't got no alcohol 'cept the drinking sort, so I'm gonna have to use it," he reminded Eddie. "Ain't no telling where my knife's been, so hope you left enough here to clean off the germs."

"Naw," Doc said, then burped. "Not your knife. You need some bolt cutters."

"What?" Eddie shrieked. "No way!"

"Shut up and pull down your pants," Doc said, then to Hardy, "Guess you better use your knife to cut a slice in his pants so the hook will slide out when he pulls them down. Then I'll show you what you need to do."

Hardy managed to slice a path in Eddie's pants to free the hook without drawing more blood. He even held Eddie's belt away so the knife cut through the waistband. For a long moment, Eddie just laid there. Then he slowly eased himself to his side and unbuckled his belt. A few seconds later, his bare butt mooned in the lantern light.

Doc started to bend over and point, and Hardy caught him right before he tumbled on top of Eddie. "Watch it, Doc," he said as he pushed the other man upright. "You don't want to end up attached to that hook yourself."

"*Hiccup*," Doc answered, then took a steadying breath and pointed without bending down. "See? The point is almost through the skin on the other side of where it went in. You gotta push it on through, then snip off the barb. Then you can pull it back through."

Hardy opened his tackle box and dug through it. Victoriously, he held up a small pair of bolt cutters. "Have to use these to get hooks outta big catfish now and then," he said.

Then he glanced down at Eddie's ass and shook his head. "Don't know if I can do this, Doc. I ain't one to mess around with another man's ass."

"Won't take you a second," Doc said. This time, he farted, and Hardy waved his hand across his face.

"Damn it, Doc. You gotta do that again, give me a warning. Or walk off a ways first!"

"Yeah, Doc," Eddie said. "I can't get away from the smell."

"Huh," Doc said in an irritated voice. "You don't need me anymore anyway. You know what to do." He turned to walk away, then fell flat on his face. Instead of rising, he burped again, then snuggled his head on his upraised arm. Immediately, his gurgling snores sounded.

"Passed out," Hardy said. "Well, let's get to this. And if you tell anyone I did this, I'll hunt you down and stake you out somewhere for the Grassman to find!"

"I ain't telling nobody, damn it, Hardy. I don't want folks to know where I got hooked any more than you want them to know where you had to take it out of me. Get to it!"

Hardy bent over Eddie. He made a quick motion, which must have shoved the hook on through Eddie's skin because Eddie let out another yowl of pain. Then Hardy poured some whiskey from the bottle over the wound, took a big slug himself, and set the bottle down. He reached out with the bolt cutters, and clicked them a couple time first.

"Do it!" Eddie insisted. "The damn booze is burning as much as the hook is paining!"

Hardy lowered the bolt cutters and snipped. But he said, "Hell, that metal's strong. I'm gonna have to...." He sighed and reached for Eddie's butt cheek with his free hand. He grabbed the hook, then used the bolt cutters again. Eddie screamed, and the tip of the hook glinted in the lantern light when Hardy tossed it into the water. Hardy followed it with the other piece of the hook he extracted from the wound.

Then Hardy laid the bolt cutters down, picked up the bottle and took another deep swallow.

"You gonna put some on my ass," Eddie demanded, "or drink it all?"

With a sigh, Hardy tipped the bottle and poured whiskey on Eddie's butt cheek. "Waste of good booze," he muttered.

Eddie got to his feet and pulled his pants up. "Hurts like hell and it's probably bleeding. I'm gonna go in the camp house and find me some paper towels and tape."

He climbed out of the boat, and as he stomped away, Hardy saluted him with the whiskey bottle and said, "Thank you very much, Hardy, for getting the hook outta me." Then he sat down on the edge of the boat and turned his attention back to the bottle.

Free Eagle glanced at Patches to see him scanning the camp area again. "The show is over," he said. "We can leave."

"I'm trying to figure out who all's here and who might be missing," Patches said. "And thinking of who could've done this to me, who probably wouldn't have."

"I would not trust any one of those three we watched just now behind my back."

"Me, neither," Patches replied. "Hardy ain't quite as bad as Eddie, though. And Doc's been the town drunk for so long, it's hard to remember what he was like sober. Rest of them down there must be passed out like Doc, though. None of them stirred when Eddie was hollering."

"They cannot see us," Free Eagle said as he stood. "We can go down and identify them for you."

Patches rose and nodded at Free Eagle. "I appreciate you doing this with me."

Free Eagle shrugged. "It helps pass the time," he said as the two of them wandered down the hillside to stroll among the various inebriated fishermen.

* * *

I actually managed to grab two whole hours of sleep before the smell of coffee woke me. Sniffing, I was halfway out of the bed before I even realized I was getting up. Caffeine does that to me. My morning greeting to anyone pre-coffee is, "Ugh."

Glancing around the room, I saw that Trucker and Miss Molly were already gone. The other twin bed was also empty, which meant Granny was up. Guilt over my elderly friend being up and about after the same amount of sleep that I'd had kept me from crawling back in bed and cuddling my pillow.

I grabbed some clean clothing from my suitcase and stumbled down the hall to the shower. A few minutes later, somewhat refreshed and wearing my favorite jeans, I headed down the stairs to the kitchen. Twila and Granny must have heard me stirring above them, because there was already a steaming cup waiting for me on the table.

"Oh, wow," I said as I picked it up and realized it was a latte. "Have you been out to the coffee shop already this morning, Twila?"

"No," she said. "I bought one of those machines like you use a while back and learned how it works. I still prefer iced coffee drinks, but Mikala likes lattes like you. She showed me how to make them."

"Thank you," I remembered to say before I took a swallow. I tried to hide my surprise, but when I looked at Twila, she was grinning. "It's really good," I admitted.

"I know you expected it not to taste as good as the ones you make for yourself. But you forget, I've watched you prepare those for years. I even put some honey in it."

"Thank you, thank you," I said again. I was starting to actually wake up.

"I still says it's a waste of good milk and coffee to mix them like that," Granny said. "But to each his own. Jist don't ask me to pay them there coffee shop prices. I can make a whole pot for what they want for one cup."

"That's one reason I make it at home," I told her.

"You bought 'nuf of them on our trip to keep them in business for a month," she reminded me.

I shrugged. It was an old argument between us. To change the subject, I asked, "Where are Trucker and Miss Molly?"

Twila smiled and motioned for me to come with her. Taking my latte, I followed her onto the back porch and looked out the screen door. In the yard, Trucker and a gray and white pig about a third his size were playing tag. Trucker would bound toward Harley, poke him with his nose, then whirl and race away. Belly nearly dragging the ground, Harley would frolic after Trucker. The dog slowed down to let the pig catch him, then they reversed the game.

Miss Molly sat on a nearby iron bench beside one of Twila's flower beds, tolerantly watching the other two animals.

"Miss Molly was actually playing tag with them a minute ago," Twila said. "But she probably decided such antics were beneath her as a cat."

I laughed. "That sounds like her. I'm glad Trucker and Harley are getting along, though. I was worried."

"Jess brought Harley down this morning and they sniffed each other for a minute or so. Then, when Jess let Harley out into the yard, Trucker wanted to go, too. And Miss Molly. We watched them for a bit, but it was pretty clear they had decided to be friends."

"How is Jess this morning?" I asked.

She grew quiet. "It's going to take a while," was her only answer.

"What's the latest on the investigation?"

"Granny was up before me," Twila said as she turned to go back in the kitchen. "And Jack dropped by for a few minutes and talked to her. I'll let her explain."

I joined Granny at the table again, and she shook her head. "Ain't much. Jack said they ain't no closer to findin' out who killed that poor man than they was last night. I asked him iffen he thought one of them ghosts prowling around might've done it. But 'bout then, he decided he best grab a cup of coffee and hightail it back to see that there sheriff."

I glanced over at Twila. "Jess is going to have to talk to Patches at some point."

"I know," she agreed. "But let's give him a little more time. I'll talk to him this afternoon and see if he's changed his mind. You know him. He will do what needs to be done. He just has to believe it's his own idea first."

I chuckled. "It's amazing how we have to manipulate our men."

Granny burst into a full-blown laugh. "You girls needs to remember somethin'," she said when she could talk. "Sometimes it's best to let them there men think they be manipulatin' us instead. Works easier that way."

"You've got a point, Granny," I said. "Now, what are we going to do this morning?"

"Go over to Mikala's, if that works for you two," Twila said. "I talked to her a while ago, since I was sure she'd heard about what went on here last night. She assured me that if I didn't feel like coming over, if I thought I should stay with Jess, she would understand. But I told her that I'd like to keep working on her problem. Especially now that you and Granny are here."

"What about Jess?" I asked.

"Tell you what," Granny broke in. "I'd just as soon stay here and do some cookin' for y'all. How 'bouts I do that while you two takes care of your ghost business. Did you get those things I called you about, Twila?"

"I did," Twila assured her. "You know I love your gumbo and crawfish pie. I can hardly wait."

"We'll have it tonight. And iffen Jess gets hungry while you two is gone, I'll fix him up somethin'. Fact is, I'll get him in here and feed him whether he says he's hungry or not."

"Speaking of hungry," Twila said to me, "neither one of us ate much for breakfast. All the rolls are gone, but I can fix you some toast. Or we can stop by Yoder's Restaurant with Mikala later."

"Yoder's," I immediately decided. "I want some chicken and dumplings."

CHAPTER 10

Mikala's house surprised me. It was ranch-style, painted white with red shutters. The cleared land looked like only an acre or so, and woods encroached in the back. The small detached garage appeared large enough for one stall, and the little barn probably couldn't hold more than a cow or two. The tiny rail fence corral attached to the barn was empty.

I wasn't exactly sure what I'd expected; perhaps more along the lines of a larger farm home. Then I recalled that she lived here alone, so she probably had her hands full keeping up the house, let alone any animals.

I'd ridden with Twila, and she parked in front of the detached garage. I was still examining the setting as she got out of the car.

"You coming?" she called in the open door.

"Huh? Oh, sure. I was just seeing if we had any company yet."

"We will," she assured me. "Did you put salt in your pocket?"

I got out and said to her across the top of the car, "Of course. But I'm still confused as to why you want us to carry your consecrated salt. Won't it keep whoever we're trying to contact here too far away from us to talk to?"

She shrugged. "I don't know. Something told me to carry that salt today, and I always pay attention to those types of warnings."

I nodded. So did I, and now I understood completely. I'd learned long ago, when I first started delving into the paranormal with Twila as my mentor, not to ignore those little voices that sometimes intruded into my thoughts.

Her comment made me recall a time I'd been in a hurry to get to a luncheon with a friend and couldn't find my keys. Looking back, I realized one of my spirit guides had hidden them to delay me. I'd heard that little voice, too, but I really wanted to talk to this friend about some of the problems I was having with Jack at the time. So I ignored the voice, and assumed Howard had hidden the keys. Howard forgot about the extra set I kept out in the garage. I left the house right on time, much to my dismay.

Mine was the only car on a long stretch of the country road. If I'd left a few minutes later, the puppy would have already run across the road and been safe. As it was, I lost control when I swerved to miss the little thing, and ended up front bumper first into a tree. Somehow, I was able to get out of the car and rescue the puppy from the highway. I held him until his owner came running from the house across the road. Then I pretty much collapsed in my car until the ambulance came. I didn't fight the paramedics that day. Even I had to agree my dizziness wasn't normal.

I got to see the friend, but she came to pick me up at the hospital ER, after the doctor was finished checking me over.

I made it a point to remind myself once again not to overlook even a faint warning from my guides as Twila and I walked from the garage to the house. A small, elderly lady opened the front door, and I assumed she must be Mikala. She was still very beautiful, and I couldn't stop myself from wondering whether that gorgeous black hair had just refused to turn gray or she helped it hold its color. I didn't see even one light hair in the intricate braid coiled around her head.

Brown eyes gleamed intelligently, and even though Twila had told me Mikala was nearly Granny's age, there were very few wrinkles on her face. Her complexion was clear and her skin satin smooth. I did spy an age spot or two on her hands as she held them out to greet us, but they were hardly noticeable.

"Twila," she said. "I'm so glad you made it. And you must be Alice."

She clasped my hands, then dropped them and pulled me into a hug. "I'm so glad you're both here," she said when she stepped back.

"More trouble?" Twila asked with a frown.

"Not in the house," Mikala said. "Come on in."

As we walked through the tidy living room and into a gleaming, clean kitchen, she said, "The protection packets and medals are doing wonders in the house, Twila. I've been getting excellent sleep at night."

She motioned us to the table, where there were already coffee mugs waiting and...wonder of wonders, a plate of Nichols rolls.

Mikala saw me drooling towards the rolls and laughed. "Twila told me they were your favorites, Alice. So help yourself. I made you a latte, too, and one for me. Just let me nuke them."

I'd already eaten half a roll when she set the coffee mug in front of me. I sighed and said, "This is heaven. Maybe I'll come stay with you a night or two before I leave."

"You're welcome anytime," she assured me.

"Finish what you were saying," Twila said. "It sounds like something is going on outside the house."

Mikala nodded. "Even more than usual. This morning, I went out to take care of Balboa and he was gone. Someone had opened the corral gate."

"Balboa is Mikala's escape-artist donkey," Twila explained, although I'll admit, I hadn't been listening too closely. I was trying to decide if Mikala would think me piggish if I took a second roll.

Twila laughed and scooted the plate of rolls closer to me, then asked Mikala, "Have you found him yet?"

"He's over at my neighbor Sonny's place. Sonny called me just as I came back in the house after finding Balboa missing. But I had to ask Sonny to keep him for a while. All the food and hay in the barn is ruined. Someone turned on the water spigot to the trough Balboa drinks from and let it run. The water overflowed and flooded the barn. It soaked the feed sack and wet the hay. Luckily, I only had a couple bales left and the feed sack was almost empty. I'll call today and have them bring out more."

"Why would someone do that?" I asked, more attentive now that I'd finished that second roll. "If it was a ghost, doesn't he like your donkey?"

Mikala sighed. "It rather looked like someone threw a childish fit in the barn. There were tools tossed all over the place. Maybe he...or it...turned Balboa out to protect him. Or maybe the donkey escaped on his own." She shook her head. "The floor's awfully muddy. It will take a while for it to dry out."

Twila stood. "Come on. We're going to see if we can contact this ghost...or whatever it is."

"Ah...whatever?" I asked anxiously. "If it's something besides a ghost, we might not want to contact it."

"I was just joking, Alice. It truly is Walking Bear, because I've seen him. And this time I brought some things with me in the trunk. Stuff I hope will help us handle a problematic ghost."

She walked out of the kitchen and through the back door, Mikala following closely. I reluctantly decided I'd better join them. I justified munching that third roll as keeping my energy up in case we had to fight.

The barn wasn't much bigger than a large-sized utility shed, a third of it taken up by a stall evidently meant for Balboa. There were some shovels, a pitchfork and other tools scattered in the mud, and the door to a tiny room was open. Inside, we could see an open gunny sack of feed and hay scattered around. Mikala was right. The floor was a sea of mud.

"We'll help you clean up before we leave," Twila said. "But for now, do you mind if we bring that little patio table and chairs over here by the barn door?"

"Whatever you need," Mikala said.

The table and chairs were made from light metal, and we soon had them sitting in front of the door. Twila left us for a moment, saying she was going to get some things from her car.

"I assume Twila has told you about the other Native American guy we've already had contact with," I said to Mikala.

"She called me early this morning," she replied. "Free Eagle is definitely one of my many-times-great grand-uncles. But I don't understand why he would be causing trouble like this. I've always respected the land, and from what I understand about our beliefs, that's what counts. I should be considered a good caretaker, not someone to cause problems for."

"Have you seen Free Eagle around here?"

"No," she replied. "I really don't *see* things, just sense them. Oh, I do hear them now and then. However, what I hear never makes any sense, so I guess that's not a strong gift for me."

Twila returned, carrying a small satchel, which she set on the table. She removed a large vase containing a white candle and placed it in the middle. Then she took out a plastic bag of sea salt.

"Both of you please sit down and stay quiet while I do this part," she said.

We obediently sat in chairs and kept respectfully silent as she walked around the table, scattering salt and murmuring protection chants. After completing the circle, she returned the salt to her satchel and stood behind the empty chair for a few seconds, head bowed. I closed my eyes, also, and grounded myself, silently asking my own guides for additional protection, as well as assistance. Before Twila sat down, she took a box of wooden matches from the satchel and lit the candle.

Once in her seat, Twila reached for our hands. Mikala appeared to know what was expected, since she held her hand out to me on my other side. I waited for Twila's lead, knowing there were various ways she could conduct this attempt to contact whoever was causing the trouble. She sat quietly, eyes closed, for a length of time that eventually stretched into five minutes.

I hadn't realized I'd closed my eyes until I heard a faint noise and opened them.

"Oh, shit," I breathed as I stared in horror at the tools that had been lying in the mud. I glanced quickly at Twila to see a look of horror on her face. The tools were standing upright in the mud, quivering as though on the verge of launching themselves at us.

"Will the salt protect us?" I whispered.

Instead of answering, Twila quickly shoved the table over and jerked Mikala with her as she dove to the ground. I went too, just as the tools rushed us. We sheltered behind the table as two shovels and a pitchfork flew overhead. Then something hit the table with a thud, followed immediately by another thud.

We clung to each other, the table barely enough protection.

"We've got to get in the house," Twila said, about the time I looked behind me to see what had happened to those shovels and the pitchfork. They were standing up again, quivering.

"Run!" I screamed as I lunged to my feet.

We grabbed Mikala between us and, instead of heading for the rear of house, raced across the back yard toward the front. I would have, and could have, gone faster, but I wasn't sure about Mikala, and we weren't about to leave her. I kept glancing over my shoulder, but the tools didn't attack again.

The three of us scrambled up the steps and in through the front door. Twila slammed it behind us and turned the deadbolt lock. Then she stomped on through the living room and into the kitchen.

I noticed she had grabbed her satchel, and she tossed it onto the kitchen table and started digging through it.

"I'll be damned if I'm going to let that piece of protoplasm get the better of us!" she fumed.

"What are you going to do?" I asked, grabbing her arm to hold her still. "That thing's dangerous! The salt should have stopped those tools!"

"I didn't use our strongest chants and protections," she admitted. "I wanted whatever it was to be able to communicate. But all he did was throw things and try to scare us."

"Try?" I said with a shiver. "He did a hell of a good job of it."

"But he did communicate," Mikala said. "Didn't you hear him?"

We both stared at her in astonishment.

"I never heard a word," Twila said. "Did you, Alice?"

"Nothing," I admitted. "What did he say, Mikala?"

"He said, 'Go. No bother.' Another word after that, which sounded like 'me-kee.' And some other things, but I couldn't quite understand them."

Twila frowned. "That doesn't make sense. I'm not denying you heard something, Mikala, but I can't grasp why neither Alice nor I caught it. Could you tell if it was the same voice you've heard before?"

Mikala contemplated for a few seconds, then nodded an affirmative. "I think it was. He has this sort of rumbly, growly voice. And it's like he's straining to be understood."

"At times," I explained, "communication across The Veil is difficult. The vibration levels are so mis-matched, even our spirit guides have trouble getting messages through in a way we can understand. Yet you had no problem just now."

"I don't know how to explain it," Mikala said.

"It definitely sounds like a warning, though," Twila said. "The entity appears to be telling us to leave Mikala alone. It's possible he wants to protect her."

"Then why is he causing all this trouble?" I pointed out.

Twila shrugged without a verbal answer. She dug in her satchel again and pulled out a plastic bag filled with several pretty pieces of flower-covered material. I recognized what she had instantly. I'd helped her consecrate the asafetida and tie it into those handkerchiefs we had found at an estate sale. Although we'd enclosed the asafetida in plastic before we tied it up, and kept the hankies in a thick plastic freezer bag, I caught a faint whiff of what some herbalists called 'devil's dung.' Despite the name, it was a powerful deterrent to negative entities, or even antagonistic ghosts.

"Do you really think we need to use that?" I asked.

"I don't know," Twila admitted. "But since it got past the salt, we need to be sure we're protected."

"Why?" I asked, then backed away from her satchel, shaking my head. I knew exactly what she had in mind, but asked anyway. "You aren't planning to go back out there?"

"Do you have any other way in mind to find out what's going on here?" she asked.

"Crap," I muttered, but I stiffened my spine and said, "I want two hankies."

She handed them to me, and I stuffed one in my bra, the other in my jeans pocket.

"You need to stay here this time," she told Mikala. "I want to see what happens if he has to communicate with Alice or me."

"It's my property," Mikala reminded her, but she didn't sound like she meant to argue too intensely.

"And you agreed to let me do whatever was necessary to help you," Twila said.

Mikala immediately gave in. "You're right. I guess I'll just feel responsible if anything happens to either of you."

Twila patted her shoulder. "We know the dangers."

I bit back my retort. Twila knew very well I wasn't the bravest person in the confrontations we had with some of the nasty things we encountered. Even though I tried my best, I'd been known to flee.

Twila caught my aversion and shot me a warning glance. I immediately closed my eyes and did some breathing and mental adjustments. I'd learned another thing from both her teachings and my own few cowardly retreats. One did not go into a confrontation with a troublesome entity with your own emotions in turmoil. Not over either a personal problem or fearing what you were on the verge of encountering. I needed to calm myself and have faith Twila would use the finest defenses possible for us.

As we left the kitchen and walked slowly toward the barn, I asked Twila, "Do you think this is...you know."

She shook her head. "It's not a demon or a devil. At least, I'm about ninety-nine percent sure it's not. You know how they can trick a person. Appear as something totally innocent. This one, though, acts like he's dealing with some very human traits. Like that temper tantrum when he trashed Mikala's barn. But, like a human who cares for animals, he turned Balboa our first."

"Where on earth did she come up with the name Balboa for a donkey?"

Twila chuckled. "She likes history."

"Oh." I halted. "Wait, Twila. I'm sensing something."

She had already taken another step, but returned to my side. We had worked together for so many years, she knew to stay silent while I contemplated. After a long minute or so, I shook my head.

"Did you hear anything at all?" I asked.

"Nothing," she said. "But...ah, wait."

A moment ago, I'd heard a quiet murmuring, which had intermittently spiked into what I thought was an intense insistence for acknowledgement or response. Given Twila's listening attitude, it now seemed directed at her.

She eventually shook her head, also. "I can't understand him."

"Well." I nodded toward the barn. "He's pissed again."

One of the shovels stood on end. At least it wasn't the pitchfork, I mused as I prepared to duck. However, whoever held the shovel didn't throw it. Instead, the shovel started battering the doorjamb on the barn.

Twila marched forward. "Quit it!" she ordered. "You're going to damage Mikala's barn! And she can't afford the repairs!"

The shovel halted in mid-air, then dropped to the ground. Then a heartrending cry echoed inside the barn. A second later, the cry flew past us, toward the woods, as though the ghost was rushing away in a ball of emotional pain and defeat. We both stared toward the woods until the cries died.

"You know," I said, "he sounds like a teenager who isn't getting his way."

"You're right," she agreed. "And I don't understand it."

"Do you think this one's Free Eagle's brother?"

"I believe so," she said. "If he's the same one I've tried to communicate with before. If we could get Free Eagle to hang around long enough to question him, we might find out for certain. Right now, let's see if we can clean up some of this mess for Mikala."

I wrinkled my nose at the mud, then looked down at my nearly new tennis shoes. They sparkled nice and white in the sun, but if I waded in the mud, they would never come clean. Twila walked over to the table and sat down. When she started untying her own shoes, I felt better. Not that I was a selfish person who resented despoiling a pair of shoes to help someone out. Well, not too selfish.

A few seconds later, we both had our shoes safely on top of the table and were wading through the mud to retrieve the tools. After we hung them tidily on their wall hooks, I turned to see if we'd missed anything.

Too quickly. My right foot slid out from under me.

"No!" I yelled as I whirl-winded my arms and tried to regain my balance. Twila was right there beside me, but do you think she would help? Instead, when I reached for her, she hurriedly backed away so she wouldn't tumble with me. The next thing I knew, I was face down in the mud.

I convulsively wiggled around until I got up on my hands and knees, spitting out mud so I could breathe. Then I tried to blow the clogs out of my nose, but had to wipe the back of my wrist across my nostrils.

And ended up losing my balance again and landing right back in that slimy, gooey mess. At least this time I fell on my side, not my face.

Still, this was black mud, farmland mud, and I could just imagine what I looked like. I spit out another dab of mud and said, "I hope like hell there's no donkey manure in this mess!"

I backhanded my eyes to clear my vision and tried to clamber to my feet. A wooden pole appeared in front of me and I jerked back when I realized it was the pitchfork. At first, I thought the ghost had returned for another attack. Then I glanced up and saw Twila holding the handle.

"Grab it to steady yourself," she said.

I glared at her for an instant. There was no doubt about the amusement and full-fledged laughter in her brown eyes. She was biting her lip, also, as though to hold back her hilarity.

I grabbed the pitchfork handle, and she stepped away again as I struggled to regain my feet. I made it halfway before I slid down into that damned mud again. Then I firmed my spine and lunged up. I pulled the pitchfork free, set it down a foot way, then followed it. Stomping my feet behind the pitchfork as I used it to steady myself, I made it out of the mud, into the yard.

I set the pitchfork against the side of the barn and growled, "If you want that damned fork over there where it belongs, take it yourself."

Twila let loose with her laughter. I glared as she hooted and giggled, alternately pointing at me and bending over to hold her stomach.

"You..." she said around her gasps. "You should see...."

I drew myself up in exasperation, dragging in a breath as I did so. Or tried to drag one in. My nose clogged and my coughing fit rivaled a drum beat. I managed to honk out the mud, then glowered around the yard until I saw the water trough inside the corral. Without any hesitation, I marched over to it and slid right into...

...some damned icy water! I hadn't felt water that cold since I'd visited a friend in Minnesota and tried to swim in the lake where she lived. I gasped, but wiggled around to wash off the mud. I even laid my head back and swirled it to help clean my matted hair.

When I climbed out of the water, Twila stood there holding the hose. She'd already washed off her feet, and now she lifted an inquiring eyebrow over one of her still twinkling eyes in a silent question. Sighing in consent, I turned my back and let her hose off whatever I hadn't left behind in the trough.

By the time she was done, I was shivering violently.

"Aachoo!" I sneezed. Then sniffled.

Ah, crap, I'd forgotten about that asafetida packet in my bra. I must have hit the side of the tank as I swirled the mud away and damaged the plastic inside the hankie. The smell of it wet was even more nauseating than dry devil's dung.

"Pe-yew!" Twila said. "Toss that bag on the ground."

I dug it out of my bra and tossed it, then removed the one from my jeans pocket. It joined the other one, but I could still smell it on my body.

"It'll take hot water to get that odor off," Twila informed me, as if I hadn't already realized that.

I coughed again and waved my hand under my nose, wishing I could strip off my blouse and bra right then and there. Instead, I felt myself engulfed in something large and soft.

I gathered the quilt around me as I turned. Mikala stood beside Twila. I bit my tongue to keep back the nasty comment about hoping the smell would waft that far.

"I saw what was happening," Mikala said. "And I've turned the heat up in the house. Let's get you inside and in a warm bath."

"Aachoo!" I answered.

The two of them kept their distance from my smelly self as they led me back inside, then down a hallway and into a bathroom. I grasped the quilt tightly as Mikala bent over the tub and turned on the spigots. I didn't even notice Twila leave, but by the time I'd reluctantly given up the quilt, undressed and settled into the blessedly warm water, she had returned.

"Here," she said as she handed me a large mug filled to the brim. "I made you a hot toddy. That will help take away the chill and, hopefully, ward off any cold."

I accepted the mug and took a long swallow. She'd made it just right, not too hot to drink yet warm enough for both the liquid and alcohol to start chasing my chill from the inside out.

She'd added enough Crown Royal, also. By the time I'd finished the mug, my buzz was chasing away the irritation and embarrassment over my tumble—all right, tumbles—in the mud.

While I drank, I was aware of her and Mikala gathering up the dirty quilt and my clothing. Instead of thanking them, I thoughtlessly held out the mug to Twila. "Another, please."

She laughed and took the mug. I laid back in contentment until she returned. But instead of giving me the refilled toddy when I held out my hand, she set it on the bath vanity.

"Let's wash your hair and get you out of the tub," she said. "Then you can have another drink. I'm making them pretty strong, even for you. And I don't want to have to try to pull you out of that water if you can't make it yourself."

"Oh, o.k.," I said grumpily before I realized how rude that was. "Ah,

I'm sorry," I went on. "I know it wasn't your fault I was so clumsy. And I know I must have looked...looked...."

I should have known better. I made the mistake of peeking over at Twila. Once again, she was trying to suppress her laughter. A second later, we were both lost in one of those shared hilarity bouts we sometimes experience. She laughed, I laughed, we hooted and howled. It was a full five minutes before we were able to control ourselves. Luckily, I'd had enough sanity left to not swish around in the tub and flood the bathroom.

Mikala had set shampoo and other toiletry items on the tub rim, and I reached for one of the bottles. Then slid another look at Twila.

"Don't you dare bother my drinkie-poo," I said in an imitation of Granny.

It was a simple sentence, but it set us off again.

About fifteen minutes later, I was finally clean and comfortable, wearing one of Mikala's gowns and robes while I waited for my own clothing to come out of the dryer.

"Now," Twila said as she handed me a cup of coffee at the kitchen table instead of the third toddy I was hoping for. "We need to get down to business."

"If you say so," I replied with a disgruntled sigh. I'd rather have gone back to her house and rested again, or perhaps talked her into sharing her stash of booze.

Someone once said be careful what you wish for. Just then Mikala's phone rang.

CHAPTER 11

Mikala answered, then held the phone out to me. "Granny wants to talk to you."

A stab of fear zapped me. Granny wouldn't have made Jess look up Mikala's number and contact me in the middle of an investigation unless it was an emergency.

And it was.

"Now, Alice, don't get your panties in a twist...too much," Granny said. "I'm sure they's all right. Didn't look like they was headed off against their will, nothin' like that."

"What are you talking about, Granny?" I half-screamed. "Is something wrong with one of my animals? Trucker? Miss Molly?"

"Well, sorta both. And that there pig—"

"Both!" It was a full-blown scream that time. "Both my animals are hurt? Granny, where are they?"

"Like I says," she said, "I don't think neither one's hurt. They was following like they was having fun."

"Following who?" I yelled, then noticed Twila had her head beside mine and lifted the receiver away from my ear an inch so she could also hear.

"Not a who," Granny said. "Or I don't think it's a who. I sort of thought it might be a what, but—"

"Granny!"

Twila took the phone. When I tried to grab it back, she plastered it to her ear and turned aside. "What's going on?" she demanded.

Then I heard a couple "uh huh's" and an "all right" before she handed the phone to Mikala and took my arm.

"Sorry, Mikala," she said as she pulled me out of the kitchen. "We need to go. I'll call you later."

In the car, I immediately started demanding an explanation, despite the fact Twila floored the gas and tore out of the driveway, her little red car flinging gravel and digging ruts behind. She's normally one of the slower drivers on the road, and I wasn't exactly sure how capable a speedster she was. However, I kept urging her both to go faster and tell me what the hell had happened.

Finally, after she turned onto the highway and brought the car out of its skid, she said, "It sounds like your Grassman paid us a visit."

"Grassman? My Grassman? What do you mean?"

She flew past a slower vehicle on the two-lane road, ducking back into her lane a safe distance from the oncoming pickup. But the other driver still blared his horn. I quickly glanced at the truck as it went past, in a corner of my mind realizing it looked like Jack's. There were more important things to think about just then, though.

I opened my mouth to demand more information, but had to grab the dash when Twila rounded a curve and slammed on her brakes again. In front of us, the Amish buggy horse plodded along as though it had the right to be blocking the road. Which it did, of course, but now wasn't the time.

I could see the semi headed toward us in the oncoming lane, and I whispered a prayer instead of a demand. Twila jerked the wheel to pass —thank goodness on the right. The car wobbled in the gravel, and she somehow maintained control and brought it back onto the pavement in front of the horse. When I glanced in the side view mirror, I saw the Amish man shake his fist at us as he fought the rearing horse.

"Sorry," Twila murmured in an insincere tone.

"What about Trucker and Miss Molly?" I asked, the fear for my pets a trembling pit in my stomach. "And Granny said something about Harley."

"She said the Grassman led them off into the woods."

The next thing Twila veered around was a tractor pulling a disk down the road. At least the farmer had sense enough to keep as much of his vehicle over on the side as he could. Still, I wouldn't have wanted my hand in the space between Twila's car and the disk blades. The red wouldn't be paint flecks; it would be my blood.

It wasn't that far from Mikala's to her house, but it seemed forever.

"What—?" I began again, but she cut off my question.

"I don't know any more, Alice. Just that Granny said the Grassman led the animals off. Please. Let me concentrate on my driving."

I shut up, except for a gasp when she slammed on the brakes and skidded into her driveway. By then, I was even more frozen with terror, imagining all sorts of dire danger to my animals.

Twila bypassed the garage and pulled to a stop beside the back door. Granny waited in the yard, one of Jess's nasty-looking double barreled shotguns in her hands.

"Omigod," I breathed. My shaky hand could barely tighten enough on the door handle to release me from the car. At last, I got the door open and nearly tumbled back into the car when my legs gave out. But Twila was already over by Granny, and I needed to see what they were saying.

I didn't even realize I was still wearing Mikala's too tight bathrobe until I rushed across the grass to where they stood. The wind whipped the robe apart, and I retied the belt. Granny immediately handed Twila the shotgun and took my arms.

"Now, lookee here, child," she said. "Like I told you, it didn't look like them animals was in any danger. They was following that thing like he was that there Pied Piper. Easy goin' and happy like."

"Do you know what the Pied Piper did, Granny?" I asked.

"Guess not really. Jist what I see on TV."

I had enough sense left amidst all my worry to see that Granny was trying to soothe my fears, despite the fact her own eyes were filled with tears. No sense telling her the piper was leading those children off to who knows where.

If that thing has hurt those animals, I'll see it in hell. I slid a glance at the shotgun in Twila's hands.

"Let's just say the Piper didn't have anything good in mind, even though he was acting very merry," I told Granny. "Which way did they go?"

"Into them woods behind where y'all found...Patches."

I pulled away from her. "I'm getting dressed. Then I'm going after my animals."

Just then Jack's pickup barreled into the yard and braked beside us. It had been him on the road. He'd evidently recognized Twila's car and that she was driving hell-bent-for-leather, and followed us.

He surged out the driver's door and around to where I stood. "What's wrong, *Chère?*"

My attempt at bravery crumbled. I kept back the moan of fear but flung myself into his arms. "The Grassman's got Trucker and Miss Molly. And Harley."

He held me tight in one arm, but pushed my face back to stare down at me. "The what?" He glanced at Twila. "I thought you didn't believe in that thing."

"I don't...didn't," she answered. "But Granny saw it happen. And it appears to be the same thing that brought Patches' body here. That Hoof and Alice went off tracking last night."

Was it only last night? I pushed out of Jack's arms. "I'm going to get dressed. I'll be right back."

It suddenly seemed to dawn on Jack that I was wearing a robe. He looked me up and down, and refused to relinquish his hold as he said, "Weren't you dressed when you left here?"

"It's a long story, Jack." I forced myself to slide free. "Twila will tell you."

* * *

The woods are deadly, dark and deep, I paraphrased. *But I give you my promise I'll find you before I sleep,* I told my two pets, hoping maybe it was true that animals sometimes had psychic abilities.

I carried one of Jess's shotguns loaded with double ought buck and a slug, which might prove a decent weapon against a monster the size of the Grassman. Twila had given it to me when she chose another shotgun for herself. Jess had an entire cabinet full of guns: rifles, pistols and shotguns. If I hadn't thought it would slow me down, I'd have carried a second gun with me. I wasn't about to mess with this thing that had kidnapped my pets.

Oh, god, I hope it was only a kidnapping. I didn't dare let myself think about what else could happen. Though I'd read a lot about the Grassman, I didn't know whether he was a vegetarian or....

As if sensing my thoughts, Jack slipped an arm around my waist. "Easy, *Chère*. We'll find them."

"Please let it be in one piece," I couldn't keep from saying.

"Don't even think stuff like that," Granny said from behind Jack.

Twila had spent very little time trying to reason Granny into staying at the farmhouse. I hadn't bothered. I knew Granny would come along with us, if that's what she'd set her mind on. If she grew too tired, she wouldn't hold us back, and I hated the thought of leaving her behind in the woods. However, when Twila had found out she'd forgotten about Jess's doctor appointment that day, and he'd already called a friend for a ride and left, nothing would make Twila wait at home, either. I knew she would remain with Granny if necessary.

Jack had opted to only bring his handgun, and he'd strapped the holster and belt outside his shirt for easy access. Granny might have been comical, had it not been for the seriousness of our quest. She held her walking stick in one hand, and the weapon she chose bobbed on her back in its harness. I'd been surprised how light that AR-17 was when I'd inattentively handed it to Granny upon her request. But Twila explained that Jess had modified it himself, with a new lightweight stock.

The four of us weren't the best trackers in the world, but I'd done a little research for my writing. Though it was slow going, I was able to find traces of either dog paw prints or little pig hooves in the dirt. Faint traces, but enough at each fork in the trail to figure out which way the parade of smaller animals had gone. The side of the trail was matted down in spots, as though the Grassman were walking in leaves and underbrush to conceal its tracks.

I didn't see any cat tracks, and finally I got up the nerve to ask Granny, "You're sure Miss Molly was with them?"

"I'm sure," she said softly. "That there thing was carryin' her."

I groaned, and Jack tightened his hold on my waist in comfort. However, a few steps down the trail, we hit another Y. Left led deeper into the woods. A couple times earlier, we'd heard traffic noise to our right, so I assumed there was a road there.

I slipped out of Jack's hold and, propping the shotgun butt down in the dirt, squatted to examine the trail. "This doesn't look right," I said.

Jack knelt beside me. "What?"

I pointed. "See? There's a dog track that looks like it's headed towards the road. Why would he go that way? And...." I gasped and quickly stood to walk over to what I'd seen. "That looks like it might have been made by the Grassman. Like the ones Hoof and I saw last night."

Jack gazed at the track. The width would have held Jack's and my feet side-by-side, all four of them, with room to spare. There were definitely toes on the front, toes several inches long.

"Oh, man," Twila said. "He's huge."

"Alice is right, though," Jack mused. "Why is he heading toward the road instead of further into the woods?"

"Y'all waits right here." Granny toddled down the left fork.

I watched her closely, since no matter how many times she insisted she didn't need a caretaker, she was in her eighties. She seemed to use the walking stick casually, rather than as an aid, proving she wasn't tiring yet. I loved her as much as my animals, and it would hurt terribly if she got injured helping me. I shook my head and blinked at the AR-17 dangling from her slight figure. No way would I protest the weapon being too big for her. She might use it to enforce her choice.

Several yards down the trail, Granny held onto the walking stick and bent to examine something. Then she turned and waved for us to join her.

"I figured it out," she said with a decisive nod when we grouped around her. "Lookee here."

She pointed down at the trail, and I saw another Grassman print. This one emerged from the underbrush on the side of the trail. Then Granny moved her hand to indicate another track further down the trail —a lot further.

"See's?" Granny said, now pointing at the underbrush. "My husband used to read them there westerns a lot. When I didn't have nothin' else myself, I'd pick up one of his. Read once 'bout how them Indians would trick folks. Called it layin' a false trail."

"I see," Jack agreed. "We've been paying attention to the main trail. It planted that track to the right, then slipped into the wood and circled around. Came back in here, on the other fork."

"What about my animals, though?" I asked as I scanned the trail. "I don't see their tracks anywhere."

"He's probably carrying them," Twila put in, and we all nodded in concurrence.

"Trucker weighs a little over a hundred-fifty pounds," I said, and Jack took my hand and gently squeezed it.

Granny's the one who mentioned the elephant in the room...or on the trail. "That thing we been trailing's big 'nuf to carry Trucker without breathin' hard."

I muffled a groan of fear, then caught Twila's gaze. One of our unspoken communications flew between us, and I stiffened my back. The two of us had faced a lot of negative stuff over the years. A damn Grassman monster wasn't going to defeat us.

Without another word, I headed down the trail at the front of my posse.

We walked for another hour or so, never once losing the trail. Either the Grassman wasn't that smart, or he did indeed think he'd covered his tracks. Within a few hundred yards, the dog and pig tracks intermingled with the Grassman's huge prints, confirming our assumption that he had carried the animals for a while.

Twice we stopped to rest. Once when I noticed Granny using the walking stick steadily, and once when even I had to admit I'd started to tire. We'd had no idea how long we would be tracking that thing, but Twila had reminded us to grab bottles of water from the case on her back porch. The one other thing we women began to need hadn't crossed our minds as we gurgled the water freely.

"Don't s'pose none of y'all brought any tissues?" Granny inquired.

"Why?" poor Jack asked.

Granny eyed him mischievously. "Well, Mr. Man. You can hang it out wherever you want and shake it dry. But even when we women drip-dry, we ain't got it all off."

Jack blushed furiously, and our laughter, though faint, broke a little of the fear and tension.

"Actually," Twila said as she pulled out a handful of white from her jacket pocket, "I grabbed one of Jess's jackets to wear. And he always stuffs paper towels in them to take into the woods when he's hunting."

She tore off two of the towels and handed them to Granny. When she glanced inquiringly at me, I nodded and accept two more.

"Your skeeters out yet?" Granny asked Twila.

"I've seen a few," Twila told her. "Why?"

Granny hardly ever wore blue jeans or trousers. She had a huge assortment of pretty house dresses, some checkered and others with flowers. The dress hems varied, also, anywhere from ankle to below-knee length.

Now she plucked at the skirt of the dress with paisley-pink roses and an ankle length hem to help protect her legs from scratches. "This here's one of my newer dresses," she said. "And I sure don't like the idea of it gettin' torn up in the briars on the side of this here trail when I go off for some privacy. But I'll do that, 'cause I have to. Worst is, I don't like thinkin' I might be scratching my backside all night 'cause of skeeter bites. Ones I got when I hadda hike it up to bare my bottom. I need's my sleep at my age."

Jack exploded in uncontrollable coughs, which none of us mistook for anything but what it was: boisterous laughter he was trying to suppress. Twila and I both giggled, and I clapped my hands over my mouth to try to control myself. We both stared at Jack, who waved his hand at us and hurried on down the trail, around the next bend and out of sight.

We could still hear his chuckles, and Granny shrugged and said, "Now I won't hafta go off in the woods."

As she relieved herself on the side of the trail, I unsnapped my jeans and did the same on the other side. Twila started to put the towels back in her pocket, then evidently changed her mind and joined us.

A few moments later, the three of us started down the trail toward where Jack had disappeared.

Twila asked Granny, "Any skeeters bite you?"

"Nope," she replied. "Thankee for askin'."

"I've got some stuff for bites in our first aid kit," I said. "Some new stuff on the—"

The smell hit us first. Twila and I raised our shotguns as we rushed forward rather than retreat. I glanced over my shoulder and saw Granny halt long enough to pull her AK-17 around to grip it in her gnarled hands before she followed us. She caught up to where Twila and I stood just around the bend, waving our guns back and forth.

There was no sign of Jack. Only his Beretta lay amidst a scuffle of footprints: boot prints from Jack and two large Grassman tracks.

I drew in a breath to scream his name, then thought better of it. That thing might be close, watching us.

Beside me, Twila growled, "That son of a bitch. We're gonna find him, and when we do, he's gonna wish he's never heard of the Three Female Musketeers!"

As one, we turned and looked at each other. Guns in one hand, we held out our free hands and placed them over each other's. Twila went first, then Granny, then mine on top.

"Hooyah!" Granny said in an imitation of the Marine's call to battle.

Then we dropped hands and marched forward.

* * *

"Are you sure this is necessary?" Free Eagle asked Patches as he stared at the two-story, red-brick building across the parking lot.

"Told you that you don't have to go with me."

"Our way was better," Free Eagle said. "We let our bodies replenish the earth."

"Well, I didn't make any plans for mine. Figured I'd have some time yet."

"Would it not be better for us to spend our time trying to uncover who killed you?"

"Probably," Patches said. "But part of the reason I didn't go into that light was because I hadn't made funeral plans."

Free Eagle glanced down at Patches' legs. "Your legs are both here now, in this spirit body."

"Yeah, but I didn't know that at first," Patches said. "It's just...I can't explain it. Never was good at putting my feeling's into words. I just want to go see if I can find out what they did with my body."

"I shall go with you," Free Eagle said. "But why here?"

"Since I was murdered, the law might have made them do one of them autopsies, like on TV. And they've gotta have a morgue here. Somewhere private, where they can keep bodies till the undertaker picks them up. Can't have them folks who haul the dead around just roll a stretcher into a patient's room. Tote someone off and ride them down the elevator along with the visitors."

"Do you even know your way around in that hospital building?"

"Nope," Patches admitted. "I ain't been in there since they cut my leg off. You can bet there's a morgue there, though. They probably have a toe tag on me, saying which funeral home's gonna come for me. I want to know where I'm being sent."

He walked across the parking lot to a hospital entrance. The sign overhead said *Emergency*, and there were two of those large square trucks sitting outside, which Free Eagle had learned over the years carried wounded or dying people. The vehicles roared down roadways, a piercing scream sounding to clear other traffic out of the way.

Free Eagle had seen a lot in the hundreds of years he roamed. Of course, it didn't seem like that long. Time didn't mean nearly as much in his state as it had when he lived. At times it did grow boring, and he'd taught himself not only the English language but also how to read it. When someone invented that television, he enjoyed it for a while, except for those stupid cowboy and Indian shows. If he tried to change the channel, the people would just change it back. Movies were better on those big screens. Unseen, he could choose which show to sneak into and watch.

Inside the hospital, there were words on the walls, painted inside arrows indicating direction. No one paid any attention to him and Patches. They were both invisible. Free Eagle could have materialized, had he been in the mood for playing a joke. However, there were two man and wife couples there, carrying sick children. It might have been fun to scare the adults, but he had no wish to frighten a child.

"I don't see any sign that says *Morgue* on it," Patches mused. "I doubt they'd advertise that, though. Let's go through here and see what we can find."

They walked on down the hallway, passing both open and closed curtains on the right. They heard moans and groans of pain, and once a whimper that sounded like it came from another child. A woman dressed in a loose, pale-blue top stuck her head out from behind that particular curtain just as another woman rushed through the door at the end of the hall. Frantic, the second woman called, "Bobby? Where's Bobby?"

"Here," the nurse called. "This way."

Patches and Free Eagle paused to watch the woman race to the curtain and waited until they heard a little boy's voice cry, "Mommy," before they walked onward.

The hallway dead-ended against a wall. They studied the arrows again, but neither set showed them the way to the morgue.

"You know," Free Eagle mused, "when I watch those television shows sometimes, the room where they keep the dead bodies always seems to be in the basement."

Patches snapped his fingers, although they didn't make a sound.

"You're right. Let's see if we can find a down elevator."

"Why do we need an elevator?" Free Eagle asked.

Patches stared at him. "Right again. Well, I guess you are. If we can walk through doors and walls, I guess we can float through floors. I ain't tried that yet."

Free Eagle dissolved his ghost body and slipped downward. He found himself in a room full of overhead pipes with a concrete floor, no Patches beside him. He sighed and ascended.

"I saw you go," Patches told him when he re-joined the other ghost. "But when I tried, I just stood here."

"It is not the morgue under this floor anyway," Free Eagle said. "We can go on, if you want."

"Yeah, we probably need to find an elevator until you get time to show me how to do what you just did," Patches said as they chose the left hallway to explore.

At the end of that hall, they found the elevator they were looking for. A young man was already there, a gurney beside him. He pushed a button beside the silver doors, and when the bell sounded and the doors opened, he shoved the gurney onto the elevator.

"Sheet's covering the body on that stretcher," Patches said. "Probably someone dead he's taking to the morgue."

Patches and Free Eagle hurried forward, both making it onto the elevator before the doors closed behind them. Although Free Eagle continued to maintain invisibility, the man beside the stretcher shivered as though the temperature had dropped. He quickly glanced down at the body, then moved as far as possible away.

Seconds later, the doors opened again, and the young man hurriedly shoved the stretcher out. Patches and Free Eagle followed, and this time, Free Eagle saw an arrow pointing to the right, the word *MORGUE* inscribed on it.

Sure enough, the man pushed his stretcher that way.

Inside the morgue, the man left the body in the middle of the room and sat down at a desk. As he began filling out some sort of paperwork, Free Eagle stared around the room.

"It seems strange there are no other bodies here," he mused.

Patches pointed to one of the walls, where it appeared there might be a safe. At least, there was one of those circular handles like he had seen on bank vaults in those western movies.

"This hospital ain't been updated in years," Patches said. "So doesn't surprise me they just have a big cooler to keep folks in. Other places, they have slide-out drawers. Still, it'll be easier to check just one room, instead of having to stick our heads into a bunch of drawers."

Free Eagle nodded. After a glance at the attendant to see him still bent over the paperwork, he walked over and through the door with the circular handle. Inside, he saw two more stretchers, the shapes beneath the white sheets indicating they both contained bodies. He sighed and lifted the sheet from an elderly man's face. Definitely not Patches.

When he turned toward the other body, he saw Patches already there, shaking his head as he dropped the sheet back in place. "Ain't me," he said.

"So where else would you be?" Free Eagle asked.

"Have to be a funeral home. There's only two in town, so we won't have a lot of space to cover."

Back outside the door, they saw the attendant close a manila file, then stand up from the desk. He walked over to the door and spun the handle. But when he jerked on it to open the door, nothing happened.

"Shoot, it's stuck," he muttered. He spun the wheel again and pulled —a little too hard. The door flew open and smacked him in the face, the force also knocking him to the floor. He slid backward on the slick tile surface and hit the cart.

Which rolled across the floor and hit the desk at the perfect angle to release the lever on the side of the cart that collapsed it.

It collapsed. The body rolled onto the desk, then started to slide off.

Instinctively, Free Eagle followed Patches when he rushed for the desk. They each grabbed a side of the body and kept it from tumbling head first onto the floor. Instead, they respectfully lowered it back onto the stretcher. Free Eagle, with his developed abilities, even reached under the cart and pulled it back up.

"We forgot to check this one," Patches said as he pulled the sheet back from the body's face. Beneath it lay an elderly woman, her wrinkled face peaceful. "Not me," Patches said, turning away without placing the sheet back over her.

Remembering the attendant, Free Eagle glanced over at the man. He sat there on the floor, his face as white as the sheet over the body. He stared at the now exposed face of the woman, then planted his feet on the floor and pushed himself up the wall. Never once taking his eyes from the stretcher, he edged down the wall, toward the door to the room.

When he reached it, he let out a scream that would have risen every dead body in the room, had they been capable of rising. Then he barreled out the door, still screeching.

"Huh," Patches said. "Bet he'd have hollered louder if he could have seen who saved the body from falling and moved the sheet."

"Perhaps he did," Free Eagle said with a sigh. "At least one of us. The effort of helping with the body and pulling the stretcher back up made me lax in keeping myself invisible."

Free Eagle had never seen any reason to take on a different form. He liked the way he appeared when he wore his paint and feathers.

Patches ran his gaze up and down Free Eagle's body. "If I had time, I'd feel sorry for the fellow. You're enough to scare the crap out of anyone."

"We painted ourselves for our own satisfaction, but also to frighten our enemy."

"You probably did that pretty good. But now we best go check out the funeral homes."

Free Eagle frowned. "Tell me. I know the people of your time usually have someone in their family make the arrangements for their burial. Who would be doing yours?"

Patches' face creased in sorrow. "I really ain't got no one other than those couple distant cousins you saw on the river. 'Cept my buddy Jess, who won't have nothing to do with me now. Well, there's my niece, Janie, who fell for one of them Amish fellows a year or so ago. They got married, and she joined their life, so we ain't stayed in touch as much as we used to. But the sheriff knows about Janie, so he might have gotten hold of her."

The door burst open again, and two men in security uniforms came through, followed reluctantly by the attendant. Pistols in hand, the guards aimed around the room.

"There's no one here," one guard said.

"That's what I said," the attendant replied. "So how'd all the crap I told you about happen?"

Free Eagle motioned for Patches to follow him and they walked through the wall into the hallway.

CHAPTER 12

"O.K., now what?" Twila asked as we stood at the foot of a rock-covered hillside.

We hadn't seen a hint of Jack's boot prints. The animal footprints had ended a few dozen yards back, and the Grassman tracks had continued to the base of the hill. Now there was only one way to go—up.

If Jack had been with us, he could have climbed the hill, albeit with an effort. I doubted any of the Three Female Musketeers could accomplish that feat. It sloped upwards at a nearly vertical angle, and sharp boulder edges poked through the weeds and underbrush.

"That thing's strong enough to carry a full-grown man, a dog, cat and pig up that hill," Granny mused. "I wish we'd've asked Jess if he had one of them scuddie missiles hid somewhere. We might need it."

I couldn't even muster up a chuckle, although I knew Granny was as serious as a heartbeat.

"We'll just have to walk along the hill until we find an easier path up," Twila said. She shouldered her shotgun, which, like mine, had probably seemed to gain at least ten pounds as we steadfastly marched down the trail. "You and Granny go one way, I'll go another."

"No way in hell," I told her. "We are *not* splitting up."

"But there might be a path closer one way than the other. We'll lose time," she protested.

"I don't care," I retorted. There were occasions when I did exert myself over her I'm-older-than-you bossiness. Infrequent, but they did occur. This was once I wasn't backing down. "If you try to take off alone, Granny and I will follow you."

"Then which way will we go first?" she gave in.

Granny reached in her dress pocket and pulled out a coin. "We'll flip this here nickel. Heads, we go left. Tails, right."

"Works for me," I said with a nod.

Granny did her best to hold the coin in her gnarled fingers, but it wobbled back and forth. Just as I started to reach for it to help out, she thrust her thumb upwards and the nickel flew into the air. We watched it sail up, then down...and hit the side of one of those blasted rocks. It ricocheted and landed hidden behind another one rock.

"Poop," Granny said. "Someone look back there and see how it landed. And don't cheat and turn it over."

I peered behind the rock. The ground was in shadow, and I leaned forward, bracing myself on a large boulder as I tried to see which face was upright.

The boulder gave way with a groan, and I barely caught myself before I ended up bashing my nose. I scrambled back and stood beside Granny and Twila, all our mouths gaping in astonishment.

The hillside to the right of the boulder opened up as though someone had installed a huge garage door. What we had taken as rocks, weeds and underbrush turned out to be a very realistic landscape painting. It slid back on a pair of overhead tracks, exposing a hole at least ten feet wide and twelve feet tall.

It was dark inside that hill. Extremely dark. As Granny would have said, had she not been as dumbstruck as Twila and I, it was as dark as a well digger's ass. There was no way to see what might be waiting on us in there, or how far we would have to go before we found out what the hill was hiding.

Once again, though, Granny had no qualms about speaking the obvious. "We found that thing's hidey hole."

"I think so," I agreed.

"Who's going first?" Twila whispered.

"Anyone bring a flashlight?" Granny asked.

I drew in a breath and said, "My animals and husband are in there. I'm going in."

I marched forward, the two of them right behind me. It dawned on me that neither Twila nor Granny had corrected my mistake about Jack. He was my ex right now, but the longer that monster had him in its clutches, the more I realized how much I loved the man.

A few feet inside, I was forced to halt and hope my eyes would adjust at least somewhat to the stygian blackness. Within a few seconds, I was able to make out a slight variation in the distance. The black appeared to have a tiny sliver of deep, dark gray in it. The cave must open up back there, perhaps to a larger cavern with lighter colored rock. Or perhaps to something else. The only way to find out was to walk on.

"I think we need to keep going," I said softly. "But I don't know how quiet we can be, if we can't see."

Behind us, the garage-door mural thudded to earth.

We muffled screams, mine drawn from a burst of fear that almost split my chest open.

The blast from Granny's AR-17 lit up the area, but only for a split-second. She had aimed at the door and pulled the trigger, and the recoil threw her small body into Twila. Both of them fell to the floor.

The fall evidently triggered a reflex action in Granny's finger, because another blast of firepower lit up the cave, these bullets ricocheting from the ceiling.

I dove for the AR-17 and managed to jerk it out of Granny's grasp before any of us died. After that, I didn't hear a word from either of my two companions.

"Twila? Granny?" I whispered into the pitch blackness.

When neither of them answered, I somehow found the courage to tentatively reach out and feel around the area where they had fallen.

"Twila? Granny?"

My fingers encountered something hard and slick, and I jerked my hand back. At first, I thought I might have touched a boot toe. All three of us were wearing tennis shoes, but Jack wore boots. I gasped in horror as the thought went through my mind that maybe he was lying there. I wouldn't let myself think about whether he was hurt or maybe....

I forced myself to reach out again and touch whatever it was. This time, I felt around a little more.

"What the hell?" I muttered as my fingers outlined what had to be a huge toe. Not a boot toe, a human toe!

Then the odor hit me. The gunpowder dregs filling the cave had probably overpowered it at first.

The Grassman was standing there in front of me!

Instead of running, I grabbed that AR-17 again and rose to my feet. I jammed it toward where I thought that monster stood, and the barrel pushed into something soft. Hopefully, it was the Grassman's belly, but given his height, it might have been his upper leg...or a little higher.

I screamed, "Where are my friends and animals? You either take me to them this minute, or I'm going to fill you so full of lead, you won't be able to walk!"

So much for foolish bravery. Something flicked the AR-17 out of my hands, and the next thing I knew, I dangled so far off the ground, my feet waved through empty air.

"Let me go!" I yelled as I reached around my waist to pull at the hairy hand on my belt. "You son of a bitch! Let me go!"

My threats didn't even faze the monster. It carried me off, deeper into the hill. I continued to fight and yell, squirming and gagging in the odor as I gasped for breath in anger and fear. It was probably a good thing we'd peed on the trail. Otherwise, I might have added my own smell to that terrible odor.

Maybe it grew tired of my curses, because it shifted its hold, and I found my nose sunk in a pile of matted, stinking fur. Right before I threw up, I realized it was lighter around me. The beast gently set me down on a large log. My hair hung in my face, and I batted it back to stare around, just as Trucker placed his forelegs beside me and whined.

"Trucker! Oh, Trucker!" I grabbed him and buried my face on his neck. Something squirmed beneath my arm, and I loosened my hold enough for Miss Molly to crawl into the hug. She licked her scratchy tongue across my check, and I realized I was crying.

"Oh, you wonderful animals," I said. "I was so afraid...." Then I frowned and looked around again.

Across from me, Granny, Twila and Jack sat together. Other than a nod of three heads to acknowledge they saw me, not one of them spoke or made a move. A huge *thing* at least eight feet tall stood just in front of them. This one was female. How did I know? The breasts poking out from the dark green matted fur told me. She had a few vines trailing from her head like hair, and...I gasped in surprise. She wore a braid of flowers across her forehead.

If you overlooked the hair-covered features, she didn't appear that mean. Her brown eyes were soft and soulful, as though she were sorry about something. Or perhaps grieving.

We were in a tiny clearing, surrounded by huge trees. I could hear water trickling somewhere, but I didn't see any sign of a creek. The underbrush was thick in places; in other areas, where the trees were farther apart, a person might be able to carefully walk.

I desperately wanted to rush over and be with the others. However, the smell beside me reminded me I wasn't alone, either. Dredging up courage, I stared to my left, where the odor emanated. This one was even taller than the one with breasts, probably nine feet. Obviously, the lore written on Grassmen underestimated their heights, probably because no one had ever gotten close enough for a true look.

I couldn't stop myself from staring between its legs, trying to determine if it was a male, since I didn't see any sign of breasts. Thankfully, at least for my sense of embarrassment, the fur there curled and clotted thick enough to hide any genitals. Straggles of vines also intermingled with the dark fur on him, too, trailing down here and there.

On up, his chest was muscular and broad, as wide as the shoulders above it. Arms as huge as the tree-trunk legs fell past its waist, ending in four-fingered hands, a thumb on each, like my hands, only several times larger. The neck fit the rest of his body, thick and sturdy, holding up a head that left no doubt as to the gender.

Where the female appeared more docile, this one's eyes stared down at me with all the haughty intenseness of an alpha wolf. No one would mistake him for a gorilla; his face was far too human-like. Even his nose was slender, with a slight hook as though it had been broken, set above a mouth just visible behind the green hair. The incongruous thought hit me that it looked like he maybe shaved that hair off to be able to eat more easily.

His forehead was high and intelligent, far different than drawings I'd seen of early man. Now I realized the eyes were a shade lighter than the female's, more of a dark hazel. He continued to stare down at me wordlessly.

I decided to at least take a chance on speaking to the others. "Can...?" I cleared my throat so one of them could hopefully hear me. "Can they talk?"

"I don't know." It was Twila who answered. "They haven't said anything yet, just made what we should do clear with motions."

On the side of the clearing, brush rustled. Trucker immediately abandoned me to rush over and greet the little Grassman who skipped out of the woods, Harley grunting and following along behind. Miss Molly also jumped off my lap, prancing over to the toddler, tail held high.

The small Grassbaby squatted to play with Trucker. As I watched in astonishment, both my pets and the pig began a game of tag. Trucker nosed Baby Grassman and raced away. Baby Grassman lunged toward Miss Molly to tag her, but she meowed and jumped too far back for him to reach. Closer, Harley wasn't so lucky. Baby Grassman whirled and touched him, then took off after Trucker.

The underbrush didn't even rustle next. One, two, then three more Grassmen emerged from the woods around us. They were all nearly as large as the one who stood beside me. Still stood there, I confirmed as I looked up.

The Grassman wasn't gazing down at me. Instead, he smiled as the little one played with the animals. Had I not known better, I wouldn't have been afraid of this vision of fatherly love.

When I examined the new beasts, they appeared to also be male. They ignored all of us and walked majestically over to join the one beside me.

What followed was a full blown conversation, although I couldn't understand a word of it. I'd never been that interested in other languages, so I had no idea whether it might be their own personal lingo or related to one of the dialects in use elsewhere in the world. Since they seemed totally involved, I eased up from the log, preparing to join the others.

A hairy hand landed on my head. Not hard, but the pressure left no doubt I was to remain where I was. I obeyed.

They hadn't protested my earlier question, so I called, "Are you all right, Jack?"

"Hush, *Chère*," he said, which totally ticked me off.

"I was only concerned—"

"Shut up," he said this time.

I crossed my arms over my chest and glared at him. Then I realized he was staring at the beasts beside me as though paying attention to what they were saying. I slid my gaze away from Jack, to Twila and Granny. Both of them shrugged, indicating they had no idea what interested Jack.

We found out when the conversation beside me subsided. Immediately, Jack stood and said something in what sounded similar to the language the beasts used. The more melodious tone of Jack's voice identified his dialogue: Cajun French. I'd heard him speak it once in a while, mostly in the night when we were alone, although I'd never bothered to learn any of it. The sound of the beasts' voices was a lot more guttural, though.

All four of the Grassmen beside me stared at Jack. He said something else, and the one who had carried me strode across the small clearing to squat in front of Jack. In voices too low for me to understand—not that I could have anyway—the two of them continued their conversation for a short while.

Jack finally said to me, "You can come on over here, *Chère*. They won't bother you."

I eased up off the log, carefully eyeing the other three Grassmen beside me. The one with Jack said something, and I took a few steps. When none of them tried to stop me, I ran. To Jack, of course. I knew I should check on Granny and Twila, but Jack held out his arms.

"Are you all right?" he asked.

"Are you?" I replied, running a hand down his cheek.

"All three of us are O.K.," he said with a nod at Twila and Granny. "These things don't seem to want to hurt us. I think somehow they connect us to the animals the little one is so wrapped up in."

I frowned. "They can't have my animals."

"Let's just see where this goes, *Chère*. At least we can communicate with them now."

"They speak Cajun French?" Keeping a firm hold on Jack's waist, I twisted in his arms to stare at the Grassman beside us.

"It's not really the exact Cajun language," he said. "But it's close enough that we can understand each other. They want us to go with them to their camp."

I gulped, and Twila and Granny joined us. Jack pulled Granny close with one arm, and Twila squeezed in beside me. Jack reached across my shoulders to enclose her in our little group.

"Do you think it's safe?" Twila whispered to Jack.

He shrugged. "Don't think we have much choice. This one did say they weren't gonna hurt us. We'll just have to take his word. He's got my pistol, and I don't see any of y'all with weapons."

The Grassman said something, and Jack replied. To us, Jack said, "He wants to know our names. It would be a good idea if each of us said our own, to show him we're willing to get along with them."

I lifted my gaze up to the one beside us, way up, and met his eyes staring down at me. I gulped again, touched a hand to my chest, and said, "A-alice. I'm Alice."

"Twila," Twila said beside me, imitating my gesture of hand on chest.
"Jack," Jack said with a nod.

Granny didn't hesitate. She pulled free of Jack's hold and marched right over to the Grassman. She only came up to his muscular thigh, and holding her elderly hand out to shake with him, she said, "Granny. And who you be?"

I swear the mouth beneath that green fur tilted up as the Grassman gazed down at Granny. He tenderly took her hand and said, "Bob."

Jack's laughter rumbled in his chest, and despite my lingering fear, I had to bite back a giggle myself. Who would have guessed this thing would have such a everyday name? Further introductions, though, confirmed that they were all called common names as Bob turned to point at each of his companions.

The female he told us was Kate, and the other three were each Tom, John, and George. We all followed his gaze when he looked around the clearing for the little one. When we saw him, I realized why it had gotten so quiet. He was curled up on the ground beside Trucker, Miss Molly and Harley, worn out from his game of tag.

"Rascal," Bob Grassman told us.

Granny repeated all the names, ending with, "Rascal, huh? He's a cutie pie."

Well, I wouldn't have gone that far, but Granny glanced at Jack and said, "Can you tell him that for me?"

Jack nodded and repeated a few words. This time, Kate walked over and squatted down by Granny. She said something, and Jack told us, "She said, 'Thank you for saying that about my little boy.'"

Granny reached out and patted Kate on the shoulder. "You be welcome."

It didn't appear Jack had to translate that, since Kate carefully stroked a finger over Granny's gray hair.

Then Kate walked over and picked up Rascal. She led the way, and the rest of us fell in behind her. I could tell Bob was still on guard, however, because he took up the rear position, behind everyone else.

CHAPTER 13

The faint trail was wide enough for us but underbrush and limbs brushed the Grassmen as they passed. We didn't walk very far. I'd been wondering where the other females were, since I didn't think that one could be a "wife" to the other four, if this hidden culture even had wives. We found our answer when we emerged into another clearing and saw three additional women and two more little ones.

One of the women had an arm in a sling and a bandage on her shoulder. And...one of the little ones was pure white, an albino. When the toddlers halted their play and the white one glanced at us, I could see the pinkish eyes.

Wonder if this one is related to the white Yeti's some areas report seeing? I mused to myself. But not knowing if my writer's curiosity would seem rude, I didn't ask.

It appeared they all ate from a communal pot, since a large black kettle hung on a tripod over a surprisingly smokeless fire. The aroma from the kettle smelled delicious, and I remembered that Twila and I had never gotten lunch at that wonderful Amish restaurant we loved.

"I wonder where they sleep," I said.

"Betcha I know," Granny said. She walked over to what I had taken for a large tree and drew back a curtain colored to match the bark. This exposed a huge hole, with a room in it. What I had taken for a tree was a cleverly disguised concealment for sleeping space.

Granny peeked in, then turned around with her finger to her lips. "Shhhhh. They's three more little 'uns asleep in there." She gently dropped the camouflage drape in place and rejoined us. "Prob'ly them big 'uns sleep outside to protect them chillun."

I nodded. "And I would be willing to bet that when someone does sight a Grassman, he's showing himself to lead them away from where his family is. Then they probably move the camp, like the Native American's used to do."

Bob Grassman said something to Jack, and he replied, perhaps telling Bob what we had said. Bob spoke again, and Jack explained, "He says you two are very smart. That's how they live."

"Those pictures are so realistic, though," Twila mused.

Without waiting for the translation, Bob again spoke to Jack and received a reply. Jack explained, "Bob says that there is always one member of each generation that has this painting talent. He doesn't know who looks over them and makes sure it happens, but someone does."

"Like our God," Granny said with a nod as I looked over at the little albino Grassman. He seemed too tiny to do such realistic painting, and I didn't see any colored specks on his fur.

A muted clanging noise interrupted our curious questions and Bob's answers. One of the females tapped a spoon on the side of the kettle. The young ones ran obediently over to sit on the ground and eagerly reach for bowls of soup. My animals, and Harley, too, were given bowls. Harley and Trucker made short work of theirs, but Miss Molly dipped her tongue in, drew back, then went for another lick. It was like she couldn't decide if she enjoyed this new taste or not.

A few moments later, we, also, had full carved bowls, along with wooden spoons. I was halfway through mine before I realized there was no meat in it.

"They're vegetarians," I said to Twila, sitting beside me on a log.

"Works for me," she said. "This is yummy."

Noticing the female who had dished out the soup watching. I smiled and patted my stomach to indicate the food was delicious. A huge smile split her face. I guess females everywhere enjoy having their cooking praised.

As soon as Jack finished his meal, Bob took the bowl and handed it to the female cook. Then he indicated for Jack to follow him. The two of them walked off into the woods. At first, my heart pounded in fear, but Twila shook her head when I made a move to follow them.

"It's all right," she said. "I don't think he's in any danger."

"I hope not," I told her. However, I couldn't eat any more. When the female wasn't watching, I poured the rest of mine behind the log.

We spent the next half-hour watching the mothers take care of their young. The ones napping inside the hidden room woke up, but they didn't wail like human babies sometimes did. Instead, one stuck his head out from behind the curtain-picture and caught a mother's attention. I understood immediately why they didn't make any noise. A cry at an inadvertent moment would expose their hiding place to any humans who might be in the area.

The mother was busy eating, and when she started to put down her bowl, Granny motioned with one hand and stood. "Goes ahead and eat. We'll git the young'uns up."

Even if the female didn't comprehend the words, she understood the universal language of mothers. She nodded at Granny in an indication for her to go ahead. Since we'd seen three babies in there, Twila and I both eagerly stood to accompany Granny.

The babies all gazed at us wide-eyed but unafraid when we entered the sleeping quarters. The light was dim, but we could clearly make out the soft mats and three little ones sitting up on them, eyes huge and shining as they waited to be picked up.

"Aw, look at them cuties," Granny said as she scooped one up. If we compared the Grassbaby to a human, it might have been three months old. The smallest, it was still an armful for Granny. Twila and I picked up the other two, who might have been six months old.

The softness of the dark green grass covering the baby's skin surprised me. It was as silky as a human baby's, and the little one smelled fresh and clean. I cuddled it and cooed like a fool, while it gaped a toothless grin at me. Then it reached up and patted my cheek, and I felt such a tender stab of love, I almost dropped the little thing.

We carried the babies out of the sleeping quarters into the sunshine. They blinked, and mine hid its little head against my shoulder until its eyes adjusted to the light. I instinctively stroked my hand down the silky strands covering its head to soothe it. When the female I assumed was its mother came over and reached out with a smile, I reluctantly gave her that bundle of new life.

A moment later, all three of the babies were suckling at a mother's breast. We returned to the log and watched in fascination as they carried the babies around while they worked. They had already taken the soup kettle off and hung up a container of water. When it was hot, they washed the bowls and set them in a ray of sunshine to dry.

I had on my watch, and on the half-hour, Jack and Bob returned. I didn't see them carrying anything, so they hadn't been fishing or picking plants for more soup. They both came over to where we women waited.

"Bob explained what's going on," Jack said. "We're free to go, and can take the animals with us, even though Rascal will miss them. All Bob asks is that we keep what we've seen to ourselves, especially their location. Plus he'd like our help on something."

"Why, we sure as shootin' will help these fine folks," Granny said. "What's he need?"

* * *

"I do not understand why we did not go see if your body was in the other funeral home," Free Eagle grumped to Patches. "While we were searching anyway, we should have looked there."

"'Cause it just ain't a place I better be," Patches said in irritation. "I'll find out for sure if Janie's the one handling things. And where she stashed me until she has a service. If it's in that funeral home run by old Judge Abbot, I'm gonna find some way to get her to move me."

Free Eagle sighed. "And how are you going to communicate with her?"

Patches' shoulders lifted in a defeated shrug. "This business of being a ghost is for the birds. Guess I'll probably just have to listen in and hope they talk about me. This here's a small community. Word of my murder's probably spread to every ear in the county, and some out of it."

"And then what?" Free Eagle prompted.

"I got you with me. Maybe we can figure out something."

"This place looks too peaceful for us to disturb them."

They stood on the edge of a woods, gazing out onto cleared land. In the distance, a man dressed in a blue shirt, black trousers and wearing a flat-brimmed black hat guided a beautiful pair of horses as they dragged a plow through the soil. Furrows of black earth flowed behind them.

Free Eagle instinctively tried to draw in a breath. He couldn't in his state, but that didn't keep him from being able to smell the wonderful odor of freshly-turned earth. As a warrior, he hadn't helped the women in their duties raising or gathering plants and food provided by the land. He and Walking Bear, with other men of the tribe, made sure there was always enough meat or fish. However, the women dug up soil in their summer camp to plant seeds they saved from fall harvest. His own wife, Moon Dove, did so, also. When no other men were watching, he would help her dig up the ground.

He missed Moon Dove immensely, and as soon as Walking Bear saw reason, he was going to pull him along that golden path the Twila woman was capable of making happen. Then he would hold the love of his life again.

Patches was already halfway across the field by the time Free Eagle came out of his memories. He was headed towards the farmhouse, not the man and horses. Free Eagle blinked and was beside Patches in an instant.

Patches was stubborn, so Free Eagle didn't bother to argue any more about disturbing these mostly peaceful people. They were not completely harmonious, of course. There were squabbles and in-fighting, even as there used to be in his tribe. Some of the men were overbearing and too many of them fought to be chief. The women enjoyed their gossip, as did the men.

However, the Amish lifestyle kept them too busy to allow much time for quarrelling. From dawn to dusk, they toiled, longer in the summers during the lengthier days. They also raised fine horses, something Free Eagle's tribe had not had when he lived.

"The women are usually around the house most of the day," Patches said. "Let's check the kitchen first."

The back door was open, and even the screen propped, so they had easy access to the kitchen. Again, Free Eagle was glad he had retained his sense of smell. Wondrous aromas rose from the pots on the stove. An abundance of baked goods lined the windowsills and cabinet tops. There was also a heaping pile of fried chicken in a black oven pan. Free Eagle saw glimpses of the crispy skin where the white towel used to protect it from flies didn't quite cover it.

There was only one woman in the room, appearing to be in her mid-twenties. She wore a dark blue, floor-length dress and white apron. A white net bonnet confined her blond hair, the strings dangling past her shoulders. Wisps of hair, damp in the kitchen heat, escaped the bonnet as she bent into the open oven and removed two pies with golden crusts.

"Those smell like apple pies," Patches said with a look of yearning. "And that's my niece Janie taking them outta the oven."

"She has no one to talk to in here," Free Eagle pointed out. "So we cannot find out what she knows of your death and the storage of your body."

Patches frowned and said, "Yeah. That's a problem. Hey." He turned to Free Eagle. "I've heard Jess swear that Twila can read minds. I sorta thought that was hog wash, and one day I even asked her about it. She just laughed and said she read body language, not minds. But she's said some creepy things to me now and then. Can you read people's thoughts?"

"Sometimes," Free Eagle admitted. "But it's more like talking between my mind and another's. It still needs to be a back and forth conversation, and one person needs to start it."

Before Free Eagle could stop him, Patches hurried over to the kitchen table, where Janie was getting ready to set the pies down on top of a newspaper. He grabbed the paper and the pies clunked onto the tabletop instead. Given his undeveloped abilities, Patches lost control of the paper, and the pages whooshed around the room.

"Dang," Patches said as he tried to capture one certain page.

Janie scowled at the back door. Then her face creased in puzzlement as she evidently realized there was no breeze. She thinned her lips and started gathering up the paper.

Patches managed to grasp one page before Janie did.

"Ah," he said. "It is today's local Heartland. They only publish once a week, but today's the day it comes out. And here's my story."

At first Patches held the paper out so Free Eagle could see it. He nodded at the glaring headlines: *Local Man Killed on Brown Farm.* Then Janie gasped. She was watching the newspaper page, to her eyes, hovering in the air.

"You better get her to look at what you want before she runs out of here," Free Eagle said.

Patches hurriedly folded the page to outline the article and held it out toward Janie. Wrong move. The young woman screamed and turned to run. Her apron caught on a chair, and she and the chair tumbled to the floor.

"Darn, Janie," Patches said as he hurried over to her. "I didn't mean for you to get hurt."

Patches laid the paper on the table and leaned down to help his niece. Janie shivered violently and jerked her apron off over her head, leaving it dangling from the chair as she scrambled to her feet. This time she made it out of the kitchen, but her screams echoed.

"When we come close to those still living," Free Eagle explained, "they feel us as something very cold."

Patches nodded. "I'll try to remember that." He grinned at Free Eagle. "And use it when I need to." He nudged at Free Eagle with his elbow, and since they were both ghosts, the elbow bit into Free Eagle's ribs.

Free Eagle laughed and agreed, "It is a good trick when needed. But perhaps we should leave."

"Naw," Patches said as he winked and gathered up the rest of the newspaper. He folded it neatly and laid it beneath the front page. "I'm sorry I scared her, but now maybe we can get the info I need."

Sure enough, Janie and an older woman peeked around the door frame.

"That's Janie's mama-in-law, Mandy," Patches told Free Eagle. "Like I told you, Janie married into the Amish. That don't occur too often—one of what the Amish call *English* marrying into their faith. But it is known to happen."

Mandy straightened and walked on into the kitchen. "What are you talking about?" she asked Janie, who still stood by the doorjamb. "This paper is not flying all around. It is lying on the table."

Janie gasped and cautiously left her post. At the table, she let out a tiny yelp and pointed. Her eyes closed and she started to wilt into unconsciousness.

Mandy reached for both her niece and the nearest chair. She managed to help Janie into the seat, then patted her gently on the cheek.

"Janie, Janie," she said. When she didn't get a response, she carefully leaned Janie against the table and hurried over to the sink. She had to prime the pump with a can of water left there for that purpose, and work the handle up and down furiously, before she had a glass of water. Back at the table, she dipped her fingers in and flicked water on Janie's face.

Finally, she was forced to tip the glass up and drizzle water on Janie. Her daughter-in-law regained consciousness with a gulp of fear. She wiped her face with one hand while her feet dug into the linoleum floor and scooted her chair away from the table. Her index finger on her other hand pointed at the newspaper.

"See?" she said. "See what the paper is folded back to?"

Mandy leaned over the table. "It is the story of your uncle's death. I am sorry for the loss, child. I know you cared about the man. But we are going to honor him the best way we can when we have his service here tomorrow."

"That's why I was baking apple pies to add to all the other food we'll need," Janie said in a tearful voice. "They were Uncle Patches' favorites. I always took him a pie at least once a month."

"She did, too," Patches said. "Me'n Jess put away many of Janie's pies."

Janie sobbed and covered her face. Mandy wrapped her arms around her and patted her on the back, murmuring soothing noises. They weren't talking now, and Free Eagle contemplated how to find out what Patches needed to know.

He waved a finger at the table and the paper rustled, the top page with the article on Patches' death sliding free of the rest. The sound caught Mandy's attention, and she forwent comforting her niece to back away.

Janie dropped her hands. "See?" she said to Mandy. "I told you! That paper is moving all on its own."

"Perhaps you should come over here with me," Mandy said.

Janie straightened her shoulders bravely. "What if it's my uncle, trying to tell me something?"

"Janie, your uncle has gone on. He is in Glory now."

"What if he isn't?" she insisted. "What if his ghost is still here?"

"There are no such things," Mandy insisted, and Patches harrumphed. As though they had heard the sound, both women turned and stared toward where the two ghosts stood.

"I think she heard me," Patches s said in awe. "Can you get her talking now?"

For a moment, Free Eagle concentrated. Then Janie slowly said, "You know it's not true about there being no ghosts. Remember what I saw after Mama died?"

"She did not respond," Free Eagle said at the same time Mandy insisted, "It was a dream. Come, let us leave this room for now."

Janie stood. "I have a lot of work to do still. If Noah comes in and finds his lunch not ready, he'll tease me mercilessly about not learning how to cook the Amish way. And I still need to cook the ham and turkey. We'll probably need more lebkuchen cookies, also."

Mandy lifted her long skirts and walked out of the kitchen. "I have my own work waiting, too," she said over her shoulder. "I must get back to it."

As soon as Mandy disappeared, Janie gazed around the kitchen. Then she walked back to the stove and set the coffeepot onto one of the burners.

"Too warm for coffee," Patches mused. "Rather have me a cold beer."

"These people do not drink alcohol," Free Eagle said.

"I know that. They don't know what they're missing."

Janie grabbed a large bowl heaped full of potatoes that still needed peeling and dumped them into the sink. She moved the pump handle up and down, but no water emerged.

"Darn," she murmured. "Mandy used all the priming water. I'll have to go out to the well for more."

Free Eagle smiled and pointed his finger at the pump. A strong stream of water gushed out, and Janie covered her mouth with one hand. She stared in astonishment as the water poured out of the pump spout, the handle never moving.

This time, instead of fleeing, she turned a circle to stare around the kitchen. "Uncle Patches?" she asked so softly even the ghosts could barely hear her. "Are you here?"

"Now," Patches urged. "Tell her what we need to know."

Free Eagle whispered, "He misses your pies."

Janie backed up until her rear hit the table. "You're not my uncle. That's not his voice."

Hurriedly, Free Eagle said, "He is here with me, but he is not able to speak to you on his own yet."

"I don't see you," Janie said.

"We are both here, I assure you," Free Eagle replied.

Staunchly, Janie held her ground and said, "Then tell me something only Uncle Patches would know."

156

Patches laughed and said, "Tell her the only thing worse than a spoiled apple is one with only half a worm in it."

Free Eagle repeated what Patches said, and Janie smiled widely. "It is him! He told me that after I bit into an apple one fall. Tell him I love him. And I will see that he has a proper burial. Noah's family has agreed he can have a plot in their graveyard. They're even building him a casket. That's where Noah is now."

"Where are you keeping him until then?" Free Eagle hastily asked.

"In the ice house," Janie said with a sigh. "The Walker Funeral Home wouldn't take him. He and Daniel Walker got into a fist fight in Calvin's Bar last month. And I knew he wouldn't like to be in the one Judge Abbot owns."

"I'd forgotten all about that fight," Patches said. "Man, what goes around comes around."

"It does," Free Eagle said.

"What?" Janie asked. "I don't understand."

"I was saying something to your uncle," Free Eagle explained.

"Why is he...and you, too, I guess," Janie said. "Why are you both still here? Why haven't you gone on? Uncle Patches' best friend, Jess, was at the bait shop sometimes when I came around to fish growing up. I've also talked to Jess's wife, Twila, several times. I know you're supposed to go into The Light when you die."

"It is a long story on my end," Free Eagle told her. "And your uncle has something to do first. Then he will go on, I assure you."

"That's good," Janie said. She picked up a potholder she had dropped on the table, then one of the pies. "I doubt you can eat this now, Uncle Patches. But I wish you would at least take it with you. I made them for you. Well, in your memory."

Patches looked yearningly at the pie, then Free Eagle. "I ain't able to lift something like that."

Laughing, Free Eagle carefully approached Janie, staying back far enough to, he hoped, not chill her. He carefully took the pie, leaving the potholder behind.

Janie stared wide-eyed as, to her eyes, the pie floated away in mid-air.

"Tell her I gotta go, but I love her," Patches said.

After he repeated the words, Janie said, "I love you, too, Uncle. I'll see you again someday. And don't worry. I'll take care of everything here."

The two ghosts walked out of the kitchen, with Patches only glancing over his shoulder once as they left, a longing look at his niece.

Outside, Patches said, "Wish I could have hugged her at least. But I'd probably have chilled her like walking into the ice house. Come on. I know where it is."

Free Eagle glared at the field, where the horses were now plowing a furrow back towards the house. Behind them strolled Walking Bear, appearing to enjoy watching the man and horses work. "You will have to go alone," he told Patches. "I am going to try to talk some sense into my brother once again!"

"Hey," Patches called as Free Eagle left. "You've still got my pie!"

CHAPTER 14

After we returned to Twila's house, our animals safely in tow, I pulled her aside and said, "Why don't you let Granny have free run of your kitchen to cook us up something? We can have a glass of tea on the front porch."

"Want to talk, do you?" she whispered with a sly smile. "Frankly, I think that's a good idea."

A few moments later, Granny was happily busy at her favorite chore, feeding people. Jack had seen through Jess's workshop window and realized his friend was back from the doctor's appointment. He disappeared after promising the two of them would come inside soon for a delayed lunch. Twila and I carried our tea onto the front porch, where we both sat in the swing.

Before I could voice a word of my concern, Twila said, "I know, Alice. How the heck are we gonna find out which one of those sleaze balls who roam the woods shot Bob's daughter? She was the one with her arm in a sling. Daisy."

I took a sip of my tea and nearly spit it out before I realized what it was. Smiling at Twila, I said, "Long Island Tea. Wow. Don't let Granny know that's in the fridge. We might not get any lunch."

"If she put her mind to it, I'll bet Granny could drink both of us under the table. I thought we needed a drink ourselves, and I keep a jar in the back of the fridge. Jess thinks it's one of those flavored teas I like and doesn't bother it." She swallowed a quarter of her glass before she leaned back and pushed her foot on the floor to set the swing swaying. "Now, we need to do one of your mental lists to see what all we've got going on here."

I drank more tea and felt the heat of the vodka, rum, gin and tequila ease my tension. Then I lifted a finger and said, "Let's go by the timeline. Number one is the situation at Mikala's. That's what brought me here in the first place."

"Right," she said, then held up her second finger, which sort of looked like she was getting ready to flip me the bird. "Next is Patches' murder. And I don't care how much you protest that you're not going to get involved in another murder case, we're neck deep already in this one."

I sighed, then added finger three. "Free Eagle. I'll leave Patches' ghost in with number two. Four is trying to help Bob Grassman...." I giggled. "I still have trouble with his name. Anyway, we have to help him find out who shot his daughter."

"There's a five." She stuck her thumb in the air. "Free Eagle's brother."

"And there's lots of a's, b's, and c's under each and every one of those," I added. "Why is Walking Bear causing Mikala trouble, and why can't we make contact with that ghost?"

"Yeah, and why's Patches still hanging around? He wants to talk to Jess, but I just don't see that happening. Jess doesn't want anything to do with ghosts, and Patches is well aware of that. In fact, I don't tell Jess much about what I do anymore. Not since he had that experience at your house."

"I chastised Teddy for appearing to Jess in the bathroom," I said. "He even agreed to apologize to Jess. But that would have made things worse, him appearing twice to Jess."

Twila nodded. "Whatever Patches is after, it has to do with what he took out of that safe in his shop."

Her comment sent a flash of remembrance about the scene into my mind. "I'm not sure it was Patches who broke into the hiding place," I told Twila.

"What?" she asked. "This is the first I've heard of that."

I started to repeat what I'd said earlier about us not having time to talk with all the other crap going on around here, but I held my tongue. She must have caught my drift, though, because she immediately said, "Sorry," and indicated for me to continue.

I sipped the tea, then said, "I'm pretty sure the pickup barreled off before I heard the wall slat over the hiding place splinter. I think some-one...or some*thing* else actually broke it open. Patches might not have had the ability yet."

She chuckled. "This ghost stuff is so weird. I mean, Patches evidently had the ability to drive his old pickup. The pickup no one's found yet, I might add. But he couldn't get to something that might be the reason he stayed on this side of The Light."

"Yeah, weird," I agreed. "But I'm not in any hurry to travel to the other side and get answers."

"Me, either."

"Do you think now that Jess has had a little bit of time to deal with Patches' death, he might sit down and try to help us figure that out?" I asked.

Twila shook her head negatively. "Not us. But he would probably talk to Jack."

"Good idea," I said, lifting my glass and realizing it was empty. "Darn, wonder if Granny would think it weird if I went back in and got us another drink?"

"No need," Granny said as she opened the screen door, a pitcher and another glass in her hand. "I found that there *tea* y'all didn't bother to offer me a glass of and poured it in here. I got the gumbo on the stove, lettin' all them flavors mix. So I figured I deserved a little drinkie-poo, too."

She set the pitcher on the small table beside one of the rocking chairs on the porch, then poured her glass full. When she sat down in the rocker, evidently not about to fill our glasses due her pout, I got up from the swing.

"I'm sorry, Granny." I patted her shoulder. "We just had too much on our minds and forgot our manners. We should have made you a glass of tea, too."

"You should have," she agreed with a nod, then took a long swallow from her glass.

Despite what Twila had said, I knew Granny didn't always hold her alcohol well. It depended on why she was drinking. We usually had a drink each evening together, unless I was working hard on my writing. I had a battery-operated candle in my front window, which I would turn on to signal Granny to come in after her evening walk. If it was off, that meant I was deep into writing and had forgotten to light it. On those evenings, she didn't disturb me.

Granny was a lot more understanding about my writing than Jack had been. Instead of interrupting me during the day, she would leave treats on my porch. If she did bother me, it was for a good cause. Woe the cat feeders on the porch be empty or the water dishes dry. I could expect a tap on the study window. It didn't matter what type of heavy scene I was writing, I'd gasp with the realization that my pets might be hungry and feed them.

"What can I do to apologize?" Twila asked, joining me beside the table. She picked up the pitcher and refilled hers and my glasses.

Granny held out her glass, which was already half empty, and Twila obligingly refilled it. Taking a sip, Granny said, "I figger that's a good nuf apology."

We laughed at the twinkle in Granny's eyes. She'd been kidding us all along. She knew as well as I did that when we came to visit Twila, we were not guests, but family. We could avail ourselves of anything she had to offer.

"Now," said Granny. "What's we talking about?"

Twila and I returned to the swing, and I repeated the list of things we'd been pondering as we all sipped tea. I was more cautious with that second glass. I'd been drunk with Twila once before on her Long Island Tea, and I didn't care to repeat the experience. It was a long way up that staircase to the bedroom I used, especially crawling on my hands and knees.

"Well," Granny said when I was done, "iffen Jack can't get Jess to open up to him, mebbe I can."

"He likes you, Granny," Twila agreed. "But I think he *dislikes* messing with the paranormal a lot more."

I tried to hide my huge yawn behind my glass. The tea and my lack of sleep were working on me. My eyelids drooped, and then my head followed suit.

* * *

When I woke up, I was lying on the swing seat, although my feet dangled off the end. Someone had covered me with one of the afghans from Twila's living room. I glanced at my wristwatch to see nearly an hour had passed. The smell of Granny's gumbo drifted out the front door and pulled me upright as quickly as the smell of coffee in the morning did.

Then I froze, still gripping one of the chains that held the swing to the porch roof.

The Native American man who sat in the rocking chair where Granny had been didn't move. It wasn't Free Eagle. This man wasn't wearing paint like his brother. But he looked every bit as fierce.

His body was toned and fit, and he wore a loin cloth. Black hair hung down his back in two braids, no feathers in his hair. He stared at me, a frown on his handsome face as though he were concentrating on trying to voice something. I could see his throat muscles working, but nothing emerged from his mouth or telepathically into my mind.

"What...?" I cleared my throat, but that didn't help the fear as I stared at the bow in his hand, an arrow negligently grasped with it. The shaft held a deadly arrowhead on the end.

"What do you want?" I finally managed.

C-c-c-cook-cookies! The voice in my mind sounded triumphant, as though Walking Bear—because that's who it was—had accomplished a major feat.

"Cookies ," I repeated aloud with a nod. "We have some cookie dough in the house. Can I go bake you some?"

C-c-c-cookies! he projected to me, this time in a threatening tone. When he stood up, shaking the bow and arrow at me, I hurriedly rose and eased behind the swing. Not that those slatted boards would protect me from a ghost bent on making its wishes known. That was when I also remembered I hadn't asked Twila for another protection packet after we left Mikala's.

"I have to go inside to bake cookies," I reiterated.

He sent me a sentence of stuttered words I assumed were in his native language, since I couldn't understand even one of them. But I did read his body language, or thought I did. He walked over to the edge of the porch as he spoke, notched the arrow in the bow and sent it flying upwards. Forgetting my fear for a moment, I stared in awe as the arrow transformed into a shower of blue feathers. Each and every one of the feathers disintegrated, except one. When it floated down, I instinctively held out my hand. It landed gently on my palm, and I curled my fingers.

Cookies, Walking Bear said, then disappeared.

When I opened my hand, the feather still lay there. I quickly gazed around to try to see where Walking Bear had gone, but I already knew he was back in his own dimension, invisible to me.

And he had singled me out for something. I'd had enough experiences with ghosts to know that when they zeroed in on someone to fulfill a desire they had, they would never give up. Maybe he'd left so I would have time to bake his cookies. Or maybe he had something else in mind.

"I don't even know what kind of cookies he likes," I muttered. I started to throw the feather down, then changed my mind and stuck it in my jeans pocket.

My stomach reminded me there was gumbo on the stove, and I moved cautiously around the swing, keeping an eye out just in case Walking Bear appeared again. Time didn't matter in his world, and maybe he thought I could whip up those cookies in a flash.

If cookies were what he really wanted. Ghosts had trouble communicating sometimes. I still didn't understand why this one couldn't speak more clearly, though. He'd had plenty of time on this side of The Light to develop—

"Omigod," I murmured as I hurried through the door to talk to Twila.

Five minutes later, I'd searched the entire house and couldn't find anyone else at home. Jack's pickup was gone, also, and I hadn't heard him leave. The Long Island Tea had relaxed me so much I'd gotten a deep hour of desperately needed sleep.

Or perhaps it wasn't the relaxation but the alcoholic haze that did that. I shrugged. Whatever. I marched beck into the kitchen to have some gumbo and wait for the others to return from wherever they had gone.

I'd only eaten two spoons full of gumbo when I felt the sensation of not being alone. For someone like me, that meant I really wasn't alone. But by damn, I wasn't going to let a stupid ghost interrupt my meal. Granny's gumbo was second only to the Nichols rolls as a food love-of-my-life.

Still, I stared around the kitchen as I ate. I snagged a large shrimp and chewed on it as I cautiously turned around in my chair to look behind me. No one there. And no one on the other side of the kitchen when I scooted around to look that way.

I was only half through the bowl when it slid across the table and nearly tumbled off the other side of the table. Furious, I stood and kicked the chair backward as I jammed my hands on my hips and turned a circle.

"Leave my damned food alone!" I screamed. "I've had just about enough of y'all's paranormal bull crap! Twila and I only want to help when we mess around in your world. So either leave me in peace to eat my food, or you won't like what I bring back from my bedroom to help me throw your ass out of here!"

The bowl slid quietly back across the table and stopped right where I'd had it. The spoon dipped in and out of the bowl, then hovered above it, full of gumbo and rice, roux dripping.

A peace offering, I thought as I pulled the chair back in place and sat down again. I took the spoon and swallowed the contents. Then I finished the rest of the bowl and drank the remaining tea in my glass—regular sweet tea this time, with the four slices of lemon I'd added.

I picked up my napkin and wiped my lips. Then I scooted the chair away from the table and sat there with my arms crossed. "Who's here and what do you want?"

Free Eagle visualized beside the back door. "I followed my brother here. I thought he might try to contact you."

"You had a poor way of contacting me yourself," I warned. "Didn't your mother teach you any manners?"

Free Eagle looked down at the floor. "I am sorry. It becomes very wearisome at times, trying to fill the hours. I seldom find someone who senses my presence."

"I thought time didn't mean as much in your state of being."

"Maybe not as you think of it," he said. "However, what if you had been wandering for several hundred years? One can only watch so many movies and play so many of those new video games."

"You play Dungeons and Dragons?" I asked in astonishment.

"No, I like the Wii," he said.

I wrinkled my nose in distaste. "Such a waste of time."

"Not when time is all you have," he reminded me.

I immediately changed my attitude. His words about wandering for so many years had made me understand him better. All right. They even gave me a stab of sympathy for him. And as Twila had reminded me more than once, that sympathetic emotion should be held at bay when we dealt with the supernatural. Still, I'd seen her compassion for lost souls over the years.

Staring at Free Eagle as I contemplated how much of what had happened on the porch to reveal to him, I drank more tea. Then, even though I'd made my decision, I rose and refilled my glass from the pitcher of non-alcoholic tea in the refrigerator, just to make him wait.

Twila's voice sounded in my mind, but this time it was a memory, not a telepathic communication: *Discipline. We have to make sure we discipline them, or they can cause havoc.*

Back in my chair, I motioned for Free Eagle to sit across from me. He walked over and didn't bother to pull out the chair pushed up close to the table. Instead, he sat down and waited for me to speak again.

Instead, I laughed. "Do you know how silly you look with only half your body showing above the table?" I asked.

He glanced down, then without any indication of movement from him, the chair scooted backward with him riding in it. When it stopped, he was sitting at the table like a regular person. Or ghost, whatever.

"That's better." I drank more tea and wiped up a small puddle of condensation on the table with my napkin before I set the glass down. Ghosts don't breathe, so it wasn't a huff of breath from him. More like an irritated sigh. Ghosts definitely have emotions.

Sympathy reared its head again. I gave in and asked, "Is your brother mentally handicapped?"

Free Eagle frowned and shook his head negatively. "I do not know what you speak of. He has no handicap. He is able to move as well as you."

"Maybe as well as *you*," I threw back at him. "However, there are plenty of things you ghosts can do that I can't." When he started to speak again, I held up a forestalling hand. "I didn't mean a bodily handicap. I meant, is Walking Bear's mind slow? Does it take him time to think about stuff? More time than a regular...ghost."

Understanding dawned in his eyes. "I see. Yes, but we only called it being one of the special ones. Those who kept one part of themselves in the land of our ancestors, instead of being wholly here. Or *here* as we were when we lived. Perhaps I should say *there*."

"I get it," I said to cut off his explanation. "Walking Bear did come to see me on the porch a while ago. He wanted some cookies."

I watched his expressions closely as he puzzled over what I'd said. "Cookies?"

Suddenly, he stared at me as though seeing me for the first time. He studied my face, then ran his gaze down my chest and focused on my hands. I started to remind him once again about manners, but held back, sensing he might be on the verge of revealing something important.

"Ah," he finally said. "You do remind me of Ruth."

I didn't bother to ask him for further explanation. Instead, I cocked an eyebrow in inquiry.

"Ruth Troyer. Her last name was as much a problem for my brother to pronounce as *lebkuchen*. Could he have said kuchen?"

"Koochin?" I repeated.

"That is what it does sound like," he said with a nod. "It is a word from the peaceful people. The ones you call Amish. Ruth lived in a settlement near the land we were forced onto by the ones who make your laws. She was one of those women who took much pleasure in the little ones, even those of us from the nearby tribe. She made what Walking Bear was only able to say as kuchen."

"*Lebkuchen,*" I repeated. "What are they?"

"Honey cakes," I heard someone say from the doorway behind us. Twila walked into the room, carrying two paper sacks of groceries in her arms. "They're a German Christmas treat the Amish make." She set the sacks on the table as she said, "Sort of like chewy gingerbread. Delicious."

"My brother thought so," Free Eagle said. "But Ruth made them all year for the children."

"What brought all this up?" she asked me.

"I saw Walking Bear on the porch. And Free Eagle came by looking for him."

She finally acknowledge the Native American. "So someone baked *lebkuchen* for your brother when he was a child?"

"Yes, but not only when he was a child. He visited her well into his manhood." He hung his head and shook it. "I believe when Ruth died is when Walking Bear began fearing death. I was with him when he could not find her one day and we saw a burial going on behind the peaceful people's church. The wooden box they use was already shut, but the elderly man who was wed to Ruth pleaded for one last look. So they opened the box for him to say a last goodbye, then closed it and lowered it into the hole. Walking Bear could not believe it when they began covering his Ruth in dirt. It took me several days to find him after he ran away screaming and crying."

The "Ah," of understanding was mine this time. I looked at Twila. "I think I've figured out one part of our puzzle. Walking Bear is mentally handicapped. That's why we can't understand him. He has trouble speaking words. That must also be why our discipline abilities don't work well on him."

To Free Eagle, I said, "Walking Bear is probably desperately afraid of death now. That's why he won't cross into The Light. He's afraid it will mean he'll be put in a hole and covered with dirt."

He cast me a respectful look. "Perhaps you are right. I had not thought of Ruth and the funeral for many years."

"But why is he so focused on me?" I asked. "I burn water. I hardly ever try to bake cookies."

Twila laughed, but even though she didn't say anything, I knew what she was thinking. We'd uncovered our great-grandmother's molasses cookie recipe once, and nothing would do but I try to make them myself. Since it was winter in Ohio, it took Twila two days to get the burnt smell out of her kitchen, and she also had to wash the dining room curtains.

As I recalled, we were drinking Long Island Tea that day, too.

Free Eagle actually blushed. It had to have been a deep embarrassment, because I could see it even through the paint on his cheeks.

"What?" I demanded. "Is the reason Walking Bear is demanding honey cakes from me something humiliating?"

"You have reminded me about courtesy twice," he said evasively.

"Look, we need to figure out how to help your brother cross over so he'll quit acting out his frustration at Mikala's," I insisted.

Twila began sorting the groceries on the table, although I knew she was paying close attention.

Free Eagle glanced at my hands again, then my hair. "You have a slight damage to your finger."

I held up my left hand and studied the fourth finger. "I slammed my finger in a car door once," I explained. "The nail never grew back right.

It's split partway down. The doctor said the only way to correct it was to have it entirely removed. It doesn't bother me, so I've just lived with it."

When I glanced quickly at him, I caught him examining my face instead of my finger. "What else? I don't consider my finger that embarrassing."

He clamped his mouth shut and turned his head aside. "Nothing," he said.

Twila stepped in and said, "You can cooperate or leave. You've been following me around long enough to know I'm not making a threat. I'm promising I can run you off."

I could see the irritation in his expression, but that didn't excuse what he said next. "Ruth...the lives were hard on the women. Their bodies aged faster than women of today. Their hair grew gray without the dyes you use."

I gasped and stood to lean over the table towards him. "Are you saying I look like Walking Bear's friend Ruth? And that I'm *old* looking?" Then I slapped my palms to the side of my face. All of the women in our family kept their hair coloring well, except one or two. I'd started noticing a graying at my hairline in front of my ears a couple months earlier. Deciding to try to keep the natural color I was perfectly happy with, I'd meant to pick up some of that hair coloring that professed to "only cover the gray." But I'd gotten involved in the new book and forgotten.

Sheesh, I wondered if Jack had noticed the stupid gray infiltrating the hair he always loved to run his hands through? He'd called it a shower of silkiness one night when we were—

"We need to go back to the store," I told Twila just as Jack and Jess walked into the kitchen.

"Damn it!" Jess yelled, face blanching. "Twila, get that damned spook out of here!"

Free Eagle stood and faced Jess. "I know your language enough to understand what you call me is insulting! I am a warrior and will not be called your names!"

"Crap," Twila said the same moment I muttered, "Oh, shit."

CHAPTER 15

Instead of retreating, as I thought he would, Jess rushed Free Eagle. He caught the ghost by surprise and swung at him. Free Eagle only stood there staring haughtily when Jess's fist flew straight through his face. Jess's impetus sent him stumbling past the ghost.

Jess shivered with the cold contact, but immediately turned and picked up a chair to swing at Free Eagle. "Get out of here, spook!" he yelled, brandishing the chair threateningly.

"Ah...Jess," Jack said, cautiously moving across the kitchen toward his friend. "Let's let Alice and Twila handle this."

"This is *my* house, too," Jess declared. "I want him out of here! Out!"

"Go on," Twila said with a wave at Free Eagle. "Leave for now."

Free Eagle drew himself up and glared at Twila, then Jess. "Warriors do not take orders from those of lesser status."

"You ain't any better than we are, you blasted freak of death!" Jess swung the chair. He had to know it would go the same way as his fist, but he evidently wanted to make his point.

The chair did as expected, the force of his swing carrying Jess close enough to the ghost to experience the chill associated when other-dimensional entities, which use up available energy to materialize. Twila sighed and backed up her order with something that worked.

She dug in her jeans pocket and pulled out a protection packet. Then she walked straight up behind Free Eagle, who was now sneering at Jess, and tapped him on the shoulder. Her finger penetrated, but got his attention. When he turned to face her, Twila dangled the protection packet from one finger and flicked the fingers of her other hand at him.

The ghost disappeared with a roar of displeasure.

The kitchen settled into quiet as Twila returned the protection packet to her pocket and slid an arm around Jess. "I'm sorry, honey. I didn't invite him in. He just showed up, and we were trying to question him about something while we had the chance."

Jess hugged her back. "I know. I know you wouldn't purposely piss me off. Let's just have a drink and forget it."

For an instant, a short instant, it appeared we would do exactly that. Then Granny walked in from the front of the house, the same direction Twila had come from. She had a bag of groceries, too, but Patches was courteously carrying it for her.

"Lookee who I found," she said.

Jess was out the back door in a flash, not bothering to order this ghost out of his house.

As he strolled after Jess, Jack said, "Let me know if y'all get that one to answer any questions. I'll go stay with Jess. He's got a bottle of Jim Beam in his workshop, so we'll have our drink out there."

Patches levitated the bag of groceries onto the table, then started out the back door after the men. He didn't even get halfway across the kitchen before Twila stepped in front of him, the protection packet in her hand.

"No," she said. "Jess isn't ready to talk to you, Patches. You'll have to wait."

"How long?" Patches whined. "We need to discuss something."

"What?" I demanded, drawing his attention to me. "You're hiding something that I'm starting to feel the rest of us need to know."

"We was talkin' outside while he practiced carryin' my grocery sack," Granny said. "He ain't sure who did this to him, neither."

"That's not what I meant," I told her. "I don't think he knows who killed him. However, I think whatever he's not telling us has something to do with *why* he was murdered."

I turned toward the ghost, saying, "You need to come clean." All that was left of him, though, was a faint mist as he disappeared.

Granny said, "He's been practicin' that disappearin', too. Says he's jealous of that there handsome Free Eagle bein' able to do things he cain't."

"He won't need any of those abilities if he'll just cross over," Twila said. "Where he belongs. His hanging around here is too hard on Jess. Shoot, I doubt I'll even get Jess to the wake this evening, let alone the service tomorrow. He'll be afraid Patches will be there."

"When did you find out about a wake and service?" I asked.

"I ran into Mikala at the grocery store. She and Janie Yoder were talking and Janie said she hoped we would come. They'll have the burial early tomorrow morning at the Amish cemetery."

"And I promised to make bread pudding to bring," Granny said as she dug into her grocery sack. "So y'all go ahead and clear outta the kitchen. I'll fix something for supper, too, while I'm at it."

Effectively banished, Twila and I headed for our favorite haunt: the front porch. Not before we each grabbed a large glass of iced tea, though. However, we didn't even get a chance to sit down in the swing before the sheriff's car pulled in.

"There's your newest admirer," Twila said with a wink.

"Oh, gag," I said. "Let's tell him where Jack and Jess are and get rid of him."

Hoof parked his patrol car beside Twila's little red compact and strolled over to us, thumbs cocked in his belt. Perhaps he thought *strolling* made him more masculine. It didn't. The more I saw of him, the more he reminded me of the ranger in the Yogi Bear cartoons: trying to look like someone in charge when any small jolt would throw him off balance.

"Just the ladies I want to see," he said as he came up the steps, ending my hope of sending him to spend time with the men. "I was wondering if you were planning to attend the wake for Patches this evening?"

Since we hadn't confirmed our plans, I let Twila answer, although Hoof had directed his attention to me.

"We plan to," she said. "At least, most of us. I'm not sure about Jess."

Hoof turned his gaze toward her and nodded. "I understand. Jess doesn't handle things like that real well." Then he refocused on me. "I've been hearing about your books for years, Alice. People talk because you're a hometown girl. I got to thinking that, since you obviously know lots about crime investigation...."

His words trailed off and he glanced over at the other side of the porch, where the swing began to sway back and forth in a much stronger manner than the slight breeze could justify.

"Huh," Hoof said. "If I didn't know better, I'd say someone was sitting in that swing."

I forced a laugh, because I'd already realized Patches had been waiting outside. "I don't see anyone there. Your eyes must be playing tricks."

He threw a brief glance at Twila and replied, "On the other hand, word is that people don't always see what you two do." Gaze back on me, he said, "Like out at the bait shack."

Ignoring that, I said, "You sounded like you were getting ready to ask me to help you in your investigation into Patches' murder. Let me tell you right up front, I'm not interested. If I do happen to find anything out, I'll let you know. But I only write about fictional murder, not real life cases."

"I see," Hoof said. "But this one's different. It's something that happened to people you really care about, right?"

I took a swallow of tea as I debated how much time I'd get in jail for knocking an officer of the law down a set of steps and telling him to get his ass off my property. Only, it wasn't my property and I really didn't want to get arrested. On the other hand, I hated to be manipulated.

Twila slid an arm around my waist and squeezed briefly before she said, "Why don't you tell us what you have in mind, Harv?"

Hoof grimaced. "God, I hate that name."

I told myself I needed to keep quiet, especially since I didn't understand why this man rubbed me so wrong. It didn't work. I lost the battle to at least get in a verbal low-blow. "I can see why," I mused. "Harv Hoof. Gee, I couldn't imagine being your wife and called Mrs. Harv Hoof."

Twila had been taking a swallow of her own tea and it squirted from her mouth along with her laughter. Since Hoof had definitely encroached on our space when he approached to talk, the tea ended up all over his newly-pressed uniform shirt and dripping down his face.

He glowered as he wiped his face, and when Twila said, "Oops," and placed a palm over her mouth, I lost the restraint on my own laughter. Especially when Twila turned her head to wink at me from the eye hidden from Hoof.

We both doubled over in another one of those shared-hilarity-episodes. I clutched my stomach and stumbled over to collapse in the nearest rocking chair. Twila tried to take another swallow of her tea to control her giggles, but she choked and spit the tea on the porch. Then she captured her glass in both hands to try to steady the liquid swirling round and round from her movements and ended up in the chair next to me.

"We're sorry," she managed to say, but when I quirked an eyebrow at her as if to ask whether we really were sorry, we both lost it again.

I had enough sense left to set my glass on the table between our chairs so I could free my hands and try to stifle my laughter. Twila attempted the same, but her glass missed the table and fell on the porch.

Where the liquid spilled across the board slats, straight toward Hoof's boot.

He did a quick tap dance to try to keep the tea off his boots, and ended up doing what I'd wished. His foot came down on the second step instead of the porch, and he lost his balance.

I had no idea if there was a law against laughing at a sheriff in Ohio, but if so, it was lucky for us that Hoof didn't fall. He managed to stagger on down the steps and stand at the foot of them, still glaring at us.

"I'm so sorry," Twila said again. "Oh, my, you have to understand. It feels so good to laugh after all the tension around here. I'm just sorry it was at your expense, Har—"

There she went again, off into gales of giggles at the mention of his name. And there I went, right along with her.

Hoof raised his voice over our merriment. "I thought maybe you ladies would like to know that I have a person of interest in mind as to Patches' murder." He turned and started towards his car. "But I guess not."

"Wait!" Twila jumped to her feet and ran after him, with me following more slowly. She took Hoof's arm. "I really am sorry. If you want, I'll take your shirt and wash and iron it. You can wear one of Jess' shirts while I do that. And we really would like to know what you've found out."

A mollified expression on his face, Hoof patted the hand she had on his arm. "I apologize, too, Twila. I know you're under a lot of stress right now. And don't worry about the shirt. You two ladies can help me in another way."

As I joined them, I asked, "You have a suspect?"

"They call it a person of interest these days," he reminded me.

I started to tell him that I, too, watched TV, but knew that would set us off into more gales of laughter. So I bit back the words and tried to look like I admired his investigative abilities. As Granny would say, *You ketch more flies with honey than vinegar.*

"Who is it? And how can we help?" Twila asked.

"You did say that you're going to the wake tonight, right?" Hoof asked.

"Alice and I will," she assured him. "Probably Granny and maybe Jack, since he knew Patches. Like I said, I'm not sure about Jess. He'll probably decide at the last minute."

"This is confidential," Hoof said quietly. "I'd like you two to keep your ears open. Do a little undercover investigating for me at the wake."

"Wouldn't Jack be better for that?" I asked.

"Not really, since the men and women stay separate at these Amish gatherings."

"You're saying your sus-person of interest is a woman?" I asked.

"First I need you two to promise this will be kept confidential," he reminded us.

I chewed my bottom lip and looked over at Twila. Given her stance, I could see she had her arm behind her back, fingers crossed. I didn't know if that would stand up in court if we were arrested for lying to a policeman, but I stuck my hand behind me and did the same.

Then we both said within a split-second of each other, "I promise."

"O.K.," Hoof told us. "I just found out that Patches had this huge life insurance policy on himself. A hundred thousand dollars! And guess who the beneficiary is?"

Twila shrugged. "I have no idea. He only had one relative that he was close to. His niece, Janie."

Hoof pointed an index finger at her. "Bingo!"

Twila's expression would have murdered a lesser man, or one with a few more points on the IQ scale. However, I hadn't forgotten that Patches was sitting on the porch.

"That's the stupidest thing I've ever heard you say," Twila raged at Hoof as I glanced toward the swing.

Ghosts can sometimes have enhanced hearing, but I was hoping Hoof's voice had been too low for Patches to catch. No such luck. The ghost surged into visibility and let out a roar as he jumped over the porch railing. He headed toward Hoof, shaking his fist.

Patches was fast, but Hoof was quicker. He was in the patrol car, foot on the gas before he even thought to say goodbye. He must have left the engine running in the car, because Twila and I had to jump out of the way when he floored the pedal and twisted the wheel to turn around in her yard. He left some ruts, although he kept in the driveway for the most part.

For a second, I thought Patches might go after Hoof, or maybe even

Twila herself would. I grabbed my aunt's arm to keep her with me, but she shook me off.

"Did you hear him, Alice?" she said angrily. "How could he even think such a thing?" She stared around until she saw Patches, standing in the driveway, still glaring in the direction Hoof had gone. "Patches! Get over here!"

The ghost ignored her, but only for a brief second. Then he turned and stomped toward us.

"What are you going to do about that?" he demanded. "He's gonna try to arrest my Janie!"

"Surely he wouldn't have the balls," I said.

"I don't know," Twila mused. "It's an election year. But on the other hand, lots of Amish vote. And they're a major block of our population in the county."

"Well, we need to get out there and find out who did murder me," Patches said. "'Cause if he arrests my Janie, he's gonna have a haunted jail like no one's ever seen!"

"Your appearing to him like that should warn him," I said to Patches. "And I've vowed never again to get involved in a murder investigation, except in my books."

"I don't think we have a choice, Alice," Twila told me.

"We always have a choice." I left them both standing there and marched up to get my tea on the porch, wishing it was Twila's Long Island Tea instead of regular sweet.

CHAPTER 16

I half-glared at Twila across the top of my car, which I'd parked along the driveway leading to the Yoder homestead. "I thought I had a choice," I muttered.

She ignored me and opened the back passenger door to help Granny out. I, in turn, silently surrendered in face of her disregard and assisted Mikala, who had called and asked to ride with us. Jack and, hopefully, Jess would be coming along behind us. Afraid Jack would tell Jess and upset him even more, Twila had asked me to keep quiet about our *undercover* assignment, so I hadn't mentioned anything to Jack.

Mikala and Granny walked on ahead. Granny carried her traditional offering for a bereaved family: a basket Twila had given her and which she had filled with a pound cake and a few jams and jellies she bought at the local bulk outlet. At home, those would have been replaced with her own hand-made jellies, but over a thousand miles from her panty, Granny had no choice. Mikala carried a cardboard box containing a pan of Granny's delicious bread pudding and two loaves of bread she herself had baked.

Numerous black buggies, horses still in the traces, lined the wooden fence in front of the farmhouse and barn. The two other cars and mine stood out oddly, especially one car riddled with rust.

I immediately overcame my small pique at Twila as I realized I'd have no one to explain all this fascinating stuff if I stayed mad. I said, "That one buggy must belong to a large family. Look how long the bed is, and it's covered over to keep the weather out."

"This Order doesn't maintain a church as we know it," she explained. "Or use a funeral home to store their dead. That buggy's the hearse. It will take the body back to someone's ice house to store until the actual funeral tomorrow."

"Oh," I said quietly.

We had delayed behind Granny and Mikala by mutual consent. There was no doubt why we were waiting, but so far, Patches hadn't appeared.

"I've never been to an Amish wake or funeral," I murmured to Twila.

"It will be a bit different because Patches isn't one of their Order," Twila explained. "But since he's Janie's uncle, the family will gather to support her grief."

"Will they have the service at home tomorrow, too, like the wake?"

"Yes." A different family hosts all the others each Sunday. Someone brings their wagon full of benches to the selected house. The service for Patches won't be as large as a Sunday service, but the close relatives will be here for Janie."

"Is there anything I need to remember, so I don't get embarrassed?" I asked. "You know how I am about making a fool of myself sometimes, due to lack of information about someone else's beliefs and rituals."

Twila chuckled. "The Amish are used to dealing with us English. You'll be fine if you just remember your regular manners."

I huffed and said, "I always keep my manners in mind and act with politeness and respect."

She smiled secretly, but evidently decided not to go down that path of reflection. More than once, I'd allowed my temper to override courtesy.

"And just about every time I did forget," I muttered clearly enough for her to hear, "you were a part of it right there with me."

"True, and occasionally we had a lot of fun, even when those Texas Rangers almost hauled us to jail. Let's get on inside," she said as she walked toward the farmhouse. "Maybe Patches isn't going to show."

"I doubt that," I warned as I followed. "He doesn't seem like the type to miss his own wake."

"You're probably right," she agreed. "He's just staying out of sight for now. But I'm also wondering why Hoof isn't here. Isn't it part of an investigation to show up at things like this? To see if maybe the murderer comes by to gloat?"

When we heard another vehicle coming down the driveway, we paused at the foot of the porch steps.

"Ah, there's Jess and Jack," Twila said. "Let's wait here for them."

Jack pulled in beside my car, and both men got out. "Wow," I said when I saw them dressed in black suits and white shirts. "They clean up good, huh?"

"They do," she agreed. "Even without ties. Jess doesn't even own one."

"I've only seen Jack in a tie a couples times," I admitted. "He abhors them, too. And I like that open-shirt space below their chins."

Our men's faces didn't reflect their handsome attire, though, Jess's more so than Jack's. Jess's morose expression indicated he would rather be riding naked through town on horseback like a male Lady Godiva. Jack's countenance showed his concern for his friend, and he walked close to Jess, ready to support him if needed.

Neither of them spoke when they reached us. Instead, they nodded, and Jess took Twila's arm, Jack mine, to walk up the steps. Twila and I both wore black skirts, mine borrowed from her closet. She only owned one black blouse, though, so my subdued maroon tunic was the only spot of color in our group besides the men's white shirts.

The large living room inside the farmhouse had been cleared of all furniture. Blue-clad men were already carrying in the wooden benches for tomorrow's service, placing them in two rows, separated by an aisle in the middle. From what I'd read about Old-order Amish gatherings, the benches held men on one side, women on the other. For the wake this evening, the coffin with Patches' remains was set on the back wall. Two sides of the six-sided wooden box were folded down, exposing a white-sheet-covered body from the waist up.

A young woman stood talking to Granny and Mikala beside a long table against the opposite wall from the coffin. All types of food layered the table, including cold-cuts, homemade breads and desserts.

"That's Janie there by the table," Twila said to Jack and me. "We need to give her our condolences first."

We followed behind Twila, Jess as reluctantly as me. When Jack realized the two of us were lagging, he halted and waited. He slipped an arm around my waist, but gave Jess a pat on the shoulder.

"You sure you're up to this?" he asked Jess.

Jess nodded and reluctantly walked on to join Twila and Janie. Jack squeezed my waist, and I smiled up at him.

"Thanks," I said. "I handle funerals pretty well, but I don't even know this guy or these people. I feel a little awkward."

Jack stifled a chuckle. "You do so know the deceased, *Chère*. He was in the kitchen just a while ago."

His attempt at easing my stress worked, and I chuckled as we continued on over to the group around Janie.

"This is Alice," Twila said, taking my arm and tugging me closer. "And her husband Jack." I slipped a look at Jack to see if he'd noticed Twila's reference to him, and found him smiling back at me as Twila continued, "Janie Yoder was Patches' niece, his closest relative."

Janie grasped hands with me, then Jack. "Thank you for coming." To Jack, she said, "I know Uncle Patches' enjoyed fishing with both you and Jess. I just wish he'd had more days of it. He was so young."

"Only sixty-three," Jess said in a low voice. "Way too young to die, and especially like this."

I hugged Janie and said, "You have my deepest condolences. Death is hard to bear at any age."

Jack added, "My sympathy, too, Janie. I remember stories Patches told us about you. He loved you very much."

"Thank you," Janie said again, sniffing back the tears Jack's words had fostered.

"You're so good to take on his burial," Mikala said. "The rest of that riffraff related to Patches would probably say just toss him in a hog pen."

I frowned and whispered to Twila, "I thought Janie was the only relative."

"There are a couple distant cousins," Twila murmured back. "But like Mikala said, they're riffraff. And in my mind, that's a polite term for them."

"Maybe one of them—"

"Shush," Twila said. "We can talk about that later. I'm sure Hoof has checked them out."

"Please," Janie said, waving a hand at the laden table. "Have something to eat. My mother-in-law, Mandy, even made some lebkuchen cookies." She picked up a nearby plate of large, round cookies that smelled like a mixture of gingerbread and molasses and were topped with a white glaze of frosting.

I shared a glance with Twila, hers indicating to me that I shouldn't talk about where we had just heard about those cookies. Instead, I reached for the plate to take it from Janie.

"You've probably got several people you need to talk with," I said. "We can help ourselves."

She gave me the cookies, then before moving away said, "There's a family story about these cookies. I can't imagine why I'm thinking of it right now, but I am."

"You mean the one about the Native American child your great-great-great grandmother took under her wing?" Mikala asked. "Did you know that Walking Bear was also an ancestor of mine?"

"No," Janie said. "What a coincidence. I heard that Walking Bear was mentally challenged. Is that true?"

"I heard the same story," Mikala said. She looped her arm with Janie's, the two of them continuing to chat as they strolled away.

I quickly glanced around to see if anyone was watching, then grabbed a napkin and folded it around several of the cookies. Then I realized I had nowhere to hide them, and shoved the package in Jack's coat pocket.

"Shhhhh," I said when he glanced down at me in bewilderment. "I'll explain later."

He shrugged, then asked, "Are you ready to go up to the coffin?"

Jack was partially blocking my view of the coffin. I leaned aside, then drew back with a gasp. A white-bearded, elderly man was holding back the sheet. Several people had lined up to take their turn *viewing* the body.

"I guess we have to do that," I murmured to Jack. "We'll go together, right?"

He nodded, and we joined the line of people waiting their turn to pay their respects. All of them were Amish, except the last man, the one we stood behind. He was one of the non-Amish, or *English,* as Twila had said.

"I guess none of Patches' other kin showed up," I said to Jack. "Everyone here except us is Amish."

The man in front of us turned at my voice, and I realized he wore a rather shabby suit. He said, "I made it. 'Course I was just a friend of the deceased. Guess I'd be lying, though, if I didn't admit it's hard to turn down an excuse to come around where there's Amish cooking."

He looked us up and down, then held out his hand to Jack and went on, "I don't believe I know you two. I'm Roy Morrow, but just call me Doc."

Jack shook hands and said, "Jack Roucheau, and this is Alice Carpenter."

"Oh, the author," Doc said, dropping Jack's hand and holding his out to me. "I'm very glad to meet you." When I accepted his handshake, he added his other hand on top of our clasp. "We don't get many celebrities in our little town."

As he spoke to me, I thought I caught a hint of whiskey on his breath beneath the stronger scent of peppermint. He seemed steady enough on his feet, though, and I courteously shook hands.

"I'm not much of a celebrity," I said with a small laugh. "But thanks for thinking that."

The line shuffled forward a few feet, and I realized we would soon take our turn at the coffin. I had to give a stern pull to retrieve my hand, and I hurriedly wrapped my right arm around Jack's waist. I wasn't exactly sure why I didn't care for Doc's courteousness. I told myself I was just bothered by our proximity to Patches' body.

I didn't mind communicating with ghosts, which are only made up of the energy that once animated the body they wore in life. Shoot, over the years I'd stood up to my share of them. Outsmarted them, outmaneuvered them, and overcome them, forcing obedience to my will. Yet I immensely disliked having to look at a body without its life force.

At the crime scene, my unrelenting nausea at the sight of blood explained my aversion. However, my disinclination to view actual bodies even after they were clean, tidy and prepared for burial was a life-long trait.

When Doc started to say something else, Jack interrupted him. "Your turn, Doc."

I could have sworn the man's face whitened when Jack said that, but he spun away too fast for me to be sure. The elderly man at the coffin had replaced the sheet again. It dawned on me that he covered the face in between each view. He looked at Doc, and I noticed Doc's shoulders stiffen as he nodded a yes.

I twisted my head to the side as soon as the elderly man reached again for the sheet, and even closed my eyes. Jack held me close as we waited several long moments before I heard Doc's footsteps moving away. Then it was mine and Jack's turn.

Jack tightened his grip on my waist, then indicated for the sheet to be pulled back. Gritting my teeth, I made myself gaze at the body.

Of course, he looked exactly like his ghost, though his gray hair and beard were now neatly brushed and trimmed. He wore a white shirt, which I was glad had been buttoned all the way up to hide the knife slash on his neck. Still, like all bodies, to me at least, he appeared cold and stone-like, as though molded from sculptor's clay. His eyes were closed, and I surprised myself by remembering the ghost's eyes were blue.

The sheet was pulled back far enough to expose his hands, crossed together on his upper chest. I felt Jack move beside me and smiled as he laid a bright yellow and black fishing lure between the two thumbs on the chest.

Then Jack softly patted Patches' shoulder and murmured, "Thanks for the good times, buddy."

Jack's hold guided me away from the coffin, but not before I noticed another gift someone had laid down for Patches. It was a small, crystal angel, kneeling with wings unfurled.

As we walked away, I noticed the next people in line were Granny and Mikala. Behind them, Twila stood with her arm around Jess, his around her. Jack paused, and I knew we both were going to stay close to the coffin for now, in case Twila needed our help.

She didn't, though. They took their turn at the coffin, but Jess shook his head negatively when the elderly man motioned once more as though to pull down the sheet. Jess removed a small, card-sized envelope from his jacket pocket and slid it beneath the closed part of the coffin lid. Then he patted the shining wood and led Twila toward us.

"We're not going to eat," Twila said. "I think we'll stroll around outside for a while. But you and Jack go ahead."

"I think I'll do that," Jack said. "*Chère?*"

"I am a little hungry," I admitted, and agreeably walked with Jack over to where the food was laid out.

I only put two pieces of cold cuts and a slice of bread on my plate, along with a spoonful of potato salad. However, before I could look for a place to sit, Granny appeared beside me.

"You're gonna get some of my bread puddin', ain't you?" she asked. "I ain't never seen you pass it up."

"I was going to come back in and get dessert," I assured her.

"Back in? There's plenty of places to sit in here," she said with a nod at the benches.

There were already several people sitting there, eating from their filled plates. As I'd thought, they were separated, men on one side, women the other. They didn't seem bothered by eating in a room with a dead body, but my stomach curdled at the thought. If I didn't get outside with the food, none of it would ever find its way into my belly.

Jack knew me well enough to understand I wouldn't touch a bite of food while I was in that room. "I'll make sure we get our share of your bread puddin'," he promised Granny. "I'll get Alice settled, then come on back before I even start on my plate. I don't wanna take a chance of it bein' gone."

"I'll fix you a couple bowls and have 'em ready," Granny said.

We carried our plates onto the wide front porch of the farmhouse. Evening was falling, but the night chill was still at bay. Doc had already claimed the swing, and two women occupied the rocking chairs on the opposite side of the doorway. I sat down on the top porch step, and Jack set his plate beside me, then returned to the house.

While he was gone, I fixed our sandwiches. Jack, too, had picked up cold cuts. We'd both added some mustard we found at the end of the table to the bread, and I only had to put the meat between the slices. There were plastic spoons, forks and knives folded into napkins, and we each had a set. Jack's plate also held baked beans, olives and pickles, and his serving of potato salad was much larger than mine.

I was tempted to pile everything on Jack's plate, since my hunger had now vanished, but I set both plates behind a porch column next to me. Leaning against the column, I gazed out at the carefully groomed lawn and the buggies and horses lining the fence beside the driveway. Here and there, golden specks of light flickered on and off, early lightning bugs showing off in hopes of finding a mate.

At first, I'd felt all right after viewing the body, but my mood had deteriorated as I moved down the table. I kept seeing that shirt buttoned around Patches' neck, the cold, frozen look of his face.

Well, of course he looked cold, I mused to myself. *They're keeping him in their ice house. I'm glad I'm not the one who has to use that ice in drinks this summer.*

Suddenly I realized I wasn't just thinking about cold; I actually was cold. I gritted my teeth to keep from making a scene as I whispered to

Patches, who had appeared beside me on the steps, "You need to make yourself scarce. I don't want Jess to see you!"

What do you think I been doing'? he mentally said. *Just because I'm dead don't mean I lost my manners. I still want to talk to Jess, but I ain't about to cause no disruption at my own wake.*

My writer's mind kicked into gear, and I couldn't help myself. To keep anyone from overhearing us, I dropped into telepathic communication, also.

What's it like, being here at your own wake? I moved around so I could see him, hoping none of the other few people wandering the yard noticed my interest in the rose bush beside the steps. One person did, though. Out in the yard, Twila was strolling toward me with Jess. Her eyes widened when she caught sight of me, and of course, the ghost beside me. She hurriedly took Jess's arm and changed direction, toward one of the buggy horses.

Patches leaned forward, elbows on his knees. *It's sorta weird. You know, you always talk about what you'd do if you was able to come to your own funeral. But being here ain't no fun. I keep looking around to see who's here, who ain't. Makes a fellow realize a few things he should've thought about while he was still alive.*

Didn't you see The Light? I asked curiously. *And want to go through it?*

Course, Patches replied. *But there was one thing I couldn't leave here without settling first.*

What? I demanded. *It must have something to do with why you were killed. You need to tell us, so we can expose whoever murdered you.*

He nodded. *Yeah, I need to tell someone. But you've gotta get Jess to talk to me first. We're sworn buddies. I can't—*

Jack emerged from the front door, and I quickly glanced toward him, then back beside me. Only the rose bush next to the steps was visible.

Jack didn't have our bread pudding in his hands. Instead, he held his hand out to me. "We need to move, *Chère,*" he explained. "They're taking Patches back to the ice house."

I barely had time to grab Jack's hand and rise before the front door opened again. A man emerged, then held the screen door. Jack led me over beside the swing, where Doc was sitting alone, his now empty plate beside him.

Six men carried the coffin out and down the steps. All strong and muscular, probably from their long work days in the fields without modern machinery, they easily held the handles. Face tear-streaked, Janie followed. The handkerchief she held appeared soggy, and a young man who was probably her husband walked beside her.

"She really cared for Patches," I observed to Jack.

Mandy, the woman I'd been told was Janie's mother-in-law, came next, accompanied by another blue-clad man. The small group made its way to the hearse-buggy and stood reverently as the coffin was placed inside.

One of the pallbearers walked around the buggy and got into the seat. A few seconds later, the horses plodded off slowly, pulling the hearse back to wherever the ice house was located.

I glanced up at Jack to see him frowning at the swing. But he didn't say anything until we'd returned to the porch column and retrieved our plates. We walked on down along the porch railing instead of returning to the steps and set our plates down

Jack glanced back the way we'd come. "Where I come from," he said with a trace of dislike in his voice, "men stand up to show their respect when someone dead is carried past them. We even pull our cars to the side of the road when a funeral procession goes by."

I followed the direction of his gaze to see Doc still sitting in the swing. From what Jack had just said, I realized the man hadn't stood when they carried the coffin out. But before I could voice my own disgust, another car drove down the driveway.

Hoof didn't bother to pull in beside the other three vehicles. He left his patrol car in the middle of the drive and got out. Without even a glance at the farmhouse porch where we stood, he headed towards Janie Yoder.

I gasped when I noticed a pair of handcuffs dangling from one of Hoof's hands.

CHAPTER 17

"**J**ack!" I whispered in horror. "It looks like he's going to arrest Janie!"

"Now, *Chère*, he doesn't have cause to do that."

I grabbed Jack's shirt front and continued frantically, "He thinks he does. He came by Twila's earlier, when you and Jess were in the workshop. He said—"

Hoof didn't bother to keep his voice down. "Janie Yoder, I hate to do this, but you're under arrest."

A defensive expression on his face, the young man with Janie stepped in front of her. "What are ye talking about? My Janie has done nothing against the law."

"Now, Noah," Hoof said as Jack and I hurried across the porch. When we went down the steps, we barely missed a young child, who barreled past us and into the house. "I don't want to have to arrest you, too. For interfering with a law enforcement officer."

Hoof reached out to push Noah aside. Janie's husband was about the same height as Hoof, but I'd have been willing to bet he was twice as strong. He planted his feet and crossed his arms over his chest, refusing to budge as Janie peeked around his side.

"I will know what the purpose of this arrest is before I let ye lay a hand on my Janie," Noah said.

Jack and I weren't the only people heading for the confrontation. Everyone else in the yard was either already gathered around Noah, Janie and Hoof, or on their way. The little boy must have alerted those in the farmhouse, because a parade of blue-clad women and men hurried out the front door. I glanced over my shoulder once and noticed Doc getting up from the swing. Instead of walking towards us, though, he went down some steps on the far side of the porch to the driveway.

As we reached the sheriff, I spared one last glance at the farmhouse, trying to see if Granny was among the people emerging through the door. She was, Mikala right behind her.

"Hey, Sheriff," Jack said in an easy voice. "These folks are pretty upset about this. Maybe if you'd give them a little more information, it would help."

Granny stalked past me and planted herself beside Jack. I noticed she'd retrieved her walking stick from the car at some point, indicating her arthritis pain was flaring up. At least, I assumed that was why she had it gripped in one gnarled hand, although in the brief glimpse I'd had of her coming out the door, she'd been carrying the walnut carved stick and walking energetically.

"You betcha life he best tell us what's goin' on," Granny said. She shifted her walking stick to her left hand and place the other one over her heart. I expected her to start singing a rousing *Star Spangled Banner*. However, she only pursed her wrinkled lips and glared at Hoof as she continued, "We watch TV and know our rights under our Constitution!"

Hoof ignored Granny and scowled at Jack, then at me, holding tight to Jack's arm. "Maybe down south you have to lay all your evidence out before you go to trial, Roucheau," he said. "But here we don't tell them nothing except a judge signed an arrest warrant."

Jack stifled a sigh, and before he could say anything else, Noah said, "Then I assume ye do have one of those warrants. I wish to see it."

"Yeah, you gotta show it," Granny snarled. "Like on TV."

"We don't watch TV," Noah said in an aside to Granny.

Granny winked at him. "What 'bout during them there *rumspringin'* years, when y'all goes out carousin' and jumpin' round 'til you decides whether or not to join your church? When you and Janie here met?"

Noah blushed slightly and wrapped an arm around Janie to pull her to his side. Janie stared adoringly up at him, which heightened Noah's blush as he glanced about to see if his fellow Amish noticed her look of love. The Amish weren't a people who showed their affection much in public. Not to other adults, anyway. I'd noticed them slavishly shower their children with love and affectionate words.

"Where'd you hear about *rumspringa?*" I asked Granny, hoping to prolong this confrontation when I noticed Hoof tarrying beside us instead of pushing Noah to hand Janie over. Maybe delaying things would keep the crowd of people calm.

"*Rumspringin', rumspringa,* whatever," Granny said. "Us women talk 'bout lots of things in the kitchen whiles we keep the food a'comin' to fill you folks' bellies. Mandy and Mikala was talkin' 'bout it whiles I heated up some Jack Daniels sauce for my bread puddin'. The Amish give their teenagers a one and only chance to see how the rest of our big, bad world lives. They can partake of all the sins they want, even run around with us *English.* But eventually, they gotta decide which is best for them: the Amish way and the church, or our world, full of all them sordid sins."

The myriad of wrinkles crisscrossing Granny's face like a roadmap deepened when she slipped a wink at Noah. "I'd be willin' to bet you did your share of that there *rumspringin'*, Noah. 'Specially 'cause that's when you met your Janie."

"That he did," Hoof said with a nod. "I remember one night he left his buggy beside the road and went riding off on his horse bareback when I turned my lights on behind him. Had some little girl behind him on the horse. One who looked a lot like Janie, only she was wearing blue jeans back then."

"Ye didn't have no reason to be stopping me," Noah defended himself.

"How'd I know that if I didn't talk to you?" Hoof demanded. "I'd just had a report of a buggy like yours at the liquor store."

"All our buggies look alike," Noah said.

"But not all the teenagers driving them get one of those old panhandlers to go in a liquor store and buy beer for an underage kid," Hoof said.

Noah glanced down at Janie, and no one could have missed the shared mischief in their gazes.

"Well, from what I understand," Granny broke in, "that there *rumspringin'* time is to sow them wild oats. Like my dear departed husband used to say, we all needs some good times to look back on when sittin' in our rockin' chairs. Wonderin' iffen we'll ever get one more poke in the sack a'fore they plant us in that box."

Even Hoof blushed this time, but he seemed to remember what he was here for. He harrumphed and grabbed for his shirt pocket. Then he patted his chest, as though the warrant might have migrated inside his shirt and down to his stomach.

"I had the danged warrant right here," he muttered. "Must have fallen out in the car." He pointed at Noah, including Janie in the gesture. "You both stay right here. I'll be right back."

As he started toward the car, Jack called, "I'm sure these people would also like to know what the charges on the warrant are."

"Murder!" Hoof called over his shoulder. "I'm arresting her for the murder of her uncle, Patches Henry!"

A dozen hives of swarming bees couldn't have made a buzz as loud the one that erupted amidst the people gathered around Janie and Noah. They all moved closer together, like a herd of animals gathering to protect their young. Except for Granny, who stomped after Hoof.

"Now you lissen here," Granny said, her voice discernable even over the hubbub of the crowd. "You ain't such a high and mighty sheriff that you don't make mistakes. And this one's a big 'un!"

Twila and Jess had reached us now, and my eyes flew to Twila's. My aunt moved close enough to me to say, "He can't be serious. That's the most asinine thing I've heard in years."

"He's evidently got a warrant," I told her. "To get a judge to sign off on a warrant, he has to have at least some sort of evidence."

Then I whirled around as it dawned on me what Jess had just

muttered to Jack. "Don't either of you even think such a thing!" I whispered harshly.

"What? What were they saying?" Twila asked.

"Nothing," Jess said. "I was just thinking out loud."

"Jess asked Jack if he wanted him to grab Janie while Jack ran ahead and got the truck started," I told Twila.

"Tattletale," Jess muttered.

"Jesse Terry Brown," Twila said as she took his arm and stepped in front of him. "You will not try to help someone run from the law! There are legal ways to handle this!"

"Jail ain't no place for a little girl like Janie," Jess growled. "And if Noah wants us to...." He looked over Twila's head to where Noah was now holding Janie in his arms. "What do you say, Noah?"

"We do have the sheriff outnumbered," Noah replied.

Janie gasped and jerked out of Noah's arms. "You listen here, Noah Yoder." She pointed her finger at Jack and Jess. "And you two *English*, too! I won't have you breaking the law for me. We all know this is hogwash, and I'll go with the sheriff until you can get me a lawyer."

Like hell she will, I heard in my mind. A quick glimpse of Twila's face told me she had heard Patches, too.

"Shit," Twila muttered, and I knew the situation was already out of control. My aunt never used anything harsher than darn unless....

And that unless happened just then. Hoof started to emerge from the patrol car, where he'd evidently been having trouble finding the warrant. Probably due to some interference already from Patches. Granny was still standing there haranguing him, but he ignored her and waved a pale blue envelope, the types that usually contained some sort of legal *writ*. Before he could move from behind the door, a hurricane-force wind appeared out of nowhere—except Twila and I knew exactly where it had come from—and the driver's door slammed shut on Hoof.

Unfortunately, Hoof's head was just a little higher than the door window. The top of it hit him directly on the Adam's apple. The point of impact effectively cut off his scream of pain, and the blue envelope went flying as he tried to push the door outward.

"Shit," I echoed Twila. "Look at that warrant go."

She chuckled as we watched the envelope fly high in the air, then land behind the horse tied at the farthest railing. As though the horse were in on the fun, it took that moment to lift its tail and drop a huge, steaming pile of dung on top of the warrant.

Hoof didn't notice; he was too busy trying to shout something. And every one of us knew exactly what he wanted to scream: a call for help. Yet for several seconds, not one person made a move toward the patrol car. Hoof's face reddened, and I realized he had to be gasping for breath. The door was pushing on his chest, the window strangling him.

"We can't let this happen," I said to Jack, then rushed forward, hoping like heck some of the others would follow me. Luckily, they did.

Or I thought it was lucky at first. The cone of hurricane force wind wasn't that wide, and it was centered on the door. I saw immediately that I needed to get on the other side of Hoof, where there was at least a opening to pry on. I rushed around the patrol car, three Amish men following me. Shoving my hands in the door gap, I pulled as hard as I could while I stared into Hoof's panic-stricken eyes.

The door didn't even move a scant inch, and my fingers burned and throbbed with my effort. One of the men gently pushed me aside and slipped his hands into the gap instead. Another man joined him, and they pulled. The third man scooted down the side of the patrol car and managed to stick a foot in the gap. He pushed, the other two pulled.

Then they pushed and pulled some more. The door didn't budge.

Hoof's face was now white, his lips tinged blue. Not envelope blue, but dark blue, lack of oxygen blue.

Quit it, Patches! I mentally shouted at the ghost. *You're gonna kill him!*

I don't care! Patches said back to me. *They can't execute me. I'm already dead.*

Twila joined me and the two of us opened our senses and tried to locate Patches. A gurgle sounded in Hoof's throat.

"There." Twila pointed at the trunk of the car, where I could now see Patches sitting cross-legged, a glare of anger on his face.

Twila stepped around the men still struggling to open the door before it killed Hoof. She didn't even hesitate when she got close to Patches. She pulled a protection packet out of her skirt pocket and showed it to him.

Patches only sneered at her and moved a few inches away. *He ain't takin' my Janie to jail!*

By the time the last word left his mind, Twila had untied the ribbon around the protection packet.

At first, I thought she wasn't going to need it, because Granny walked over to the car just then. She stuck her walking stick behind the window beside Hoof's neck, then said, "Couple of you strong men grab hold of my stick."

They grasped what she wanted them to do, and two of the men placed their hands on the stick and jerked. The window shattered into the small pieces of safety glass, as it was designed to do. Hoof collapsed over the door, and the men returned their attention to trying to pull it loose from his unconscious body.

Dang it, Patches said. *But they still gotta get him out of the door.*

Turn him loose! Twila ordered.

I ain't gonna do it! Patches snarled.

Oh yes you are! Twila exposed the little plastic pouch inside the outer layer of purple material in her hand. The plastic held the herbs and salt we consecrated and blessed. She ripped a hole in that with her fingernail, poured the contents into her hand, and tossed everything at Patches.

The wind Patches had conjured up was still directed at the car door, so nothing interfered with Twila's pitch. Patches screamed in agony, a sound I knew everyone there heard, not just Twila and me. The entire tableau froze...except for the men trying to pry the door open. The wind died abruptly as they strained, and they flew backwards when the door that freed Hoof.

The sheriff tumbled into the car, and Twila and I rushed over. I nearly stumbled over the man I'd forgotten was lying on the ground, but he scooted out of my way and scrambled to his feet.

For a second, the men eyed Twila and me as though we'd dropped into their midst from a space ship. "Wha...who...." one started to say. "Was that one of you ladies screaming?"

"No," I answered.

"Then who?" he demanded. Seeming to remember he was male and lord over a female, he propped his hands on his waist and tapped his foot as he waited for my response.

Irritated at his high-handedness, I said, "Just a ghost. The ghost of Janie's uncle."

His face whitened under his farmer's tan. and he and the other men left without another word. I leaned in the car and unbuttoned Hoof's shirt, so hopefully he could breathe better.

"Thank goodness he *is* still breathing," I told Twila. Then I patted his cheek to try to get his attention. His head wobbled on his bruised neck. "Maybe someone better call 9-1-1, though."

"I already called," Jack said from beside me. "Let me in there, *Chère*. We need to get him out and lying flat."

I backed away to stand with Twila and let Jack take over. Noah and another man joined him, and they eased the sheriff out.

Granny joined Twila and me, saying, "He don't looks so good. Wish I had me some of my cousin's remedy with me."

"Remedy?" I asked inattentively. One of the women had brought a blanket out, and she spread it on the ground so the men could lay Hoof on it. Off in the distance, I heard a siren.

"It's what he makes in his still," Granny said. "But it's so pure and tasty, I wouldn't be surprised iffen it didn't raise the dead."

"He's not dead, Granny," I said. "Oh, lord, he has to be all right."

Twila tugged my arm. "Come with me. You, too, Granny."

She led us down the driveway to my car. Just as we reached it, the ambulance roared into the driveway. The idiot driver didn't have sense enough to kill the siren, and several of the buggy horses reared frantically, pulling against the reins hitched to the wooden crossbars. The horse in front of where the warrant had landed stepped repeatedly in its pile of manure. I doubted anyone would be able to rescue that piece of legal nonsense now.

Men quickly left the circle around where Hoof laid on the ground and hurried over to calm the horses.

"You'd think a person living 'round here would know not to use a darned si-reen 'round horses," Granny muttered.

"At least that ruckus will make sure there's enough going on over there to keep them occupied while we do what we have to," Twila said.

"And what's that?" I asked. "Off the top of my head, I'd say we need to discipline ourselves a ghost."

"Exactly," Twila said. "He's got to understand he can't go around trying to kill people. Not that he can, but he can set up situations that will hurt someone badly. Which he just did. He thinks he can escape any punishment because he's already dead, but I've got news for him. I won't allow stuff like that in an instance where my friends are involved. He's going to have to be taken to task and reprimanded. But we have to find him first."

"We might need Free Eagle for that," I said.

"I'm in, too."

Twila lifted her eyebrows in surprise when she realized Jess had walked over beside her. "Are you sure, honey?"

"Yep," Jess said with a nod. "All this is happening because Patches wants to talk to me. Right?"

"Well, yes," Twila told him.

"Then it's time for me to end this mess," Jess told her. "I'm going with you to find that rascal buddy of mine. Find out what's so high on important that he's gotta talk to me after he's dead."

"You mean you don't know?" I asked Jess. "I assumed you were aware of what Patches wanted."

He shook his head. "Patches left a will, and I know what's in it because he asked me to be a witness. He wants the shop and land sold, Janie to get the money. There ain't nothing about that to cause a commotion over. Leastwise, nothing like what he's been up to."

"Let's get back home then," Twila said. "See if we can round us up some ghosts and figure out what's going on."

A disturbance over by the ambulance caught our attention. Hoof had evidently regained consciousness, and he was slapping at the hands of the paramedic who tried replace the oxygen mask on his face and keep him on the stretcher.

"Leave me alone," he said in a raspy voice. "I've got a warrant to serve!"

He pushed himself off the stretcher and nearly collapsed before the paramedic grabbed him.

"Sheriff," the paramedic said. "We're just trying to do what's best for you. You're in bad shape."

"Not that bad," Hoof denied. He managed to stand upright and glare at the men and women who had gathered around the ambulance. They all moved a few steps back to distance themselves from his malevolent look. "I'm here to make a legal arrest."

I hurried over to where Janie stood with Noah and whispered, "Make sure you ask him again for the warrant."

Noah pushed Janie gently at me, and I wrapped an arm around the young woman's waist. Stepping in front of both of us, Noah said, "Ye still haven't shown us that warrant, Sheriff."

Hoof wobbled away from the ambulance, toward his patrol car. He managed to make it there without falling, then stopped and stared at the damage to his door.

"Who the hell did this?" he demanded.

Unfortunately, Granny had neglected to retrieve her walking stick after the men used it to shatter the window. Hoof picked it up and shook it toward the crowd.

Granny walked over to Hoof and said, "That's my stick. And iffen it weren't for it, you'd probably be lying in that there ice house next to Patches!"

Hoof scoffed a grunting laugh. "I'd be in a proper funeral home," he said, then seemed to realize the ridiculousness of his comment. He pointed at the stick with his free hand. "This was used to damage a law enforcement vehicle. That's a crime."

Granny held out her wrists. "Then go ahead and take me in. And while youse at it, call me one of them there criminal lawyers. Iffen you ain't got one good enough for me here, I got a half-dozen grandkids who's lawyers down in Texas."

"They wouldn't be licensed to practice law here," Hoof said, but I noticed he didn't reach for the handcuffs he'd replaced on his belt at some point.

"They can get some of that there reciprocity," she said. "Just 'cause I'm old don't mean I don't know a little bit about the law."

"Yeah," Hoof muttered. "You watch CSI on TV."

"Yep," Granny said, shaking her wrists at him to get his attention.

Instead, Hoof handed her the walking stick and turned to search inside his car. After a brief few seconds, he stood up and said, "I remember now. I had that warrant in my hand when I started to get out of the car."

Twila and I grinned at each other, and she beat me to the punch as she hurried over to stand beside Granny. "The wind picked up the warrant," she said. "I know where it landed, if you want me to show you."

"Damn right I do," Hoof said.

I couldn't bear to miss this, and I quietly joined the other interested people who trailed along as Twila walked towards the buggies, where men still stood calming the horses. Hoof followed Twila down the line until she halted on the far side of the last horse. Just as Twila started to point at it, that horse calmly lifted its tail and deposited more steaming manure on top of the pile already behind its rear legs.

I was close enough to see that a small corner of blue still showed beneath the horse dung.

"Uh..." Twila said, struggling to get actual words out past her dammed up laughter. "Uh...the warrant landed down there on the ground."

Perhaps the lack of oxygen still clouded Hoof's mind. He actually bent toward the manure and reached for the corner of the warrant before he seemed to realize what he was doing. He drew back and stared at the crowd.

"Who owns this damn horse?" he snarled.

A man stepped forward. "It is mine. But if ye think I am gonna reach my hand into a pile of horse shit, ye best think again."

"I need that warrant! Your horse destroyed legal property!"

"I cannot help you, Sheriff," the man said. "Besides, my Brownie here does not like anyone messing around behind her. She has been known to kick hard enough to send a man to the doctor with a broken bone."

"Oh, fiddle-de-dee," a woman said from behind the man. "Brownie doesn't hurt me when I help you harness her."

The man looked at the chubby woman who had said that. "And that is exactly why ye put the harness on the rear end of her," he said with a smile. Then he reached for the water bucket she held in her hand. "Now, Lydia, you are not supposed to be lifting right now."

When he said that, I noticed the woman must be with child instead of plump, as her protruding stomach indicated. Another look made me re-think her age. She had at first appeared in her forties, but on closer examination, she could have been much younger.

"Oh, pooh, Samuel," she responded. "I was afraid Brownie might be thirsty. But now I think the water might be useful elsewise."

Without another word, she bent down and grabbed the corner of blue. She drew it out from beneath the manure, then immediately dunked it into the pail of water.

"Don't!" Hoof said.

Lydia pulled the sodden warrant out and tossed it to him.

"Sorry, Mr. Sheriff," she said with a wicked grin as the warrant landed on his shirt. There were still traces of manure on it, and Hoof distastefully batted it to the ground again.

"I believe ye need a readable warrant to be able to serve it on some-one," Noah said. He took Janie's hand and led her to another one of the buggies. "When you get such a thing, you can come back and see us again."

"You bet your ass I will!" Hoof shouted as he shook his fist at Noah. Noah disregarded him and helped Janie into the buggy. Then he untied the horse and climbed in after her. A few moments later, the buggy carrying the two of them disappeared down the driveway.

Hoof was already back at his patrol car, leaving the warrant on the ground. He opened the door and bent in to wipe at the seat. Little round pieces of safety glass scattered on the ground beside the car. When he was satisfied he wouldn't cut his rear end, he slid in the car, started the engine, and roared off down the driveway.

"Huh," Granny said. "He makes me want to make a citizen's arrest for him speedin' like that."

Jack chuckled. "I don't think there's a speed limit on a driveway, Granny."

"Should be," she said with an emphatic nod of her head.

"I agree with Granny," Twila put in. "But now we need to get back to the house and see what we can do about Patches."

Suddenly my stomach woke up and growled. However, I knew that no matter how longingly I thought about Granny's bread pudding on that laden table inside the farmhouse, Twila wouldn't let me take time to grab a bowl. I was right, too. She herded me and Granny toward my car, leaving Jack and Jess to follow.

"Where's Mikala?" I asked before I got behind the wheel.

"She said she was going to stay with Mandy a while," Twila told me as she helped Granny into the backseat.

I was almost to the end of the driveway a few moments later when I had to stop and let Noah and Janie's buggy pass me.

"Why are they back—?" I started to say, then laughed. "Oh, they live here. They must have been getting a jab at Hoof when they left. Showing him they knew their rights and weren't going to let him restrain them."

Twila winked at me, and Granny collapsed in cackles.

CHAPTER 18

Trucker, Miss Molly and Harley met us when we pulled up behind Twila's house. Like me, Twila had a doggy/kitty door on her back mud porch, or perhaps hers was a doggy/kitty/piggy door. The pets didn't seem resentful about being somewhat neglected since we'd brought them back from the Grassman encampment. They all three greeted each and every one of us, then Harley nudged Trucker on the rump as though tagging him "next," and the three of them raced off across the yard.

I carefully studied the woods behind Twila's home, wondering if perhaps Bob might bring Rascal to play. I knew Twila wouldn't care, but Jess kept an arsenal of guns, and I wasn't sure if Twila had told him about our adventure with the legendary supposed-monsters. We'd been so inundated with ghost situations, there hadn't been much time to make sure everyone was updated on the various threads developing all around us.

In the years we'd lived next door to each other in Six Gun, Granny had come to know me nearly as well as Twila. In the kitchen, I poured all of us glasses of iced tea, and as I set them on the table, Granny added bowls of her bread pudding. She'd evidently made an extra pan for

Twila's house, and must have heated the Jack Daniel's sauce in the microwave. Steam rose from the luscious dessert.

Jack, Jess, Twila and Granny started discussing what they were going to do in order to find Patches, but I surreptitiously blew on a spoonful of pudding. I kept my glass of tea close in case I made the mistake of gobbling it down before it cooled enough not to burn my tongue. However, the pudding was just right, and I dug in for another bite. As I lifted it to my mouth, I peered around the table at eight eyeballs trained on me.

I left them staring until after I swallowed that delicious morsel before I asked, "What?"

Twila laughed. "We should know better than to try to discuss something with you when you're eating bread pudding."

"It's my favorite dish in the whole world," I said with a nod of agreement. "Especially Granny's. You don't know what you're missing."

"My allergy to eggs keeps me from concurring with you," Twila said. "And now that I have your attention, I'll repeat our question. Do you think you could get Hoof to tell you what evidence he's got against Janie? While we try to contact Patches?"

"What?" I asked. "By myself? If I'm understanding you right, you want me to see if I can flirt with him and get him to release confidential information."

I glanced at Jack, whom I hoped might negate that idea right off the bat. After all, we were trying to become a couple again.

Or we were before we had that fight back in Six Gun.

A fight I'd been thinking was totally stupid and hoping might be behind us now.

"I think I should be the one to handle Hoof," Jack said, and my heart actually warmed.

"You'd be bound by your law enforcement ethics," Twila explained. "Even if you're out of your jurisdiction, you wouldn't feel right sharing information another cop considered confidential."

"There is that," Jack agreed. "But sometimes a guy's gotta weigh both sides of a situation."

Granny rose and said, "Y'all can handle things for a while by your-selves. I think I'll go on up and take me a little nappy-poo."

"Have a nice one," I said to her as she left the kitchen.

"Yes, do that," Twila added. Then she asked, "Are we tiring Granny out too much?"

"I don't think so," I assured her. "She takes a couple naps a day down home. She hates to miss anything, but she knows when she needs to take care of herself."

"Good," Twila said. "We'll check on her in a little bit."

I nodded agreement, then dug back into my bread pudding.

Suddenly we heard Harley squeal from outside. Not one of his playful sounds, either. This one sounded as though the pig might be in distress.

Jess was the first one out of the kitchen, and he grabbed a double-barreled shotgun left sitting by the mud room screen door. I was the last one in line. What I saw when I reached the backyard made me stifle a laugh instead of hurrying back inside to dial 9-1-1.

Of course, I realized vets weren't included in that emergency network. So while Jess untangled Harley from a bundle of rope one of the animals must have dragged out of the barn to play with, I went back inside to my pudding.

Twila's phone was ringing when I entered the kitchen. I glanced back out to see her helping Jess, so I reached for the cordless receiver. She and I were at home in each other's houses.

"Hello?"

At the same moment, my cell phone rang. I saw it on the countertop, where I'd plugged it in to charge before we went to Janie's. I lunged for it as I inattentively listened to what someone on the phone at my ear was saying. "Keep your nose outta things that could get your ass in trouble!"

I checked the cell phone display in order to decide whether or not I should answer that, then grabbed it and swiped the screen to accept the call. Before I could push the speaker button to ask Hoof to wait a minute, it dawned on me what I'd heard on Twila's phone.

Ignoring the cell phone, I said into the receiver, "Who the heck is this? What are you doing calling here threatening my aunt?"

But the line was already dead. I held the receiver in front of me to see the display, but the screen had already gone dark. I poked at the little arrows until the incoming number was displayed. That didn't do me any good, since it said *Blocked*.

I grabbed the cell phone, but that call had already gone to voice mail. Biting my lip in indecision, I tried to decide whether or not to call the others back in. However, before I reached the mud porch, Trucker and Miss Molly came through the pet door.

At first, I thought they were going to head for their food and water dishes. Instead, they sat down just inside the kitchen. Trucker appeared to be watching something.

I realized what it had to be when Jack's suit coat rose from the back of the chair he'd been sitting in. Some darn ghost had managed to avoid my senses and snuck into the house while I was busy with the phones! Whoever it was had probably caused the disturbance outside, entangling poor Harley and hoping the distraction would clear the kitchen to make his raid.

Because I realized who this had to be.

"Walking Bear," I ordered sternly, "put that coat down!"

The coat never wavered. The only thing I noticed was a bulge in the pocket I'd slipped the cookies into. Then the napkin-wrapped bundle of cookies came into sight.

I stomped over and grabbed the cookies. "Walking Bear," I said again. "You're being a naughty boy!"

The ghost whimpered and I could see a faint outline of him. Both Trucker and Miss Molly joined me, one sitting on each side. I hoped their presences didn't mean they sensed danger from this entity, but I needed to concentrate on the ghost.

"It's O.K. for you to let me see you," I told Walking Bear. "I'm not going to punish you. In fact, I'll let you have one cookie to show you I'm not a mean person."

I held a cookie out. When Walking Bear reached for it, he forgot to maintain his invisibility, an invisibility he must have been able to hone over the years to the point where he'd slipped past my senses. Too, I defended myself, I'd been distracted.

Walking Bear looked the same as when he'd appeared on the porch, asking me for the cookies he seemed to have acquired a taste for. He wasn't carrying his bow this time, or so I thought at first. I saw it tied to the arrow quiver on his back.

I handed him the cookie, reminding myself this ghost might be hard to handle, were he antagonized rather than manipulated with kindness and my supposed resemblance to the long-ago woman who had befriended him.

"There you go," I said in a soft voice as he took the cookie.

I knew for a fact ghosts couldn't eat, so I wasn't surprised when he only held the cookie beneath his nose and seemed to breathe in the delicious smell. Of course, ghosts couldn't breathe, but one or two had told me over the years that they retained their sense of smell. Female ghosts even often carried an odor of their favorite perfume with them.

"Now," I said to Walking Bear, "won't you sit down and talk to me for a moment? It's been a while since you saw me, hasn't it?"

I wasn't referring to the brief visit on the porch. Instead, I hoped he would continue to mistake me for the Amish woman over three centuries ago and not take off running now that he had his treat.

I wasn't the one who startled him, though. Harley barreled in through the pet door, his tiny hoofs clicking across the wooden back porch slats and the linoleum kitchen floor. He skidded to a halt beside Trucker, and Walking Bear dropped the cookie. In one fluid motion, he had the bow in his hands and an arrow notched, aimed at Harley.

Trucker beat me to the defense of his new friend. He roared a challenge and attacked the ghost. Of course, he leaped straight through him, and I stepped in front of the arrow, glaring at Walking Bear.

"No!" I ordered. "You will not shoot this pig!"

Walking Bear frowned as Trucker ran around him and sat by my side, his mouth set in a snarl that matched the noise coming from his throat, his vicious fangs exposed.

"M-m-meat," Walking Bear insisted.

"No," I repeated. "This pig is a pet. You can't eat him." I patted Harley on his bristly head. The pig didn't appear to realize it was being threatened. It was enjoying friendship licks from Miss Molly. I realized she was licking the pig to show Walking Bear this wasn't a meal on the hoof.

Walking Bear sighed and replaced his bow, then shoved the arrow back into the quiver. I bent down and handed him the cookie from the floor. Since he couldn't eat it anyway, it didn't matter if it had picked up a few germs. Not that Twila would tolerate a germ living on any surface in her house. The ghost smiled at me as he lifted the cookie to his nose again.

"Now, sit down and let's visit," I told Walking Bear.

"He does not have time for a visit."

I jerked around to see Free Eagle a few feet from us and pointed a finger at him. "You keep quiet. Your brother evidently hasn't seen fit to talk to you in a long while. So let me handle this."

Free Eagle sighed, but he looked over at his brother and said, "I have missed you, Walking Bear. If you would rather speak with Alice, I will leave you alone for your visit."

"A-a-alice?" Walking Bear said. "N-no. R-Ruth."

I certainly didn't want him to leave right now, so I said, "I'm Ruth," and gave Free Eagle another stern look that promised reprisal if he kept insisting on my true identity. "Walking Bear loves my *Lebkuchen* cookies." I gazed at Walking Bear again and said, "Don't you like my cookies?"

He nodded and held the cookie to his nose.

I started wondering why the others hadn't come inside when Harley did, but all I could do was hope they recognized what was going on and left me alone for my *visit*. There were glasses of tea still on the table, and I pulled out the chair where Twila had sat.

"I can get you some milk if you would rather have it than tea," I said to Walking Bear as he sat down.

"M-milk," he said with a nod.

"Would it be all right if I sat down, too, my brother?" Free Eagle asked in a soothing tone of voice rather than in the confrontational manner he had used a moment ago.

Walking Bear must have indicated agreement, because as I went to the refrigerator, Free Eagle finger-motioned one of the other chairs out from the table. Instead of watching the by-play between the two brothers, though, I glanced out into the back yard, trying to see what the others were up to. I didn't see hide nor hair of anyone.

The pets had all wandered over to their food and water bowls to fill their bellies after all their exercise. I poured Walking Bear's milk and carried it to the table. Then I sat down to join him and Free Eagle.

Walking Bear did the same with the milk as the cookie: he held it up to his nose.

"It's nice, cold milk," I said. "You can still imagine drinking it, can't you?"

"M-magine?" he asked with a frown at me, then back at his glass.

Uh oh. How was I going to get out of this? Surely he realized he was dead and couldn't eat, didn't he? But if not, and I insisted he had indeed died, would he deny it and flee? Be afraid I would try to bury him, cover him with dirt?

Instead, I decided on another path to the conversation. "Imagine is a word that means remembering. It's sort of like when you dream. You imagine things in your dreams, don't you?"

I had no idea whether or not ghosts dreamed, but evidently they did. Walking Bear smiled and nodded a yes, then picked up the cookie to smell. Unfortunately, when he laid the cookie back down to transfer his attention to the milk, he placed it too close to the table edge. Before I could make a grab for it, it fell on the floor.

Harley had left his food bowl to see if any crumbs escaped the tabletop. He gobbled up the cookie in a flash.

"No!" Walking Bear jumped to his feet, an arrow notched in his bow.

Maybe it was the ghost's scream of anger that warned Harley he was in danger. The pig took off out of the kitchen like he had a butcher on his tail. I scrambled to my feet and swiped at the bow. Of course, my hand went straight through it, and Walking Bear released the arrow without its aim being knocked off kilter. The arrow missed Harley, though, and hit the door jamb, where it shivered from the impact for a second, then disappeared.

Trucker had seen the ambush on his friend, and he must have forgotten how his earlier attack ended. He lunged at Walking Bear before I could reach for his collar. Once again, my dog went through the ghost.

Miss Molly was pissed at Walking Bear assaulting Harley, too. She leaped onto the table with a cat-hiss of rage and launched herself at the ghost. She didn't meet any resistance either, and ended up on the floor.

"Tell your animals to cease their attacks on my brother," Free Eagle demanded as Walking Bear stood there with a puzzled expression on his face.

I didn't like the threatening tone in Free Eagle's voice, and I whirled on him. "Or what? If you try to harm even a hair on Trucker or Miss Molly, you'll wish you'd never been born!"

He huffed himself up, his chest protruding. "I have been born and I have even died. I have also gained knowledge during this death existence. He is my brother. I have spoken a vow to protect him."

I waved at Walking Bear. "Does he look like he's being hurt?" In fact, when I gazed at the ghost and then tried to locate my pets, I saw both Trucker and Miss Molly sitting side-by-side a few feet away from Walking Bear. They were staring at him, he was staring back at them.

Walking Bear pointed at Miss Molly. "W-what is t-that?"

"A cat," I explained. "Haven't you ever seen a cat?"

He shook his head, and I bent down to pick up Miss Molly. At first I thought she might order me to set her back down, and follow that demand up with an ultimatum that included her sharp claws. She only turned those blue eyes of hers on Walking Bear and settled in my arm.

I stroked Miss Molly's head as I said, "See? She's a nice cat."

The ghost tentatively reached out a hand, and Miss Molly stiffened a bit in my hold. On the floor, Trucker growled low, but only as a warning. He trained his brown eyes resolutely on the arm reaching for his life-long buddy.

Miss Molly shivered a bit, as I did, from the coldness surrounding the ghost's hand, but otherwise tolerated his touch. He pulled back, a surprised look replacing the puzzlement on his face.

"S-soft," he said.

"Yes," I agreed, setting my beloved cat back on the floor so she could join her protective companion. "Now, would you like to visit some more?"

He glanced away from me at Free Eagle. "B-brother wants me to walk into light. But light scares me. They might p-put me in the ground over there."

Free Eagle started to speak, but I motioned him to silence. "They won't put you in the ground," I promised, and continued, "Has your brother told you that you will find all the friends and family you love on the other side of The Light? The ones who are missing from your life now?"

"Y-yes," the ghost agreed. "And I am l-lonely now."

"I'll bet you are," I said. "Would you like me to help you cross over instead of your brother?"

"I do not k-know," he said. "I n-need a cookie so I can t-think about the light."

I'd laid the napkin-wrapped cookies on top of the refrigerator when I got the milk out, and I walked over and took one more out of the package. As I handed it to Walking Bear, I realized I had interrupted a conversation between him and Free Eagle.

"...we can see Mother and Father, and I can be with Moon Dove again."

Walking Bear took the cookie, lifted it to his nose, then gazed adoringly at me. "R-Ruth will go with us?"

"Ruth cannot because she is still a—"

"Ruth has to bake more cookies," I interrupted.

It was too late. Walking Bear stuck out his lower lip in a pout. "I will n-not go without Ruth!"

He disappeared, and somehow he was able to make sure the cookie went with him.

"Darn it," I fumed at Free Eagle. "Now see what you've done."

He scowled fiercely at me, but was also gone in a flash.

I sat down and pulled my bowl of pudding over to finish while I waited for the others. I'd only eaten two more spoons full, though, when Harley raced through the pet door and halted in the kitchen doorway.

"Oink, oink!"

I could have sworn I heard a distress call in his tone, and evidently Trucker and Miss Molly did, also. They both tore across the floor and flew through the pet door after the pig.

I started to take the pudding with me as I followed them, then thought better of it and set the bowl on the counter as I went onto the mud porch. Hurriedly, I pushed open the screen door and looked around for the animals, as well as Twila and the others. I didn't see a sign of anyone.

I rushed across the yard toward the barn, then hesitated, wondering if they'd gone in there or perhaps out into the woods. There were so many ghosts and creatures in this adventure Twila and I found ourselves involved in, I couldn't decide which trail to follow.

Then the three animals appeared in the barn door, so I started that way. However, the sound of a vehicle driving into the yard halted me again, and I groaned under my breath.

* * *

Walking Bear actually allowed Free Eagle to catch up to him this time. Perhaps it was because his brother was crying and upset, unable to clearly see where he was going. He was already back by the woods, though, and Free Eagle tentatively placed an arm around his shoulders. His brother allowed it and halted, sniffing sorrowfully.

"I am sorry I upset you," Free Eagle said. "It is not a nice thing for us to be as we are. Do you not think you would be happier if we went where we could be with those we loved when we were alive?"

Walking Bear looked at him with a tear-filled gaze. "W-we are dead?"

Free Eagle hesitated a moment, then nodded a yes. "It happens to everyone," he said in a quiet voice. "And when it does, we can see those who have gone before us, if we just follow the path to the land where our ancestors are now."

"Bu-but you said R-Ruth...that is not R-Ruth in that house, is it?" He turned to gaze back at the white farmhouse.

"No," Free Eagle said as he squeezed his brother's shoulder. "But we will be able to find Ruth in the land of our ancestors, if you will go with me."

"How do we do th-that?" Walking Bear asked.

"The door is in the East," Free Eagle told him. "We need to go that way."

They started to walk into the woods, but suddenly Free Eagle halted and turned around. "I think we better wait a minute. That man driving up to the house down there is the one we saw where they were honoring my new friend Patches' life. I do not like him."

"He will n-not hurt the one who l-looks like R-Ruth, will he?"

"We will wait and see."

CHAPTER 19

Hoof drove his patrol car near me before he parked. But since Trucker woofed at me and disappeared back into the barn, Miss Molly and Harley joining him, I ignored Hoof when he stepped out of the car and called, "Alice, can you take a little time off and join me for a root beer float?"

I'd loved those floats growing up, and I wasn't sure how he'd found that out. But I shook my head and waved a distracted "no" as I rushed on into the barn.

Inside the door, something grabbed my arm. I let out a shriek and flew into a frenzy, hitting and kicking at whatever it was. This case was getting to me, and I wasn't about to put up with one of the entities we were dealing with trying to capture me.

Whoever it was had more experience than I did. He jerked me back against him and covered my mouth with a broad hand. A broad male hand. And I immediately recognized the smell of Jack.

"Shhh, shhh, shhh, *Chère*," he whispered in my ear. "They've got Patches in the old tack room, trying to get him to talk to Jess."

I relaxed in his arms and said quietly but in a harried tone, "Then why did the animals bring me out here? I think there's something going on back there that Twila needs me for."

Just then, Hoof entered the barn, calling, "Alice? Hey, Alice, where'd you go?"

"Crap," I said softly. "Maybe he'll leave if he can't find me."

But Hoof walked on deeper into the barn, calling my name every few steps.

"You better get him out of here," Jack said as he dropped his arms.

I didn't have to, though. All three of the animals rushed toward Hoof. A huge dog and a large chubby pig appearing out of the dimness in the barn evidently startled the sheriff, let alone what hearing the screech Miss Molly let out did. Hoof turned and ran.

"Ah, shit," Jack said. "Let's get out there."

"The animals will run him off," I said.

"Not if he shoots them," Jack replied in a grim voice, already halfway to the barn door. Outside it, I heard him shout, "Hey, Harv! It's all right! I'll take care of the animals."

By the time I got out the door, blinking my eyes to adjust them again to the brightness, Hoof was standing by his car with the driver's door open. But he didn't have his gun out. Instead, he was staring at Harley, perched on the car hood. His tiny hoofs made slight indentations that popped right back out as he pranced around.

"How'd he get up there?" Jack asked as he reached the patrol car. Seeing that Jack had the situation under control, I stepped back into the dim recesses of the barn.

"That darn pig jumped right up on the dog's back, then climbed onto my car," Hoof said. "Get him off there, Roucheau. I've gotta go serve this new warrant."

Uh oh. Torn between heading deeper into the barn and waiting to make sure Hoof didn't try to harm Harley, I hesitated. Then I heard Twila's mental plea: *Alice, if you're hearing me, I could use some help back here.*

Huh? Twila asking for assistance? She must be involved in a desperate situation if she needed help from someone like me, who had less than half her experience. I took a step forward, then realized what I'd just heard outside. Hoof had said he was on his way to serve Janie again and take her to jail.

Hoping like heck Jack would take care of being there for Janie, I rushed on through the dark barn. I hadn't spent much time in here on my visits, but I did recall there was a room back there where the former owner had allowed a ranch hand he periodically hired to sleep. It hadn't been used since Twila and Jess bought the farm, so it was probably dirty and filled with spider webs and bird droppings. As I got closer to it, I could see the door was closed, but I heard voices inside.

"I ain't gonna talk to you until you get that meddling broad out of here!" That was Patches' voice, and he probably was referring to Twila. The little I knew of him had shown he wanted to talk to Jess in private. And with Granny napping, the only other woman who could possibly be in there—or broad, as he said—was Twila.

I knew Jess, though, and it didn't surprise me when he answered, "I ain't talking to you without her here. You're a damn ghost, Patches!"

"I know I'm a ghost. And I stayed back from that light and became a damned ghost so I could tell you a couple things you need to know. But they ain't something I want a broad to know."

"You call my wife a broad one more time and I'll walk out of here and never speak to you again. I don't care if we were pards when you were alive. She's my wife, and you'll treat her with respect. You don't hear me talking about your niece Janie like that, do you?"

"Speaking to Twila nice didn't get her out of here," Patches said in the same tone of voice. "You stand up to her and tell her to get out of men's business."

"I told you that no way in hell will I stay in here alone with a ghost. Twila's got lots more practice with your kind. She stays."

"My kind? Gosh darn it, Jess, I thought we were friends!"

"Were," Jess repeated. "You always knew how I felt about ghosts."

Alice? I heard.

I'm right outside the door, I replied. Twila and I hardly ever used this form of communication, because it was hard and we needed all our concentration in paranormal situations. Also, sometimes we would mis-read the other's mind. So I listened closely for her next remark.

...satchel in my bedroom closet.

I'd missed her first word or words, but we were close enough that my psychic senses picked up on what she wanted. Without hesitation, I whirled and raced back through the barn. A quick glance at the driveway as I ran through the back yard showed me Hoof was gone, and so was Jack's pickup. I'd been right in trusting Jack to take care of Janie.

As I ran through the house and to Twila and Jess's bedroom, my thoughts continued. Jack wouldn't interfere in an arrest, if Hoof did have another valid warrant. However, he could make sure Janie wasn't mistreated and got legal counsel as soon as possible.

Not that I thought Hoof would mistreat Janie. He really wasn't a bad person. Besides, he'd want the Amish vote in the fall.

I paused in the bedroom. Twila and Jess had separate closets, and I wasn't sure which one was hers. Thankfully, the first door I opened revealed Twila's clothing. Her satchel set right inside the door, and I picked it up and scanned the shelves above it to make sure there wasn't something else she might need. Instinct told me to grab the rope on the shelf, plus an extra canister of sea salt. Carrying everything with me, I raced out of the room.

Back in the barn, I halted. Someone had opened the door on that room a couple inches. I should have been able to clearly hear any conver-sation going on in there. However, I only heard silence. Tiptoeing forward, I bent close to listen.

I could also see part of the room through the gap. Patches was over in a far corner, standing beside a dusty chest of drawers. He had his arms crossed over his chest, a mutinous scowl on his face. I couldn't see Jess or Twila, but I heard someone breathing quietly beside the door.

"Twila?" I whispered.

"Shhhh," she said so softly I barely heard her. "Patches and Jess are in a standoff. Jess is over on the bed."

"What do you want me to do?"

"Did you bring the rope?"

"Yeah, and the satchel and an extra box of sea salt."

"Spread a circle of salt out there and put a seat inside it."

I set the satchel and rope down, then opened the canister of sea salt. Half a minute later, I had a large circle of salt spread, but I didn't see a chair anywhere. Surely Twila knew she didn't have any chairs in her barn.

Oh. She said "seat." I set the salt on the ground and went over to a bale of hay.

Those darn bales were heavy! I was sweating and my muscles ached by the time I dropped the hay in the middle of the circle. That would have to do, because I was sure Twila was already wondering what was taking me so long.

"Done," I whispered through the gap.

"Great." She raised her voice and said, "Jess, I think this conversation is over with, don't you?"

Bed springs creaked, indicating Jess had stood up. "Yeah, I do," Jess said. "Let's get out of here."

Twila shoved the door on open, but instead of stepping through herself, she waited. "Get the lasso ready," she whispered.

I had watched Twila use her consecrated lariat, but I'd never used it myself. Still, I'd do my best. I picked up the rope and shook out a loop, then stood back away from the door.

"You can go ahead, honey," she said to Jess. "I'll keep this old reprobate behind so he doesn't bother you."

Jess came through the door in a rush, just as Patches said, "Like heck you will, Twila. You stay out of my way. I don't want to hurt you."

Jess caught sight of me and the rope and, thankfully, understood what we were up to. He jumped behind the door as Patches flew through it. The ghost didn't even see the sea salt circle or the hay bale, He stopped inside the circle, though, and stared around the barn.

"Hey, Jess! Where'd you go?"

Twila emerged from the room as I whirled the lasso and threw it. I missed the hay bale, but the lariat landed well enough to encircle Patches inside its majik ring.

Patches looked down and sneered, then glanced up to see me standing in the shadows, holding the end of the rope. "You ain't got a lick of sense if you think you can lasso a ghost."

"You're wrong," Twila said as she took the rope from my hands. "I've spent a lot more time handling ghosts than you've been one. So the experience scale tips way over in my favor."

To me, she whispered, "Good job, Alice," then turned to face Patches. With an ease that must have taken hours of practice, she flipped the rope into the air. When it landed this time, both the ghost and the bale of hay were inside the circle.

"There," she said, tying the rope around one of the barn posts. "You've got a seat if you get tired. But you're not going anywhere until you tell us what you're hiding."

Patches snorted his disbelief. Then he rushed at Twila. As soon as he reached the rope, he bounced back as though someone had thrown him. He landed on the bale of hay and sat there, shaking his head.

"What'd you do?" he demanded of Twila.

"Both the rope and salt will keep you jailed until you get ready to talk to us," she told him. "Alice, you and Jess come on. Let's leave him here to think for a while."

Patches watched us in disbelief as we walked away. "Wait!" he called after a few seconds. "Wait! You can't do this to me!"

We ignored him and left the barn. Outside in the sunshine, I stopped.

"What are you going to do if someone sees a ghost captured in your barn?" I said to Twila with a laugh.

She chuckled. "We'll deal with that if it happens."

"Hoof was just here," I told the two of them. "I think Jack probably followed him when he drove off. Hoof said he had another warrant for Janie."

"Damn it to hell," Jess said. "That little girl wouldn't hurt a fly."

"Let me go leave Granny a note and tell her where we've gone," I said, but before I could start toward the house, the back door opened and Granny emerged.

219

"What's goin' on out here?" she asked. "All them cars comin' and goin' woke me up, so I guess there's somethin' happenin'."

"We'll explain as we drive, Granny," Twila said. "Who has a set of car keys?"

We were all still dressed in our funeral attire, so I was pretty sure neither she nor I had keys in our skirt pockets.

"I'll go get my purse while the rest of you get in my car," I said.

I found my purse in the kitchen, and as I started out the door, I noticed the message light on Twila's phone blinking. Rather than take the time to call her back in to check her messages, I punched in her passcode, since we both shared that info on our different phones, landlines and my cell.

"You have one message," the mechanical voice informed me, then went on to say, "First message."

After that, Janie's voice came on: "Twila, we've decided to go ahead and have Uncle Patches' burial this evening, in case I can't come to it tomorrow. I hope you get this message so you can all come."

"End of messages," the voice-mail woman said, and I replaced the receiver and ran out to my car.

"There was a message from Janie on your voice mail," I told Twila as I slid into the driver's seat.

She and Jess were in the backseat, and she leaned forward and asked, "What did she say?"

I started the engine as I told her about the change in the burial service.

"Then she'll be right where Hoof can find her," Twila said with a sigh.

"Uh..." I began, then glanced at the barn.

"Huh uh," she said with a stern shake of her head. "I'm not letting him loose to go to his funeral. He'll throw another fit and disrupt things again when Hoof serves that warrant."

"I agree," I said. "I just thought it was worth bringing up."

"We've got enough on our hands without that ghost causing another disturbance. At least we have one of the troublemakers corralled."

"Corralled," I said with a laugh as we drove down the driveway. "Yep, he's corralled all right."

Free Eagle waited until Alice's car disappeared before he led Walking Bear out of the woods and across the pasture to the barn. The darkness didn't bother him, since he could see just as well as in daylight.

"I do not see anything in there," he told his brother. "But they were in this barn for a long time."

Walking Bear wandered on into the recesses, then called back, "I-I have found someone."

Free Eagle hurriedly joined him and ran his gaze around the lariat and salt circle before he looked at Patches. "What is this, my friend?"

Patches stood up from the hay bale. "I've gotta get outta this darn trap! Twila did it to me. See what you can do, will you?"

Free Eagle glided a tentative step toward the rope, but halted a good three feet back, shaking his head. "I cannot get any closer. What did you do to make your friend Jess's wife entrap you like this?"

Patches sighed. "I just told her to keep her nose out of men's business."

"I cannot see her doing this only because you said that," Free Eagle responded.

"Well...." Patches shook his head. "It was Jess, too. I need to talk to him alone, and Twila won't let me."

Free Eagle lifted an eyebrow, and Patches' shoulders dropped in defeat. "All right. Jess won't talk to me without Twila around."

"What is so important that you cannot tell your friend about it in front of his wife? I know of very little I would not speak of in front of Moon Dove." He grimaced. "If she will even talk to me now."

"W-why do you think M-Moon Dove will not speak to you?" Walking Bear asked.

Free Eagle stared at his brother, contemplating whether or not he could handle the truth. Now that they were together again, he did not want Walking Bear to leave in anger. It might take him another hundred years to find him.

"I w-wish to know, my brother," Walking Bear said.

"I fear she will be angry with me because I did not join her in the land of our ancestors for so long," he admitted.

Walking Bear hung his head. "B-because you w-waited for me."

Free Eagle pulled his brother close. With them both ghosts, it was good to be able to touch and hold him. "I do not regret it, Walking Bear. I would do it again. And you know Moon Dove cares for you, too. She will probably only be teasing with her anger."

"Look," Patches said. "You two can get all lovey-dovey later. For now, figure out some way to get me out of here."

Free Eagle drew himself up and glared at Patches. "I will not tolerate you taking my beloved's name in disrespect like that."

"Ah, crap," Patches said. "That ain't what I meant. You just don't understand English."

"I understand your tone and manner," Free Eagle snarled. "You can find your own way out of your trouble."

Arm still around his brother, he took him with him as they dissolved.

"Wait! I'm sorry!" he heard Patches call. But he ignored him.

There was a small waterfall near one of the trails he had used when he lived. He and Walking Bear settled on a fallen tree there to watch the silvery water cascade down the side of a rock cliff in the hillside. Already there were a few flowers growing in the fertile soil around the falls; wood violets, he recalled Moon Dove calling them.

Although he had never for one moment forgotten his wife, his memories seemed to be growing stronger now that he and his brother were close again. He actually bent and picked one of the violets and held it close to his face so he could smell the delicate scent.

"M-Moon Dove l-liked those," Walking Bear said.

"Yes," Free Eagle agreed.

"We can s-see her now?"

"We have to find the light," Free Eagle said, inattentively sticking the violet into the leather pouch hanging from the belt across his chest. "We can go through it and—"

"No!" Walking Bear stood up from the log. "I do n-not want to go into l-light. It scares me. They c-can come to us."

Free Eagle stood and tried to keep his irritation out of his voice. "Do not be foolish."

He knew immediately he had used the wrong word. In life. he had fought several battles with another child who dared call Walking Bear a fool. But this time when Walking Bear shot him a disbelieving look in response to his careless and hurtful words, then disappeared, Free Eagle went right after him. He would not lose his brother again.

CHAPTER 20

"Where's Jack?" Granny asked me from the passenger seat beside me.

"I think he followed Hoof," I told her. "The sheriff got a new warrant and was going after Janie again."

Surprising me, though, I saw Jack's pickup travelling towards us within seconds of pulling out of Twila's drive. We both braked our vehicles, but he was already past me. Jack knew me well enough to understand him backing up would be the better choice. My skills at navigating a car in reverse were well known to be lacking. Since I didn't want to end up in one of the water-filled ditches along the road, I waited where I'd stopped.

Jack already had his window rolled down when he stopped beside my car, as I did. "Hoof got a call as he was getting back in his car to leave Twila and Jess's," he told us. "He said there was a burglary in progress at a house over by the county line. He figured he better get by there and make sure his deputies didn't need help. He didn't figure Janie would be running anywhere."

Jess leaned forward in the backseat. "Are you sure that's where he headed?"

"Yeah," Jack said with a nod. "I followed him a ways. He drove right past the Yoders."

"Well, we got a phone call from Janie," I told him. "She said the burial was going to be this evening. She's afraid they'll arrest her before she can see Patches to his final rest."

"I'll follow you there," Jack said.

Before I could shift back into drive, one of the back doors on my hybrid opened. In the rear view mirror, I saw Jess get out and walk over to the passenger side of Jack's truck.

"We'll see you at the Yoders," Jack said as he drove away to find a place to turn around.

I let off the brake and drove on down the road. "You'd swear we were Amish," I said with as much teasing as I could force into my tone, given we were on the way to a funeral. "Men separating from women."

Twila chuckled. "When you've been together as long as Jess and I have, you understand when a man needs to be with another man even more than his wife."

I didn't even try to respond to that truth. Instead, I mentally counted up how long I'd known Jack, and ended up with five years. We'd married way too soon after we met, a bare three months. But we'd been so much in love, there didn't seem to be any reason to wait. He asked me and I said yes. That was that.

The marriage lasted two years, and it had been well over two years since our divorce. Adding in the four months lately when we'd been trying to see give our relationship another chance, I had close to five years.

Even if we did get married again, we would never be able to count as many years together as Twila and Jess. I sighed as I flipped on my blinker and turned into the Yoder's driveway. Jack's truck followed me, so he must have been able to turn around quickly. When I halted after the last buggy at the fence, he parked behind me.

Our men didn't ignore us in favor of their friendship when we were a foursome. Well, a five-some, counting Granny. Jack quickly helped

Granny out and joined me. Jess walked close to Twila as we went toward the large, two-story house where Janie and Noah resided.

Despite the fact the women and men were clearly separated in the two sets of pews in the Yoder's living room, Jess motioned Twila into a seat just inside the door. When he sat beside her, Twila started to scoot over so Jack and I could join her. But Jess took her arm and held her in place. He stood and indicated for Granny, Jack and me to go on past them to the center of the pew. Jess sat back down on the end of our group, next to the aisle, an escape route if he needed it. Twila and I both understood his reason for that: a result of his time in Vietnam.

After we were all settled, I leaned past Jack and said to Twila, "Should we have gone up to let Janie know we're here?"

"Probably," she replied quietly. "But we'll get a chance when we do the final viewing of the body."

I shuddered and peered past a dozen prayer-capped heads, just now realizing we were sitting on the women's side of the room. The casket sat in front of the pews, the sheet in place. I frowned as one of those dastardly writer's questions entered my mind. But this was one I didn't dare utter right now. I'd google it later. Unfortunately, Granny evidently noticed my puzzlement.

"Whatcha thinkin' 'bout, Alice?" she whispered. "Them there gears in your brain's grindin' so loud I can hear 'em."

"Well...." I leaned close and made sure she had her hearing aid in before I whispered, "They've had that body in the ice house for a while now."

"Oh," she said with a sage nod. "You're wonderin' iffen poor Patches is gonna start smellin' soon."

One of the women in the pew in front of us turned around and said, "Shhhhh. Bishop is getting ready to start talking."

A black-clad man walked to the front of the room. I decided to drop my inquiry to Granny for now. She probably didn't know any more than I did. Instead, I started paying close attention, letting my writer's mind absorb this new experience, even on such a sad occasion.

Granny, however, wasn't intimidated by the command of a woman half her age. "I asked Mikala the same thing," she said in a low voice. The shoulders of the woman who had ordered her to be quiet stiffened, but she didn't turn back around. Up front, the Amish bishop was dallying for some reason, so Granny didn't actually interrupt him as she explained to me, "These here Amish do have some'un's body embalmed. See, it's the law, and they cain't get outta that. So dead folks go first to a funeral home. Old Patches has got nuf perserves in him to last 'til they can get him in the ground."

Perserves? I thought. *Oh, she meant preserves like in preservation, not jelly perserves like she calls those she makes.* I'd heard Granny use the same word, "perserves," when she talked about her jams and jellies. As soon as I figured that out, my stomach lurched. I'd eaten many a jar of Granny's perserves/preserves. To associate those delicious delicacies with what had been used in the body in the casket might taint my enjoyment for the rest of my life. And I did love them dearly.

Sometimes I wished I could turn my darned writer's mind off like a light bulb and just enjoy the moment.

Not at a funeral, of course.

Shut up, mind!

The Bishop cleared his throat and a respectful silence fell. Like these plain and simple people, the service was short and respectful. There were no songs or eulogies, only a reading from the story of Creation. It wasn't long before we all rose row-by-row to file past the casket and then murmur condolences to Janie, who sat with Noah and his family.

When the last person had paid his respects, the Bishop closed the coffin. Several men picked it up to carry it down the aisle between the pews.

I kept watch for Patches, even though I didn't think he could possibly escape the majik circle. Still, my vigilance only appeared to fuel my writer's mind. I couldn't help but wonder what it would be like to watch your own funeral. Maybe Patches would let me interview him later about how he felt at the wake. For research material, of course.

Then I mentally snorted at my audacity.

Everyone fell into line behind the coffin as it was carried out and loaded into the hearse buggy. Now there were numbers chalked on the sides of the buggies, and I assumed this indicated the order in which they were to follow the hearse. A number three was on my car, a two on Jack's pickup.

Twila noticed my glance and said, "Janie murmured to me inside that she asked for her uncle's closest friends to be at the head of the funeral procession, behind her buggy."

"Do you want to ride with Jess? You two can take my car."

"I think he'd just as soon have Jack with him," she replied at the same moment Janie approached us. Her eyes were red-rimmed and puffy with grief.

"I hope it was all right with the rest of you," she said. "My putting you behind mine and Noah's buggy."

Twila pulled her into a long embrace as she said, "Of course it is."

I caught Janie's worried gaze when she glanced at me over Twila's shoulder. "It's fine, Janie. Don't worry. We're here for you. And again, I'm very sorry for your loss." I took my turn hugging her. No sense intruding on her grief by explaining the trouble we were having with her uncle, even dead.

"Thank you," Janie said when she pulled back. She waited until she also hugged Granny before she asked softly, "Is my uncle here again?"

"No," Twila told her, which we both hoped wasn't a lie. "Or, if he is, he's being unobtrusive."

Janie nodded as she was joined by her handsome, bearded husband, Noah. I knew enough about the Amish culture to understand his beard meant he was married. Until marriage, all Amish men remained clean shaven. But afterwards they let their beards grow. Another interesting fact I'd stored away was that the women never cut their hair. However, since Janie had lived as an English most of her life, the part of the bun on the back of her head that showed where her prayer cap had ridden up didn't protrude as much as on the other women.

"Thank you for being here for my Janie," Noah said.

"We're glad to do it," Twila responded.

"We'll see you all at the cemetery," Janie said as Noah took her arm to lead her to their buggy.

I frowned as I looked around for Jack and Jess, asking, "They don't have a church but they have a cemetery?"

"Yes," Twila said without further explanation.

Jack and Jess were walking towards the pickup, and they waited when they saw the three of us approach. I could tell Jess was stifling deep emotion, his eyes puffy as though he'd recently been crying. However, knowing him as well as I did, I didn't broach my sympathy. He and Jack would bear their sorrow in their own masculine way.

"We'll be right behind you two," Twila said. She patted Jess on the arm and we went on to my car.

I barely had to touch my gas pedal as I followed along behind Noah and Janie's buggy. I held my breath, though, when we reached an intersection where cars sped by at the posted speed of 55 miles per hour, some even faster. Lucky for my stress level, a man got out of the hearse buggy and stopped the cross-flow traffic so we could all pass through. Then we halted until the man raced past us and climbed back into the hearse.

We reached the cemetery in another ten minutes. A white board fence enclosed perhaps five acres of neatly maintained land, with row upon row of old and new tombstones. We could easily identify the grave for Patches: the one with a mound of dirt covered by a green tarp beside the hole in the ground.

There were no chairs set out beneath an overhead awning. Instead, the same men carried the coffin to the gravesite and set it on one of those casket-lowering devices while we gathered around. Their bishop only said: "Rest in peace." Then another man began lowering the coffin.

The mourners broke up, most of them giving Janie one more word of condolence or a hug before they went back to their own buggies and drove away. I started toward my car before realizing Janie and Jess were still standing at the grave. By now, there were two men shoveling dirt into the grave, disregarding the last two mourners.

I paused to take in the stark but beautiful scene outlined by the now-setting sun. Jess and Janie were black figures standing by the grave, the two other men bent over and barely visible against the backdrop of mounded dirt. Beyond the grave site, dozens of gravestones of various heights stretched away to the white board fence enclosing the peaceful cemetery. The prevalent Ohio woods lay just beyond the fence. For a second, I imagined I saw a flicker of movement in the underbrush.

Probably a deer, I told myself.

"If you want," Twila said, "you and Granny can go on. I'll wait and ride back with Jack and Jess."

"We're fine," I assured her. "We can wait for you."

I wasn't close enough to see, but the grave had to be at least half full by the time the last buggy, except for Noah's, pulled out—and Hoof's patrol car pulled into the cemetery.

"Shit," I said irreverently, given we were in a cemetery. "He's gonna arrest Janie right here, while she's watching her uncle be buried."

"There's not much we can do about it," Twila said, grabbing Granny as she started toward Hoof. "Don't, Granny. He'll take you with Janie."

"And you think that would bother me how?" Granny fumed. "Don't know 'bout you Yankee police, but down South we don't disrespect a buryin'." She gently picked up Twila's hand and removed it from her arm, then marched toward Hoof.

We followed Granny, with me hoping against hope she would be reasonable and only ask Hoof to wait until Janie left the grave. It was too much to expect the sheriff would let Janie go home first.

By the time we got to Hoof, Noah and Jack had joined us. Hoof ignored everyone else in preference to eyeing Granny. He stood behind the patrol car driver's door, keeping a barrier between him and the tiny barely-five-foot woman glowering at him. So far, Granny hadn't said a word. She didn't have to; her clear blue eyes glared a warning.

Jack spoke first. "I gather you're here for Janie."

Hoof barely glanced at Jack, then fixed his gaze on Granny as he said, "You know I don't have a choice, Roucheau."

"Iffen that ain't a lie, I ain't never heard one," Granny spat.

"What do you mean?" Hoof defended himself. "I'm the sheriff, and I've got a warrant to serve."

"I was talkin' 'bout you sayin' you had no choice." Granny rushed on when Hoof opened his mouth to respond. "You made the choice to charge Janie. So you're the one who stirred up this mess of cotton worms! You know what we do 'bout cotton worms down South?"

Noah stepped forward, and I could have sworn he was grinning. But I couldn't tell behind his beard.

He said to Granny, "I thank you for wanting to protect my wife, ma'am." To Hoof, he said, "I will bring Janie to you as soon as she is ready to leave here. I think that would be best."

Hoof contemplated for a few moments, then slowly nodded his head. "I'll take your promise on that, Noah."

"We will have a lawyer there, too," Noah told Hoof. "There will be no *booking,* or whatever the word is, done to my Janie until he comes. And I will want to take her home with me, so you must make sure she has...." He frowned, and glanced at Jack.

"Bail," Jack responded. "You want bail set so you can pay it and not leave Janie there in a cell."

Noah lifted an eyebrow at Hoof.

"I'll get hold of the judge," Hoof said. Then he got back in the patrol car and started the engine, a look of relief on his face as if he'd just escaped a firing squad. Which he probably had, although I was fairly certain Granny hadn't brought one of her pistols with her.

I hadn't checked her luggage, though, and we had driven up to Ohio. She understood she couldn't get a pistol through airline security, but on reflection, I wouldn't want to bet she hadn't brought one along for our drive. Just in case, she would say.

Janie and Jess finally abandoned the grave and walked over to us. Janie was glancing down the driveway where Hoof's car had disappeared, but Jess kept his eyes on the ground. When he got close, he evidently changed his mind and went on over to Jack's truck and got in.

"We'll see y'all back at the house," Jack said.

"Aren't you coming to the jail?" I asked.

He looked at Twila. "Where you gonna be?"

"I'm coming to the house," she said. "I'm sure Alice and Granny can handle things at the jail. Besides, Noah has an attorney. You have called him, haven't you, Noah?"

"I called him earlier today," he said. "But that was before the sheriff showed up again. I will have to let him know about this."

"I've got my cell phone he can use," I assured Twila. "You go with Jess."

Twila turned and walked toward Jack's pickup to ride back with him and Jess, but Jack lingered for a moment. He glanced at Granny, then me.

"On second thought," he said, "I'll drop Twila and Jess off and meet y'all at the jail."

I huffed in a deep breath, preparing to tell Jack that Granny and I sure as heck didn't need the protection of a big, bad man. But I relaxed immediately. I realized I would feel better having him with us, if only to help me keep Granny in line.

"I'm sure Janie and Noah will appreciate it," I said instead, and caught a little glimmer of laughter in Jack's deep, chocolate eyes. He pulled me close and kissed my forehead.

"See you in a bit, *Chère*."

CHAPTER 21

"Well?" Patches demanded, his body language indicating his frustration where he still sat on the bale of hay inside the majik circle. "Did you find out what was going on?"

"You will not like what I have to tell you," Free Eagle said. "But Janie's man told the sheriff he would bring her to the jail to go under arrest."

"No, damn it!" Patches stood and paced inside the circle.

He had to stay inside, since Free Eagle and Walking Bear had watched him earlier try to find any possible way to escape. Free Eagle had even suggested Patches become invisible, but the barrier continued to hold him.

"You cannot remember who killed you," Free Eagle pointed out. "If you could, it would give the sheriff the right person to arrest."

"He'd want evidence against the bastard," Patches said. "Did you find out what made him try to pin this on Janie? What evidence he has, or thinks he has? I've watched enough cop shows to know he's gotta at least have a danged motive."

Free Eagle hesitated a moment, but Patches had to know. "One of his deputies recognized the knife left by the body. A Yoder son is a blacksmith. He makes the knives they use to butcher in the fall, and no one else has a knife like them. And since you were dead, the lawyer could not keep the sheriff from reading something he called your Will."

"Gosh dang it!" Patches fumed. "He found out about that life insurance I took out a few years back to leave to Janie. He's calling that motive! I just wanted Janie to be comfortable in life, maybe go to college. She's the only good one left out of that entire Henry line of clowns!"

Free Eagle frowned. "But from what I have found out about your Janie, she chose a simple life with the peaceful people around here."

"I took out that policy before she married Noah," Patches explained. "Decided to keep it up, along with—"

A pile of loose hay rustled nearby, and Patches, Free Eagle and Walking Bear stared as it lifted into the air. The light yellow hay cascaded to the floor, leaving behind a huge pile of dark green grass and vines, taller even than the two Native Americans. And frightening enough that Free Eagle cried out and nearly joined Patches in his majik circle for protection.

Free Eagle barely managed to croak out, "What are you?"

"It's one of those things my cousin Hardy was talking about one night at the Eagles," Patches said in a voice wavering with fear. He backed up as far as he could in the circle, actually flattening himself in a spread-eagle position against the barrier.

Walking Bear smiled and said, "It is a-all right. He is B-Bob, m-my friend."

Bob spoke for a few moments, and Walking Bear nodded. "H-he has taught me h-how to understand his words. He says he was l-looking for the man called J-Jack."

Puzzled, Free Eagle asked, "How long have you been friends with Bob?"

"A l-long time." He waited for Bob to finish saying something else, then told them, "B-Bob says for me to tell you I led him to D-Daisy when she was shot. And I brought Janie to fix D-Daisy's arm."

From inside the circle, Patches said, "Janie knew about these mon...uh...nice folks? He looks like a Grassman."

"H-he is called that," Walking Bear agreed.

"Can he understand our words?" Free Eagle asked.

"S-some," Walking Bear said.

Free Eagle gazed at Bob. "The man called Jack is coming by here to leave his friend Jess and the Twila woman off. Then he will go to the jail."

Bob said, and Walking Bear translated, "He says Jack was trying to help find out who shot D-Daisy." Then Walking Bear shook his head. "I told you who, did I not, B-Bob?"

Bob shook his head negatively, and Walking Bear frowned. "I guess I forgot. I am sorry." He mentioned a name both Patches and Free Eagle knew well. Bob's eyes took on a red glow.

Just then, they heard vehicles pull up outside the barn. Free Eagle dissolved, then reappeared a few moments later, after one of the vehicles drove back down the driveway. "That was Jack and the others. The ones called Jess and Twila got out and went to the house. Jack went with the Alice woman and Grandmother."

Bob stalked to the barn door and looked out. Evidently satisfied it was clear, he raced out of the barn. By the time Free Eagle could think himself to the door, Bob was disappearing in the woods behind the house. Then Free Eagle noticed Twila hadn't gone inside with her husband, Jess. Instead, she stood near the back door, perhaps sensing there were others in her barn.

Twila walked resolutely towards Free Eagle. "What just happened here?" she asked.

* * *

The gorgeous sunset in the west had disappeared by the time we parked outside the jail. Rather than go inside, Jack, Granny and I sat in my car for a long while. It was quiet here. The county Twila lived in wasn't that large, and from what I remembered, the county seat town didn't even have a police force. Instead, the sheriff's department provided law enforcement to the entire area.

The jail was a separate building, across the street from a beautiful old courthouse constructed back in the mid-1800's. I'd always loved that old red-brick building with its bell tower on top. Since I enjoyed historical research, I had spent some time on this courthouse. The bell was actually used in the original building, built in the early 1800's. In the 1870's, that building was torn down to make room for a larger one, with the same bell.

So much history in some of these small towns.

The jail had once been a part of the courthouse, but a growing population meant the construction of a modern one-story building that wasn't nearly as pretty. We'd pulled into a parking lot beside the jail to wait for Janie. There was only one patrol car there, which I recognized as Hoof's. I supposed he didn't worry about any trouble from Noah when he turned Janie over for arrest. I just hoped we could keep Granny under control.

We had the car windows down in the cool evening, and there was enough breeze to blow away any early mosquitos that might try to feast on us. None of us spoke to anyone else, all lost down our own thought paths. I didn't know where Jack and Granny were roaming in their minds, but I was hoping Janie's lawyer would show up. Noah had called him on my cell phone before we left the cemetery, but he said the call went to voice mail.

I thought for a moment my wish had been granted when headlights flashed in the rear window of my SUV and another car pulled into the parking lot. Instead, as soon as the headlights went out, I recognized Twila's little red car. She got out and slid into my backseat with Granny.

"Anything happen yet?" she asked.

Jack turned around to glare at her. "And just what does that mean, Twila?"

She scowled right back at him. "Don't you try to pull that 'bad cop' routine on me, Jack Roucheau. I've still got a few voodoo tricks up my sleeve. Things Cat Dancer taught me in New Orleans."

For an instant, I saw a tiny bit of trepidation flash in Jack's brown eyes, but he kept his composure and said, "If you know somethin' that might happen here, you need to tell me. I'm not gonna be a part of no law breakin'."

"Is the Sixth Sense viable evidence in court?" she threw back at him. When he glanced evasively away, she went on, "I thought so. So I'm not forced to reveal anything I've only gotten hints of. Therefore, you can't have Hoof charge me for withholding evidence."

"Twila, I wouldn't—" Jack started to deny.

But finally we heard the sound of horse's hooves and glanced out the windows as Noah guided the buggy into the parking lot. He and Janie were alone, which surprised me. I even looked past them to see if any other family members had accompanied them.

Granny voiced my reaction. "You'd of thought some of her kin would come along with Janie."

"Maybe they didn't want to travel on the roadways after dark," I told her. "I imagine it's rather dangerous for a buggy, even with those rear lights and that night-glow sign I saw when we followed Noah to the cemetery."

"Could be," she agreed.

Hoof must have been watching from the window, because he stepped out the front door of the jail as Noah pulled his buggy up beside my car and got down. Noah assisted Janie from the buggy and held her hand as they walked over to where we were all getting out of my car.

"I haven't seen your attorney, Noah," I greeted him.

"He did not call you back on your phone?"

I checked my cell phone again, although I'd done that only five minutes ago and hadn't seen any missed calls. Beside, I kept the darn volume turned high, so it would jar me into noticing any communication, phone call or text. I didn't much like carrying a cell phone in the first place, but when I did, I made sure to pay attention to it.

"Nothing," I told Noah with a shrug.

Noah looked over at Jack. "You will be with us, right?"

"Sure," Jack said.

I started to reach out and hug Janie, only to realize Granny had beat me to the punch. Over Granny's shorter body, I noticed the strain and worry on Janie's face. I wished like hell I could keep her from having to go through the horrible experience of being booked into jail, something I knew about from my own recent past. But short of forcing her into my car and getting a head start before Hoof started after me, I couldn't think of any way to prevent this.

Besides, I doubted Janie would cooperate, and even if she did, we'd have to come out of hiding at some point.

But if I could keep her away until they found the real murderer....

Jack put an arm around my shoulder, squeezing me tighter than necessary. I tried to free myself, but he whispered, "Don't even think it, *Chère*."

Now how on earth had he figured out what I was thinking? I guess he did know me fairly well. I sighed and relaxed in his hold until he let go so I could hug Janie.

"Granny, Twila and I will be right with you, also," I assured her.

"Thanks," Janie said with a shiver. "I'd feel better, though, if the lawyer would show up."

"Without him," Noah asked, "does it mean we cannot get that bail for my Janie?"

"Not really," Jack told him. "It's the judge who sets bail."

"Are you coming on inside?" Hoof called.

We stared back and forth at each other. Janie took the first step toward the jail, Noah hurrying up beside her to take her hand again. We fell in behind.

Turned out, Granny wasn't the one I should have worried about.

CHAPTER 22

Avisitors area/waiting room took up the left side of where we entered the building. Office doors lined the right. No lights were on this time of evening, except for what spilled out of the third office down the hallway, where the door was open. Beyond it, the hallway continued on into darkness.

Hoof led us into the lighted office. A projection screen on a tripod stood near the back wall. Janie would have to stand in front of it for her "mug shot." I fisted my hands so tightly the nails dug into my palms as I thought of this young woman having to go through that.

First, though, Hoof went over to a desk, where he had opened a stamp pad and laid out fingerprinting cards. Evidently, this backwoods office hadn't obtained any Homeland Security funds to update to computerized booking equipment.

"We wish to wait for our lawyer, Mr. Peters," Noah insisted.

"Peters called here about five minutes ago," Hoof said. "He's over in Columbus at a fund raiser for the governor. Said it would be midnight before he got back to town, and he'd come by then. And I tried to get hold of Judge Abbot to ask him to set bail, but he's out of town for a couple days."

239

"That attorney had my number," I fumed. "Why didn't I hear from him?"

Hoof shrugged. "You'll have to ask him. He's got our department on speed dial."

"You might need a different attorney," I said to Noah.

"Does this mean you are going to put my Janie in a cell until the judge returns?" Noah asked.

"I don't have any choice," Hoof answered with a shrug. "She's turned herself in now, so I can't let her leave."

Hoof picked up one of Janie's hands and separated her index finger to push onto the ink pad. Janie whimpered.

Noah reached for her arm, and Janie shook her head. "No, it's all right, Noah. He has to do this."

I gritted my teeth as Hoof continued with the finger printing. He was on the second hand when something in the hallway caught my attention. I could have sworn a dark shadow passed the door. Of course, I was used to seeing ghosts, and a building like a jail would hold plenty of traumatized paranormal energy.

I glanced over at Twila to see her staring at the door, too. Someone who didn't know her as well as I did wouldn't have recognized the tiny smirk on her lips.

Since I was staring at the doorway with her, I saw the next thing that slipped past.

Uh oh. I quickly looked around to see where Jack was. Luckily, he was consoling Noah and assuring Hoof treated Janie respectfully. Or as respectfully as possible when being booked.

Granny was there too, on the other side of Janie. Given how close Granny pressed to our new friend, it was a wonder Hoof could even maneuver. However, Granny's wrinkles creased even deeper into a frown, and she turned toward Twila and me. Since she had her own measure of Sixth Sense, her getting a hint that something was out of place here didn't surprise me. She edged away from the desk and over to us.

When I caught Twila's gaze again, her lips quirked into a full-blown grin. She took mine and Granny's arms and pulled us away from where we stood, which would have blocked the doorway.

I expected one of those huge shadows to enter. Instead, loud footsteps echoed in the hallway, steps which sounded like hard-soled shoes or boots. The two shadows hadn't made a sound, so this had to be human. Closest to the door, I peered out.

A deputy staggered down the dark hallway. He noticed me and held out a hand, murmuring, "I think...did they...oh, man, I hope I'm dreaming."

He got close enough for some of the light to spill on him. I didn't see any blood or bruises, and his face was white enough to show even a tiny mark.

I glanced in the direction I'd seen the shadows going. There was another door beside this office. It had been closed when we came in the building. Now it stood open an inch or so.

"Are you all right?" I asked the deputy in a quiet voice.

He shook his head. "No. I...where's the sheriff?"

"He's booking someone. Where did you come from?"

"The cell block," he said as he halted in front of me. "I've got guard duty tonight, but—" He dropped his face into his hands and murmured through his fingers, "I swear, I wasn't asleep and dreaming. I swear."

By now, Twila was standing beside me, and Granny peered around her.

"I has nightmares once in a while when I nods off," Granny said. She patted his arm, but the deputy jumped away from her touch and stifled a scream.

Granny chuckled, and Twila and I shared a mischievous glance. We both knew what had this man in such a state. Granny probably did, too.

"Sorry, Mr. Deputy," Granny said. "Didn't mean to scare you."

He shook his head violently. "No! It wasn't you. It—"

"What's going on out here?" Hoof demanded. We women moved aside so he could see the deputy.

"What are you doing here, Sanders?" he asked. "Who's guarding the cell block?"

"I-I was, Sheriff," Deputy Sanders replied. "But-but-but...ah, hell, you ain't gonna believe me anyway."

"Try me," Hoof said. "And hurry it up. I've got a prisoner in here."

"Prisoner my blue butt," Granny fumed. "Janie ain't no more a criminal than me." She blinked and reconsidered. "Well, I ain't got nothin' fresh on my record, anyways."

I couldn't resist trying to delay things. I wasn't sure what Janie's rescuers were up to, but since they hadn't shown themselves yet, maybe they needed a little more time to firm up whatever plan they had cooked up.

"You've been arrested, Granny?" I asked, feigning awe. She'd told me the story one night when the two of us were on our second Crown and Seven. I held my liquor better than Granny, but not by much. I'd walked her home before I had my third drink and went to bed.

"Well..." she drawled. "T'was back when I was one of them stupid teenagers. Had them hormones runnin' hot and heavy, y'know?" She winked at Jack, drawing my gaze in that direction. Besides him standing there, Noah and Janie were in the doorway, Janie trying to clean her fingers with some tissue. Jack's ear tips actually reddened in a blush, but Noah only smiled at Granny.

"See, I was showin' off for this here boy I had my eye on," Granny went on. "He was one of them bad boys, ones your mama told you to stay away from."

"And?" I prodded when she fell silent for a few seconds. Her eyes had danced up and over my shoulder, but I didn't dare look around to see what caught her attention. Hoof and the deputy evidently hadn't seen her quick glance, and it wasn't something I wanted them to notice right now.

"Well, I had me two close girlfriends back then, and we'd heard there was gonna be a party down on the bayou this here certain night. We knew our folks wouldn't let us go, 'cause word had got 'round that them there parties had liquor at 'em. But all three of us wanted to go real bad. There was two other boys those gals had their eyes on, like I did on Mr. Bad Boy."

She chuckled, and Twila edged sideways a step, which I realized would give her a view behind me. I didn't dare move myself. I was close to Granny, and for some reason, her story had Hoof and Deputy Sanders fascinated.

"We each told our mama and daddy we was stayin' at one of the other houses," Granny continued. "But we didn't want to go to that there party empty-handed, and my old Uncle Keith, he brewed his own moonshine back then." She winked at Jack again. "We knows how to make 'shine just as good down home as them there hill folks do up in Tennessee."

Another shadow flickered in the distance far down the hallway. Then two more. The way we were standing allowed Twila to see my left hand hanging down by my side. I lifted one finger and wiggled it back and forth until I saw her stare at it. Then I added two more fingers. Her brown eyes widened a hair, but when I closed finger two and three and pointed behind her with finger one, she didn't give things away by looking over her shoulder.

"...And that there policeman wasn't fooled one bit by mine and my friends' story 'bout just bein' out for a ride," Granny was saying when I paid attention to her again. "'Specially since we'd all three took a hit of that shine a'fore we got in my old rattletrap car and headed for the bayou. Guess he smelled it on us, 'cause Uncle Keith's shine was stronger than anythin' we could've got in a liquor store."

Twila laughed. "I'd have been more afraid of my parents than the police."

"We was," Granny assured her.

The shadows down the hallway moved silently towards us. By then, I could count five of them. Two were Grassmen, the other three appeared to be ghostly apparitions.

Behind me, a door hinge squealed loud enough for everyone except Twila, Granny and me to turn and stare.

Twila and I took Granny between us and stepped back into the dimness of the waiting area.

"Is that Patches with the brothers?" I whispered to Twila.

She nodded. "I turned him loose."

"Who's there?" Hoof shouted, and his hand dropped to the holster hanging from his belt.

Bob stepped out of the office first.

"It's him!" Deputy Sanders screamed. "I saw him and another one, Sheriff! Shoot! Hurry!"

But Hoof bonelessly started to collapse. Jack tried to catch him, but Hoof hit the floor with a loud thump.

The second Grassman stepped out, and hands in front of him, the deputy tried to scuttle backward. However, his legs seemed frozen in place. He didn't have a gun, which I assumed was standard for someone guarding a cell block, and he made no move to kneel and grab Hoof's weapon.

"Uh, Bob..." Jack began.

Roar! Bob growled, straight into the deputy's face. Sanders screamed to high heaven and whirled...into a solid wall of two more Grassmen and three ghosts a few feet behind him.

"No!" he screeched. He pointed at Patches and said, "You're dead! I saw you." A puddle of urine spread beneath his feet while he aimed his finger at Free Eagle and Walking Bear, any further words evidently fear-frozen in his throat.

An instant later, I got a whiff of the pee, too, which made me wonder why we hadn't smelled the Grassmen approach. Maybe it was time for their monthly bath. Who knew? And there wasn't time to ask them now.

The deputy whirled again and dove past Jack and between Noah and Janie, into the office. He slammed the door, and the lock turned, leaving us all standing in the dim hallway.

Jack said something to Bob again, and this time he wasn't interrupted. However, instead of answering, Bob shook his head and walked over to Janie. He reached out for her, and Jack tried to step between them. Bob heaved a sigh and picked Jack up with no problem.

"Hey, you'll be in a lot of trouble if you don't stop!" Jack insisted, forgetting to use his Cajun French and pushing at Bob's arm.

Bob handed Jack to the Grassman beside him. That one deposited

Jack in the office where the two of them had been hiding. He shut the door and held it closed while Bob got a chair out of the waiting room. Bob shoved the chair beneath the doorknob as Jack pounded on the door.

"Uh..." I began.

"Hush yo' mouth," Granny said. "Lessen you wants to go in there with Jack."

"We're all going to be in trouble for helping in a jailbreak," I whispered.

Twila just grinned at me. "Yeah. But it's for a good cause."

Bob walked back over to Janie and stared down at her as Patches joined them. I moved a few steps so I could see Noah, but Janie's husband didn't appear at all fearful of either the huge beasts or the ghosts.

"We're takin' you outta here until we can find out who the real murderer is," Patches said. "You go on with our friends here, and we'll catch up with you soon."

"Uncle Patches," Janie said. "I don't know if this is the right thing to do."

Noah said, "They lied to us about waiting for our attorney. And the sheriff will put you in a cell until this judge decides to come back."

"Right," Patches said. "And if that old reprobate Abbot finds out it's my niece he needs to set bail for, he might stay away another week!"

Bob gently picked Janie up, and she sighed and settled in his arm. He headed for the front door of the building, and the rest of the Grassmen and ghosts walked down the dark hallway in the opposite direction.

Hoof stirred and moaned. By the time Bob reached the door and turned around to see what the noise was, Hoof was sitting up, staring around. Twila grabbed my hand, and slipped an arm around Granny. We all hurried to the front door, where Bob had now disappeared.

"Wait," I said as I tried to jerk my hand free. "I need to let Jack out."

"No time," Twila insisted. She dragged me down the steps, Granny with us. Then I saw what Twila sensed that made her in such a hurry.

The doors were open on my car, and Trucker and Miss Molly peered from the back seat. In the driver's seat, Bob hunched over the steering wheel, his huge body barely fitting in the car. It looked as though he was trying to figure out how to start my hybrid vehicle.

"No you don't!" I yelled at Bob. "You probably don't even know how to drive!"

I reached in my pocket for my keys, then remembered I'd left them on the console. The hybrid didn't have an ignition switch, just a button to push. But the keys had to be close enough to the button for the engine to engage, and lying on the console only a few inches from the button darned sure made them close enough.

"Gentlemen," Janie said loudly with a grin as she reached over to push the ignition button, "start your engines."

The low, nearly silent hum meant the hybrid engine had engaged. I rushed toward the car, but Bob slammed the driver's door shut. Twila shoved me into the back seat, which Trucker and Miss Molly vacated by bounding into the hatchback area. Twila pushed me so hard, I hit the door on the other side, then Granny was next to me, Twila next to her, and the passenger door closed.

Barely in time, too. Bob shifted the car into drive and gave it some gas. I looked out the rear window, past my dog's huge body, to see Hoof on the steps, his pistol drawn. Lucky for us—or him, if he'd shot at us and hurt either of the animals or any of the passengers—he dropped the gun to his side. Before we were out of sight, I saw Jack join Hoof.

The car jolted over something, and behind us, the parking lot receded, along with the concrete speed bump that marked the edge of it. Bob had driven right over the bump. The car moved faster.

I grabbed my seatbelt and snapped it, then reached down beside me to find the belt for Granny. Between us, Twila and I secured her, then I turned my attention back to the front seat.

"Bob!" I insisted. "Or Janie. Whichever one can understand me. What the hell are you doing?"

The car veered around a corner, sliding me towards Granny. Only the seatbelt kept me from squishing her into Twila.

"Bob, damn it—"

"He's not going to answer you, Alice," Janie said. "He has to concentrate on his driving. And I need to help him. So please don't distract us. We don't want to wreck your car."

My mouth dropped open. I was speechless, rare for me.

Beside me, Granny chuckled. "You best listen, Alice. We don't wants to end up in a ditch."

"Or get caught by the law," Twila said with a giggle. "Hear the sirens behind us?"

I turned my head again and heard a faint siren. However, I couldn't see anything, even the flashing lights that should have been visible in the darkness.

Bob steered the car onto the bridge that divided the town from a smaller village on the other side of the river. On the bridge straightaway, he floored the gas pedal. The hybrid launched itself forward like an obedient steed, throwing us back in our seats. Trucker hit the rear hatchback with a thump, but when I worriedly looked at him, he was already sitting up, tongue hanging out and eyes gleaming in excitement.

That's when I noticed another animal behind Miss Molly and beside Trucker. That darned pig must have already been in the hatchback when we got in.

"Harley's back there," I said to Twila as Bob came off the bridge and slowed down to turn onto an entrance ramp. He headed down the ramp to the four-lane that ran on this side of the river, accompanied by Granny's "Wheee!" of pleasure.

"I think they came with Bob and the ghosts," Twila said with a smile. "Maybe Bob brought them so they could visit with Rascal. Besides, they don't want to miss the excitement."

"Excitement?" I snarled. "It's not your car being driven by a being that's never been behind a wheel before!"

"He's seen TV programs," Janie said.

"Omigod," I muttered as I curled my hands over my face. Not looking didn't last long, though. The car picked up more speed, and I gasped and clenched the armrest on one side, the edge of the seat with the other hand.

Bob barreled out onto the highway and headed east. Suddenly I realized the hybrid's automatic headlights weren't on. It hadn't mattered on the bridge, which had pole lights lining it. But now we flew through darkness.

"Tell Bob he needs to at least turn on the headlights," I ordered Janie.

She said something to Bob, and after he replied, Janie told us, "He says he can see fine. And he doesn't want to make us easy to find."

I groaned and didn't distract our driver by arguing. Being what he was, Bob probably did have keener vision than a human. That didn't abate my stress level, though. To keep my mind occupied, I tried to figure out where we were. It had been a long while since I'd explored the towns and surrounding woods with Twila. I tried to puzzle out where he was going but made the mistake of glancing at the speedometer.

It hovered past ninety. I didn't dare scream at Bob again. I was too afraid of intruding on his concentration and sending the car into a spin. Luckily, right now we were passing flat pasture land. We couldn't get hurt too badly if we left the road. Could we? I recalled a teenage friend who'd lost control and gone through a pasture fence. She'd spent months in the hospital and rehab.

Unfortunately for my tiny peace of mind crumb, we left the pasture behind and headed into woodland. The siren behind sounded closer, and this time when I looked, bubble lights flashed in the distance.

Janie said something in Grassman language and pointed out the windshield ahead of us. Bob slammed on the brakes, and we skidded down the road, taking months of wear off my brand new tires. At least I hadn't had to pay for them. The Grassman twisted the wheel and slid the car sideways into an intersecting road. Gravel spewed when Bob floored the gas pedal again and zoomed down a road that hadn't seen asphalt in its life.

"Hi ho, hybrid!" Granny yelled.

I clenched my fists to keep from throttling Granny, but I wasn't making any promises—silent or verbal—about what I'd do if she kept encouraging Bob.

Hoof must have had time enough to turn into the intersection road without sliding a hundred yards. The siren sounded even closer.

"You might as well tell him to pull over, Janie," I pleaded. "They're gonna catch us in a minute."

Janie ignored me, but Bob did slow down. The speedometer only read fifty when he braked and turned into another road. This one was filled with potholes, but Bob seemed to know where they were located. Instead of us bouncing up and off the low ceiling on the hybrid, he weaved in and out, from one side of the road to another. Janie had grabbed the *oh-shit* bar above her head to keep herself in place, but Twila, Granny and I slid back and forth so fast, I was surprised sparks of static electricity didn't shoot out beneath our butts.

"Uh oh," Granny said, covering her mouth. "Think I'm gettin' car sick."

I managed to throw a comforting arm around her. "Please don't throw up in my car, Granny. Surely we can't go on much further."

The barrier of trees in front of us put truth to my words. Bob slammed on the brakes and the car skidded to a halt at a dead end. Road-less woodland stretched in front of us, trees packed closely and underbrush rampant.

The siren behind us grew closer.

Granny picked up a huge sewing bag I'd noticed her load into the car back in Six Gun. God, was that only three days ago? She reached inside it and pulled out the huge revolver she kept beside her bed for protection.

CHAPTER 23

Twila gasped and carefully took the revolver from Granny's hand. "We're not going to shoot our way out of this, Granny." Twila shoved the pistol back into the sewing bag and dropped the bag into the hatchback.

"You're prob'ly right," Granny agreed, much to my relief. "And my belly's better now."

I glanced back to see the bubble lights not that far away. Frankly, I was grateful they would soon catch us. I was ready to spend the rest of the night somewhere safe, even in a jail cell.

Bob opened the driver's door and wrestled his huge body from behind the steering wheel. Now the interior lights shone, and we saw Bob lift one huge arm and motion at the woods.

Five huge Grassmen stepped into sight, two on the side where Bob stood, the other three on the passenger side of my car.

"No!" I insisted at the same moment Bob said something to Janie. I grabbed for the door handle, but Janie quickly pushed the button to engage the childproof locks. Those of us in the backseat were now effectively trapped.

Bob slammed the driver's door, leaving us in darkness again. He and the other Grassmen lifted the car onto their shoulders. They trotted forward like Egyptian litter bearers, the car swaying back and forth in time to their gait. I looked behind, but was fairly certain we were out of sight by the time Hoof's car skidded to a halt at the road's dead end. Still, the patrol car's headlights shone enough for me to see Hoof alone get out of the vehicle.

Though I continued to try to peer behind, in case Jack got out, Hoof disappeared a second later, leaving only moonlight for illumination. Endless midnight blackness extended a couple feet from the car.

I thumped back into my seat and grumped, "I didn't see Jack."

"Then we're lucky, at least for a while," Twila said as she stared out at the closest Grassman's shaggy head. "He knows where the Grassmen live."

Janie twisted around in her seat. "You've been to their camp?"

"Yes," I told her. "And I'd guess you have, also."

"She cared for Daisy," Twila said. "And you also understand them, Janie."

Janie shrugged. "I've always had a gift for languages. I picked up Noah's Pennsylvania Dutch with no problem, and Noah taught me what he could about Bob's language. His family has known about the Grassmen for ages."

I realized Granny had grown unusually quiet, her hand hovering close to her mouth. "Are you getting carsick again?" I asked her.

She nodded. "Sorta seasick, this here car swayin' like 'tis.

Twila handed something to Granny. "Here, take this. It will calm your tummy."

"Is that something natural?" Janie asked.

"Yes," Twila replied. "I make tablets for indigestion from fennel seeds."

"I hope it works," I murmured in a worried voice. "I'm sorry you're getting sick, Granny. But it will probably be worse if you have to ride back here smelling vomit."

Granny chewed for a few seconds, then nodded her head. "Think it's doing me some good." She looked sideways at me and added, "Don't want to mess up Alice's new car."

"Oh, pooh," I began, then continued the comment in my head: *I don't want you to mess it up, either.*

Twila interrupted my thoughts to ask Janie, "How long have you yourself known about them?"

"Only since the day Noah asked me to go with him and help Daisy," she said. "I was pretty shocked when I got to the camp. I mean, after all, things like Big Foot and Grassmen are supposed to be just myths."

"Myth, schmith," Granny said. "They's lots of real things people don't believe in. Like ghosts."

The car stopped swaying, and we all looked out the front windshield. Suddenly I remembered how the four of us had had to walk along that narrow cave path when we wound up in the Grassman camp.

"There's no way they can carry my car through that cave," I said with a frown of concern. "Can you warn them about that, Janie? Please?"

"Cave?" she asked. "Noah and I didn't go through a cave."

"Then hopefully there's another way in there," I said.

"If not, Alice," Granny said, "I'll be your witness when you explain things to that there insurance man."

I groaned, but managed to keep the sound silent.

Fortunately, they didn't try to maneuver the cave. Right then, anyway. I breathed a sigh of relief as two of the Grassmen disappeared from sight as though walking down a river bank. The other four handed the front of the car downward, and we had to brace ourselves against the tilt. Janie grabbed the *oh-shit* bar, and we pushed on the seatbacks in front of us while our litter bearers descended. A moment later, we were being carried along a creek bed amidst splashes of water.

Sheesh, I thought to myself. *I should be able to hear splashes. Twelve huge feet are hitting that water!*

Safe from hanging against the seatbelt, Janie looked at us and said, "It's surprising none of you are acting scared."

Twila laughed. "Oh, Janie. I'll admit, I didn't think Grassmen existed until recently. However, Alice, Granny and I have seen plenty of things no one else would believe. I'll bet even you draw the line at imagining time travel could be real."

Janie smirked. "Now you're teasing me."

"I'm not," Twila denied. "But we better discuss that later. Look." She nodded her head toward the windshield.

Ahead of us, a flow of lanterns stretched into the distance. They were carried by a line of Grassmen who, according to what I could see of their sizes, included men, women and perhaps teenage children. As we reached the back of the line, I saw youngsters on the shoulders of some of the creatures. The last two Grassmen stepped aside so Bob and his friends could convey my car on through.

We passed by at least twenty more Grassmen, and that didn't count the children and babies. When we reached the front of the line, all four of us gasped at the sight revealed as the leading creatures moved aside.

The end of a pole sat on Walking Bear's shoulder. We could see straight through the ghost to a man hanging upside down, hands and feet tied securely on the pole. It looked like Free Eagle's hairdo on the head of the person on the other end. Patches trudged along to the left of the dangling man. Every once in a while, he angrily slicked a stick through the air, barely missing the captive.

I squinted at the trussed up man's head, which sagged loosely from his body, oily hair nearly brushing the ground. He looked familiar, but the dim lantern light made recognition difficult.

"What on earth?" Twila asked. Then she added, "That's Doc Morrow hanging on that pole!"

"Where you think they's carryin' him to?" Granny asked in Janie's direction. "I thought these here Grassmen was a tribe of vegetable eaters. You ever hear of them bein' cannibals?"

"I haven't," Janie replied. "But like I said, I haven't known about them long."

My stomach curdled. "Do you have another fennel tablet?" I asked Twila.

She dug in her satchel and opened a small, smoky bottle. I threw the tablet she handed me into my mouth and chewed as Twila responded to Janie's comment.

"I very much doubt they're taking Doc somewhere to barbecue him. But who the heck knows? Here we are in the company of supposedly mythological creatures and three ghosts. I doubt any human has ever communicated with Grassmen long enough to get a handle on how their minds work. And as long as Alice and I've been hunting ghosts, we still get surprised by their actions."

"So you're saying don't be surprised by anything that happens?" I asked in a worried half-whisper.

"Yes," was all she answered.

Even Granny appeared in shock for the rest of our bizarre journey. None of us said another word as we travelled at least a half-mile further on the creek bed. I assumed the Grassmen were using the water to hide their trail, doing everything they could think of to keep their existence and whereabouts secret.

A warm breath feathered my left ear, and I reached back to pat Trucker. Apparently deciding the humans had finally noticed the animal passengers in the back, Miss Molly crawled over the seat into Granny's lap. Harley took a hint from Trucker and stuck his head over the seat next to Twila. She raised a hand to scratch his head. Still, nothing broke the solemn silence other than Miss Molly's purrs as she nestled comfortably on Granny's lap.

At last the lead Grassmen climbed out of the creek, followed by the three ghosts and their captured prisoner. I braced myself for the tilt as our litter bearers followed suit. However, the two rear creatures lifted us high enough to keep the car level as they climbed up a bank noticeably lower than the ones we had been travelling through.

The line didn't stop. Now we were on a faint trail through the trees and underbrush. The Grassmen and ghosts continued walking so long, I finally started to drift off to sleep. The lack of rocking motion in the car startled me into full wakefulness.

We were in a clearing that looked as though it would strain at the seams with all the members of our party. Our litter bearers turned and set the car down on the far side of the clearing, the windshield facing inward so we could see what was happening. Bob opened the driver's door, which turned on the interior lights. He said something to Janie, then walked away. Beside me, I heard the reassuring click of my door lock disengaging.

Or I thought it was reassuring for a split second. Now what the hell were we supposed to do? Get out and watch them torment their prisoner? I once again cursed my vivid writer's imagination as I recalled all the tales of how the Native Americans tortured their captives, both white men and members of rival tribes. They had ways of bringing the prisoners close to death over and over, until they begged to be killed and put out of their misery.

Janie opened her door, and Twila and I both followed suit. However, Janie was the only one who got out of the car. We stayed put, as did each animal we tended.

"Leastways we gots some fresh air in here," Granny murmured quietly.

None of the rest of us, animals included, responded.

The Grassmen who had lanterns carried them around the clearing and set them down. When they were finished, we could see the entire area fairly clearly. At first, I couldn't figure out what was going on. Several Grassmen gathered in one spot in what looked like two rows of six, an even mixture of males and females. Walking Bear and Free Eagle laid Doc on the ground and pulled the pole out as Patches untied Doc's legs. Doc sat up, a frozen look of terror on his face. He didn't try to stand.

"Good lord, they're going to try Doc," Twila whispered.

"Try to get him to do what?" I asked before it dawned on me what she meant. I gasped, and she didn't bother to explain after she looked over and saw understanding in my eyes.

CHAPTER 24

Twila's explanation of what was about to happen fired my curiosity enough to slide out of the car and get a better view. *This is actually a new experience for me,* I justified. *Shoot, I might use it in a book some day.*

Trucker bounded out to sit beside me, and Rascal saw him. The little Grassman struggled in his mother's arms until she set him down to scuttle over and wrap his arms around the dog. When he pulled back, Trucker slurped his face.

The next thing I knew, Harley was beside Trucker, and Rascal gave the pig a hug of its own. I glanced down to see Miss Molly sitting on the edge of the backseat, a tolerant expression in her blue eyes. She didn't make a move to join the others, though, not even her good friend Trucker. Only occasionally did Miss Molly deign to enlist in rambunctious play, and she evidently wasn't really sure yet whether the larger animals were preparing for a bout of toss and tumble.

It amazed me how I was beginning to differentiate amongst the huge Grassmen in ways other than adults and children: a lighter shade of green here, a cowlick there, skinnier and pudgier figures on some of the females.

A murmur of voices beside me drew my attention. Free Eagle and

Walking Bear were in a low-voiced discussion, with Walking Bear pointing unswervingly at Doc Morrow and saying something about cowards. I blinked for a moment when I realized both ghosts appeared quite highly visible, wondering what that was all about. But then Bob walked over in front of the twelve "jurors" and spoke, his voice strong even though I couldn't understand more than a word here and there.

"What is he saying?" Twila asked Janie.

"He's telling them why they brought Doc here," Janie answered. "It seems he's the one who shot Daisy."

Bob motioned to Janie, and she slid out of the car. "Excuse me," she said to us. "I think they want me to interpret."

"Bob must have found out about Daisy's attacker some other way," I said as Janie walked away. "We were supposed to see if we could help Jack get that information for him."

"Actually," Twila responded quietly while Bob and Janie were talking, "Bob found out from Patches and Walking Bear. I'd explain it to you, but it's a somewhat long story and we probably should be quiet. Besides, I think we're going to hear it directly from them, which will be more interesting."

Bob walked over and sat on a downed tree, conveniently felled in the spot where a judge could orchestrate a courtroom. Patches, Walking Bear, and the female Grasswoman with her arm in a sling gathered on the right of the makeshift podium, along with another large Grasswoman. A male Grassman reached down to pick up Doc. He carried him over to where Janie stood to the left of the ghosts and Grasswoman, and when he refused to stay on his feet, sat him on the ground. Doc buried his head on his knees, but refusing to face his jurors wasn't allowed. The Grassman's shoulders heaved in what appeared to be a gesture of frustration, and he pushed Doc's head up. Then the Grassman pulled the red handkerchief out of Doc's back pocket and tied it under his chin and around the top of his head. Huge hand on the top knot, he kept Doc's face up.

Doc whimpered and tried to hide his eyes with his hands. The Grassman shoved Doc's hands away and murmured something to Janie.

Janie bent to talk to Doc, and whatever she told him made his shoulders quiver, then stiffen. He didn't make another move to hide his face.

The Grasswoman, whom I'd decided was the prosecutor for this trial, spoke for a minute or so, then gave Patches a gentle push forward, even though her hand went through the ghost. Patches walked over to stand beside Judge Bob, in the position a witness would take in a trial, although there was no chair for him. Another Grassman had apparently been appointed Bailiff, and he carried a black book to Patches. The ghost didn't need Janie to translate. He placed his hand in position on top of the Bible and said, "I sure do swear to tell the whole truth."

Doc tried to mutter something, but the handkerchief held his mouth shut. The Grassman beside him, whom by now I'd figured out was acting as Doc's attorney, untied the knot on top of his client's head, allowing him to speak.

"What's going on?" Doc asked Janie. "What's he holding that book up there for?"

"Can't you see the witness?" Janie asked.

"What witness?" Doc grumbled. "All I see are these creatures. Ain't I supposed to be able to confront my accusers?"

Judge Bob frowned, and the activity in the clearing ground to a halt for several long seconds as Janie explained what Doc had said to the judge. Then she looked over at us with a shrug. "Doc Morrow can't see Uncle Patches, so I don't know what they're going to do now."

"I can help, if Judge Bob wants me to," Twila told her as she walked toward Janie.

Janie didn't have to translate Twila's offer. I was beginning to believe the judge understood more of the English language than he was letting on. He waved a hand and gave a permissive nod to Twila.

Approaching Patches, Twila held her arms outstretched with palms facing upward as she called out a spell I recognized as one Cat Dancer had taught us in New Orleans. When she finished, she cupped her hands and ran them down the sides of Patches' head, shoulders and legs. Behind her hands, Patches solidified into stronger visibility.

Strong enough for Doc to see him, evidenced by the gasp of alarm from Doc and his high-pitched voice as he squealed, "You're dead!"

"I guess you can see Uncle Patches now," Janie said. Doc only nodded a yes in reply.

Patches seemed to know what he was meant to testify to. When Doc's attorney Grassman waved a hand indicating for him to speak, Patches told his story in English, with Janie murmuring a translation for the jury.

"I didn't know 'til a few hours ago that something I'd overheard was important to these Grassfolks," Patches began. "I was with Jess and Twila at the Eagle's Club one night when we went there for the fish fry and free beer. Me and Jess had stepped outside for a smoke, and Hardy, one of my no-good cousins, was outside doing some bragging. He was already drunk, so he wasn't keeping his voice down."

Patches glared over at Doc. "Seems Doc and Hardy was out hunting coons one night. They followed their dogs too deep into the woods to get back real easy in the dark, and the dogs ran off and left them. So they fell asleep on the river bank. I guess this poor little gal—" Patches pointed over to where Daisy stood, her arm still in a sling. "I found out she was named Daisy from my new friend Walking Bear, and that she's our judge here's daughter. Anyways, Daisy had come to the river to wash some diapers out. Something woke Doc up, maybe the water splashing. He didn't stop and think. He just grabbed his gun and shot."

"Did Doc's buddy see Daisy, too?" Janie asked in response to something the Grassman beside her said.

"The shot woke him up and he got a glimpse," Patches replied with a nod. "Hardy went with Doc to try to find the trail. Said he saw footprints in the river mud and blood in the underbrush. But they never caught up to Daisy."

"I just found out about all this a while ago myself," Twila whispered. "That's part of the reason I turned Patches loose."

"Then Jess knows about the Grassmen?" I asked softly.

"He does now," she replied with a smile.

The prosecuting Grasslady spoke to Janie, and Janie asked Doc, "Do you have any questions?"

"Ain't you supposed to be my lawyer?" Doc appealed to Janie. "Why ain't you standing up for me and asking questions?"

Before Janie could answer, Judge Bob spoke, reaffirming to me that he was conversant in English. When he finished, Janie told Doc, "The judge says you are being tried by their rules for a crime you committed against one of them. That you'll get your chance to testify. Besides," she added with a nod at the Grassman beside Doc, "he's your lawyer. I'm just an interpreter. And probably a witness."

"It ain't fair me having a lawyer I can't talk to," Doc whined.

Bob said something else, and Janie translated, "The judge also says that you have your choice of whether or not you want a trial or to just accept your punishment without a chance to tell your side."

Doc drew himself up and turned toward Bob as he said, "Sounds to me like you've already decided to punish...." His bravery dwindled and he shrank in stature as he stared from Bob to the jury panel of twelve more Grasspeople, then around the clearing where more creatures and their young stood. Slowly, he hung his head.

His lawyer Grassman reached out with the cloth in his hand, prepared to tie it back around Doc's jaw and head. But Doc saw it and quickly lifted his head.

After a nod from Judge Bob, Patches continued, "Doc only wounded poor Daisy, and she was able to make it back home. Janie's man Noah brought Janie to the camp to fix Daisy up so she didn't get blood poisoning or an infection and die."

Bob said something, and Janie didn't bother to bend down to Doc as she translated, "The judge wants to know if you admit to what you did, Doc."

Doc must have found some measure of bravery, because he said, "Dang it, I've watched TV shows. Everything he's saying up there is total hearsay. He didn't see me do nothing."

The prosecutor Grasswoman tossed a trailing vine out of her face and spoke to Janie. After Janie translated, the Grasswoman fixed Doc with a nasty grimace as she said something else.

"She says she is not done with her witnesses," Janie told him. "And Bob's still waiting for you to answer his questions about whether you admit to what you did."

Anger clouding his expression, Doc spat, "Well, what would you do if you woke up and saw one of these deformed monsters gettin' ready to attack you?"

Then Doc evidently realized he was spouting off to Bob, who was not only the judge but one of the "deformed monsters" Doc was vilifying. "Oh, shit," he said, jumping to his feet and racing toward the edge of the clearing.

He didn't get far. Trucker bounded over and cut him off, and Doc skidded to a halt. Trucker bared his fangs and uttered a low growl. For a second, Doc swiveled his head between Trucker and Bob, then appealed to Janie.

The lawyer Grassman said a few words, and Janie interpreted, "He wants to know if you have anything else to say to defend your actions."

Doc shook his head, and Bob motioned for Patches to continue.

"I ain't got much more to say," Patches told Bob. "'Cept I'll sure miss goin' to them fish fries. Those Eagles can cook up a good mess of catfish. Me and Jess usually caught enough on our trotlines for them to have one at least once a month."

"Too bad he ain't still alive," Granny murmured. "I'd cook him up some Southern Fried Cat so good he'd—"

Miss Molly whirled and arched her back at Granny, hissing through bared, pointed teeth.

"Oh, oh, oh, sorry, Miss Molly," Granny soothed. "I meant cat*fish* not *just*cat. Forgives me, will you, pretty please?"

Mollified, Miss Molly settled down and allowed Granny to pull her onto her lap and continue her apology with soothing strokes.

In the clearing, Patches walked away from the witness area, and the female Grassperson prosecutor gave Janie a nod. The young Amish woman didn't hesitate. She took her place as a witness and echoed Patches' oath on the Bible, only adding, "So help me God."

"I can't add much to what Uncle Patches said," Janie began. "Noah and some of his family have evidently known about the Grasspeople for a long while. I woke up one night and saw Noah missing from our bed. I found him in the barn, gathering some first aid supplies. When I asked him if he needed some help doctoring one of the animals, he laughed at me and said he did."

She looked over at Daisy with a loving smile. "At first, I was scared to death. But everyone was so nice to me, and I was really glad I could help Daisy, so she didn't lose her arm."

Doc's attorney looked down at him, and Doc said, "I'm just making the same objection. She didn't see me do nothing."

Janie left the witness area, and the next person the prosecutor called was Walking Bear. I glanced over at Doc to see if Twila would need to do another visibility spell, but Doc clearly tracked the Native American with his eyes.

Walking Bear appeared somewhat hesitant, and he stopped to scan the clearing. His gaze focused for a moment on his brother, and I tuned in on their telepathic exchange.

You can do this, Free Eagle said.

Yes, Walking Bear replied. *It is the right thing. What R-Ruth would want me to do.*

For a second, it appeared the Bible confused Walking Bear, but he evidently recalled what the others had done. He raised his right hand and placed his left on the book.

Keeping his eyes on Free Eagle's encouraging face instead of looking at Doc, Walking Bear said, "I was f-following this man and the other one the night P-Patches is talking about. Then I saw D-Daisy coming and decided to talk to her and help with her w-wash. We had not been at the river more than a m-minute when that one—" Walking Bear drew his eyes from his brother's and pointed unerringly at Doc. "The one they call Doc shot my friend Daisy!"

For a second, I thought Walking Bear would break down. I wouldn't have been surprised to see a tear track down his cheek. However, he stiffened his shoulders and went on, "She was hurt bad. T-there was b-blood. I wanted to hurt the man who did it, b-but I had to help D-Daisy get away. When she was safe, I went to find my friend Noah."

"Do you want to ask Walking Bear any questions?" Janie asked Doc.

"This is a farce!" Doc said angrily. "It's not legal for ghosts to testify! I can see through him, so he's a ghost, too. Just like Patches!"

Bob sighed and spoke. Janie translated, "Judge Bob says you keep forgetting you are being tried by their rules. Do you or do you not have anything to ask Walking Bear?"

Doc turned his head as he once again took in his surroundings. Then he reached in his pants pocket and pulled out a silver flask that somehow hadn't been lost during his transport. Before anyone could stop him, he opened the flask and swallowed its contents.

He belched, and Janie waved her hand beneath her nose and stepped away, as did the lawyer-Grassman. I noticed Janie put a protective hand on her stomach.

"She's pregnant," I whispered to Granny and Twila.

"I've knowed that since I laid eye on her," Granny replied quietly. "She's got that look."

"You're better than we are, Granny," Twila responded. "I'm like Alice. I didn't realize until she laid her hand over her baby."

"When we gets outta here, I'll teach you how to recognize them baby signs," Granny said.

The whiskey in his flask must have given Doc at least a small measure of courage. He burped again, then glared at Judge Bob. "I only did what any red-blooded man would do when he woke up and saw a monster big enough to eat him almost on top of him!"

Even from where we watched the proceedings, I saw the twinkle fill Daisy's eyes, and a silent communication flew between her and Walking Bear. The ghost stood up, an arrow notched in his bow and aimed at Doc. The attorney Grassman walked away a few steps, and while Doc's attention was centered on Walking Bear, Daisy slipped behind the others in her group. She tiptoed over behind Doc, grinned an evil sneer that bared both her upper and lower teeth, and lifted one arm as though getting ready to pounce.

She tapped Doc on the shoulder and when he jerked around fearfully, she growled. *ROAR!*

"Aieeee!" Doc screamed as the entire clearing, including Granny, Twila and me, erupted into gales of laughter. During the lack of attention on him, Doc raced across the clearing away from where we stood, into the woods on the other side. Both Free Eagle and Walking Bear were laughing so hard, it took them a second or two to realize Doc was escaping. Free Eagle disappeared in the wink of an eye, and I had no doubt Doc would soon return to face the remainder of his trial.

He did. An invisible Free Eagle dragged him kicking and screaming back into the clearing in less than a minute.

"Stop! Help me!" Doc yelled. "Something's got me! Help!"

More chuckles inundated us as we realized Doc's fear left no doubt he couldn't see his captor. Finally, there were only a few snickers now and then among the jury and spectators. Free Eagle picked Doc up under the arms and stood him where he'd been before his escape attempt. Doc froze in place, staring first at Walking Bear, who shook his bow and arrow and sneered at the prisoner.

Then Doc made the mistake of peering over his shoulder. Daisy let loose with another *ROAR!* When Doc frantically swiveled his head looking for another escape route, Free Eagle bent toward his ear and went, "Boo!"

Knees wobbling, Doc whimpered and whipped his head around to face Judge Bob. Lawyer-Grassman walked back over to Doc and nodded at the judge to continue.

After Bob spoke, Janie said, "He says that since you don't seem to have any questions, he's going to turn your fate over to the jury."

Though basically the jury whispered together, as though trying to be somewhat secretive, once in a while a laugh or a solemn sound stood out. Finally, one of them turned to gesture for Daisy to join them.

Granny said, "That's what's missin' from that there so-called justice system we got. The people who suffered the wrong oughta be in on pickin' the punishment!"

"Granny, sometimes you really hit the nail on the head," Twila said.

A few moments later, Daisy left the jury circle and the Grasspeople resumed their deliberations. Everyone else in the clearing appeared to be as fascinated as I was. They watched the jury, perhaps wanting to catch more than a chuckle or two, maybe a comment loud enough to foretell the decision. Finally, one member of the jury walked over to Judge Bob.

"Now you're gonna get it for hurting one of these fine folks," Patches said. He stood behind Doc, rather than over at the prosecuting table. "I hope they—"

Doc whirled and swung at Patches. When his fist went through the ghost, he yelled, "This is all your fault! You should've stayed dead! If you weren't a ghost, I'd kill you all over again!"

The tableau in the clearing froze for what seemed like an eternity of silence. Then Patches screamed, "You murdering bastard!"

CHAPTER 25

Patches swung.

 Doc ducked.

But it didn't matter. Patches' fist would have gone through him, as did Doc's fist when he threw a punch at Patches.

Patches danced away, and when Doc rushed to follow, fists swinging, Patches swung again. The punch didn't hurt Doc, but it distracted him. Patches lowered his head and dove straight through Doc's belly.

Shivering violently, Doc grabbed his stomach with one hand and turned to face Patches, his fist on his other arm trembling with the cold. Patches backed away, forcing Doc to pursue if he wanted a chance to throw another ineffective punch.

"Come on, you sleazy murdering son of a bitch," Patches taunted, dancing around with his arms up in a boxer's stance. "You've got fifty pounds on me. You ought to be able to take me easy enough."

"You're a damn ghost!" Doc yelled. "How am I supposed to kill you again?"

Patches stopped abruptly. "Oh. Right." Then he launched himself at Doc's legs.

Doc jumped, but Patches' back still went through Doc's feet. When he landed, Doc teetered for a second, as though his feet were asleep. Which maybe they were, due to the paranormal cold. Doc crashed to the ground, and Patches immediately stood over him.

"Get up, you murderer!" Patches said. "Take your whipping like a man!"

I whispered to Twila, "Are we just going to let this go on?"

Granny giggled and answered instead of my aunt. "You tell me how you're gonna make a ghost stop fighting his killer, and I be glad to help you out."

"Oh, we can do it," Twila assured her. "But I'm having too much fun watching them."

I bit my lip, but couldn't hold back my words. Perhaps I'd spent too much time around a cop. "This is a serious business," I said. "Doc pretty much confessed to Patches' murder...twice. We need to take Doc in to face justice. And clear Janie's name."

"Oh, just one more minute, Alice. Please," Twila said, a huge smile on her face. "This entire situation has been stressful. Watching this is almost as good as meditating away tension."

I laughed and shook my head. "You know, I do believe it is."

By now, Doc was on his feet, cautiously backing around the circle the Grasspeople had formed. They stood shoulder to shoulder, eyes shining with excitement in the reflected lantern light. Here and there, children sat at their parents' feet.

Patches pursued Doc, though not too closely. Instead, the ghost satisfied himself with throwing a jab at Doc's head every few steps. Doc jerked back each time, to the point I started wondering if he would soon suffer whiplash.

I chuckled. Granny was jabbing her fists in one-two punches, imitating Patches. Every few seconds, she would bounce up on her tiptoes. I caught Twila's gaze, and we both grinned. I did ready myself, in case I had to grab a hyped-up Granny, if she decided to head into the fray and help Patches out.

I forgot about her, though, when I again grew enthralled with the fight. Doc went on the attack, throwing wild punches at Patches as he braved the cold energy, head down and screaming, "You useless piece of trash! Go to hell, where you belong!"

Patches stood his ground, and when Doc hit him this time, he groaned at the impact. A surprised look on his face, Patches fell to the ground, barely scrambling away before Doc's larger body fell on top of him.

"Oh, crap," Twila said as Granny and I both turned questioning gazes on her. "Cat didn't tell me that part of the spell."

"What part?" I asked before the explanation dawned. "You mean when we use the spell to help a ghost visualize, it keeps working? Eventually gives him back a physical body?"

"It looks that way," Twila said. "Do you have your cell phone with you?"

"In the car."

"Is Cat's phone number in your contacts?"

"Yeah, but I don't know if I can get a signal out here. I'll try."

With one swift glance into the circle to see both Doc and Patches now circling warily, I hurried to my car. Given his new guardedness, Patches evidently understood that his re-formed body could take punishment.

At first I couldn't find the phone. Then I remembered stuffing it in the seat back, because the lump in my jeans bothered me. I pulled it out and hurriedly swiped the screen.

I couldn't read the icons on the phone screen, so I bent back inside to use the car's overhead light. It appeared the phone had nearly a full charge, and I recalled having it on the charger in Twila's kitchen.

I searched the contact list for Cat's number, stood back up and pushed the little phone button to place the call.

Cat answered immediately. "What's going on, Alice? I can sense something, but it doesn't seem possible."

It didn't surprise me that Cat's psychic senses had picked up on something happening to us. When she cared about someone, her gifts were way stronger than mine or even Twila's. The jump from Ohio to New Orleans would be child's play to her.

"Since when does stuff in the paranormal world have to seem possible?" I asked with a sigh. "We've got a confessed murderer fighting the ghost of the man he killed. Twila used your spell earlier to make the ghost more visible, so he could testify at the trial—"

"Wait a minute, wait a minute," Cat interrupted. "You had a ghost testify at a trial and didn't call me so I could watch?"

"It's a long story, Cat. Look, I promise I'll call you and tell you all the juicy details as soon as I can. Right now, I need to know how to reverse the spell Twila used to make the ghost visible to his murderer."

Only silence sounded for so long, I held the phone away to see if the server had dropped the call. We were still connected.

"Cat?"

"Uh...I'm trying to figure out how to tell you this, Alice. Is Twila there? You said she's the one who cast the spell, right?"

"Yes and yes," I told her.

A cheer went up from the circle of Grasspeople, who had only watched silently until now. I didn't even want to think about what caused such exhilaration.

"What was that?" Cat asked. "It didn't sound like people cheering."

"It's a group of Ohio Grassmen," I said, and waited for her reaction.

"Oh," was all I got back. Then she went on, "The spell can't be reversed until it has run its course. You'll have to ask Twila which version she used. One will last an hour or so, then Twila can undo it by speaking it backwards. The other one...."

Dread at what was coming next filled me as I waited for Cat to continue. Her words fulfilled my foreboding.

"The other one isn't easily reversible. I might have to come up there and help you both, and I'm at the airport right now, on my way to be with my daughter through the last week of her chancy pregnancy. I can't possibly get away for at least two or three weeks."

I started to ask her which spell was which, but she said, "I have to hang up. It's last boarding call."

And the call did disconnect then, even though I called, "Cat! Cat!"

I stuffed the phone in my pocket and hurried back to the circle to pass on the bad news.

"Well," Twila said with her usual logic after she checked her wristwatch, "we've got a half hour left before I can try the reversal. If it doesn't work, then we'll know it's the other spell."

In the circle, Doc lunged for Patches, and the ghost stepped aside fast enough to land a swift punch to Doc's jaw. Doc hit the ground, where he stayed for a long moment. At first, I assumed Patches would pounce on Doc, but he only stood there swaying back and forth.

"He ain't used to his new digs," Granny said. "He's gettin' tired."

"New digs?" I repeated. "Oh, you mean his body."

She frowned. "Yep. But I suppose it's his old digs, y'know?"

Suddenly Patches looked down at himself. But it wasn't his upper body he was examining. Instead, he bent down and groped one of his legs.

"Hey," he said as he felt up and down it. "Welcome home. You feel lots better than the leg I've been using lately."

"What's he talking about?" I asked Twila.

"He lost that leg to gangrene a few years ago," she explained. "I think he's saying the leg that goes with his firmer, physical body feels better than the one on his ghost body."

Doc noticed where Patches' attention was focused, too. He didn't bother to get up. He swept his legs around to knock both Patches' legs out from under him. The ghost—or was he not a ghost now? Darn, I was confused. But Patches hit the ground with an oomph of pain.

Doc scrambled toward Patches, but Patches wasn't done for yet. He landed a kick on Doc's jaw, then rose to his feet as Doc rolled away groaning. Doc came to rest nearly at our feet.

"You had enough?" Patches spat in a defiant voice, although the tone contained a measure of hope that maybe this was over with.

At first, Doc only rose to all fours, head hanging, as though he were indeed ready to concede the fight. However, the crafty killer had one more trick up his sleeve. He thrust himself to his feet, grabbing Rascal as he went. He held the Grassbaby around his stomach with one arm, the other hand clenched in the fur on Rascal's head.

"Don't anyone try to stop me!" he yelled. "Or I'll break this one's neck!" He glanced around the circle, then settled his gaze on Patches. "And you tell them I can do it, asshole! Tell them we learned how in Nam!"

Patches slowly nodded. "He's right. He can do it."

The silent black flash that whizzed by me was a hundred-fifty pounds of angry Trucker. He timed his lunge perfectly. He grabbed the hand Doc used to hold Rascal's head in a mouth filled with vicious fangs. His impetus carried him past Doc, the hand going with him. Doc screamed and released Rascal, but Patches was already diving forward to grab the Grassbaby.

It all happened within a couple seconds. Then Patches was on the ground, Rascal cradled safely on his stomach. But I'd heard the groan of pain from Patches when the Grassbaby landed on him. Even in his toddler state, Rascal had to weigh well over a hundred pounds.

Trucker shifted his hold on Doc to clench the man's upper arm tightly in his mouth. My dog backed up, pulling a screaming Doc across the circle. I followed, making no attempt to call Trucker off. Doc deserved every bit of punishment he was suffering.

Trucker knew exactly which person to take Doc to, but then, he had watched the trial with us. He dropped his burden in front Judge Bob. As soon as Doc realized he was free and made a move as though to stand, Trucker growled, low and vicious. My Trucker didn't need to speak human to get his point across. Doc froze, lying on his back, his gaze shifting between the savage countenance of the animal who guarded him and the face of the tall, legendary beast above him.

I sensed someone behind me and glanced over my shoulder to see Patches standing there.

"Hell of a dog you've got there," he murmured.

"Thanks," I replied. "By the way, do you have any idea why Doc killed you?"

"I think so," Patches said with a nod. "Let me think on it a minute before I say anything."

Doc must have heard our low conversation, because when I looked back, his gaze was ping-ponging a triangular path: Patches and me, the dog, and Bob. Bob wasn't doing much of anything except cupping his face in one hand in a thinking position. We all waited for his conclusion, and while he thought, Twila joined me, one hand holding Rascal's and Harley at her heels. Then came Granny carrying Miss Molly. Trucker's circle of love was complete now, and I didn't even want to think about what he would do to Doc should the man try again to harm one of us.

Bob lowered his hand and motioned to someone in another area of the circle. Janie came over and he said to her in accented English, "I need you to write something down."

Janie replied, "I'll need some pen and paper."

Being a writer, I tried never to travel without writing materials. I took a step forward and said, "There's a tablet under the driver's seat of my car. And some pens in the console."

"Will you retrieve them, please?" Bob asked politely.

I hurried back to the hybrid and found the tablet and pens easily enough. I grabbed three pens, knowing from experience the first one would run out of ink right in the middle of writing down what I considered a fabulous plot idea. Sometimes it took two more tries to uncover a workable pen.

Back in front of Bob, I realized my stress level had again escalated. I stood for a few seconds, drawing in breaths and breathing out slowly, as I stared at the situation I'd landed in. There must have been thirty or more Grasspeople, male and female adults, teenagers, toddlers and children. Then there were three ghosts and the man who had taken one ghost's life. Intermingled with them was an Amish woman whom we'd broken out of jail, and Twila and Granny, my usual faithful companions in any bizarre phenomenon I found myself in. Oh, and I couldn't forget the animals: my Trucker and Miss Molly, and Twila's pet pig, Harley.

What a state of affairs we'd found ourselves in this time. Things hadn't coalesced yet, either. We still had to get back to civilization and drop a murderer off for justice, as well as help three ghosts cross into The Light. And all I wanted to do was catch up on my sleep!

I carried the tablet over and offered it and the pens to Bob. He cleared his throat to draw everyone's attention, since they were carrying on several separate conversations.

"Janie will take the pen and paper," he said when things were quiet once more. "And she will write down the words the one on the ground will say, so he can confess his crimes. He will also sign his name, as they do in those television shows."

I couldn't help myself. "Do you have television in your camp sites?"

Bob nodded. "The satellite signal is good for that. Sometimes on our computers, too."

Computers? These fascinating beasts used computers?

"But...but...." It would be totally rude to ask the next question bursting into my mind.

"Go ahead," Bob said. "You want to know something else?"

I asked, "Don't you have to pay for a satellite signal to view TV and operate computers?"

He chuckled and winked at me. "There are ways."

Bob stepped around Trucker and nudged Doc with one huge foot. "You may sit up now. You will speak the words for Janie to write down. And do not try to lie."

Doc made one more round with his eyes before he cautiously zeroed in on Trucker and pushed himself up. But when he started to try to rise further, Bob put a hand on his head.

"Sit, not stand."

Doc made absolutely no attempt to disobey.

CHAPTER 26

The Grassmen didn't appear to have a bit of trouble carrying my car through the woods back the way we'd come. I sat behind the steering wheel, Twila beside me, Granny and Janie in back. Once in a while, Janie sniffed and blew her nose in one of the tissues from the box I kept in the car. She had said a tearful last goodbye to her Uncle Patches before we climbed into the car. She really did love that old reprobate.

The animals made themselves comfortable in the rear hatch area. I'd stuffed the keys securely into my jeans pocket, so no one else could drive my car once I got it back on the road. Notwithstanding Granny's offer to bear witness, my insurance wouldn't cover a non-licensed Grassman.

I doubted Doc enjoyed the journey, since he was strapped to my luggage rack on top, like a deer hunter bringing home a kill. Only this prey was still alive.

We'd left the camp with a few minutes to spare before we could try to reverse the spell on Patches, so we would have to wait until we got back to Twila's for that. Hopefully, the ghost would cooperate. Twila hadn't been able to talk to Patches about what we needed to do, since he and the two Native American ghosts had disappeared somewhere while the Grassmen were loading Doc on top of my car.

"It shouldn't be much further to the road," I told Twila. "We're climbing out of the creek bed now."

"Another ten minutes or so," she agreed.

However, we only navigated a little over half that distance before the Grassmen set my car down and silently disappeared into the surrounding forest.

"Hey!" I called before I realized my window was up and they probably couldn't hear me. I opened the door and repeated, "Hey! Come back here and take us on out to the road!"

Not one of them responded, and Twila nudged my shoulder. "Look straight ahead."

I easily identified the faint flickers of light as the overhead bar on a cop car. Perhaps more than one. Unfortunately, I'd seen too many of those in my rear view mirror before I slowed down or risked losing my license.

"Probably Hoof," I said. "He's probably searching for us for breaking Janie out of jail. But we can deliver the real murderer to him now."

"That's not gonna help you much if Hoof decides not to drop the charges against all of you." By the time Jack had finished his sentence, I was staring at where he stood beside my open door.

"How...where did you come from?" I asked inanely, just as Noah emerged from the woods, followed by a small gray animal with huge, long ears.

"Why, Mikala's donkey, Balboa, must have wandered again," Twila said as she stared past me. "She'll be glad you found him, Noah."

About then, I began to realize the forest was light enough for us to see the men and donkey without the assistance of any lights. Dawn was getting ready to break, and it should be easy enough for us to direct Hoof to where we had Doc trussed up on my car. But—

"Shit," I said with a half-moan. "How am I going to get my car out of here?"

"We'll worry about that after we find out what Hoof's got in mind," Jack said. "You won't be needin' it if you're servin' a few months in the women's prison."

275

"Oh, you're just mad because we didn't include you in our escape, Jack," I said. "I tried, but I was afraid Bob would take off without us."

"You left your keys in the car again, didn't you, *Chère*?"

"Well, yeah," I admitted.

Jack breathed a sigh, then took my arm and helped me out of the car. The next thing I knew, he held me so tightly I could barely move.

"Damn you, *Chère*," he said. "Do you know how worried I've been?"

I slipped my arms around his waist and cuddled even closer. "I'd have come back and let you out if I could have. You missed all the fun."

He pushed me back and glared. "Fun? You call what's been goin' on around here *fun*?"

I giggled and nodded. "I'll tell you all about it, if I don't forget half of it while I'm incarcerated for several months."

"You ain't gonna be incar—"

He kissed me, his lips demanding and heated at first, transmitting his anger and worry to me. Then they softened, and he held the back of my head as he kept kissing me until I forgot where we were and who we were putting on a show for. My legs weakened, and I tightened my hold on his waist, but I still started to slide to the ground.

If Jack hadn't come to his senses, we might have put on a totally inappropriate show for our spectators. He laid his forehead against mine. "This isn't the end of your apology," he whispered.

I smiled and moved my lips close to his ear. "I hope not. It's been a while."

Jack groaned and pushed me away.

"Gosh dang it," Granny said from inside the car. "It was just gettin' to the good part."

We both ignored her, but Jack's chuckle rumbled in his chest. Keeping one arm around me, he stared at the car roof. "Isn't that Doc Morrow?"

"Yes," Twila told him. "And if you two are done—" Twila's door opened and Jack and I moved a few steps so we could see over the front of the hybrid. Jess stood there, and he snapped his fingers in an order for Twila to get out. Meekly, she complied.

"Gol'damn you and this ghost business," Jess muttered.

"It was your friend's ghost who started it this time, honey," she said. "And it wasn't only ghosts. There were a few Grass—"

He covered her mouth with his hand. "I don't want to hear about those monsters roaming the woods. I still like to camp out overnight on the river fishing."

She removed his hand and stood on tiptoe to kiss him. "We've only got a couple things left to do in order to wind this up."

Jess heaved a sigh. "Well, hurry it up. I'm ready for you to be home for a while."

"Awww," I heard Granny say from the back seat. She nudged Janie. "I thinks your man is waiting for you, too."

Janie slid out the driver's side to greet Noah. I wasn't surprised when Noah only slipped an arm around Janie to hug her close. The Amish weren't public with feelings for their spouses. Janie would have to wait for her welcome home.

"Are you all right, wife?" Noah asked in a whisper.

"We're both fine," she said, caressing her stomach.

"Both?" Jack asked. Before I could explain, he said, "Oh," his gaze on Janie's tummy. However, her loose dress hid her pregnancy well.

"We better get movin' here," Jack said. "I think I've figured out a way we can get this prisoner to the sheriff and clear y'all's names."

"We have a written confession," I said. "He admitted to shooting Daisy and also killing Patches."

"What?" Jack released me and took a step toward the car, an expression on his face that I wouldn't have wanted to be on the receiving end of.

With a low growl of loathing, Jess came around the front of my car, followed by Twila.

"Now, honey," Twila said as she grabbed her husband's arm.

He gently removed her hand and pushed her over to stand beside me. Then he said to Jack, "Whatever you've got in mind for this bastard, I want in on it."

On the top of my car, Doc sniveled. He stared at Jess and Jack, eyes full of fear. I didn't feel a bit of sympathy for him.

"I believe I will take my wife and wait at home for you to tell me what we should do next," Noah said. He still held Balboa's lead rope, and now Janie sat on the donkey's back. "I know a way through the woods that will keep us out of sight of the sheriff. I will also get word to Mikala that I have her donkey."

Granny slid out of the car and toddled over to Noah. "Now, iffen your name was Joseph, we'd be remembering that Christmas journey when the ass carried such a precious cargo."

"Actually, my middle name is Joseph," Noah said with a smile. Then he glanced at each of us as he continued, "I wish to thank all of you for helping keep my Janie out of a cell." He looked up at Janie with an expression of total love. "She probably would have made the best of it, but it would have torn me up. I might have forgotten my faith and our non-violence teachings."

Jess and Jack both shook hands with Noah, with Jess saying, "You ever need someone who doesn't believe in turning that other cheek to help you, you come directly to me."

Noah chuckled and nodded. "Hopefully, this is the end of it."

He led Balboa away down a faint trail in the underbrush, Janie on the donkey's back. Just before they disappeared, Janie turned and waved at us. I didn't dare look at the others, afraid the tears would spill out of my eyes. It was hard enough to hold them back when Granny hummed, "Silent night, holy night," for us all to hear.

Even before Granny finished the song, Jess was untying Doc from the top of my car, Jack assisting. They pulled Doc down none-too-considerately, and Jack turned him around to re-secure his hands behind him with a plastic tie he pulled from his jacket pocket. It didn't surprise me that Jack had a tie with him. He always carried a lot of just-in-case cop things.

"Now," Jack said when he finished with Doc. "Where's the confession?"

I leaned into the car and retrieved the notebook from where I'd placed it between the driver's seat and the console. Jack opened it and read what was written there, nodding as he did so. I recognized the amazement in his voice when he said, "Pretty darned good job," and drew myself up in a huff, prepared to tell him we weren't stupid just because we didn't have his training.

He defused my defensive attitude when he said, "Alice must have helped y'all write this. She's obviously learned what needs to be in a confession from the research she does to make her books so good."

He lifted an inquiring eyebrow, and I actually preened for a second or two. "Well," I said. "I did have a little input."

"Input, schminput," Granny said. "She made sure this here murderer got it all down slick and right, so there wouldn't be no doubt what he done. Hope he spends the rest of his useless life behind bars."

"Actually," Twila murmured, "Ohio still has the death penalty. They use lethal injection."

Doc leaned against the car, shoulders heaving in sobs. But he didn't utter even one word of remorse.

"Effin bastard," Jess said. "It'll serve him right." He frowned at Twila. "Did he ever say why he did it?"

"He did," Twila told him. "I'll tell you all about it when we get home. I'm tired and hungry."

"I'll fix us up a good ole Texas breakfast," Granny said.

Jack smiled at Granny. "With that waitin' for me, I'll get movin'." He reached in his pocket and handed me a set of keys, pointing the way Noah had gone with his other hand. "My truck's over there. Hoof wouldn't allow Noah or me on the search, so Noah took me back to the house. Jess can show you where it's parked, and I'll take care of your prisoner here. I should be able to get a ride back with one of the deputies. I'll just remind the sheriff about the positive publicity that solvin' Patches' murder so quickly could bring to his next re-election campaign. I think I can talk him into not revealin' how it all came about, since he wouldn't want his constituents to think he believed in ghosts and the Ohio Grassman. They might not want a loony sheriff in office."

"Excellent," Twila said. "And I'll bet the Amish will praise him for keeping on the case to clear Janie's name."

"I'll be sure and mention that, too," Jack told her.

"Well, not to be a party pooper," I said, plopping my hands on my hips, "but how the hell am I going to get my car out of here?"

CHAPTER 27

As usual, Granny did herself proud on the food, and it would have been very easy for me to take my full tummy and head back to bed. However, although I didn't really believe the Grassmen would come back and take my unguarded car to their camp, I prodded and poked until the hybrid's rescue was in the works.

The men grumbled and griped, but went to the barn for the four-wheelers. Twila stayed behind, since we still had to gather those ghosts and tie up the last thread of our adventure. She was scraping scraps into a bowl for Harley as I left the kitchen, and the pig never took his eyes off the food. Miss Molly decided to catch up on her lost sleep. My cat got even more bitchy if she didn't get her full twenty hours. Trucker, though, trotted along with us.

I got behind Jack on one four-wheeler, and Jess called Trucker up to ride with him on the other. Jess went first, since he knew the cross-country way to where the Grassmen had left my car, and Trucker happily sat there, ears blowing behind him in the wind, mouth open in a grin of enjoyment.

Shoot, I might have to buy a four-wheeler when I got home. Or better yet, have Jack bring his over and give Trucker a ride now and then.

Of course, if we ever reached a decision on our relationship, maybe the four-wheeler would already be at my cabin. Or maybe not, if that decision went a different way. I caught myself musing about which direction I wanted that decision to unfold as we flew across a pasture. Finally, we turned down a narrow country road I recognized.

Once in the woods, the two men hitched up heavy ropes while I sat in the driver's seat to steer. It was a good thing the four-wheelers were the strong, mulish type men prefer. It took several tries to get the car out to the highway, where I inspected it thoroughly.

"I guess it has a good paint job," I said to Jack after I walked around the car. "I don't see even one scratch." I frowned. "Not even the one that moron in Tennessee keyed in the paint."

"I buffed that one out one day when you left the car at the house, Alice," Jess said as he rolled up the ropes and tossed them into a tool box attached to his machine. "Only took me a few minutes. It wasn't that deep."

"Why, thank you, Jess," I said. "The car's perfect again."

Jack quickly turned away, but I'd seen his grin before he could hide it. I grabbed his arm to keep him from escaping.

"What did that silly expression on your face mean?" I demanded.

"Oh, shoot, *Chère*. I'll tell you, if you promise not to get mad. I was hoping...." He winked at me.

He didn't have to tell me what he meant. I hadn't forgotten whispering in his ear as dawn broke.

Blushing, I said, "I'll do my best."

His smile devastated me nearly as much as the sleepy, knowing look in his dark brown eyes. "I was just thinking that a car of yours finally made it through one of yours and Twila's *adventures* in one piece."

"Hey," I said, looking at my hybrid once more, "you're right." I patted the car's fender, as I went on, "But we're not quite done yet. I need to get back to help Twila with those ghosts."

"What else do you need to do?" Jack asked, getting on the four-wheeler.

"Convince them to cross into The Light," I said logically, as though even a neophyte like Jack should have understood that.

He only nodded and dropped his machine into gear to follow Jess, who was already nearly out of sight, Trucker still relishing his ride.

I got into my car and pushed the start button. The faint buzz of the battery-powered end of the engine was reassuring, since I'd almost asked Jack to wait and make sure the car would start. I stroked the dash as a thank you, then pulled the floor shift into *Drive*.

I should have known Jack's comment would jinx me. Anxious to get back to Twila, I hit the gas a little too hard. The rear of the car slid in the gravel.

Crunch!

"Oh, shit," I muttered as I jammed on the brake. I'd forgotten about that one tree close to the back of my car. If I'd gone straight, as Jack had briefly mentioned when he released the ropes, then turned, I'd have been fine. But no, I had to get in a hurry!

By the time I'd hit the brakes, I was already halfway on the highway. Pulling on out, I maneuvered partway off the road and hit the four-way-flashers. I crossed my fingers as I got out, hoping maybe the damage wasn't as bad as I feared.

It was. There was no way to hide the large dent in the rear fender. Biting my lip, I decided I'd only be semi-honest with the insurance adjuster. He would probably raise my rates on total suspicion that I did drugs if I mentioned Ohio Grassmen were the reason we had to drag my car out of the woods. I'd just reveal the part of the story about sliding in the gravel.

Still, I probably should get another book on the market to pay my already outrageous premiums.

* * *

I backed the car into a spot beside Twila's garage, hoping I wouldn't have to explain the damage before Granny and I started back to Texas. As I hurried toward the house, a flicker of motion drew my attention. Then I caught that faint hint of a whisper in my mind, calling my name. *Alice.*

I headed across the pasture to the edge of the woods behind the house. Twila, Granny and the two men stood around the area where Bob had left Patches' body. Even the animals were there; evidently Miss Molly had either caught up on her sleep or realized something was going on that she didn't want to miss.

As I drew closer, I kept watch for the three ghosts, but didn't see even one of them.

"What's wrong?" I asked when I reached the group and saw a frowning Twila with hands on her hips.

"They're being stubborn," she said with a hint of irritation in her voice. "We might have to go looking for them."

"Shoot, Twila. It would take us weeks to travel around to all the places they might be languishing."

When she glanced at me, I shook my head negatively. She'd already decided what we had to do, and it wasn't something I was comfortable with. Hoping to change her mind, I said "We haven't practiced that enough to be good at it. Soul traveling should only be a last resort."

"I agree," she replied. "I'm not happy to have to do it, either, without Cat's guidance. But we can't let them get away with ignoring us. Granted, they can refuse to go into The Light, but we're obligated to do the best we can to change their minds."

She was right, as usual. It was part of our code of ethics. We knew far too many supposed paranormal investigators who were just out for the excitement of the ghost hunt. They would descend on naïve homeowners, identify ghosts in residence, and antagonize and provoke the paranormal entities into anger and a desire for retaliation. Then the foolish idiots would run off and leave the poor human residents to cope with the result of their stupidity.

The two of us never left a haunted location in worse shape than when we arrived, as some of those unprincipled individuals or groups did. We believed in leaving peace behind, or at least, giving that our best shot. Just because this was Twila's home didn't mean I could retreat from that important obligation.

I sighed. "Where are we going to start from?"

"Right here," she said as she sat down in the tall grass and motioned for me to join her. "I've already told Jack and Jess to keep an eye on us, warned them what signs to watch out for and how to counteract them, if necessary. But as long as we stay together, we'll be fine."

I took a deep breath and sat beside Twila. We both removed our shoes and curled our legs together in front of us in semi-yoga positions. Then we laid our hands palms up on our knees and closed our eyes.

Neither of us had any trouble leaving our bodies and heading out for a reconnaissance bit of soul traveling. We had each practiced that with Cat Dancer's supervision, but never just the two of us alone. Twila hadn't had any trouble returning to her body, either. I was the one who got lost in the wonder of it, perhaps due to my inquisitive, creative mind. Once Cat had sent one of my Spirit Guides after me to figuratively take me by the nape of the neck and toss me back into my physical body.

As I felt myself leave the chains of my human body behind and enter the joy of being an entity of energy, I made an ardent vow to keep my mind on business this trip.

I glanced aside to see Twila with me. We couldn't communicate with body language, but we were easily able to understand each other. She wanted me to stay with her, rather than us splitting up to cover more territory. That suited me just fine, and I relaxed, feeling much safer in her company.

We checked out the bait shop first. There was no sign of the three ghosts, or even Patches himself. However, that reminded me of something.

We never found out what was hidden in the bait shop, I telepathed to Twila. *I wonder if it had something to do with the motive he said he wanted to think about before he told us.*

I sensed her give a mental shrug. *We'll have to find them in order to figure that out.*

We kept our focus on staying aloft and watching for the ghosts somewhere down below. They were tied to the earth and unable to do as we did. Ghosts could indeed travel; however, not this way. Our senses were also more highly attuned than when in our physical bodies, so the ghosts would be unable to hide from us indefinitely. It might take us a little longer than someone like Cat, who had much more practice, but we would find them.

Twila led me over the Grassman camp, but they were going about their daily business of living, no ghosts in sight. We even checked out the river bank, to see if Patches had talked Free Eagle and Walking Bear into going fishing with him. No luck.

As we started to leave there, I noticed a beautiful, red covered bridge around the river bend. Covered bridges fascinate me. There are so few left in Ohio, and I'd visited most of them. I didn't recall this one, though, and wondered why Twila hadn't told me about it.

In this state of being, it wouldn't take that long to check it out. Twila would never miss me.

As soon as I got closer, I realized this one would be difficult to get to after we returned to the physical. The road on both sides of the river had been abandoned. Grass and weeds grew up through the few feet of asphalt the highway department hadn't dug up and carted off for fill dirt elsewhere.

Still, we could ride the four-wheelers, I told myself when I saw another county road not far away. *I'll just delay my trip home long enough to come here with Twila.*

Satisfied that I'd remember where this covered bridge was located, I turned to apologize to Twila for getting distracted. But Twila's ball of energy wasn't anywhere in sight.

Twila! I mentally called. *Twila!*

No response.

Oh, crap. I was in trouble now. She would be exasperated with me, and knowing her, she would come up with some punishment to fit my crime: the crime of disobeying one of the laws we'd been taught. We weren't supposed to go off alone until Cat had time to allow us to solo under her supervision. Then and only then would we receive our soul travel diploma.

Twila!

Shoot. I should probably go back into my body and wait for her. After she got over her pique and dealt out my reprimand, we could head out again. It wasn't as if the ghosts were on any sort of schedule.

I spun my energy ball as I tried to see which way I needed to go to return to my body. Agitated when everything looked strange to me, I spun faster. A second later, I realized I couldn't stop myself. The world whizzed and circled past me so fast, it blurred. Then I was falling.

If I'd had any breath or need to breathe, I'd have held it as I waited for impact. Shoot, I didn't even know if impact would hurt in this state. Or what would happen if I ended up speared on a tall tree or fence post. Would my energy dissipate into a zillion small balls, with no way of putting them all back together to make *Alice* again?

I jolted to a halt. The first thing I did was glance below. Not more than fifty feet away, a layer of treetops bunched closely waited to splinter me. If something like that were possible. I directed my sense of sight upwards. There was no mistaking who that other ball of energy belonged to. Twila had rushed to my side and halted my journey before I shattered into Humpty Dumpty. But my senses told me she wasn't very happy she'd had to save my wayward butt, even if the faint hint of anger-red in her energy ball hadn't indicated her displeasure.

I'm sorry, I told her with what I hoped was the proper measure of remorse.

Her energy ball expanded with a sigh of either relief or disgust. I hoped it was relief.

I won't do it again, I promised. *Honestly. I'll stay right beside you.*

You better, she warned. *Next time I might not be able to stop you.*

If I'd had a mouth, it would have dropped open in astonishment. *You were hiding to teach me a lesson!*

Not deigning to reply to that obvious truth, she told me, *I've found our ghosts.*

She led off without even a glance behind to see if I followed. Of course, I didn't dare break my promise. But as soon as I could, I wanted to go visit Cat and get my solo license. No way did I want to take another tumble like that.

Not that far from where our bodies waited for us, the ghosts were walking single file along a trail. Since we couldn't communicate with them in our state, I tagged close when Twila headed over to where Jack, Jess, Granny and the animals waited.

I always hated the jolt that meant my weightlessness was gone, and which reminded me of the extra five pounds that hung on my hips. I took a few moments to reacquaint myself with my body, then opened my eyes to see Jess and Jack worriedly hanging over the two of us.

"What?" I asked Jack. "We're back, safe and sound."

"I'd rather not go through that again," Jack said. "Jess and I were debating how long we should wait before we started mouth-to-mouth. Or got the paddles in my first aid kit."

"Mouth to mouth, huh?" I whispered to Jack, which sent an interesting blush up his neck.

"I told 'em they'd end up sendin' you to the Maker a'fore you was supposed to go," Granny said, although the wink she gave me indicated she'd heard my flirtatious comment. "Thought I was gonna have to order Trucker to stand over y'all's bodies."

"Well, that's all it looked like was left there," Jess said. He didn't bother to temper his anger and fear. "I was getting ready to go look at coffins!"

Twila put her arms around him. "Sorry, honey. I forget how things look to someone not used to what I do. But I'm fine now. See?" She laid her head on his chest and snuggled close.

I waited for Jack to reach for me and get his own cuddle, but he was definitely back in cop mode, perhaps to combat his blush.

"What did you find out?" he asked. "Are the ghosts already gone?"

"No," I explained. "They're over there in the woods. I'm not sure what they're up to. It looked like Patches was carrying a shovel."

Jess snapped his fingers. "I know what Patches has been trying to hide. Bet you they're headed for that burial mound just over the next rise. Come on."

Jess led, the rest of us, including the animals, trailing after him. Barely a minute later, I recognized the trail the ghosts had been following, which we had seen from the air. Shortly, the ground began an upslope. It wasn't a big hill, and within a few minutes, the animals gathered around us as we stood on the crest and stared down at a smaller, man-built rise. The three ghosts were on top of it, and Patches appeared to be having little success using the shovel to dig a hole.

Jess pointed at the mound. "That's one of those Indian burial mounds Ohio's got so many of. I'll bet Patches is trying to bury the antique he pulled out of the river on the end of one of his hooks when we were fishing last year. The one he told me he'd already buried."

"Antique? Fishing?" I asked, but Jess was already heading down the hill toward the mound.

The ghosts saw us, but not one of them made a break for it. In fact, they all waited for us to collect at the foot of the mound, then Patches spoke.

"What'd you do to me?" he asked Twila. "I feel like I'm myself again, but I ain't got no weight to speak of. I can't get this shovel to work." Then he noticed Jess and said, "Hey, Pard. You gonna finally talk to me?"

"As long as you talk from up there," Jess said in a grumpy voice. "Are you trying to bury that antique? The one you said you already took care of, so we wouldn't get charged with stealing ancient artifacts?"

"Yeah," Patches said with a slight nod as he looked away from Jess's glare. "I wanted to talk to you in private and see if you could find out who got it out of the safe when I couldn't. I remembered what Doc and me were arguing about right before he killed me, and I was afraid Doc had managed to come back and get it. Got worried that if he got caught with it, he'd tell the law that you and me gave it to him. Get you in trouble. Didn't want your wife to know I'd done something that might bring the law down on you."

Jess shook his head. "Twila would have understood. But how did Doc find out about it?"

"It wasn't until I saw Walking Bear with it that my memory came back." Patches stepped aside so we could see the pretty pottery cow on the ground. The paint was faded to near invisibility, but we could tell the cow sat with its legs crossed, a screw-on head concealing the interior of its tummy where the cookies would have been placed.

Patches continued, "I didn't really tell Doc about it directly. He said I was talking when I was coming out of that there anesthesia the day they cut my leg off. I guess folks say weird stuff then. But mostly the nurses and docs just ignore them."

I started to ask Patches a question, but Twila nudged me. When I looked at her, she barely shook her head in a caution for me not to interrupt this exchange between Jess and Patches. I understood immediately. The discord between them was yet another thread that needed tied before Patches crossed over.

Granny, Twila and I all backed up a few steps to let Jess and Patches work this out. When Jack saw us move, he silently joined us. I quietly snapped my fingers at Trucker, and Miss Molly followed him to my side, Harley tagging along with her.

"Walking Bear's the one who took it from the bait shop," Patches explained. "He was able to get into the safe when I couldn't."

"I-I did not steal," Walking Bear said. "It was m-mine."

"Right," Patches said. He explained to us, "It belonged to Walking Bear. His Amish friend, Ruth, gave it to him, and he used it to store the cookies she baked for him. He lost it one day in a storm, so guess that's how it got into the river for me to catch. Now he wants it buried before he goes with his brother to their hunting grounds."

"How'd Doc fit into all that?" Jess reminded him.

"Well, see, Doc was getting pretty desperate for money. If he'd of just quit drinking, he might have went back to practicing medicine. But the way things were, he couldn't even pay to renew his license. All his relatives had had enough of him. I caught him in the bait shop when I came home early one night from fishing. He was trying to figure out the combination to my safe, him being one of the few folks who even knew I had one."

290

When Patches fell silent, Jess prodded, "Doc must have been pretty desperate to kill you over it."

Patches shook his head sadly. "Yeah, it happened that same night I caught him in my shop. I was so pissed off, I chased him off into the woods, hollering what I was gonna do to him when I caught him. That I was going to call Hoof and have him arrested for breaking and entering. Thing was, I'd had a few drinks, too, and I stumbled over a log and knocked myself out. Next thing I knew, I was dead. I guess that there Mr. Bob Grassman was watching what was going on. He told me about it while I was with them. Said he knew I was Janie's uncle and that I was friends with you. He didn't realize what Doc was gonna do until too late to stop him. So he brought my body to where you'd find me."

"You've met those Grassmen that Twila told me about?" Jess shook his head and glanced at Twila. "I thought maybe she was teasing me."

"Nope, they're real," Patches said. "They was with us when Doc admitted what he'd done. But Doc tricked himself when he killed me. 'Cause that got the law keeping an eye on the bait shop, so he couldn't get back in there and try to steal anything. Gave Walking Bear time to get it that night I tried and couldn't do it."

He shook his head. "Them ghosts get bored and then curious. They find out lots following folks around to see what they're up to."

"Sounds like the jar's special to Walking Bear, so no one needs to be misusing it."

"You're right, Pard," Patches said. "We need to bury it here, since we can't take it with us." He looked at Twila again. "So I'll let you folks bury this, if you promise you'll do that. And I need to be put back like I was, so I can cross into that there Light with my new friends."

"Uh...well...." Twila shared a what-do-we-do-now? glance with me.

"Between the two of us, we should be able to figure out—"

I hadn't noticed Patches leave the mound and appear closer to us. "Figure what out?" he asked Twila. "Can't you put me back like I was? I don't want to be stuck like this cause you pulled some of your wacky stuff!"

A guilty flush stole over Twila's face, but Patches had crossed the line. Trucker growled low in warning, and Jess took a step towards us, but sweat beaded his brow—probably at the thought of having to be in such close proximity to a ghost—and he froze in place. I stepped between Twila and Patches and, hands on hips, leaned close to give the ghost a measure of discipline.

"You listen here, you...you...ghost!" I said. "If it wasn't for Twila helping out at the trial, the person who murdered you might still be on the loose. And make no bones about it—"

"I ain't got no bones no longer," Patches broke in, his tone indicating he wasn't being suitably chastised. "Way I am, I ain't no ghost nor a person neither one. I can't even work that shovel."

"I can," I said. "And so can the rest of us. We'll bury the cookie jar for Walking Bear, not for you. And if you don't watch your attitude, you'll find out what we really can do to you. Keep on spouting off and Twila and I will make sure you do a heck of a lot of wandering all by your lonesome for a lot of years before you see The Light!"

"Can you make sure he can't haunt us?" Jess asked. "I don't like the way he's behaving, either. He knows better than to piss me off by saying something hurtful about my wife."

"Oh, crap, Pard." Patches held out his hands in an apologetic manner. "I'm sorry. Really."

"I'm not the one you need to apologize to," Jess growled.

Patches gazed sincerely at Twila. "I'm sorry as a blue tick hound who treed a possum instead of a coon, lovely Twila. I'm just a little on edge, and my mouth's outrunning my brain. Please forgive me. I promise I won't do it again." He frowned, then shot Twila a sly grin. "I really won't say anything mouthy if I can get myself on the other side of that Light and out of your pretty red hair."

Twila chuckled. "Apology accepted, Patches. Now, let's see if we can reverse the spell."

"If!" Patches cried, but he immediately backpedaled. "No, no, no, I didn't mean that. I'll do whatever you need me to do."

"It's not you who needs to do it," Twila told him. "It's me, but Alice will help. First, let's make Walking Bear happy."

She looked over at our men, but neither Jack nor Jess moved to climb the mound to help bury the cow cookie jar and put it to rest. Instead, they stared at the two fierce looking Wyandotte warriors who had been waiting patiently, glanced at each other, then seemed to get extremely interested in something on the ground.

Granny took the shovel from Patches' hand. Instead of handing it to one of the men and ordering him to get busy, she toddled over to the mound and started to climb. Jess and Jack hesitated a long moment before they rushed forward and tried to take the shovel from her. Granny slapped Jack's hand away, then Jess's. She glared at them, propping her hands on the shovel to hold herself steady on the side of the mound.

"Both you big strong men has gots a yellow streak up your backs when it comes to dealin' with ghosts. Now you wants to save face 'cause an eighty-somethin'-year-old granny showed you up. Don't you know we is way more powerful than a ghost? Ain't you learned nothin' in the years you been the men in your women's lives? Ain't you listened to anythin' they said?"

They stuck their hands in their blue jean pockets and hunched their shoulders in embarrassment. Neither of *our men* liked the fact that we dealt in the paranormal. They tolerated it, because if they didn't...well, we would do it anyway. Despite their dislike of what we did, however, we loved them dearly. To us, they were two of the most handsome and loveable men alive. Besides, they knew when to shut up.

"Now," Granny said, "I'll let y'all help me up this hill, but I'll do the diggin'." She allowed Jack and Jess each to take one of her arms.

"Do you want me to carry the shovel?" Jack asked respectfully.

"I gots hold of it just fine," Granny replied.

The three of them climbed on up the mound. It took them nearly five minutes to make it to the top of the rise. By that time, Trucker and Harley were waiting. Perhaps the animals understood the word "dig." Trucker loved throwing dirt between his rear legs, and Harley might have sensed a chance to root around.

Granny motioned a finger at Walking Bear. "Do you want to hold that there jar one more time?"

293

He nodded, and went over to where the cookie jar lay. Bending, he picked it up, then glanced over to see Free Eagle watching him.

"I guess you think I am still childish for caring about a silly cookie jar," Walking Bear said without a hint of stutter. "For wanting the cow buried before I go."

His brother glided up beside him. "I love you, little brother. It never mattered to me that you did not grow up. You gave me much gladness being as you were. You helped me remember all the things that were fun when we were small. Made me stop and watch the new animal young each spring. I helped you gather flowers for our mother, the mushrooms you knew our father enjoyed. I would have missed very much in my life without having you to make me recall these things."

Walking Bear smiled and handed the cookie jar to Jess, who was the closest to him, so he and Free Eagle could share a manly hug. Jess nearly jerked back and dropped the cow, but Granny muttered something in time for him to grab a firm hold. He did shiver from the proximity to Walking Bear's paranormal coldness, but the Native American ghosts didn't notice. Instead, they patted each other on the back in one of those awkward, gestures that men didn't seem very comfortable making, then turned to look down at where Twila and I stood.

"We are ready to go," Walking Bear said.

"Are you sure, my brother?" Free Eagle asked. "If you wish to wait until we see the gift Ruth gave you buried, I will be glad go after that."

"I am still afraid, but not as much as before," Walking Bear said. "My fear is less now because you are with me. And I do not want to make you wait any longer to see your Moon Dove."

Twila smiled at them, and murmured to me, "These two will be easy. Do you want to do the crossing?"

"I'd be honored," I said.

I left her there with Patches and walked up the mound to stand beside Free Eagle and Walking Bear. "I'll bet you two can tell me which way is east," I said.

Walking Bear pointed to his left, and we all faced that way. Over the years, Twila and I had gained confidence in our ability to help lonely souls find peace, so I only had to lift my hand and say, "I have souls who would like to cross into The Light. Please open a door and show them the way."

Immediately, a bank of clouds above us in the blue sky parted. A light shone out from the fissure and expanded toward us until a golden sidewalk descended, ending a few feet in front of us. Most of the time, the souls were somewhat leery about this being real, and both of the brothers hesitated.

I pointed at the fissure in the clouds to draw their attention upward. I knew they would see what I did: people gathered there, smiling and excited to have them join them.

"Moon Dove," Free Eagle said at the same moment Walking Bear raced forward calling, "It is our mother and father!"

Free Eagle hurried after his brother, catching him at once, because Walking Bear stopped halfway up the golden walkway to turn. I'd expected that; seldom did it not happen.

"Thank you all, and goodbye!" both of them called with a wave. Then they rushed forward into the arms of their waiting loved ones. As usual during such an awesome experience, tears tracked down my face. Granny sniffed, too, and Jack and Jess each coughed, as men do, like they were covering up their emotions.

Although all of the souls, including the two brothers, disappeared from the fissure in the clouds, the walkway remained.

"Do you think I could go, too?" Patches asked Twila, the measure of respect still holding sway in his voice.

"You can try," Twila said.

She and the ghost walked up the mound to join us. But when Patches tried to continue onto the golden sidewalk, he couldn't even step one foot there. When he turned to gaze back at Twila, there was a deep sorrow in his expression, rather than the anger I'd halfway expected.

"We'll have to un-do the spell," Twila said.

Shoulders slumped, Patches glided over and stood before her. Unexpectedly, Jess handed Jack the cookie jar and came over to stand with him.

"Don't worry, old Pard," Jess said. "Twila can fix it."

"Well, while you two does your duty," Granny said, "me'n Jack'll keep y'all's promise to that there nice Walking Bear."

They both went over to where Patches had first been trying to dig, and Jack again made the mistake of reaching for the shovel. Granny lifted it, and I started to hurry forward and catch that sharp instrument before she could whack Jack over the head. Instead, she glared at him, her tiny figure a picture of David confronting Goliath. Jack backed up and said, "Go ahead, Granny. I'll stay here just in case you need help. Just in case, you know?"

Granny stuck the shovel into the ground and pushed on it with one foot. She managed to removed a miniscule amount of dirt and dumped it beside the hole she had begun. Trucker and Harley evidently smelled the dirt, but also realized they better not interfere with Granny. They laid down beside the small pile, Trucker with his muzzle on his front paws, Harley with an oomph as he folded his legs under him. Miss Molly had been sitting on a nearby rock, sunning herself, and she jumped down and regally stalked over to climb on Trucker's back. She curled herself up there and went to sleep.

"Oh, dear," Twila whispered to me. "This might take her a while. We might have to bring out some lanterns."

I chuckled. "We'll deal with that when we have to, Twila. Right now, we need to send Patches on."

"Yeah, before that there pretty path closes without me," Patches said worriedly.

"The path will be there whenever we need it," Twila assured him. "You stand still here and let me try to reverse that spell."

CHAPTER 28

An hour later, sweat poured down Twila's face. But Granny looked as fresh as if she had just dressed for the day as she continued to dig small portions of dirt and dump them on her slowly growing pile. I swiped my brow the same time Twila did. We'd both been trying to reverse the spell, unwilling to give in to the reality staring us in our sweltering faces.

Trucker and Harley had long ago given up their hopeful gazes on the hole they hoped to help dig and wandered over to where Miss Molly once again sunned on the rock. They laid beneath her, relaxing under the beautiful blue sky with puffy clouds floating lazily across it in the slight breeze.

Finally, I said with a huff of frustration, "We might as well face it, Twila. You used the spell that Cat will have to help un-do."

"You said Cat's going to be unavailable for two weeks," she reminded me.

To give him credit, Patches had held his peace at the five failures we had suffered. He hadn't faded a bit; he still looked as solid as the rest of us. Plus each time he tried to walk up the golden path, something blocked him.

I'd seen numerous full-bodied apparitions in my paranormal life, yet there was something even more defined about Patches. I couldn't put a name to it, however. Perhaps I was sensing the lack of success plaguing us.

"There," Granny said from over beside the hole. "I thinks it's deep enough now. Why don't you do the honors and put Missy Cow where she belongs, Jack."

"Let's take a break," Twila said. "Pay our proper respect to the cookie jar."

"Good idea," I agreed, wishing we'd thought to bring something to drink with us.

Sensing something going on, the animals rose to their feet and came over to sit by the grave as Jack placed the cookie jar reverently in the hole. When he stood, Granny said, "Well, who's gonna give her a moo-logy?"

"Moo-logy?" I asked, then nodded my head. "Oh, since she's a cow, she gets that instead of a eulogy. Good thinking, Granny."

We waited for someone to speak. Glancing around after a few seconds of silence, I realized everyone was looking at Jack. When he noticed us, he backed up, holding his hands out defensively.

"Huh uh. Not me. I didn't even know the cow." A chuckle made its rounds, and Jack guffawed loudly when he realized what he'd said. "Well, I didn't," he said around his laughter. "I mean, poor Missy Cow's a little bit older than I am."

Patches stared down at the cookie jar for a few seconds as his laughter halted and an expression of contemplation filled his face. At last he stepped forward. "I think this might be something I'm supposed to do. So I'll stand in for my friend, Walking Bear."

Patches bowed his head as though deep in thought for a minute or so, then began, "We're gathered here to honor a fine cookie jar. One that gave my friend Walking Bear lots of joy. She came to him from a real nice Amish lady named Ruth, who made sure the young lad who never did grow up always had plenty of cookies to eat. I'm sure Ruth did a lot of other things for our friends, but this here cookie jar seems to have been a symbol of it all. We bury this cookie jar, Missy Cow here, with the folks she meant the most to. Amen."

"Amen," we echoed. Then Granny's cracked voice rose to sing, "Amazing Grace, how sweet thou art." We all joined in for the rest of the hymn. Even Trucker lifted his muzzle for a few howls, and Miss Molly added that "meowser" she didn't realize set people's teeth on edge. Harley satisfied himself with a few grunts, which I'd have sworn were on tempo with the song. Surely pigs didn't understand music, though. Did they?

If I'd been drenched in happy tears before, the ones that rolled down my face now made a mockery of the previous deluge. I'd always had trouble handling that beautiful old hymn at funerals. Somehow, it embodied exactly what life after death was all about.

My eyes were too blurred to see who slipped an arm around me and held me close. However, I recognized every inch of Jack, from his physical shape to the clean masculine odor I associated with him. As the last notes of the song faded and drifted off into the silent Ohio hills, Patches took the shovel from Granny. She allowed him, and nodded in concurrence as he began covering Missy Cow with dirt. Leaving the ghost to his work, she came over beside Jack, and he drew her close with his other arm.

Twila noticed it first. She nudged me and nodded toward Patches. I smiled in relief. The more dirt the ghost replaced in the hole, the more he faded into mistiness. By the time he patted the shovel on top of the small mound to pack the dirt in place, I could barely see him.

"Patches," Twila said softly. "I think you should try to go into The Light now."

He stuck the shovel in the dirt beside the cookie jar grave and frowned at her. "What makes you think it'll work now? Not that I'm disbelieving you," he hastened to add, although I didn't see Jess scowl at him. "But I don't feel any different than I did."

"But you were able to use the shovel," Twila pointed out.

He stared at the grave, then looked back at her with a smile. "You're right."

"Look down at yourself," she said.

When he did, he jumped into the air with a whoop that echoed all around us. "Then you think I can go now?" he asked when he landed and gazed at the golden path.

"I think what you did tied up the last thread of your present life," Twila told him.

Patches nodded, but he didn't make a dash for the path. Instead, he walked slowly toward it. At first, I thought perhaps he was worried that he'd be blocked again. However, one glance at his face showed me how wrong I was. His expression mirrored the deep measure of awe he felt. He didn't halt until he had taken his first step onto the golden sidewalk, proving to himself the barrier had fallen. Then he looked at Jess.

"This is it, old Pard," he said. "I want to thank you and your pretty wife for all you done for me."

"You're welcome," Jess replied.

"Now maybe you won't be afraid of ghosts any longer," Patches said in a joking manner.

"Don't bet your afterlife on it," Jess growled. "You want to come back and tell anyone you made it over there fine and that you're happy, you appear to Twila. She can give me any message you want to pass on."

Patches laughed and nodded his agreement. "The thanks goes for the rest of you, also. I appreciate everything each and every one of you did for me."

"Aw, get going, Patches," Jess said. "Your real leg's probably waiting over there for you." Then he gazed directly into Patches' eyes and said, "See you later, Pard."

Patches nodded, then turned to look up the path. I couldn't help myself. I looked, too, as I'm sure each and every other person in our small group did. I breathed a sigh of relief when I didn't see a lone leg standing amidst the people gathered to welcome Patches.

He whooped again and raced up the path. As with the two Native American brothers, he received a warm welcome and they all disappeared back into the depths of the wonders that existed on the other side of the Veil.

The golden path receded this time, rolling up on itself until it reached the fissure in the clouds. Twila and I turned away, but Jack kept his hold on me and pointed toward the sky.

"The opening's still there, *Chère*. Why hasn't it closed?"

"It will," I assured him. "When there aren't any more souls in the area who want to go into The Light. Until then, it will wait and see if it's needed again."

Jack took my hand and pulled me with him down the mound. Giggling, I tried to jerk free, but he held on in a near death grip.

"Jack," I said when we reached the bottom of the mound and started up the other hill. "You won't be forced to go up the path. You'll have a choice when it's your time."

He kept dragging me with him as he said, "That's not it at all. I figure Jess and Twila will stay with Granny, and looks like the animals are happy enough to wander along with them. With Granny to take care of, it'll take them a lot longer to get back to the house than us. I thought I'd help you move your things into the room I'm in. You can stay a few more days, can't you?"

Laughing with delight, I quit pulling against him.

"I believe I can," I said as I raced over the top of the hill with him and down the other side toward the farmhouse.

AFTERWORD

Welcome to the fourth book in my *Dead Man Mysteries* series. I'm sending our (sometimes) fearless crew of intrepid ghost hunters off into a different world this time, Yankee-land, where Twila lives. You only need to scratch the surface of any state to find all sorts of interesting historical facts. Ohio, like the rest, has a fascinating history. Both Aunt Belle and I are descendants of some rough and rowdy hill folks, including a few moonshiners here and there.

My family lived in the middle house of the three belonging to our families. On one side was my great-grandmother, Alice; on the other, my grandmother, Mary, grandfather, Brady, and Aunt Belle. I grew up hearing tales of escapades about the men in our family. Supposedly, my love of fast driving in my earlier years may have been inherited. There were a few stories about midnight, lights-out escapes from pursuit by the feds. As far as I know, none of our menfolk were ever caught in their moonshining activities.

We raised a lot of our own food back then, too. That meant hours of plowing and hoeing in the springtime. Another tale I recall is about the forgotten keg of moonshine the plow unearthed one year. I can't speak from experience, but supposedly it was some pure, smooth whiskey. The men's eyes grew dreamy when they spoke of drinking that 'shine.

Looking back on my childhood, I'll bet the women were involved in their share of adventures, also. Their tales were just kept quiet due to propriety. I won't reveal how closely Granny's tale in this book comes to what might have happened in our teen years. I'll let you guess.

Ohio also has its share of folklore. As a tomboy, I spent hours and hours in the woods or on a creek bank. I even camped out overnight in the hills when we "ran" our fox hounds. There were many tales told around campfires about mysterious beasts in the woods. Who knows? Maybe the ones in this book are real. Ohio definitely has enough hills and wilderness for them to be possible.

I hope you enjoy this new *Dead Man* crew adventure.

Boo!
T. M.

ABOUT THE AUTHOR

T. M. Simmons lives in a haunted house on the edge of the East Tex
Piney Woods, which she and her husband share with a variety of p
and paranormal residents. In between writing cozy mysteries and ot
stories, she delights in scaring herself silly during otherworldly enco
ters and visits haunted building and graveyards during both dark
full moons. Her husband goes along sometimes to protect her fron
bumps in the night, although he's been know to spy a ghost and r
rather than confront. She also pursues paranormal entities with he
real-life Twila, Aunt Belle Brown, and they are Lead Investigators
Supernatural Researchers of Texas paranormal investigative tean
motto is, "Leave Peace Behind," and the team seeks to leave peace
people who are dealing with troubled hauntings, as well as
ghosts. Simmons is extremely willing to discuss her experien
anyone she can corner.

Sign up here for the T. M. Simmons newsletter and receive a co
Thrall Bound, a Short Story; only available to newsletter sub

https://ghostie3.wixsite.com/index1

www.iseeghosts.com

facebook.com/tranam.simmons

twitter.com/TMSimmonsauthor